The School of Starting Over

The School of Starting Over

Lisa Swift

hera

First published in the United Kingdom in 2020 by Hera

This edition published in the United Kingdom in 2020 by Hera

Hera Books
28b Cricketfield Road
London, E5 8NS
United Kingdom

A CIP catalogue record for this book is available from the British Library.

Print ISBN 978 1 80032 113 7
Ebook ISBN 978 1 912973 22 4

Look for more great books at www.herabooks.com

Printed and bound in Great Britain by Clays Ltd, Elcograf S.p.A.

For Nana

Chapter One

Plip. Another chunky droplet landed in the metal pot by Nell's knee.

There was a spray of splashback from the now almost full pot. She blinked it out of her eyes and shuffled out of range.

What even was the pot? What the hell was it supposed to be for? Nell had found it in a cupboard in the kitchen. It was squat and made of brass, with an ear-shaped handle attached to each side.

Casserole dish? Chamber pot? Spittoon?

Anyway, whatever its intended purpose, right now it was finding gainful employment as a rain-catcher: one of several pots, pans and bowls she'd salvaged from the kitchen to catch the drops invading her new home via the hole-ridden roof.

'Well, Colin,' she said to the sheep lying contentedly at her side, resting one hand on his warm fleece, 'here's another fine mess I've got myself into.'

She jumped as her phone vibrated in her pocket.

'Dad. Hi,' she said when she answered, trying not to grimace.

'Well then?' he demanded in his usual gruff tone. 'How is it?'

'It's... great. Like I said, loads of potential.'

He snorted. 'Yeah, I get it. In other words, it's a dump.'

Nell winced. 'I prefer the term "fixer-upper".'

'Are you going to invite me over to have a look now you're moved in, then? Or am I still banished?'

'Not yet. Wait till I've done it up a bit first.'

'You can't do it all on your own, can you? At least let me get a look at that dodgy roof.'

'Dad, please. I want to do it myself. I need to.'

'If you'd just hung on a bit before laying out your bloody life savings on some half-derelict barn in the arse-end of nowhere, something was bound to have come up round here,' he told her sternly. 'You know me and Leanne have got room for you for as long as it takes to sort yourself out with something.'

He didn't say 'I told you so', but Nell heard it all the same.

They'd had this conversation a dozen times. Her dad was wilfully oblivious to the fact that she'd rather be anywhere than living back with him and his wife.

First there'd been the break-up with Shawn, and having to move out of the flat they'd been sharing in Manchester, with all the stress, heartache and misery that comes when a long-term relationship ends. Then, hot on the heels of that little life-changer, she'd had to leave her job at the school where she'd been working. At twenty-eight, Nell Shackleton had found herself suddenly single, homeless and unemployed. Rock bottom, she'd told herself: the only way from there is up, right?

Except, she realised, it wasn't quite rock bottom. Real rock bottom would only come if she let herself weaken and agreed to move back in with her dad. That would be too big a step back; a return to the safe, closeted world of childhood. If she wasn't going to let this break her, Nell needed her next step to be forward.

'And does our Freddie know you offered me his room?' Nell asked her dad. She couldn't imagine Freddie would be any too pleased at arriving home from uni for the holidays to discover his big sister kipping in his bed.

'Freddie's grand on a camp bed in the box room. He's only home every few months anyway.'

'Dad, look, we've talked about this,' she said gently. 'It's kind of you to offer, but I'm an adult. I need to make a fresh start.'

'You could've made a fresh start here. Lots of good schools around Leeds.'

'What I mean is, I need to stand on my own two feet. I can't expect you to look after me whenever life drops me on my backside, can I?'

'Breaking off a two-year engagement right before the wedding is a bloody long drop, love,' he muttered.

'Well, it's done now anyway. Deeds are signed. For better or worse, I'm here.'

'You'd have been better off staying put in Manchester, where there's decent jobs. There's nowt for you in the country but rain and horse shit.'

'I like the country. And I've got a decent job – at least, I will have from Monday.'

'Hmm. You're a clever girl, Nelly. You'll be wasted in some tiny village school with a bunch of inbred farmers' kids.'

'It's not *All Creatures Great and Small*, Dad,' she said impatiently. 'There's more to rural life these days than cousin marriage and cow-fisting.'

He sighed. 'I don't mean to talk this new start down, pet. I know you're excited about the house and the job and every-thing. You seemed to make the decision in a hell of a hurry after splitting with Shawn, that's all.'

'It's a good job,' she said, snuggling against Colin's warm fleece. 'And Humblebee Farm was a bargain. I'm a homeowner now – that's something, right? How many single women in their twenties are on the property ladder?'

'Hovel-owner, more like.'

'I'm not like you, you know. I'm a country girl at heart.'

He scoffed. 'You've never lived in the country in your life.'

'Yeah, but I always wanted to.' She flinched as a blob of rainwater landed on her nose, brushing it off with her thumb. 'This is my dream, Dad. Be happy for me, please.'

'I worry about you, that's all,' he said with another sigh. 'Is the place even habitable? I thought you said half the slate had come down.'

'The bedroom and kitchen are fine. The living room...' She glanced around at the pots and pans dotted across the stone-flagged floor, catching water. 'Well, I'm sure I'll have it fixed up in no time. Got to go, Dad, I need to save the battery till I can get to a power socket.'

'Don't forget Monday, will you?'

'Monday?'

'Leanne's birthday,' he said, with a trace of exasperation.

She flinched. 'I know, I hadn't forgotten. Card and flowers are on their way.'

'You will give her a ring too, won't you?'

'Can't I text?'

'Nell, I think your stepmother should be worth more to you by now than an emoji and a couple of kisses.'

'It's just... I never know what to say to her.'

'Well "happy birthday" would be a good start,' he told her sternly. 'Don't let me down, Nelly.'

She sighed. 'I won't. Bye, Dad.'

When she'd stashed her phone away, she pushed herself up from the floor, rubbing her buttocks to try to inject some feeling back into them.

She could lie to her dad but not to herself. Truth was, she was ready to cry.

When she'd first come to look around Humblebee Farm, an old farmhouse out on the moors that rolled high above the little Yorkshire village of Leyholme, it had been a glorious day in August. The air had been heavy with the scent of clover, the moors purple with new-blooming heather. The estate agent – and this guy had been a born estate agent – had used words like 'idyllic', 'charming', 'ramshackle'...

Well, Nell was only human. Bloody hell, there'd been roses around the door, for God's sake – actual pink roses, climbing over the stone front like they'd escaped from a chocolate box. She'd been swept away on a tidal wave of romance and air-castles that was just too delicious to resist.

The house had previously been the property of a retired farmer, Ted Preston. As he'd grown old he'd sold off his land to the other farms peppered through the hills, but Farmer Ted had stubbornly stayed living in his farmhouse until the very end, apparently unconcerned as it fell into disrepair around him. After his death the place had been inherited by some great-nephew, a Londoner who just wanted it off his hands. Nell had thought he must be mad to let it go for such a low asking price and snapped it up right away before he changed his mind.

Best of all was that she knew it was the last place Shawn would ever have wanted to live. He was a townie through and through, wrinkling his nose at anywhere you couldn't get a sushi platter and an Uber. On the day the sale had completed, Nell had felt an infinite amount of satisfaction at the idea of living anywhere Shawn would have hated.

Not so much earlier this evening though, when her taxi had dropped her off at the end of the dirt track that led to Humblebee Farm, suitcases in hand, in the middle of a torrential autumn downpour.

With the sky a glowering charcoal, the farmhouse was no longer idyllic. It felt bleak and forbidding. The roses around the door were long gone, just a mess of black, ugly briars clawing at the lintel. As the taxi pulled away, Nell almost had to stop herself from chasing after it with cries of 'Don't leave me!'

And the inside – sweet Jesus, the inside.

The kitchen wasn't so bad: no hot water or electricity, but there was a working gas cooker, a kettle, even a few tins in the cupboards. The bedroom was grim and cold, but dry. But the living room… ugh. Bare, sodden with rainwater, with a pile of soggy kindling next to an open fire she knew she had no chance of lighting.

And then there was her new roommate Colin, a friendly Swaledale sheep who'd barged in through the broken back door and seemed to be claiming squatter's rights. She'd tried to shoo him out at first, but when the clouds exploded into thunder and lightning she'd taken pity on him and told him he could stay till the storm was over. Actually, she was kind of grateful for the company. Good old Colin.

She carried a couple of pans of rainwater through to the kitchen and tipped them down the sink, set a tin of beans with pork sausages to warm on the hob for her tea and returned to the living room to put the emptied pans back in position.

Nell sighed as she sank back down to the bare floor.

'Oh God, Colin,' she whispered, resting her head against him. 'I think I've made a terrible mistake.'

—

'Got a surprise for you,' Xander's mum Anne told him when he stumbled into the kitchen on Monday morning, rubbing sleep out of his eyes.

He smiled uncertainly. 'What?'

'Here.' She opened the fridge and whipped something out with a flourish. 'Ta-da! Not for now, obviously. We can have it with our tea later, celebrate your first day, and then you can take what's left for the staffroom tomorrow.'

Oh God. She hadn't. She hadn't… baked.

'You really didn't need to do that,' he said, meaning every word.

'Of course I did,' she said, beaming as she put it down on the table. 'It's not every day your son becomes a headmaster, is it?'

'Headteacher, Mum. We don't really call them headmasters these days.'

Xander fished his glasses out of his dressing gown pocket so he could see the cake more clearly. It was shaped like a mortar board, white icing spelling out the message *Congratulations on your promotion, Alexander! #ProudMamaBear #AllGrownUp #Blessed.*

He was starting to rue the day he'd helped her set up that Instagram account. The woman was a hashtag junkie.

'Well, headteacher then, if that's the PC thing now,' she said. 'And the youngest Leyholme's ever had to boot. Don't tell me that's not worth celebrating.'

'Third youngest. And I'm only acting headteacher.'

She shrugged. 'That's close enough.'

'Mum – it's a lovely cake, thank you. But you do realise this is only temporary? I'm the caretaker head, that's all. I just have to keep things running smoothly until Jeremy's back on his feet.'

'They still picked you, didn't they? Out of everyone?'

Oh right, out of everyone. If you didn't count the three other staff members he knew had turned the job down before him. Normally it would fall to the deputy head, but as luck would have it, she was off on maternity leave. Xander – quiet, unambitious Xander Scott, who'd been perfectly happy teaching Year 3, thank you very much – had been dead-man's-bootsed by the school governors into a position no one else had wanted. He didn't want it either, but a sense of duty and general inability to say no had forced him to accept. It hardly seemed like an occasion that called for cake.

He looked up into his mother's proud, hopeful eyes and forced a smile. 'Yeah, Mum. They picked me.'

'Of course they did,' she said, ruffling his dark hair. 'They know talent when they see it.' Her expression brightened. 'And maybe Jeremy won't get back on his feet. Then the job could be yours permanently.'

'Mum!'

'Oh, don't sound so scandalised. I don't mean I wish him dead or anything awful,' she said, waving a hand. 'But a heart attack, that's not good, is it? High time he started putting himself first – took early retirement and spent some time with the grandkiddies. He's fifty-nine, and if you ask me he looks every day of it.'

'He's a very competent head.' *And rather him than me...*

'Well, so will you be. More than competent. Exceptional. You know they put that on your school report once? *Exceptional.* I've got it upstairs in Dad's bureau.'

Xander winced. 'You kept my old reports?'

'Of course I did. They're in the bottom drawer with your nana's premium bonds.'

He could remember a few choice phrases from those reports himself. It hadn't been all exceptionals. 'Could be so much more if he only believed in himself,' his Year 10 class teacher had observed mournfully. And from his Biology teacher: 'Alexander would do rather better if he spent more time properly studying the reproductive system diagrams and less time doodling beards on the testicles'.

Thanks, Mr Allen. Actually, he'd learnt quite a lot about reproduction while he'd been adding the beards. Well, the theory, anyway. It had taken him a fair while longer to get to the practice.

'It doesn't work that way anyway,' Xander told his mum. 'If Jeremy retired, the school governors would have to advertise the post. And they'd get a lot more experienced applicants than me.'

'Well, experience isn't everything, is it? The parents know you, the staff respect you – what stranger can say that? You'd walk into it.'

He smiled. Only his mum, of everyone in the world, could have such blind, unshakeable faith in his abilities.

'I'm glad you think so,' he said.

Anne put the cake back in the fridge and opened the cupboard above the cooker. 'So what do you fancy for breakfast, clever clogs? Croissants? Toast? Cereal?'

'I'll make it.'

'No, let me, I like looking after you. The novelty of having you home hasn't worn off yet.'

'Mum, please. I'm thirty-one, for Christ's sake. I feel about five when you run round after me.'

Her face crumpled and he sighed.

'I mean, I'm grateful, course I am,' he said in a soothing tone, standing so he could give her a hug. 'It's good of you to put me up till I get myself sorted out. But I don't want to be treating the place like a hotel, do I? Bad enough you won't take any rent.'

She smiled. 'When you were a teenager, me and your dad were forever telling you to stop treating the place like a hotel.'

'And I learnt my lesson, you see?' He guided her by the shoulders to a chair. 'Here, you sit down. I'll make us both breakfast.'

'So what's on the agenda for your first day then, Mr Scott?' she asked as she took a seat.

'I just want to project vibes of "new boss, same as the old boss" really, reassure staff and parents it's business as usual while Jeremy's recovering. I think everyone's still in shock, with it being so sudden.' He grabbed a box of muesli and poured out a couple of bowlfuls. 'Oh, and there's the new Reception class teacher starting today as well. A Miss Shackleton.'

–

As he brushed his teeth after breakfast, Xander couldn't help remembering a naff joke his dad had told him when he was small.

A mother goes to wake her son for school and finds him crying.

'I don't want to go to school,' he sobs. 'The children hate me, the teachers hate me, everyone hates me. Please don't make me go, Mummy.'

'But you have to go to school,' his mother says. 'You're the headmaster!'

Xander spat his toothpaste into the sink, feeling a strong urge to vomit. He leaned over the toilet, retching, but nothing came up.

Christ almighty. What had he let himself in for?

Chapter Two

Nell reached up to pat some flyaway strands of hair back into place. Her first day in a new job and she was walking round with a giant ginger bird's nest on her head.

And she'd had to work even for the horrible up-do she was currently sporting. Over an hour it had taken her to boil enough water in her four biggest pans, one on every gas ring of her hob, to have a hot bath – well, lukewarm bath by the time she'd got the tub half-full. She'd had to leave her voluminous mop to dry naturally then cram it full of hair grips and spray, just to hold it in place. Not the best look for a dashing young professional.

Oh, how she missed her GHDs...

Her first task in her new home really needed to be getting the old boiler replaced so she could have hot running water. Then the lecky, allowing her to once again embrace straight hair and a fully charged phone. And she needed to get the roof fixed, keep out the wind and rain – the two big tarps she'd chucked over the worst patch, weighted down with half-bricks, were OK as a temporary solution but they could only do so much. And the back door, of course. She couldn't sleep easy knowing it was open to any rapist, murderer or sheep who might choose to pop in.

Her scooter was arriving this evening, she'd arranged to have it couriered over from her dad's along with some of her other possessions. Once she had that, perhaps she could join a gym over in Halifax. She'd be able to grab a shower there, maybe sit in the sauna for a bit to warm up before heading back to her freezing moorland shack.

As worried as she was about the falling-down farmhouse she now called home and her ill-considered, possibly doomed decision to start a new life here in Leyholme, she couldn't help feeling a little better as she strolled towards the village school. She could see it in the distance: a squat Victorian building in blackened sandstone, capped by a little belltower.

There was a fresh, fecund mix of scents after the recent autumn showers that seemed to go with the first day at a new school, somehow: old leaves, fresh-dropped conkers, wet soil, with just the faintest hint of woodsmoke from somewhere in the distance. Nell breathed in deep lungfuls, taking in her surroundings as she walked.

To her right was a post office, the sign outside proudly proclaiming that it was community-run and staffed by volunteers. An old mechanics' institute seemed to function as a village hall – the place was currently decorated for some sort of Halloween event, festooned with orange and black bunting while a row of carved pumpkins lined the path leading to the front door. A little further up the road was a cheery-looking pub, The Highwayman's Drop. Dick Turpin reference? She'd have to look up the history of the place sometime.

There were shops too – a corner shop, butcher's, hardware store, bakery, even an old-style apothecary (although these days it just seemed to deal in all-natural soaps and bath salts), with an assortment of coloured glass bottles filling the windows. Rowan trees lined the pavements, shaking in the knife-edge October wind that swept down off the moor.

It was exactly the sort of place she'd always dreamed of making her home in – well, a bit colder and damper than her fantasy village maybe, but close enough. Shawn would've popped a vein if she'd told him this was where she wanted them to live.

She slowed down as she passed the warm, fragrant open door of the bakery, falling into step behind a gang of kids lined up in pairs ahead of her – what they called a walking bus. They were all in hi-vis jackets with *Leyholme Primary School* printed on the back, two adults at the front and another bringing up the rear.

'OK, time to cross the road,' one of the parents leading the bus said when they reached the zebra crossing. 'What do we do first, you lot?'

'Stop, look and listen,' the kids chanted dutifully.

Nell drew level with the woman at the back, thinking she should probably introduce herself. A lot of the kids in the bus looked around Reception age.

'Hiya,' she said. 'Are you one of the school mums?'

'Oh God, don't talk to me.' The woman ran a hand over her brow. 'I mean, sorry, do talk to me. Just don't talk to me about school. It's been one of those mornings, first day back after half-term and all that.'

It didn't look like it had been one of those mornings. The woman was country chic in her jodhpurs and stylish wellies, her caramel-highlighted blonde hair curled and glossy, make-up pristine, huge *Breakfast at Tiffany's*-esque sunglasses perched on her nose. Her harassed tone was distinctly at odds with her immaculate appearance. Nell realised she'd reached up to pat her stupid fluffy nest again and yanked her fingers away.

She shook the manicured hand the woman offered her. 'Nell.'

'Jolene. You sing, you die.'

Nell laughed. 'For everyone's benefit I'll try to restrain myself.'

Jolene's plump, glossed lips spread into a smile. 'Nice to meet you anyway, Nell. You new to the area?'

'New as they come. I only moved here on Friday.'

'Is one of the breakfast club yours then?' Jolene asked, nodding towards the kids clutching lunchboxes and schoolbags as they filed over the crossing.

'Well, you might say some of them are, between nine and half three at least. I'm the new Reception teacher.'

Jolene examined her with more interest. 'You're Miss... no, don't tell me. Miss Shackleton, right?'

'That's me.'

'Well, rather you than me, hun.' She watched the kids as they mounted the pavement again. 'I mean, we adore them, obviously, but they're little sods sometimes.'

Nell smiled. 'Parents always say that, I've learnt not to believe a word of it. Which one belongs to you?'

Jolene pointed out a swaggering lad marching at the head of the walking bus, two or three girls jogging at his heels. 'That's my Morgan. Did you ever see a five-year-old who could flirt like that? Takes after his father.'

'Does he?'

'Mmm. Daddy's long gone now though. The two things were not unconnected.' She frowned, looking over her shoulder. 'Hey, can you hear something?'

It all happened in a bit of a blur. There was a frenzied yapping, then a streak of reddish-brown fur shot past Nell, heading straight for the crowd of kids.

One of the little girls shrieked and broke formation. She ran past Nell and Jolene, out into the road – right into the path of a huge Range Rover just cresting the brow of the hill.

'Red!' the girl yelled. She fell on the frisking dog and hugged it round its neck. 'Aww, you missed me.'

Nell didn't stop to think. She dashed out into the road, and in an instant she'd grabbed the girl's hand and the dog's trailing lead and swept them back to the safety of the pavement.

'Sweetheart, you mustn't ever do that!' she panted, dropping to her haunches to talk to the child. 'It's very, very dangerous to run into the road. Don't you know a car could come and knock you down?'

The child blinked. 'But I had to get Red. She's not s'posed to run off.'

'Is this Red?' Nell asked, resting a hand on the still ecstatic spaniel.

The girl nodded. 'She's my dog,' she announced, beaming around the other kids with obvious pride. 'She wants to come to school too.'

The walking bus had stopped, the children watching the little tableau with interest. Jolene was standing with the other parents, and Nell had the horrible idea they might be treating this as some sort of test of her abilities.

'She can't come to school, my love,' Nell told the child. 'It's a school for humans, not dogs – they have their own schools, you know. What's your name?'

'Can't tell you,' the little girl said, jabbing a thumb into her mouth.

'Why not?'

' 'Cos you're a stranger,' she mumbled through a mouthful of thumb.

Nell smiled. 'That's OK. I'm your new teacher, I'm not a proper stranger.'

The girl looked up at Jolene, who nodded to confirm the truth of the statement.

'It's all right,' she said, smiling encouragingly. 'Go on, sweetie, tell her your name.'

'Milly Madeleine,' the child told Nell.

Nell looked at her for a second. 'OK then, Milly Madeleine. Do you know where Red came from today so we can get her back there?'

That question answered itself as a petite woman in her early forties, her pixie-chopped auburn hair giving her a look of Julia Roberts playing Tinkerbell, came barrelling around the corner with arms and legs flailing.

'Red! Red, you little – arghh! There you are!'

The woman came running over, panting heavily.

'Oh God… so… sorry,' she managed. 'She… got away from me in the park. Sorry, sorry, sorry.' She glanced at Nell, noticing her hand on Red's collar. 'Who are you, then?'

Nell blinked. 'I'm the new Reception teacher. Who're you?'

'Stevie, Milly's mum.'

'Milly's mum,' she muttered. 'Hey, do you know your dog ran into the road?'

'And Milly followed,' Jolene said. 'It's lucky Miss Shackleton here was on her toes. She's a hero, Stevie. Pulled them out of the path of a speeding car.'

'Oh, it wasn't quite as dramatic as all that,' Nell said.

'Oh my God!' Stevie dropped to her knees and pulled Milly into a hug. 'Mill, you know not to do that! Stay with the bus, duckling. That's what it's for, to keep you safe.'

'But Red was—'

'Never mind what Red was doing. Red's a naughty dog to run away from me. Now go on, get off to school – and for goodness' sake, do as you're told and stay safe.'

She stood up and nodded to Nell. 'Well, looks like I owe you one, new Reception teacher. Thanks.'

'Um, my pleasure.'

Stevie disappeared down the road, running to keep up as the tiny furry thunderbolt dragged her in the direction of the park.

'Phew. Nothing like a bit of drama on your first day, eh?' Nell said to Jolene as they got moving again.

'Oh, wherever you find Stevie Madeleine, you'll always find drama.'

'How come?'

'Who knows? That's the thing, she never seems to be the cause of it. Stevie's just one of those people, you know? Trouble follows her around.' Jolene lowered her voice. 'We're rather proud of her at Leyholme. It's not an enormously diverse school community, sad to say, but we do have Stevie and Milly. She's our only gay parent.'

Nell frowned. Jolene talked about Stevie as if she was the school mascot or something; some sort of trophy. Not knowing quite how to respond, she was relieved when they reached the school gates and the conversation came to a halt.

–

'Red Madeleine, you are a bad, bad, bad dog,' Stevie scolded as they headed back into the park. 'And you know I only say that because I love you.'

Red looked up at her with tongue lolling cheerfully. Unlike some of her kind, she didn't seem to feel any shame at being told she was a bad dog. If anything, Stevie reckoned she took it as a compliment.

Stevie sighed and knelt to give her a stroke.

'You and Milly could've been hurt today. And if anything happened to either of you, the last little unbroken part of my heart would crack into bits. Do you understand that, you moronic canine?'

Red lunged forward to give her face a big, wet lick.

'Nope,' Stevie said to no one in particular, wiping off the drool with a tissue. 'Not a word.'

'Oh wow, what a sweetheart! Is she yours?'

Stevie looked up to see who'd spoken. A beaming woman with dark, wavy hair stuffed into a ponytail, dressed in combat trousers and a fitted *Firefly* hoodie, had materialised by her side. At her feet were six dogs of varying sizes, shapes and breeds, their curious eyes fixed on Red.

'Probably truer to say I'm hers,' Stevie said, standing up. 'For all the notice she takes of a word I say, the little hellhound.' She glanced down at the dogs around the woman's feet. 'I feel a bit inadequate now I've met you, with my paltry single dog.'

'Oh, they're not all mine. I'm a professional.'

'Professional what, dog-wrangler?'

The woman laughed. 'Basically. I walk them, if you can call that a career. All girls, so we don't have any slip-ups with the unsnipped ones.' She nodded to a little border terrier who'd deigned to turn around and present her backside to Red for inspection. 'This is the only one that actually comes home with me. My Life.'

'Yeah, it can feel a bit like your world revolves around them sometimes, can't it?'

'No, I mean, that's her name. Life.' The woman grinned, her mouth dimpling at the corners. 'It's a joke. Geddit?'

Stevie hesitated, then groaned. 'Life's a bitch. God, that's terrible.'

'Isn't it? I've got a million of them.' She nodded amiably. 'I'm Deb, by the way.'

'Stevie. And this is Red. She's in the doghouse this morning so don't be too nice to her.'

'She's a beaut,' Deb said, crouching down to tickle Red's ears. 'Cocker?'

'That's right.'

'You'd think I'd get bored of them, wouldn't you, with half a dozen a day to see to. And yeah, I pick them all up and I'm like "ugh, dogs". But then I see a new one and I'm like "ooh, dog!" You know?'

Deb stood up again, beaming happily. Stevie smiled back. She couldn't help it: Deb's carefree grin was infectious.

She struck Stevie as one of those people who could be sheltering in a bunker, waiting for the apocalypse, and still manage to stay upbeat. On full beam, the woman could dry out a wet weekend in Morecambe.

'Hey,' Stevie said. 'Are you booked up right now, dog-wise? I'll actually be in the market for a sitter myself soon. I've got a kid who does it for pocket money, but she's off on a gap year or something after Christmas so I'll be stuck come the January term.'

'You mean it?' Deb said. Stevie wished her eyes sparkled like that when she thought about work.

'Of course. You and Red seem like you're good pals already.'

'Six is my limit, but I do have a vacancy coming up. Young Sadie here's moving away. I'd love to take Red, if you're sure you trust some random stranger you just met in the park to take care of her for you.'

Stevie breathed a sigh of relief. She'd been really quite worried about finding a new dog-walker. Red had a reputation

around the village for being flighty and over-excitable, with
this morning's running-off episode just one in a long line,
and Stevie couldn't imagine even Leyholme's most hard-up
residents queueing to take her on. She wasn't entirely convinced
her current dog-walker was really going off on her travels either.
There was a good chance the girl had just decided to go into
hiding.

'In the interests of full disclosure, I should warn you she can
be a bit of a handful,' Stevie told Deb. 'Full of energy, never
does as she's told, always off chasing after something...'

'I had an ex like that once,' Deb said, laughing. 'Don't worry,
Stevie, we'll get along fine. Hang on.' She reached into the deep
pocket of her combats, pulling out a mess of coppers, dog treats,
poo bags and other clutter. She fished a business card from the
debris. 'Here. Drop me an email and we'll get it set up.'

Chapter Three

Xander sat back in his chair, staring at the emails on his computer screen. They seemed to have gone a bit blurry.

To be honest, he wasn't one hundred per cent sure what exactly it was he was supposed to be doing. None of the governors had fully briefed him and there'd been no time to arrange any training after Jeremy had been taken ill without warning during the half-term holidays. So far, all he'd done with his morning was answer a few emails, read through a wad of paperwork that had been dumped in his in-tray and scoff chocolate Hobnobs from Jeremy's secret stash in the desk drawer.

He'd started the day well enough, delivering an invigorating speech in the staffroom – at least, he hoped it had been invigorating. The theme had been keeping calm and carrying on while Jeremy was in hospital. Not quite the St Crispin's Day speech from *Henry V* maybe, but it had seemed to reassure people. But then he'd been shuffled off by the school secretary and closeted in the headteacher's office, where he'd been feeling a bit lost ever since.

He'd glanced longingly through the open door of his Year 3 classroom when he'd passed it earlier. Mrs Benedict, the supply teacher the governors had engaged to cover for him while he was covering for Jeremy, had been giving a lesson on fractions. Xander never imagined the day would come when he'd miss teaching fractions, but as she'd written up definitions for numerators and denominators on the smartboard, he'd longed to run in, grab the pen from her and take over.

Some of his pupils had spotted him there, excited whispers of 'Mr Scott' hissing through the rows. A few even waved to him. Xander had almost sobbed.

On Jeremy's desk – well, Xander's desk, for now, anyway – was a framed newspaper article with a photo of Jeremy, Mr Illingworth, shaking hands with the Education Secretary when he'd visited the school last year. Xander remembered it well. They'd got new flowerbeds planted especially for the occasion and Caroline Fairchild, the Year 2 teacher, had been discovered hyperventilating into a paper bag in the art cupboard.

Shit, what if the bugger decided to pay another visit? Now, on Xander's watch? Or... bollocks, Ofsted. Just the word had the power to set his stomach muscles knotting. That'd be just his luck, if they suddenly announced a surprise inspection.

He took his mobile from the desk drawer and tapped out a message to his best friends Sara and Justin, who lived in Leyholme's neighbouring village of Morton with their infant son.

**Drink at the Bull later, you guys?
Could do with one after today.**

The pair weren't just his best friends: they were pretty much his only friends still in the area. Most of his mates from secondary school had disappeared after moving away for university, off to jobs further afield. He'd almost done the same himself when he'd finished studying for his PGCE at Manchester Met, but then his mum had introduced him to Marie, and Marie was in Leyholme, so back in Leyholme he'd eventually found himself. It had to be the ultimate irony that Marie, who'd always claimed she never wanted to live anywhere else, had eventually left the place for good, while Xander, who'd dreamed of nothing but getting out since childhood, had been the one who couldn't drag himself away.

His phone buzzed five minutes later with a reply from Justin.

> **Sorry mate, bit short notice for us to sort out a babysitter. Why don't you come round ours? There's a beer in the fridge with your name on it.**

Xander sighed as he sent back a yes. He was at that age, he guessed. The age of crying kids and dirty nappies, with unscheduled trips to the pub a far-distant memory. Even a swift half after work now seemed to take weeks of organisation.

At least, for Justin and Sara it did. Not for him, of course, with only his mum to go home to.

He seemed to have been left behind somewhere along the way. He'd always assumed... but then Marie had left, and at thirty, Xander's life had unexpectedly hit the reset button. Marriage, kids – all the things he'd hoped he'd have one day, suddenly off the agenda. Forever, perhaps.

The dynamic with his best friends had changed too. They were the same as ever, always pleased to see him. But he was very aware that what had been double dates had transformed into a couple and him in these post-Marie days. That added up to three, and everyone knew what three made.

So his friends were doing the grown-up stuff – marriage, parenthood – while Xander was back in his old room at Mum and Dad's, lying in the dark every night naming the constellations just like when he was a kid. There was a whole universe up on his ceiling in sickly glow-in-the-dark green, stuck there by his dad back when little space-mad Alexander – who was totally going to be an astronaut and would never dream of going into anything as *yawn* as teaching – had just started primary school himself.

Oh yeah, that reminded him. The new Reception teacher. He was probably supposed to welcome her to the school or whatever. He picked up the phone and dialled the extension number for the school secretary.

'Um, hi,' he said when she picked up. 'It's me.'

'Oh, hello, love,' Mrs Rhodes said in her familiar motherly tone. 'How's the first day going? You all settled in?'

And that was the other problem with being the third-youngest head Leyholme Primary had ever had. Half of the staff had been here longer than him. A handful had been here since he'd been a pupil. Pink-rinsed school secretary Janet Rhodes was a classic case in point. To her, no fancy job title could stop him being little Alexander Scott, who got told off for picking his nose during assembly and wore a patch over the left lens of his glasses.

'I suppose,' he said. 'Have you heard any more about Jeremy?'

'Afraid not,' she told him in that dirge-like sing-song people always seem to use when talking about illness or death. 'Still in hospital. No news on when he'll be ready for visitors.'

'Should we send flowers or something? I mean, as a school?'

'Done and dusted, pet. Mr Theakston organised a whip-round on behalf of the board of governors. I ordered a lovely bouquet off Interflora this morning.'

'How come no one told me? I'd have liked to contribute.'

'Oh, well, he forgot, I expect. Was there something you wanted, Alexander? Tea or coffee? I can bring you in a cup.'

'No — yes, I mean, not tea, but yes, there's something. Could you ask Miss Shackleton to pop over at break time? I want to check she's settling in all right.'

There was silence.

'Mrs Rhodes?'

'Yes, I heard.' She lowered her voice. 'Have you met her yet?'

'No, not yet. She wasn't there earlier when I addressed the staff — I suppose you were giving her the guided tour. Why?'

'It's just that she's very... you know.'

'Do I?'

'Yes, you know. Young. I thought you should be fore-warned.'

Xander frowned. 'Why do I need warning about her being young?'

'Well, maybe I don't mean young. Bonny, then.'

'Mrs Rhodes, I don't think this is really... could you just send her up, please? Thank you.'

When he'd put down the phone, he groaned deeply and let his head fall onto his folded arms.

He was woken from a half-doze an indeterminate number of minutes later by the sound of a throat clearing. A young woman with – well, frankly *enormous* hair was standing in front of his desk, arms crossed.

'I wasn't sleeping,' he said, wiping a bit of saliva from the side of his mouth.

'Right.'

'Honestly. I always drool when I'm giving up the will to live.'

The woman looked puzzled. 'Sorry, I'm looking for the headteacher, Mr Scott. Is this the right office?'

'Er, yes.' Xander blinked, still in a daze. 'I'm it. Him. Hey, don't you knock where you come from?'

'I did knock. Then there was no answer so I just barged in. You did send for me, you know.' She examined him sceptically. 'Are you sure you're the head? You seem awfully young.'

'I'm older than you.'

'You also seem very... er, perturbed, if you don't mind me saying so.'

'Listen, if you'd been in the staffroom earlier things could have been very different. I gave a speech. I was masterful. I mean, teacherful.' He sighed. 'Sorry, it's my first day. I'm not incompetent, I promise. Just terrified.'

The woman regarded him for a long moment. Then her face relaxed into a smile. 'I know just how you feel.'

He stood and came round to the front of the desk, presenting her with a hand. 'Xander Scott.'

'Nell Shackleton,' she said, shaking it.

Her touch was firm. Warm. And… and why was he thinking about that?

Get a grip, Xand. It's a handshake, for God's sake. You're not taking her out to bloody dinner.

He perched on the edge of his desk, trying to look more relaxed than he felt. His tummy had gone a bit twisty.

Mrs Rhodes was right, Nell Shackleton was young: mid to late twenties at a guess, a pile of fluffy red hair pinned on top of her head. And as for bonny – well, it probably wasn't appropriate for him to notice, what with him being her boss and all that, but it was hard not to when she was right in front of him. With her green eyes and wild, flaming hair, she looked like a medieval warrior princess or something.

'Celtic,' he muttered.

Nell blinked. 'I'm sorry?'

He grimaced when he realised he'd spoken out loud. 'Er, Cel— *Sell*tic. The football team,' he said, hurriedly correcting his pronunciation to a soft C. 'Just remembered there's a match on this week.'

'Footie fan, are you?'

'God, no, can't stand it.'

'Right. OK then.'

Generally speaking, Xander felt awkward around women his age. And men his age. And everyone, of any age. He knew he was burbling, making a total cock of the conversation, yet there was an expression of wry amusement in Nell's eyes that made him feel it was all going to turn out OK. There was something oddly reassuring in the notion she didn't take him seriously. Perhaps because that made two of them.

'So how's your first morning been?' he asked, indicating a chair for her. 'I'm told you started your day by saving a walking bus full of children from a speeding articulated lorry.'

She laughed as she took a seat. 'Chinese whispers travel fast. It was just the one child. And I didn't exactly save her, just scooped her off the road when she wandered out.'

'Quick thinking, anyway. Have the Reception kids been behaving for you?'

'Bar a few tears, one damp-pant incident and Henry Benson sicking up glitter glue in the reading corner, they've been good as gold.'

'Good,' he said absently. He couldn't help watching the way her mouth curved while she spoke, making every word sound like laughing. 'That's… good.'

She frowned. 'Sorry, am I boring you?'

He pulled himself together.

'No. No, of course not. I've just got a lot on my mind today.'

She examined him through one narrowed eye. 'Mr Scott—'

'Christ, please don't. I can't take being Mr Scott on top of everything else.'

'Well, Xander then. Are you OK?'

'I'm supposed to ask you that, aren't I?'

'You're being very odd, you know. And no offence, but you look kind of stoned. Maybe you should go home if you're not feeling well.'

He sighed. 'Nell, if I told you I never wanted this job, what would you think of me?'

'I wouldn't think anything of you. If you don't want it, how did you end up with it?'

'I was the best candidate. Also the only candidate.'

'Oh.'

'It's like the Fates were conspiring against me,' he told her, the words for some reason just dropping out of him. 'This time seven years ago, when I came to work here, I wouldn't even have been eligible for this position. That was when the education authority decided to scrap the requirement for teachers to have the NPQH in order to qualify for a headteacher role. Then our deputy head went off to have a baby, Jeremy got sick, and… well, long story short, here's muggins holding the bloody fort till either Jeremy can come back to work or the governors find someone better.'

'I'm sorry. Sounds like you've been stranded paddleless up the creek a bit.'

Xander took his glasses off and rubbed his eyes. 'I really shouldn't be telling you this, should I? That's all I need, to scare off the kind of Reception teacher who snatches children from the jaws of death on her first day.' He blinked hard. 'I'm exhausted, that's all. Worry and lack of sleep. Come see me tomorrow and I promise I'll be the calm, professional, not-at-all-insane headteacher you've always dreamed of working for.'

She smiled. 'Oh, I don't know. For some reason, I quite like the idea of working for this one.'

'Ach, you're just trying to make me feel better. But thanks.'

Nell stood up. 'I'd better get back. I want to grab a coffee before the bell goes. Bit short on sleep myself today.'

'You came from Manchester, didn't you? When did you move?'

'Friday.'

'Bloody hell, three days ago, is that all? You've hit the ground running. Are you living in the village then?'

'Yes – well, about a mile out. Humblebee Farm.'

He laughed. 'Stop.'

'Eh?'

'That was a joke, right?'

'Um, no. Why should it be?'

'But Humblebee Farm – Ted Preston's old shack? You can't seriously be living in that broken-down old place. It's falling to bits.'

She drew herself up. 'It was an investment. A great one, thank you very much, Mr Xander Scott.'

'Right. OK,' he said, rubbing the heels of his palms in his eyes before putting his glasses back on. 'Didn't mean to cause offence.'

'Forget it. It's fine.'

'Right,' he said again. 'Well, my door's always open and all that jazz – I think that's the sort of thing I'm supposed to say. Shout if there's anything you need.'

'If I think of anything, I'll let you know.' She flashed him another quizzical look, and he self-consciously rubbed his fingers through his hair. 'Look after yourself, eh?'

'Er, thanks. You too.'

Once she'd left, Xander sank back into his swivel chair, not quite sure what had just happened.

He knew he'd just made a proper tit of himself in front of a new teacher, telling her far too much about his feelings towards his new role, but for some reason he felt better than he had since he'd been given the unwelcome news he was about to get dropped into the acting headteacher job. He hummed a jolly tune as he helped himself to another Hobnob from the desk drawer.

Chapter Four

Nell prodded the lifeless hearth, trying to coax some flames from the Jenga tower of fizzling kindling she'd constructed there. But there was nothing. Just unpleasant-smelling black smoke disappearing up the chimney, polluting the atmosphere with all its fossil-fueliness. She might feel guilty if she wasn't so bloody cold.

It wasn't like she hadn't done her research. She'd spent the whole of her dinner break on her phone, watching YouTube videos showing the correct way to light an open fire. Miming laying out the kindling, newspaper and logs until she thought she had it down. On the way home, she'd stopped at the corner shop and heaved a big bag of fresh, dry kindling and a couple of logs up the hill to the farm.

But the fireplace, like the gaping maw of some taunting, flesh-ravening beast, laughed silently at her with every attempt to get the flames going. Eventually she was reduced to setting light to pieces of individual kindling, one at a time. They burnt out within minutes, but it was a bit of warmth.

At least it wasn't raining, thank God, and the huge pillar candles she'd dotted around the living room cast a mellow glow that made the place look almost homely. Nell could have a cold but dry night snuggled into her giant floor cushion under two or three of her warmest jumpers, a couple of duvets and her hot water bottle: making plans for the house, reading by candlelight, thinking about her new job.

It had been a good first day, that strange interview with the acting head bloke aside. The Reception kids were pretty amazing. Well, kids that age were always amazing, which was why she'd wanted to teach them. But these ones... maybe it was the rose-tinted, half-drunk feeling of being in a new job in a new place. Maybe it was the fresh country air. But her new class had endeared themselves to her right away: even cheeky, charming Morgan Hancock and little Olivia Cross, who delighted in telling 'Knock Knock' jokes that all had the punchline 'poo' before collapsing in fits of giggles.

Nell smiled at a picture she'd Blu-Tacked to the wall. It was a child's picture of a gigantic orange stick figure, apparently with limbs twice the length of a regular human's, balancing a couple of other stick figures – one on four legs, one on two – as something on wheels sped by. The little girl she'd pulled from the road, Milly Madeleine, had drawn it for her. It was her first gift from her new pupils.

She frowned as a muffled tapping started at the back door. No one would be calling on her now, would they? Anyway, she didn't know anybody.

The wind? Nell had blocked the broken door with a heavy box of her stuff that had arrived in the removal van earlier, but it wasn't exactly secure. She'd better go check.

She fumbled for her torch and headed to the kitchen. Then, on second thoughts, she went back to the fireplace and grabbed the poker to take along too.

Once she'd heaved the box out of the way, the door swung open of its own accord and a woeful little face looked up at her.

'Oh. You again.' She put down the poker and bent to tickle Colin between the ears. 'Don't you have a home to go to, eh?'

The sheep stared up at her, his eyes full of silent pleading.

'Colin, come on. I've been scrubbing for days to get the stench of sheep poo out of the living room. I'm sorry, but you can't treat the place like you own it any more.'

Colin let out a long, plaintive bleat, holding eye contact.

'No, now go on. Stop looking at me like that,' she said, trying to sound stern. She waved her torch beam towards an adjoining field where a number of straggly clouds were floating about, separated from her garden by a gappy, crumbling drystone wall. 'Look, there's all your little mates happy enough, see? It's not raining now. Hell, it's not even cold – it's colder in here.'

Colin's expression suggested he didn't believe a word of it.

'Honestly it is,' Nell said, fully aware she was standing in her kitchen defending herself to a sheep. 'This house is solid stone, you know. Brrr. Now off you go. I'll see you around, eh?' She tickled his ears one last time, Colin tilting his head in appreciation, before closing the door and dragging the box back into position.

In the living room, she took a match to a couple of candles that had gone out and settled down with her book again.

Nell had never read *Wuthering Heights* before, but felt it was appropriate reading material for someone living in a half-derelict farmhouse on the Yorkshire moors. However, she'd just reached the bit where the child-ghost of Cathy Earnshaw knocks at the window, demanding entrance to her mortal home. The candles cast long, eerie shadows into every corner of the room, dancing on the walls and the thick panes of her own window, and Nell was starting to question whether Emily Brontë had been such a clever choice for her evening read after all.

She nearly jumped up the chimney when another faint tapping started up, at the front door this time.

'Ugh. That bloody sheep,' she muttered, patting her thundering heart.

She unlocked the front door and yanked it open.

'Colin, mate, I swear to God— oh.'

'Um, hi.'

On her doorstep was the school mum she'd met briefly earlier, Stevie Madeleine, holding a bottle of white wine out in front of her. Red, the cocker spaniel that had caused so much trouble, was panting at her ankles.

'Sorry,' Nell said. 'I thought you were a sheep.'

Stevie shrugged. 'Happens to me all the time. Can we come in?'

'Well, yes, you're welcome to, but I'm afraid I can't offer much in the way of home comforts.'

Stevie and Red followed her into the living room. Stevie looked around, blinking in the candlelight.

'Bloody hell, you weren't kidding.'

'Yeah, it's a work in progress,' Nell admitted. 'So what can I— sorry, pull up a box. What can I do for you?'

Stevie plonked herself down on one of the numerous cardboard boxes filled with Nell's stuff that had been shoved against the walls while Red made herself comfy on the floor cushion. 'Call it a housewarming present,' she said, nodding to the wine at her feet. 'I really can't thank you enough for what you did today. My Milly's a dozy little sod on the roads at the best of times. I've asked the mums who supervise the breakfast club bus to keep an extra-close eye on her, but sounds like you were the only one on the ball this morning.'

'Oh, I didn't do anything much,' Nell said, flushing.

'You saved my little girl's life. My dog's too. That's something much in my book.'

'I really didn't. I just got her out of the way.' Nell changed the subject, feeling embarrassed at her increasingly exaggerated heroism. 'Where is Milly?'

'She's staying at her nana's tonight. That's my wife Angela's mum, not mine – my late wife, I should say. I don't have any family in the village.'

'Oh, I am sorry. About your wife, I mean.'

'Thanks.' Stevie picked up the wine. 'Anyway, I thought we could have a glass or two together. If you wanted to have a drink with me, that is. And if you drink.' She laughed. 'I'm making a lot of assumptions here, aren't I? I just wanted to say thanks for what you did for Mill, and you being new to the village and all, I guessed you might feel like you needed a friend.'

'How did you know where I lived?'

'Carmel in the post office told me. She got it from Anne Scott, Xander's mum. I guess Anne got it from Xander. Everyone's kind of amazed the old place found a buyer, to be honest.' She smiled at Nell's expression. 'I know. It's a cliché, but yep, we're that village. No secrets.'

'Do you know Xander then?'

Stevie shrugged. 'I know most people. And most people know me, and most people know most other people. We're—'

'—that village. I know,' Nell said.

'Now you're getting it,' Stevie said, grinning. 'I know the Scotts better than most though. Xander and his mum are old friends.'

'Look, is he – I mean, he seems a nice lad and everything. But is he definitely all there? We had the weirdest conversation today when he called me to his office.'

Stevie laughed. 'Oh God. What did he say?'

'He just sort of blathered manic nonsense at me. I walked in on him having a nap at his desk. Then he told me how masterful he'd been in the staffroom earlier and how he definitely, definitely wasn't insane. He looked knackered, I felt kind of sorry for him.'

'Well, be gentle with him, it was only his first day. And he's had a rough couple of years.'

'Has he? Why?'

'Not for me to say, really. He might tell you, when you know him better.' Stevie regarded Nell thoughtfully. 'You know, I've been a friend of the Scott family since I moved here. Xander was a shy, awkward, lanky eighteen-year-old then, earning beer money doing odd jobs in our garden. Now he's a shy, awkward, lanky thirty-something. He's always struggled to talk to girls he fancies.'

Nell laughed. 'Me?'

'Why not?'

'Come on, we just met today. Plus he's my boss.'

She shrugged. 'He's still Xander. Got wine glasses?'

'Just a sec.'

Nell went into the kitchen and dug out a couple of dusty sherry glasses. She gave them a rinse in the sink and headed back to Stevie.

'Sorry they're so tiny,' she said, handing them over. 'The crockery and stuff came with the house. Looks like Farmer Ted was a fortified wine kind of a guy.'

'Well, frequent refills can be the order of the night.' Stevie poured an incy-wincy glassful of wine and handed it to Nell. The candlelight cast a glow through the crystal, making a flickering golden ghost on the stone flags of the floor.

'Cheers then, Miss Shackleton,' Stevie said, raising her glass.

'Not sure I'm really supposed to go drinking with my school parents,' Nell said, toasting her back. 'I'll have to trust you not to grass me up to the governors.'

'Oh, don't worry about that,' Stevie said, waving a hand. 'It's a small village, everyone drinks with everyone. You know, your predecessor was the head's ex-wife. He met his current wife when she was serving as a school governor. It's that incestuous round here.'

'Xander's married?'

She laughed. 'Don't be daft. No, I mean the real head, Jeremy Illingworth.'

'Ah, right.'

'Can I just make it clear I'm not coming on to you, by the way?' Stevie said, smiling awkwardly. 'I'm old enough to be your – well, not quite your mum, I hope, but certainly a much older sister from your dad's first marriage.'

Nell blinked. 'Never would've assumed you were.'

'No. Sorry. Sexual orientation's usually the first thing newcomers get told about me so I like to drop that in, just in case someone gets the wrong idea when I show up on their doorstep waving bottles of wine.' She took a long draught of said wine. 'It was the first thing you heard about me, wasn't it?'

'Well, yes, Jolene Hancock did mention it in passing.'

'Mmm, I bet. She doesn't mean any harm, but when you're the only gay in the village it does tend to be the first thing about you that comes to mind for people.' Stevie half-smiled. 'I actually think they're proud, in a funny sort of way. Jo's the kind of person who hates being tarred with the small-town yokel brush. Born and bred in Leyholme but her heart's in New York.'

'She did seem kind of… I dunno, glam, I suppose.'

'Exactly. And when you've got your very own pet lesbian in the school-mum brigade, well, that's practically cosmopolitan, isn't it? I'm the human equivalent of a soy frappuccino and smashed avocado on sourdough. Someone to namedrop. I don't mind.'

'Don't you? I'd be pretty pissed off.'

Stevie sighed. 'Oh, they're good people. But I guess I am a bit jaded from years of being reduced to "the gay single mum".'

'So you're not from Leyholme originally then?'

'No, I grew up in Cononley. Angela was, though. We met through work and when it got serious I moved here to be with her. I think that makes it worse, to be honest, when you've come in from outside.' Stevie shivered and nodded to the fireplace. 'Have you considered lighting that, love? My nipples are about to have one of your eyes out.'

Nell smiled. 'I gave it my best shot. Turns out my inner cavewoman skived off the class on how to make Man's red fire.'

'Here. Pass us the matches, I'll soon get it roaring.'

Nell watched in awe as Stevie first deconstructed and then rebuilt her little stack of logs and kindling, creating a perfect interwoven prism. In the gaps she stuffed knotted sheets of newspaper. The finished pyramid was a thing of beauty, almost a modern art sculpture.

'How did you do that?' Nell asked in a reverent whisper.

'We had an open fire when I was a kid.' Stevie lit a match and touched it to the twisted newspapers. 'It was the only heating in the house – it heated the water tank too, so even in summer we had to light it if we wanted a bath. One of my chores was getting it going first thing every morning, before my little brothers were up.'

'That sounds a bit Dickensian.'

'It did have a workhouse vibe in the cold weather. We lived on a farm too, a working one. My mum left us when my youngest brother was tiny and Dad worked long hours with the animals, so I was left to take care of the kids.' She glanced up. 'What about you? Are your parents nearby?'

'There's just my dad and his wife, over in Leeds. My mum...' Nell hesitated. '...she left us, too.'

'Yeah?' Stevie focused her attention on the fire, which Nell appreciated. There was nothing worse than the stares of pity and surprise you tended to get from strangers after dropping something like that into conversation, as she was sure Stevie knew from her own experience. 'No contact now, then?'

'Not much. She...' Nell flinched, but pushed herself to go on. She ought to be able to talk about this with people. It wasn't wrong; wasn't shameful. It was just something that happened. 'She had an affair, when I was a kid, and it left her... in a delicate situation, if you like.'

'Delicate, as in...'

'Pregnant, yes. On purpose maybe, I don't know. She wanted another kid and my dad didn't, or couldn't, that was the muddled message I half picked up from overhearing them rowing. So when I was nine she left to start a new family with this other bloke, her lover. Totally forgot about the family she already had.' Nell gave a bleak laugh. 'Every year she sends me a bit of cheap costume jewellery for my birthday and I send her a thank-you card. And that's it; the sum total of our relationship.'

Stevie finally looked up to meet her eyes. 'Wow. What a bitch. I'm sorry, Nell.'

'Well, I guess it's always more complicated than it seems when you're viewing it through a child's eyes. Dad married again when I was thirteen.'

'Do you get on well with his wife?'

Nell stared into the fire, burning shame rising in her cheeks as she thought about Leanne.

'I wasn't much of a stepdaughter,' she confessed. 'Leanne was just like a mum to my little brother Freddie. He was six when they married so she's the only one he really remembers. Me... God, I was a pain in the arse.'

'It must've been tough, seeing someone taking your mum's place. Thirteen's a difficult age to have to share your home with someone new.'

'Maybe so, but I was a selfish little cow.' Nell winced with guilt. 'The number of times I yelled at her that she wasn't my real mum when all she was trying to do was reach out to me. The sulks I used to go into because I felt like she was taking my dad away from me.' She sighed. 'She must hate me.'

'Surely not. Not now you're both adults.'

'I don't know. We're civil enough to each other, but I drove such a wedge between us back then, it feels like we'll never be able to close the gap.' She thought back to the brief telephone conversation she'd had with Leanne earlier: little more than a 'happy birthday', an awkward silence and then goodbye. 'It's always so strained when we're together, and yet she's such a great mum to my brother. So happy with Dad...'

'And you feel like the outsider,' Stevie said softly.

'Yes,' she whispered. 'Ridiculous, isn't it? It's my mum I ought to have been angry at. She's the one who walked out on us. All Leanne ever did was try to be there for me and all I ever did was push her away.'

'Well, it's hard, that kind of rejection from a parent. It goes deep – deeper than a kid can properly understand. All they really know is the anger. Trust me, I've done this one.'

'It did feel like that. I didn't have the words, then, so I just acted out. And Leanne got the full force of it.'

'You should talk to her.'

Nell sighed. 'I'm not sure how, now. I've been so distant since leaving home.'

'It's never too late to start healing, Nell.'

'No. I guess not.' She summoned a smile. 'Thanks.'

'So how did you end up moving to this godforsaken corner of the globe then, if you don't mind me asking?'

'There was a job opening. I'd just broken it off with my fiancé and felt like I needed a new start.'

Stevie laughed. 'In Leyholme? Funny place to come looking for new starts. Why here?'

'Looking for something. Something I always felt I'd missed out on.' Nell stared into the fire. 'A place I could belong, maybe.'

'Well, chicken, I think you might find it. You certainly seem to have made an entrance.' Stevie picked up her sherry glass and finished the bit of wine left in it. 'Hey, how about we leave the place to warm up and head down to the pub? We'll freeze our lady-goolies off in here.'

'It's not that cold, is it?'

'Says Susie Seven-Jumpers over there. I'm not even wearing a vest.'

'Red's fine. Fast asleep, look.' The cocker spaniel was snoring away on Nell's cushion, back leg twitching as she dreamed of chasing rabbits.

'Red's covered in fur. Plus she's an idiot, which stops her feeling the cold.'

'Dunno, Stevie. I'm not sure I really ought to be seen necking wine in the local on my first day, having it get around that the new Reception teacher's a drunk.'

'You worry too much,' Stevie said, laughing. 'But if it really bothers you, we'll go to the White Bull in Morton. It's only half an hour over the moors, a nice little torchlight walk. I'll buy you a drink and fill you in on all the playground gossip you'll need to know if you want to survive in this place until the Christmas holidays.'

Chapter Five

'Here you go,' Justin said, dumping Xander's pint in front of him. 'On me. You look like you're ready for it.' He squinted at his friend. 'You look like you're about ready for Dignitas, to be honest.'

As arranged, Xander had headed to Justin and Sara's place in Morton after work only to find their son Jacob lying naked in a pile of Cheerios in the kitchen, beating the floor and screaming while his parents stood over him in a fluster.

'What on earth brought this on?' Xander had yelled over the din.

'He wanted Justin's coffee,' Sara told him.

'He drinks coffee?'

'Course he doesn't drink coffee, Xand, he's two. But if he sees his dad eating or drinking anything, whatever it is, he wants it. He's reached the age where he thinks it's time to challenge Daddy for alpha male status because he's in love with me. All perfectly normal, if you believe that Freud bloke.' Sara squinted at him. 'Mate, you look rough as flip, pardon my child-friendly French.'

'Oh. Yeah. Tough first day.'

'Right.' She gave Justin a little shove. 'You. Take him out for a pint, he's clearly gagging for one. Jacob'll calm down when you're out of his sight.'

Jacob, hearing his name, decided it was time for a new tactic and started holding his breath.

Justin had put up a token amount of resistance, but eventually he'd had his arm twisted with no great effort and headed to the White Bull with Xander while his wife dealt with their increasingly purple toddler.

'Cheers, Jus,' Xander said, drawing the pint to him and holding it tenderly in both hands like a long-lost pet. 'Do I really look that bad?'

'Last time I saw a face like that it was on an Edvard Munch painting. What the hell happened to you today?'

Xander took a reviving gulp of beer. 'That's just it. Nothing.'

'Nothing? Then how come you look like a reanimated three-week-old corpse?'

'I...' Xander blinked into his pint. 'Jus, I can't do it. I think I need to resign or something. It's beyond me.'

'No it isn't. You're just being neurotic, as per usual. Take a week to get into your stride before you start making decisions like that.'

'You know, I was reading in the paper about some bloke whose job it is to censor erotic uploads at one of those personalised greetings card websites,' Xander muttered. 'You reckon it's too late for a change of career?'

Justin squinted at him. 'Something did happen, didn't it?'

'Not really.' He sighed. 'OK, sort of. I mean, other than the fact I'd been awake all night worrying and my mum being, well, my mum, and not knowing what the hell I was supposed to do with myself all day, there was... this other thing.'

'What other thing?'

'Right, you remember when we were seventeen we got those fake IDs and took the train down to Manchester for a night out? Those sisters, Chloe and Siobhan?'

'Er, yeah, vaguely. Why?'

'You copped off with Siobhan and left me with Chloe. I knew I had to make sexy chitchat but couldn't think what to say, so I was racking my brains for something to talk about...'

'Ah, I remember. And the last subject you'd revised for Geography A-Level was...'

'...Icelandic herring exports. Yeah. She went to the loo and never came back.'

'So you spent your first day as a headteacher boring your colleagues to tears about Icelandic herring exports?' Justin said, frowning.

Xander took another sip of beer. It was slipping down very easily.

'Not exactly. But I may have accidentally drooled on our new Reception teacher and rambled some bollocks about Celtic FC.'

'Who, you? You don't know the first thing about football.'

Xander groaned and dropped his head to the table. 'I know.'

'Why were you talking about Celtic? Is she a supporter?'

'No, I was just thinking out loud,' he mumbled, in a voice muffled by his arms. 'You should've seen this girl, Jus. She looked like a Highland princess or something.'

'Poetic.'

'Honestly. Beautiful yet scary is how I'd describe her. Like she'd be up for either seducing you or kicking you in the nuts, depending on her mood. Wild red hair, green eyes...'

'What, like that lass over there?'

Xander looked up to see where Justin was pointing and his eyes went wide. Nell was at the bar with a glass of wine, chatting in a familiar way to Stevie Madeleine.

'Shit,' he hissed to Justin, grabbing his arm. 'Jus, that's her! Nell Shackleton, warrior princess-slash-Reception teacher.'

Justin turned to give Nell a proper examination.

'She's a teacher?' He let out a low whistle. 'I didn't know primary teachers were allowed to be hot. I thought even the young ones had to be all huge glasses and cardies, à la Miss Honey. You lucky bastard, Scotty.'

'Mate, you have to hide me. I can't face her again, she thinks I'm mental.'

'Hide you where, under the table? We'll get kicked out for lewd behaviour.'

'Seriously. Come on, we'll go sit in the snug before she sees us.'

But it was too late. Red had already spotted her old friend Xander and come bouncing towards him, tail wagging itself into a blur.

'Traitor,' Xander muttered as he fussed her. 'Tell you what, I've never approved of this trend for dog-friendly pubs.' He glanced towards the bar. 'Oh balls. Now they're coming over. Thanks, Red, thanks a bunch.'

'Excellent,' Justin said. 'You can have another go at chatting Miss Honey up then, can't you?'

'I don't want to chat her up, Jus. We're colleagues, that's all.'

'Right. Course you are.'

'I mean it. OK, she's insanely beautiful, but even if there was the slimmest chance I could get someone like her to look at me twice, I can't go out with another teacher. Not now. I'm her boss, for Christ's sake. I'll settle for learning to talk to her like a normal person and leave it at that.'

'All right, fine, then you can practise that. You take Xena Warrior Princess, I'll wingman for you and keep her fit big sister busy.' He brightened. 'It'll be good to hone my skills a bit, see if I've still got it. It's been a while.'

Xander laughed. 'What, you're going to hone your skills on Stevie Madeleine?'

'Yeah, why not?' Justin rolled his eyes. 'I know, I know, I'm a married man. It's only a bit of fun, Scotty – no touching, I promise. Be just like the old days, eh?'

Xander had hated this bit of the old days. This had been the bit where they'd found a couple of pretty girls, then Justin had gone like a bomb with his relaxed, easy charm while awkward, socially inept Xander had crashed and burned.

Not this time, though. He smirked to himself.

'Stevie's not Nell's sister,' he said.

'Oh, right. Who is she then?'

'Old friend of the family's – my family, I mean. She lives in Leyholme too.'

'Ah, OK. That's good, gives me an in.' Justin grinned, flexing his fingers. 'Better prepare yourself to watch the master at work.'

'Jus, you know she's… I mean, she's not…' Xander gave up. 'Knock yourself out, mate.'

Justin slipped off his wedding ring and summoned his old knicker-dropping, on-the-pull smile as the women approached. It didn't seem to have atrophied much in the years it had been out of action. Personally, Xander would've been content if he could just have stopped his mouth from wobbling.

'Hi again,' Nell said to Xander when she reached him. 'You know, we were just talking about you.'

What? Why? Why would anyone, and especially Nell Shackleton, ever want or need to talk about him?

'Were you?' he managed.

Stevie laughed. 'No need to look so scared, Xander. All nice things, I promise.'

'Oh. Er, good. So what brings you two out this way?'

'Wine, mainly. Nell fancied a drink away from the judgemental eyes of the playground mums.'

'So, ladies,' Justin said, nodding to two free chairs. 'Would you like to join us? Always room for more over here at Party Central, right, Scotty?'

Nell glanced at Xander. 'Are you sure that's allowed, socialising with the boss? I don't want to get you into trouble.'

'No. I mean, you won't. Er, well, I am the boss, aren't I?' Xander fixed his face into a frown. 'And I insist you sit down at once, Miss Shackleton, or I'll be forced to discipline you.'

No sooner were the words out of his mouth than he regretted them. He shot a look of horror at Justin.

That was neither small talk nor flirting. It was psychopath talk.

'I'm not a psychopath,' he said, just to clarify.

Nell blinked at him. Xander buried himself in his beer, wondering if he should give up and just go home.

'What he means is, neither of us are psychopaths and we'd love it if you joined us.' Justin pulled a chair round closer to his and indicated for Stevie to take it.

'Er, thanks,' she said, shooting an amused look at Nell.

'This is my friend Justin, by the way,' Xander told the two women. 'I apologise for him in advance.'

'So how do you know Xander, Stevie?' Justin asked her.

'Oh, we go way back. He used to trim my topiary.'

Justin snorted. 'I bet he did.' He shuffled his chair nearer to hers. 'So... will your husband be joining you tonight?'

'I should think that's very unlikely. I haven't got one.'

'OK. Your boyfriend maybe?'

Stevie laughed. 'Nope. My life is quite notoriously man-free, if that's what you're angling to find out.'

'That's good news for me then, eh?'

'Don't you think I'm a bit old for you, sonny?'

He grinned. 'Not at all, I like my girls on the vintage side. With age comes experience, right? I bet you've shown your share of lads like me a thing or two.'

'Mmm. You'd be surprised.'

Nell nudged Xander, who was laughing silently at his friend. 'You're enjoying this, aren't you?' she whispered.

'Me? Never.' He twisted his chair to face her, trying to think of something to talk about that wasn't Icelandic herring exports. 'So, um... how's the farm?'

'Still standing, thanks.'

'Nell, I'm sorry about earlier, really. I honestly didn't mean to be rude.'

'Forget about it. You were obviously under a bit of stress.' She smiled. 'And anyway, it was sort of cute.'

What? Had she just called him cute? He wasn't sure whether he ought to feel complimented or insulted.

'Thanks,' he said. 'Also, sorry about threatening to discipline you. Er, I won't.'

'You're a kind and benevolent employer, Xander Scott. Definitely not a psychopath, I can tell.'

He winced. 'I'm sorry about that too. And for anything weird I might go on to say in future.'

Nell laughed. 'Are you always this nervous?'

'Only with human beings.' He reached under the table to give Red a stroke. 'Well, the small ones I can manage. Hence, teaching.'

'I'm really not scary, you know. You should try to relax a bit.'

'No.' He smiled. 'No, I know you're not. So have you done much work on the farmhouse yet?'

'Nothing really, other than chuck a couple of tarps over the roof to keep the rain out. And Stevie was kind enough to get the fire lit for me so I don't have to sleep in my thermal knickers tonight.'

Xander tried not to blush at the picture she'd conjured. It was an odd man who could have inappropriate thoughts about a woman in long-johns, but apparently he was that man.

It was a while since he'd last had sex, to be fair. Mental images of Nell in her underwear, any sort of underwear, were water in the desert by this point.

'I'll start work in earnest tomorrow after school,' Nell said, oblivious to his flushed cheeks. 'First job's the roof, then I need to sort the back door out before my friendly neighbourhood sheep moves in for good.'

'I could help. If you like. Um.'

She blinked at him. 'You?'

'Yeah. Not that I'm any kind of home improvement expert, but if you need another pair of hands, just ask.'

'Well, thanks, that's very neighbourly of you.'

Xander finished his beer, starting to feel more relaxed as the alcohol seeped into his tired, eternally anxious brain. Nell didn't seem to be recoiling in horror at his conversation, although she did look faintly puzzled, and he hadn't mentioned herrings once. That had to be a win.

'How did you end up buying that old house?' he asked. 'We thought it'd never sell in the village.'

Nell folded her arms. 'It was a bargain.'

He laughed. 'OK, it was a bargain. That wasn't a dig, Nell. Just interested.'

'Sorry.' She uncrossed her arms. 'Didn't mean to sound defensive. I suppose I'm just a bit pissed off with people telling me what a dump they think the place is.'

'Who's said that?'

'My dad, mainly.' Nell paused to take a sip of her wine. 'I had to move out of my flat in Manchester after I split with my fiancé. Dad wanted me to go back home. Naturally he was horrified when I told him I'd spent nearly all my savings putting a deposit down on some knackered farmhouse in the middle of nowhere.'

'Well, he's got a point. Sorry. But it is in a bit of a state.'

She shrugged. 'I like a challenge. With Humblebee Farm, I've got the opportunity to really make it my own. You know, like on those telly programmes where couples do up barns in rural France then drink wine and scoff baguettes on gingham picnic blankets in the neighbouring vineyard.'

He smiled. 'We're a bit short on vineyards round here.'

'Well, maybe when it's finished I can split a bottle of plonk with the sheep in the field next door,' she said. 'Anyway, I couldn't bear to move back home. Seriously, can you imagine living with your parents again now? I'd have felt totally pathetic.'

Xander coughed. 'Er, yeah. Nightmare. Sorry, hang on a sec.'

He pulled out his mobile to make sure it was on silent, just in case his mum rang. No need for Nell to find out quite how pathetic he was.

There was an Instagram update in his notifications and he tapped to open it. He only followed one account so he already knew who it was going to be from.

AnnieGetYourGun64 House to myself tonight. Book open, gin poured. Why not, right, ladies? #GinOClock #ChinChin #CatsAway #LiveYourBestLife

The photo showed a tumbler of gin and a half-empty bottle of Gordon's on his mum's coffee table. A half-empty bottle of Gordon's that had been an almost full bottle of Gordon's when

Xander had left the house that morning. He sighed and tucked his phone away again.

'So can I tempt you to another?' Nell asked, nodding to his empty pint glass.

'No, thanks. I really have to get home and catch up on my sleep so tomorrow I can be a fully functioning headteacher.' He turned to Justin, who was muttering in Stevie's ear while she leaned away from him, grimacing. 'Come on, Jus, let's leave these girls to it. Your wife and child await.'

Stevie raised an eyebrow. 'You're married then, are you?'

'Er, yeah,' Justin said with a guilty grin. 'Sorry. Just tell me, though, was I in with a shot?'

'No.'

'Come on. Seriously?'

Stevie sighed and looked at Xander. 'You can fill him in, Xand. I don't have the energy.'

'You're the wrong shape, mate,' Xander informed his friend.

'Eh?' Justin glanced down at his chunky rugby-player's bod. 'Never had any complaints before.'

'Let's go, Jus. I'll explain on the way.'

'Oh,' Nell said as they stood to go. 'Xander. I meant to ask earlier: do we have a theme yet for 7th March? I know it's yonks away, but I want to get ahead on my lesson planning while I'm living *sans* telly.'

Xander stared at her. 'Sorry – 7th March?'

'Yeah, World Book Day. You do that here, right?'

'Oh. Yes, course we do.'

'OK. So does the school choose a theme or do we just follow the official one?'

'We choose our own, but we don't start planning until the spring term usually. I'll, er, keep you posted.'

–

When he got back home, Xander found his mum stretched out on the sofa, snoring nasally with a book in one hand and an empty glass in the other.

Gently he prised them both from her fingers. He placed her bookmark between the open pages of her book and left it on the coffee table, then took the gin tumbler into the kitchen to put it in the dishwasher.

The bottle of Gordon's sitting on the worktop was now around a third full. With a quick glance through the door to check his mum was still sleeping, Xander stuck it under the tap and added an inch of water. He shook it, then put it away in the cupboard.

Anne Scott wasn't what people pictured when they thought of an alcoholic. She never drank before five p.m; she never lied about her drinking or hid the evidence; she rarely drank until she was sick. Those were the rules, and as long as Anne abided by the rules she'd never think she had a problem. But she drank a lot, every night. Neat spirits in big, gulping mouthfuls, until they knocked her to sleep.

His mum had always been prone to over-indulging a bit on weekends, even when his dad was alive. But Xander hadn't realised quite how bad it had become until he'd moved back home after splitting with Marie.

'Mum?' he whispered, shaking her gently.

'Hm?' She blinked her eyes open, breaking into a smile when she saw who it was. 'Xander, love. How was your first day?'

'It was great, Mum. Perfect.'

'Where did you go tonight?' Her voice was slurred and thick.

'I went for a pint with Justin after work. I did tell you,' Xander said, fighting against a feeling of guilt at having left her alone. 'Have you had your tea?'

She looked puzzled for a moment. 'Tea? I don't... no.'

'You ought to eat. I'll make us a supper, shall I?'

Her eyes opened fully. 'Cake! We need to have your celebration cake. I have to cut it.'

She half pushed herself to her feet, wobbled, then sank heavily back to the sofa again.

'Let me do it,' Xander said. 'You're a bit… tired, Mum.'

'Yes. Tired. I am quite tired.'

'Why don't you lie down, eh? I'll bring you some water.'

'It's just the dreams, you know,' she mumbled.

'I know.'

Xander gave her his hand to help support her weight as she lay down. Then he headed to the kitchen, shaking with silent sobs.

Chapter Six

'Milly, please. I'm begging you.' Stevie dropped to her knees on the kitchen floor and clasped her hands together. 'Look, see? I'm literally begging you. Please eat faster. We're both going to be late.'

It was 3rd January, the first day of the new spring term, and as on every other first day of term, the Madeleine household was neck-deep in back-to-school chaos.

Milly tutted, dragging her spoon through her porridge to create swirls of golden syrup. 'Mummy, you're being very silly. Stop it.'

Keen to add to the general mayhem, Red shot into the kitchen, grabbed her favourite rubber chicken from her dog bed, headbutted Stevie in the back and shot out again, squeaking her toy excitedly.

'Duckling, I need you to hurry up,' Stevie told Milly. 'It won't look very good if I'm not on time for work the first day back after Christmas, will it?'

Milly shook her head. 'Your boss will be mad with you, I bet my life.'

Stevie didn't know where her four-year-old daughter had picked up the phrase 'I bet my life', but if she ever found out then she'd certainly be filing a strongly worded complaint.

'Exactly,' she said.

'And then you might get sacked.'

'I know. And then we'll have no money and you'll have to go live in the orphanage and they'll put Red in the naughty dogs' home.'

Milly blinked at her. 'Where will you go?'

'The naughty mummies' home, probably.'

Milly stared for a second. Then she started spooning porridge into her mouth like her life depended on it.

Stevie smiled as she stood up. She bent to kiss her daughter's hair. 'Well, I don't think it'll quite come to that, but thanks for trying to save me. Slow down a tiny bit, eh? We don't want breakfast coming back up again.'

'I made you a present, Mummy,' Milly mumbled through a mouthful of porridge.

'That was kind of you. Will I like it?'

Milly nodded emphatically, spraying droplets of porridge. She yanked something out of her pocket and handed it to her mum.

'It's a hat,' she said as Stevie unfolded it. 'Nanny and me made it for you. Put it on.'

Stevie smiled and did as she was told, perching the sailboat newspaper hat on her head.

'And you have to wear it *all day*,' Milly said, jabbing her spoon in Stevie's direction. 'All day and not take it off once. Promise?'

'I solemnly promise I'll wear it wherever the dress code doesn't specify no paper hats,' Stevie said, raising three fingers in a Brownie salute. 'Now come on, eat up.'

There was a knock at the door.

'Is it the bus?' Milly asked.

'No, you've missed the bus messing about. I'll have to take you in for breakfast club today.'

'But I'm having my breakfast now.'

'That's because you woke up and told me you were *absolutely dying* of starvation, didn't you, drama queen?' Stevie said as she hunted in her handbag for the front door key. 'And now we're late-laterty-late. You can still have a bit of fruit.'

'Who's at the door, Mummy?'

'It'll be the new dog-walking lady, Deb. She's going to be looking after Red for us in the daytime from now on.'

'Is she a nice lady?'

'She's very nice. Red likes her a lot.'

'Do you like her?' Milly asked, turning big eyes up to her mother.

Stevie hesitated. 'Yes, I think I do. She's funny, even though her jokes are terrible. And she's very smiley.'

Milly nodded her approval. 'I like smiley people.'

Stevie went to answer the door and was surprised to find Nell there.

'Oh. Hiya. Thought you were my dog-walker.'

'Ahoy there, Captain Pugwash,' Nell said, with a naval salute in the direction of Stevie's new hat.

'Ahaha. You know, with a bit of work you might be nearly as funny as you think you are. What's up?'

'Brought you something.'

Stevie took the wine bottle Nell held out to her. It was filled with tiny white fairy lights and marbled paper flowers. She flicked a switch on the side of the cork and watched the lights illuminate.

'You didn't make this yourself? It's gorgeous, Nell.'

'You teach kids long enough, you develop an aptitude for arts and crafts,' Nell said, smiling. 'It's actually your wine bottle. The one you brought me after my first day at school, I saved it.'

'You didn't have to do that.'

'I wanted to. It was nice of you to help me feel like I belonged here when I didn't know anyone.'

'Well, thank you. I love it.' Stevie put the bottle on the shelf by the door. 'Are you heading to school? You're welcome to walk in with me and Mill. I'm dropping her off today.'

'Thanks, I'd like that.'

'Here, come in. She's just wolfing down her breakfast before the Child Catcher turns up to drag her off to the nearest orphanage.'

She ushered Nell into the hallway and squinted at a figure in the distance, being yanked along by five four-legged demons on leads.

'Hang on, that's Deb, my dog-walker,' she told Nell. 'Red! Come on, you daft hound. Your new friend's here to take you out to play.'

Red came bounding down the stairs. She jumped up at Nell to give her a lick, sending her staggering backwards, then joined her mum at the door.

Stevie shook her head. 'I've never known a dog like her for causing havoc.' She took Red's lead from a hook on the wall and clipped it to her collar.

'Now you be good today,' she told Red, wagging her finger. 'Play nicely with the other dogs and no running away. I've gone to a lot of effort to get you a lovely new walker, I don't want you frightening her off with your bad behaviour on her first day.' She smiled at Deb as she approached the house. 'Hiya. Nice to see you again.'

'Hey-up,' Deb said, beaming as ever. She nodded at Stevie's hat. 'If you've got the chips that came in that, I'll have one.'

Stevie flushed and yanked the thing off her head. 'Sorry. Present from my daughter.'

'Nah, put it back on, it suits you,' Deb said. 'The Steve Bell cartoon brings out your eyes.'

Stevie laughed. 'You're sweet.'

'Is the gorgeous Red all ready for me then?'

'Yep, here you go.' Stevie handed over the lead. 'I'll be back around four if you'd like to drop her off after that.'

'Will do. Have the kettle on, eh?'

Milly had crept to the door and was staring open-mouthed at Deb and her many canine companions.

'Oh, this is Milly, my daughter,' Stevie said, resting a hand on Milly's head.

'Hiya, tiny,' Deb said, grinning.

'And this is Nell,' Stevie said, jerking her head in Nell's direction.

Deb peered over Stevie at Nell. Her full-beam smile seemed to flicker a notch. 'Right.'

'Are all these dogs yours?' Milly whispered.

'Not all of them. Just this little one.' Deb pointed out Life, the border terrier. 'You can stroke her if you want. She likes being stroked.'

Milly crouched to run her hand over the dog's fur and Life wagged her tail appreciatively.

'Red likes being stroked too,' Milly told Deb.

'Then I'll be sure to stroke her lots till you and your mummy get home. If that's OK?'

Milly hesitated a moment, then nodded.

'Right, I'll be off then,' Deb said to Stevie. She shot another look at Nell. 'Um, yeah. See you later, Stevie. Bye, Milly, nice to know you.'

When she'd gone, Stevie shut the door. 'One thing off the list,' she said to Nell. 'Mill, where are your school shoes?'

'Jeffrey's got them on.'

'Well, Jeffrey can just take them off again. Go get them.'

'Jeffrey's her big bear,' she told Nell when Milly had bounded off to her room. 'He's got into cross-dressing just recently.'

'So who's your dog-walker?' Nell asked. 'A friend?'

'No, not really.' Stevie started yanking her coat on. 'It was a bit random, I met her in the park and we got chatting. She had a vacancy coming up, I needed a new walker, so here we are. I just hope Red doesn't put her off.'

'Right.'

'What?' Stevie said. 'Why're you looking at me like that?'

'There just seemed to be a bit of… you know.'

'No, I don't know. Explain.'

'You know.' Nell waggled her eyebrows.

Stevie pursed her lips. 'Stop that. There is no "you know". I'm fresh out of "you knows", now and ever after.'

'Come on. Everyone needs a bit of "you know" in their life.'

Stevie bent to pull her boots on. 'You're barking up the wrong tree anyway, love. She's not gay.'

'How do you know? She was giving me some major jealous evil-eye over your shoulder there. And what was all that business with the hat?' Nell nudged her. 'Some pretty saucy flirting, I'll warrant.'

'That was just messing. She isn't a lesbian, I promise you. I remember her joking about her ex-boyfriend the day we met.'

'She might be bi.'

'She might. But she also might not. And the statistical likelihood is that she isn't.'

'Hmm. Did she definitely say ex-boyfriend?' Nell asked. 'Because that is definitely what I remember flirting looking like.'

'She...' Stevie paused, trying to remember the conversation she'd had with Deb when they'd met over two months earlier. 'Yeah. Yeah, I'm sure she did.' She shook her head. 'It doesn't matter anyway, I'm out of the game. I've got Milly and Red in my life and that's enough for me. I'm too old for romance, Nell.'

'Come on. What are you, forty?'

'Forty-three.'

'Spring chicken, that is. You'd think you were eighty with talk like that. Why not sign up for Tinder or something?'

'No, I couldn't do that. Not after Angela.' Stevie brushed past Nell to unlock the door. 'We'd better set off before we're all seriously late.' She turned to yell over her shoulder. 'Milly! Bag, coat, shoes. It's time to go.'

—

'...and I just really don't feel the school is taking into account Robbie's needs,' Mrs Doneen said, looking at Nell over the top of hands pressed together as if in prayer. 'He's a very gifted boy, Miss Shackleton. If he isn't challenged by the tasks you set him, he will act out. It's boredom, not deliberate naughtiness.'

Nell swilled her coffee absently.

'Miss Shackleton? Are you listening?'

'Yes.' Nell fixed on a sympathetic smile and uttered the words she knew parents like Mrs Doneen always wanted to hear. 'You're quite right. Of course Robbie needs to be challenged – all our pupils do. But we do have to follow the Early Years Foundation Stage framework to make sure no one is left behind, as does every school.'

'I don't see why the bright children are the ones who have to suffer,' Mrs Doneen muttered. 'Why should they be held back by the less intelligent children? It isn't right, the way they're dragged down by the lowest common denominator.'

'I don't believe anyone at Leyholme Primary is being dragged down, Mrs Doneen. All the children learn in their different ways, and we strive to give each one the mental stimulation he or she needs.'

'You know, his father and I are convinced Robbie's on the autistic spectrum,' Mrs Doneen said, ignoring her. 'You really ought to take that into account.'

Nell suppressed a sigh. She'd taught a number of autistic children in her years as a teacher and Robbie Doneen showed none of the signs of that condition. Whereas he showed every sign of being over-indulged at home and obsessed with seeing just how far he could push his luck.

'Last year I'd have gone straight to Mr Illingworth with this,' Mrs Doneen said. 'He always had time for me. But under the new management… well, when the head of a busy school dives into his office like a frightened rabbit whenever he so much as catches sight of a parent—' She stopped herself. 'But it's only for the short term, I suppose. Let's hope so, anyway.'

'I must say, I think that's a little unfair,' Nell said, as gently as she could manage. Gentle tones while quietly seething were the first thing you learned to master when teaching Reception. 'Mr Scott has only been doing the job a couple of months. Personally I've found him to be a pleasure to work with.'

Mrs Doneen quirked a pencilled eyebrow. 'Yes. So I'd heard.'

'I'm sorry?'

'There have been sightings. The two of you...' She glanced over her shoulder at the children filing into class and lowered her voice. '...the two of you canoodling in the pub.'

Nell frowned. 'Canoodling?'

'Well, is it true?'

Nell bit back the answer she wanted to give, which was that it was none of Mrs Doneen's business who she canoodled with.

'No, it's absolutely not true. We have occasionally bumped into each other in one of the locals and enjoyed a friendly drink together, yes, but there has definitely been no canoodling. You've been the victim of village hearsay, I'm afraid.'

'Hmm. No smoke without fire, I always say.'

'Mrs Doneen, I can promise you that if I'd been canoodling with Xander Scott, I'd certainly have noticed. And of course I'd have ensured you were the very first to know.'

'I don't think there's any need for sarcasm, Miss Shackleton.'

Nell gritted her teeth and forced her irritation back under control. 'I'm sorry, but I really don't see that my private life has anything to do with my teaching methods. Mr Scott is a colleague, that's all – a colleague and a friend. Any gossip that might be doing the rounds about the two of us is purely because we're similar in age, I suppose.'

Mrs Doneen looked like she had more to say on the subject, but before she could speak, Nell stood and shook her hand firmly.

'Thanks for your feedback on my lessons, Mrs Doneen, I'll be sure to bear it in mind. If you have any other suggestions on how I ought to be nurturing young Robbie, please do let me know.'

She'd been trying her best not to sound sarcastic that time, but she couldn't be sure a teeny bit hadn't crept in under cover of darkness.

'I certainly will. And if I find out you've lied to me, if there is any kind of... of *dalliance* going on between you and your Mr

Scott, be assured I'll take it straight to the chair of governors.'
Mrs Doneen gave her a curt nod and left.

Jolene Hancock, who'd just come in to deliver the kids from
the breakfast club she helped run, flashed Nell a sympathetic
smile.

'You look like you've been Doneened,' she whispered as she
stopped at Nell's desk on her way out.

Nell smiled. 'Does it show?'

'What was it then?'

Nell lowered her voice. 'She thinks Robbie's not being
nurtured. Plus she's concerned I'm secretly having it off with
Xander Scott. Which, by the way, I'm not.'

'You should be so lucky, eh?' Jolene said, laughing. 'Don't
you worry about Karen, she's all bark and no trousers. We've
got your back if she starts giving you hassle, hun.'

Stevie was right, Nell thought as she watched Jolene leave.
For all their faults and foibles, the parents here were a good
bunch. You needed a Mrs Doneen in the mix to make you
appreciate all the non-Mrs Doneens.

When the mums and dads had all left, she clapped her hands
for quiet.

'OK, good morning, everyone. Desks please.'

Nell glanced around the room as the children took their
seats, a smile twitching across her lips. She'd missed the place
over a Christmas break spent back in Leeds with her family –
more than she'd expected, in fact. In the half a term she'd been
teaching at Leyholme, she'd grown to love her classroom, her
little universe, with its bright colours and its Comic Sans and
its happy, smiling, naughty little faces. There was nowhere she
felt so at home as right here, embedded in the simplicity, chaos
and joy of Reception.

Once the kids were seated, Nell took the register and then
allowed them to choose whatever activity they liked best to start
the day. Each sought out the table or corner they favoured,
whether it was Lego, plasticine-modelling, sensory play or

reading – although present-bragging seemed to be the main activity they wanted to indulge in that morning. After allowing ten minutes for them to get all the lingering Christmas out of their systems, Nell started their literacy lesson.

The first activity involved putting word-and-picture cards telling the story of Little Red Riding Hood into the right order. When they were all hard at work, she wandered among the desks, watching to see how they worked and interacted.

'Where's your Big Bad Wolf, Robbie?' she asked Mrs Doneen's delightful offspring as she passed the desk he shared with Olivia Cross, his best friend and ever-willing partner in crime.

'Up my bum, Miss.' Robbie slapped his hand to his mouth to stifle his giggles while Olivia guffawed appreciatively beside him.

'No he isn't. Come on, stop messing about.'

Reluctantly Robbie removed the laminated card from where it was hiding in his sock and slapped it down on the desk.

'Good, thank you. And now we'll have no more talk about bums until playtime, please.'

Olivia's hand shot into the air. 'What about poo, Miss?'

Ugh. Why were kids that age so disgusting?

'The list of banned words includes "bum", "poo", "wee" and anything else icky,' Nell told her.

'But after playtime it's OK?' Olivia asked hopefully.

'We'll see.' Maybe she could work it into their lesson on the digestive system later, just to keep them interested. Well, if you can't beat 'em...

'OK, Henry, that's good. Very neat,' Nell muttered as she passed a boy's chair, his tongue protruding from one corner of his mouth while he focused on getting the cards on his desk lined up.

'And Milly...' She blinked at Milly Madeleine in the seat next to Henry. She was sitting behind a perfect set of story cards, her arms smartly folded. 'Wow, you've finished already? That was fast work.'

Milly nodded, looking pleased with herself. 'It's my favourite story so it was dead easy.'

Nell crouched down beside her. 'Who told it to you?'

'My mummy. I think my other mummy used to tell it too, but I was a baby then so I don't remember. She's in heaven.'

'I know she is, sweetie. Can you tell me why it's your favourite story?'

Milly giggled. 'Because... because it's rude.'

Nell frowned. 'What, Little Red Riding Hood? Which bit is rude?'

'The bit...' Milly buried her face in her hands to hide her smirks. '...the bit where it says knickers.'

'Does it say that?'

'Yep. Red Riding Hood's got a gun in her knickers and then she shoots the Big Bad Wolf with it. Only it's not on the story cards so I had to miss it out.'

Nell smiled. 'Ah, I see. Does your mummy read you the Little Red Riding Hood story from a book called *Revolting Rhymes*, Milly?'

'Yeah, *Vaulting Rhymes*! That's my favourite ever book. I love all the stories.'

'How come Milly's allowed to say "knickers" when we can't say "bum"?' she heard Robbie whisper to Olivia behind her.

'Because Milly and me are talking about a book,' Nell said, turning to face him.

'Can I say "bum" if it's in a book then, Miss?'

'Er, yes, I suppose you can. If you're talking about the book.'

Robbie grinned, smug at having found a loophole. He met Nell's eyes with a glint of challenge, and she knew the little boy wouldn't rest until he'd scoured the school library for books mentioning bums.

His mum was right, he was gifted. Gifted at being a little bugger.

There was a knock at the classroom door and Mrs Rhodes, the school secretary, appeared.

'Message for you, Miss Shackleton.'

Nell got to her feet. 'OK, go ahead.'

'Alex— that is, Mr Scott, has asked if you can join him in the staffroom this break.'

'Me? What for?'

She shrugged. 'I've to give the same message to all the staff. Some big announcement he wants to make, I think.'

Nell frowned. 'Announcement?'

'That's what he said.'

'Oh God, please say he's not resigning,' she muttered under her breath as she went back to the kids.

Chapter Seven

'The thing is...' Ryan Theakston, Leyholme parish councillor and chair of the school's board of governors, took a sip of the coffee Mrs Rhodes had brought him. He wiped a fleck of foam from his odd little 1940s-style pencil moustache and put his mug down on the table. 'The thing is, Xander, a school is like a ship. And you're like the captain.'

'Right,' Xander said, wondering where this was going. Ryan had been quite pressing about needing to come in and see him the first day back. Did the board of governors want him to start wearing an eyepatch or something?

'Except you're not the captain, are you?'

'Aren't I?'

'No. Jeremy's the captain. So what does the temporary captain do while the real captain's in bed with cabin fever?'

'Er, splice the mainbrace?'

'No.' Ryan narrowed one eye. 'Maybe. I don't know what that is. Anyway, what I'm getting at is, you've got a simple job here. Scrub the decks, polish the portholes and make sure the ship doesn't go down. Don't change course, don't drop anchor and for God's sake don't go off hunting for the X that marks the spot.'

'Sorry, Ryan, but can we drop the ship thing? I'm feeling a bit seasick.'

'I'm saying you've got one job: to stop this place going under until Jeremy's back at his desk,' Ryan told him with a stern look. Xander was sensing he'd been quite proud of the whole ship analogy and resented the instruction to drop it. 'Stay on top of the admin stuff for one more term, all right? Keep the cogs turning, fight any fires that need fighting, keep your head down and don't do anything big. I came in to let you know Jeremy will be back at work after Easter.'

'Oh, brilliant. Is he recovered then?'

'Getting there.' Ryan stood up and patted the pile of paper in Xander's in-tray. 'Just keep doing what you have been doing. Busy yourself with this, answer the emails, make sure the parents are happy. And for God's sake—'

'—don't do anything big. Got it.'

'What are your plans for today then?'

'Well, what you just said, I guess. Admin, emails. Oh, and I called a staff meeting.'

Ryan frowned. 'Staff meeting? Why? That sounds big.'

'It isn't. I just want to ask for their input on the school's plans for World Book Day in March.'

'Hmm. OK, that sounds safe enough. Don't get too daring with it, will you?'

'Doubt I could if I tried,' Xander muttered as Ryan showed himself out.

As soon as the bell rang for morning break, Xander headed for the staffroom. When he pushed open the door, he discovered the other teachers and classroom assistants already congregated there, hovering anxiously.

'What're you all looking so worried for?' he asked.

'What is it? Bad news?' Frank, the Year 6 class teacher, demanded.

'No. Why, were you expecting some?'

'We thought it might be Jeremy. You know.'

'Oh, right. No, he's on the mend. I actually just wanted some input from you all on World Book Day.'

Caroline, the Year 2 teacher, exhaled slowly and patted her heart. 'You could've told us that when you sent the message, Xander.'

'Sorry, I didn't think.' He glanced around. 'So does anyone have any ideas for a World Book Day theme? Nell?'

Nell blinked. 'Who, me?'

'You were the one who brought it up.'

'I asked you what the theme was. That's not the same as volunteering to coordinate the thing. I've only worked here a few months.'

'As long as it's something to do with actual books for once,' Caroline said. 'The whole point of the day is to promote literacy. I'm literacy coordinator for this school and do you know what I got in my class last year when our theme was Bedtime Stories? Twelve Marvel Avengers, eight Disney characters, six premiership footballers, three kids who turned up in their pyjamas and an octopus.'

'Cthulhu,' Frank said.

She frowned at him. 'I'm sorry?'

'It wasn't an octopus, it was a Cthulhu. That was Edie Taylor. Her parents are big H.P. Lovecraft fans.'

'Well, at least that's from a book, I suppose,' she muttered. 'Perhaps someone can tell me why I had two Princess Anas, three Queen Elsas and an Olaf the snowman. What book are they from, *Frozen: The Novelisation*?'

'*Frozen*'s based on "The Snow Queen", isn't it?' the Year 4 teaching assistant, Kimberley, chipped in. 'That's a classic fairytale.'

'Very loosely based on. None of those characters are in the fairytale, they're pure Disney. And what about all the super-heroes?'

'They're not just from the movies, they appear in comic books too,' Frank said.

Caroline scoffed. 'Oh, *comic* books. Sorry, but I thought we were talking about literature.'

'Guys, could we just have a bit of calm?' Xander said, but as usual no one paid him any attention.

Frank drew himself up. 'And what's wrong with comic books, Caroline? Some graphic novels are genuine classics, I'll have you know. But I suppose you'd turn your nose up at the suggestion *Watchmen* could be considered literature.'

'You're right, I would,' Caroline shot back. 'Imported American rubbish, the lot of it, if you ask me.'

Xander sank into a chair, pushing his fingers into his hair. And to think he'd thought this was going to be straightforward.

'And what about the footballers, Frank?' Caroline demanded. 'Don't tell me you want to argue the case for *The Leeds United 2019 Annual* being classic literature? What else – *My Life in Football* by Kevin Keegan? The back of a Walkers crisp packet? I mean, where does it end?'

'There's a distinct whiff of "check your privilege" about all this, Caroline,' Kimberley informed her warmly. 'Not every child has the same access to books and reading. When you demand they choose characters from "proper" children's literature, you're favouring those with tertiary-educated parents. It sounds like you're sneering at some reading choices and not others, and that's not going to encourage them to read more, is it?'

'I'm sorry, but I just don't feel everything that contains words has equal value,' Caroline countered, jutting out her chin. 'Whatever they're given access to at home, our job as education providers is to broaden their minds with the good stuff.'

'And who decides what constitutes "the good stuff" – you? It needs to be child-led. Some kids are always going to be reluctant readers. Words and stories, wherever they find them, can guide them to—'

'Roald Dahl,' Nell said loudly.

The other members of staff turned to look at her.

'What?' Xander said.

'Er, Roald… Roald Dahl? Is he literary enough?'

'Well, yes, I suppose he is,' Caroline said.

'And most kids love him, don't they? No matter what their age or background,' Nell said, warming to her theme. 'He's crude and disgusting and scatological, he's dark, he appeals to the little monsters in them and makes reading fun. He expands their vocabulary without them realising but he's still easy to read, even for reluctant readers. My little brother used to gobble those books up, and as a general rule he never read anything wordier than *The Beano*.'

'So are you suggesting our theme for World Book Day ought to be the work of Roald Dahl?' Frank asked.

'That's up to all of you. I'm just putting it out there.'

Kimberley nodded slowly. 'Roald Dahl. I could certainly get behind that.'

'And me,' Frank said. 'Caroline?'

'Yes, I'd be happy with that. Just please, no footballers.'

'Right,' Xander said. 'OK, that sounds positive. Can everyone in favour of Roald Dahl as a theme raise their hands?'

There was a unanimous show of hands from the staff and he breathed a sigh of relief.

'Excellent,' he said. 'In that case, let's return to our classrooms and prepare our lesson plans. Er, Nell, can I have a quick word in Jeremy's – in my office?'

Nell followed him to the head's office and he shut the door behind them.

'Thanks for that,' he said. 'You really saved my skin there. I thought Frank was about to beat Caroline to death with his copy of *Watchmen*.'

'Happy to help.'

'Roald Dahl. It's a good idea. What made you think of it?'

'Stevie's little girl, Milly. She was talking about *Revolting Rhymes* in class this morning. It just seemed to fit everyone's requirements.' Nell smiled. 'So, confession time. You'd forgotten, hadn't you? That night in the Bull, when I asked about the theme, you'd forgotten World Book Day was a thing.'

He grimaced. 'Let's just say it wasn't top of my list of priorities.'

'Xander... you know you're better than this, don't you?'

'Me? No I'm not. Better than what?'

She gestured to a seat. Xander sat down, and Nell pulled up a chair next to him.

'Seriously, why do you always do that?' she asked.

'What?'

'Put yourself down like that. I said you were better than this and you denied it before you asked what I meant.'

'Oh. Yeah, suppose I did. Sorry.'

'And now you're apologising again,' she said, shaking her head. 'Don't let them make you be that guy, Xander. Don't be Karl Dönitz.'

'Karl who?'

'Dönitz. He was a senior member of the Nazi party.'

Xander blinked. 'OK, bit harsh. I've got my faults, but I can promise fascist tendencies aren't among them.'

'Dönitz was the supply Nazi who took over from Hitler,' Nell told him. 'He was appointed Führer after his gaffer's death with the sole job of surrendering to the Allies. A puppet leader with nothing to do but throw the towel in.'

'You seem to know a lot about it.'

'Well, I can't vouch for the historical accuracy. I got my information from a Mitchell and Webb sketch.' Nell twisted round to face him and put her hands on his shoulders. 'And I'm telling you not to surrender, Xander. To keep on fighting.'

'For Aryan supremacy?'

'For this school. For Xander Scott. Underneath that knotted cluster of neuroses and self-doubt, I'm convinced there's someone pretty impressive trying to make his voice heard. Don't let them Dönitz you.'

'The governors don't want me to do anything big,' he muttered.

'And who's the head?'

'Jeremy.'

'No he isn't, Jeremy's on sick leave. So who's the head?'

'Um, I am?'

She nodded. 'Bloody right you are. So get out there and do some heading. Talk to the kids, the staff, the parents. Make friends, be approachable, fix things that are broken. It's your job.'

'But what if I mess it up?'

'You're only messing it up by hiding in here with your paperwork. You were practically invisible last term, Xander.'

'Suppose I was a bit.' He felt the word 'sorry' forming again and bit his tongue to stop it slipping out.

'Don't you miss teaching?' Nell asked.

He sighed. 'God, yes.'

'So do some, then.' She squeezed his shoulder. 'Look. How do you fancy storytime with my kids tomorrow afternoon? Come and be our guest reader, they'll like that.'

'That sounds... nice, actually.' He looked up from his twitching fingers to smile at her. 'Thanks, Nell.'

'For what?'

'For believing in me. For thinking I'm less shit than all the evidence so far might suggest.'

'The only evidence for that is embedded in your brain.' Nell stood up. 'And as for not doing anything big – Mr Scott, what do you think to making this the best damn World Book Day Leyholme Primary's ever seen?'

–

'I enjoyed that,' Xander said as he and Nell watched the Reception kids file out with their parents after storytime the next day. 'Reminded me what it's really about. You know, that's the first bit of proper teaching time I've had since October – well, unless you count supervising that school trip to the Appersett Rope Museum, which I don't.'

'The kids loved it too,' Nell said. 'They never howl like that when I read to them.'

Xander smiled. 'Ah, well. I do the voices.'

He did do good voices. Nell hadn't been far off yelping with laughter herself a few times. His Big Bad Wolf – Welsh, in this version of 'The Three Little Pigs', for some reason – had been particularly impressive. For someone as self-conscious as Xander always seemed with other adults, he wasn't a bit afraid to make a fool of himself with the kids.

And they loved him for it, as children always do when they meet with an adult prepared to humiliate himself for their entertainment. They'd begged for a return visit the following week, which Xander had readily agreed to. Nell was hoping they might make storytime with the head a regular thing.

Xander picked up the copy of *Revolting Rhymes* he'd been reading from. 'Always a winner, eh? I used to wet myself over this when I was their age too.'

'Heh, and me. It's practically a rite of passage.'

'Good sign for this year's Book Day.' He waved goodbye to the last gaggle of kids as they left with their parents. 'See you next time, guys. Enjoy your weekends.'

'Bye, Mr Scott,' they chorused.

'And we want "Cinderella" next week!' Milly called back. 'Um, please may we have "Cinderella"?' she corrected herself, following a nudge from her mum. She giggled. 'I like it when the prince chops the ugly sisters' heads off and they roll all over the floor.'

'That child has all the makings of a future serial killer,' Xander observed when she'd gone.

Nell shrugged. 'That's kids for you. Adorable, disgusting and ever so slightly psycho. Got to love them, right?'

Xander looked at the cover of the *Revolting Rhymes* book, a Quentin Blake illustration of a wolf reading to a couple of children. 'Should see some good costumes this year. What did you do for World Book Day at your old school?'

'Oh, it was a massive thing there,' Nell told him. 'To be honest, it was more like World Book Week. We had all sorts going on: games, special assemblies and stuff. The kids and parents got really into it.'

'What school was it?'

'St Margaret's C of E, near Salford. Till I got made redundant.'

Xander stared at her. 'You're kidding. You never taught at St Mags'?'

'Yeah, why?'

'I did my PGCE placement there. Back when I was a student at Man Met.'

Nell turned away and started packing up her stuff. 'Did you really? Small world.'

'Nell, that place has got the most amazing reputation. Parents used to move from miles around just to get into the catchment area.'

'I know, it was a great school. I was sad to go, but I think it worked out for the best.' She glanced up to smile at him. 'I quite like it here.'

'Why did you get made redundant, if you don't mind me asking?'

'Falling pupil numbers. They had one more Early Years teacher than they needed, and I was last in so I got to be first out.'

'Falling numbers? I thought St Mags' was always oversubscribed.'

'Not the last year or two. Changes to the catchment area mean there are fewer eligible kids than there used to be.'

'Right.'

She finished loading her bag with folders and slung it over her shoulder. 'Hey, Xander. You busy tonight?'

'Me? No, not really, why?'

'I wondered if you fancied coming up to the farm for a chat. About World Book Day, I mean. I feel sort of responsible for it after suggesting the theme, and like I said, it was a massive thing at my last school. I thought we could, you know, thrash out some ideas.'

'What, me and you?'

'Yeah, why not? I'll order in a takeaway, get us some wine, it'll be fun. You can marvel at this amazing new invention I discovered recently: electric lighting.' She smiled at him. 'I kind of missed you over Christmas, you know. We can have a good old catch-up.'

'That sounds... great. I'd love to, Nell.'

'OK.' She patted his shoulder in a matey sort of way as she passed him to leave. 'My place at seven then.'

'Right. Shall I bring anything?'

'No, just yourself. See you in a bit, eh?'

Xander stared after her as she left, feeling a little light-headed.

It wasn't a date. It very definitely wasn't a date. It was work; that was all.

But still. Drink. Chat. Takeaway. Thrashing. Him and her, alone in the farmhouse. It wasn't a date, but it was definitely a date-lite. Supremely unobtainable Nell Shackleton, Warrior Princess, had just asked him out on a date-lite.

And... what was that about having missed him? Had she really said that?

He headed back to his office. Might as well squeeze in another couple of hours' work before he went home to get ready. It'd keep his mind off the nerves.

He couldn't believe Nell was ex-St Mags'. Anyone who'd taught there was seriously overqualified for obscure little Leyholme Primary, with its crumbling Victorian premises, declining pupil numbers and hard-won 'Requires Improvement' rating from Ofsted. With that kind of experience on her CV, Nell would easily have been able to walk into a job at some of the top schools in the area.

Yet here she was. It was a mystery all right. On fire with curiosity, Xander woke his computer and pulled up the website for St Margaret's.

Four hundred pupils, according to the homepage. That didn't sound like they'd downsized any since the days he'd been on placement there. There were still two Reception year classes. He scrolled through the News section, but there was nothing in there about staff changes or alterations to the catchment area.

Perhaps they hadn't got around to updating it in a while? Leyholme's school website had been known to sit neglected for months at a time too. Still, he'd have thought somewhere like St Mags' would be a bit more on the ball.

Xander hesitated a moment, then opened his mail client and did a search for Nell's name.

Nothing. Jeremy wouldn't have deleted them, surely?

But Nell would be short for something, wouldn't it? Helen… Ellen? She'd have used her full name on the application. He changed his search to just the surname, Shackleton.

Sure enough, there was a whole email chain between Jeremy Illingworth and Ryan Theakston, the chair of governors, relating to the appointment of new Reception class teacher Eleanor Shackleton.

Everything seemed in order. There was no mention of her redundancy, but the headteacher at St Mags' had provided a glowing reference, saying how sorry they'd been to say goodbye to Eleanor and how he hoped she thrived in her new role. Clearly she hadn't left under any sort of cloud.

Oh, nice one, Xander. The woman invites you to her place and you celebrate with a bit of light stalking. You know, paranoia really isn't an attractive quality in a man.

Mentally slapping himself, Xander closed his emails and turned instead to some of the paperwork that was cluttering up his in-tray.

Chapter Eight

Not a date, Xander reminded himself as he walked up the moorland track to Humblebee Farm. *Just a simple business meeting between colleagues. You're her boss, remember?*

For now, said a little voice. But soon Jeremy Illingworth would be back behind the headteacher's desk and… well, what then? There was no law against dating your colleagues, was there? Jeremy had both married and divorced the school's previous Reception class teacher, and they'd had other couples on the staff in Xander's time at Leyholme Primary. It certainly wasn't uncommon, not in a village school.

But even after Jeremy was back, Nell Shackleton would still be just as far out of Xander's league as she was now. They could be friends – he hoped they already were. But as for anything else… it wasn't going to happen. He needed to stop thinking about it.

Except not thinking about Nell seemed increasingly difficult lately. Xander's life didn't have many rays of sunshine, but in the few months she'd been at Leyholme, Nell had definitely become one. He'd caught himself making excuses to see her, timing his visits to the staffroom to coincide with her breaks. Actually counting the days until the Christmas holidays were over and he'd see her again.

He couldn't help it. Just a coffee and a chat with Nell – and for someone with all the social skills of a hermit crab, he found her a very easy person to chat to now his initial nerves had worn off a bit – could brighten up an otherwise grey day. She was fun. Joyful. She made him laugh.

So even though tonight wasn't a date, Xander was in his best jeans and shirt, clutching a bottle of wine. Well, it did no harm to make an effort.

He hoped his mum was going to be all right while he was out. She was up and down at the moment, with the anniversary of his dad's death coming up, but she seemed to be doing OK this week and he couldn't babysit her every night. He'd added a couple more inches of water to her gin supply before he'd left though, just to make sure she wasn't at any risk of overdoing it.

Xander pushed open the rickety gate to Humblebee Farm. The place was certainly looking better than the last time he'd seen it. It had a roof on top, for a start.

What looked like a pile of soiled wool was visible through the open door of an outhouse. Xander approached it to take a closer look, then jumped back when it let out a low *baa*.

'Sorry,' he muttered, backing away.

Keeping his distance – the thing in the outhouse was giving him a very dirty look – he knocked on the front door.

'Hi,' he said when Nell answered. 'Did you know there's a sheep in your shed?'

Nell gestured for him to join her inside. 'That's just Colin, the previous tenant. I felt bad for evicting him so I let him have the outhouse. He's become a bit of a pet.'

'Right. Oh, er, this is for you,' Xander said, presenting her with the bottle of wine.

'Thanks, Xander. I told you you didn't need to bring anything.'

'I didn't like to turn up empty-handed.'

He followed her through the house, casting an impressed glance around the cosy, well-lit hallway.

'Looks like you're making good progress with the home improvements,' he said.

'Yeah, getting there. Electricity and hot water were the biggest things, other than the roof – and I tell you what, you really appreciate them after roughing it for a bit. Hot baths, my God! Better than sex.'

Did she say this stuff on purpose? Xander ran a finger under his collar, thinking that a cold shower wouldn't go amiss, never mind a hot bath.

'I'm broke now though,' Nell went on, oblivious to his discomfort. 'Spent the last of my savings on the roof.'

'What's still left to do?'

'Ugh. Everything else. Getting the back door lock sorted might end up being a pretty pricey job, and then there's painting, carpeting, furniture. I haven't even got a bed yet, I'm on an air mattress. But I'll be home-improving on a shoestring until I've got a bit more in the pot.' She held open the living room door to him. 'Here we are.'

'Oh,' he said.

The room was packed with people, milling about chatting while a roaring fire blazed in the hearth. There was Caroline and Frank, and some of the other teachers. Stevie Madeleine, Jolene Hancock, Karen and Keith Doneen... it looked like half the village was in Nell's house that night.

'I thought it'd be good to rally the troops,' Nell said, beaming. 'Quite a few of the parents were anxious to be involved. Of course I asked Caroline along as literacy coordinator, and some of the other staff who said they'd lend a hand.'

'Right. That was good thinking.'

Definitely, definitely not a date then. As if there was any chance it could have been. *Xander, you idiot.*

'Xander, come join us.' Stevie Madeleine came forward to guide him to a little group of parents by the fire. 'We were just discussing the idea of running a book-themed fete to raise money for this literacy charity Jo was telling us about. Sounds like they do great work with kids in disadvantaged communities. What do you think?'

'It's a good idea to do something for charity, but... I don't know, a whole fete?' Xander said. 'That might be a bit ambitious.'

'We can pull it off, as long as all of us parents are willing to roll up our sleeves,' Stevie said.

'Help yourself to food, Xand,' Nell said, nodding to a table of spring rolls and other takeaway nibbles. 'White or red wine?'

'Er, red, please.'

She'd used the short version of his name, he couldn't help noticing. What did that mean?

That they were friends, probably. Friend-zoned, wasn't that what the kids called it when one of you wanted friendship and the other secretly hankered after more? So very, very platonic it was painful.

It did hurt actually: he was a little surprised by just how much. No matter how many times he'd told himself it wasn't a date, he'd still cherished a forlorn hope it might be.

Nell was nice to him – more than nice. She seemed to understand him, now they'd got to know each other. She'd said she believed in him when no one else had. She'd told him she'd missed him over the holidays – he'd been replaying those words in his head all evening. And he'd never been great at interpreting body language, but the little touches, the arm-squeezes and shoulder-pats, must mean she at least felt comfortable around him. For just one brief, glorious moment when she'd opened the door, he'd allowed himself to think that a Nell sort of person and a Xander sort of person might actually be able to fit together.

But it was work. It was just work. Fucking work.

'I'm not sure the governors are keen on us getting too adventurous while Jeremy's out of action, Stevie,' he told her when Nell had pushed a glass of red wine into his unresisting hand. 'They might not like the fete idea.'

'Oh, bum to the governors,' said Keith Doneen, who seemed to share a vocabulary with his son Robbie. 'It's our school. Bugger them, I say.'

'Yes. I actually am a parent governor, Keith,' Jolene said.

'Ah. Sorry.'

She shrugged. 'Well, you're right though. The kids'll love it, that's what matters – not Ryan Theakston and his obsession with bloody efficiency drives.'

Stevie nodded. 'This could be something really good for Leyholme, a regular addition to the school calendar for our kids to look forward to in the No Man's months between Christmas and Easter. Milly's already described to me in great detail the Red Riding Hood costume I'm apparently going to be making for her with my non-existent seamstress skills. Keith's right; sod caution! Let's go all out for the littlies while they're still young enough to appreciate it.'

'I'm just a bit worried it'll be too much for us,' Xander said. 'It'll be a lot of work. And what if it flops?'

'And what if it doesn't?' Stevie said. 'I've been saying this to you for years, Xander Scott: you really need to work on your glass-half-full mentality.'

He blinked at the half-empty, half-full glass in his hand and took a gulp of wine.

'Well, if you're all keen on the idea then yeah, I guess we could go for it,' he said, the wine helping his Dutch courage along a bit. 'Why not? Like Jo says, the kids'll enjoy it and that's the main thing. If it gets more of them reading, so much the better.'

'And they'll be raising money for charity too,' Jolene said. 'I think the Roald Dahl focus is an inspired idea. Morgan's obsessed with *Fantastic Mr Fox* at the moment.' She nodded to Nell, who was animatedly waving her arms while she chatted to Caroline and Frank. 'That girl's a diamond, Xand. I'd hang on to her if I were you.'

After a couple of hours' wine and discussion, the little group of World Book Day organisers had a solid, if ambitious, plan to work to. Celebrations would involve Dahl-themed literacy lessons on the morning of the event, then in the afternoon there'd be book-related stalls and games in the main hall, with parents and villagers invited too. Everyone present had volunteered to run something, even difficult Karen Doneen smiling in cooperation as the wine flowed, and Nell was confident they'd be able to press-gang more help from within the school community.

'Well, thanks for coming, everyone,' she said at the end of the night as she chucked paper plates into a bin bag. 'Really productive, I think. Let's get something in the school newsletter next week asking for volunteers, then we can go from there. Don't trip over the sheep on your way out.'

Stevie squeezed Nell's arm. 'Good job with this, chicken. You know, I'm starting to wonder how we ever managed in this village before we got our very own Miss Shackleton.'

Nell blushed at the praise. 'Thanks, Stevie.'

When Nell had bustled off with her bin bag, Stevie approached Xander by the fireplace and gave him a nudge.

'Oi. Go help Nell clear up,' she whispered.

'All right. Why?'

'Because everyone's going home now. If you help tidy up, you can be last to leave.'

'Why do I want to be last to leave?'

Stevie rolled her eyes. 'Good God, you're an idiot. Are all boys like this?'

'No, just me, I think.'

'Just do as you're told, Xand. For me.'

Xander shrugged. 'OK, if it gives you pleasure.'

He started collecting up bowls and glasses while the others filed out. When he had his arms full, he followed Nell into the kitchen.

'Thanks,' Nell said. 'Just dump them by the sink.'

'Here, let me wash them up.'

'You don't need to do that. Honestly, leave them, it'll give me something to do with myself.'

'Nope, I insist. I want a chance to be amazed by this lah-di-dah hot running water you were telling me about.'

She smiled. 'Well, if it means that much to you. Go on, knock yourself out.'

Xander twisted the stiff brass tap until a stream of hot water was filling the washing-up bowl. Behind him, the front door slammed closed as the last member of their new World Book Day committee left.

'Well, there'll be talk on Monday,' Nell muttered.

'What?'

'Oh, Mrs Doneen. She's got this theory...' Nell glanced across at him. 'Never mind.'

'She seemed to be in a good mood.'

'Yeah, but she was on the warpath yesterday. I think I managed to pour oil on troubled water with tonight's invitation though. She just wants to feel she's being listened to, really.'

'The wine might've helped too.'

'Definitely.' Nell nodded to the steaming washing-up water. 'Impressive, right?'

Xander shook his head. 'I don't know, *hot* water? It'll never catch on.'

She laughed. 'Thanks for helping anyway. Don't bother washing my glass, will you? Or yours.'

'Why?'

'Because I'm going to invite you to stay and have another drink with me.'

Xander looked down into the suds so he had an excuse to avoid eye contact. 'Oh. OK.'

Chapter Nine

Once all the bowls and glasses were upside-down on the draining rack, Nell presented Xander with a fresh glass of wine. He followed her back through to the living room, where she gestured for him to take a seat on the sofa.

It was an interesting array of furniture she'd put together. Nothing matched, from the modern curved glass coffee table to the twee chintz armchair. And yet 'charmingly mismatched' suited the place, somehow.

The sofa was a plush brown monster straight out of the 1970s, ugly as hell, but God, was it comfy. Xander sank back against the cushions and allowed himself to soak in the warmth of the crackling fire, letting out a deep sigh as the tension left his body.

'I think that might be the most relaxed I've ever seen you,' Nell said as she sat down next to him.

'Yeah, this is nice. It's good to get out for the evening. My mum's lovely, but she can be a bit much when you have to see her every day.'

'Your mum?'

He winced, feeling some of the tension creeping back again. 'And I did not just mean to tell you that.'

'You live with your mum?'

'Only temporarily.'

'Oh God.' Now it was Nell's turn to wince. 'And I said—'

'—you said how pathetic it must feel to move back in with your parents at our age.' He shrugged. 'Well, you're not wrong.'

'I didn't mean pathetic. I just meant... you know. It would've felt like a step back, like being a kid again.' She groaned and threw herself back against the cushions. 'I'm digging an even bigger hole for myself here, aren't I?'

Xander laughed. 'Hey. Did you just turn into me?'

Nell laughed too. 'Think I did. You must be catching. So how did you end up back with your mum then?'

'Same as you. Break-up.' He glanced around the room. 'Is that where this lot came from? Did you get all the weird furniture in the split?'

She shrugged. 'Most of this came from skips, if you want the brutal truth. People throw away some nice things, I'm broke and it seemed a shame to let it go to waste. Don't judge.'

'How did you get it here?'

'Stevie's been helping me. We make a pretty good skip-diving team actually. She's only little so I hold her ankles while she fishes out the good stuff.'

'I guess everyone needs a hobby.' He shuffled to face her. 'You two seem close these days.'

'Yeah, I love being with Stevie. We just seemed to hit it off, you know?'

'You're not... I mean, not that it's any of my business, but I couldn't help... sorry. I'll shut up.'

Nell rolled her eyes. 'No we're not. Lesbians aren't obligated to be attracted to every woman they meet, Xander. Sometimes, radical as it might sound, people with compatible genders and sexualities can just be friends.'

'So you are compatible? I mean, you're, um... are you...'

'I'm straight, if that's what you're fumbling around,' Nell said. 'Even if I wasn't, there's still the fifteen-year age gap. Plus the fact I'm her daughter's teacher. Plus the fact you're a cheeky sod for assuming.' She put on her best teacher voice. 'And we know what it makes when we assume, don't we, class?'

Xander smiled. 'It makes an ass out of you and me.'

'Yep. Except in this case, where it just makes an ass out of you.'

'Sorry. I didn't want to make a fool of myself, that's all.'

'Make a fool of yourself how?'

Yeah, Xander, make a fool of yourself how? By offering her your body? Begging to remove every item of her clothing with your teeth? The wine must be going to his head.

'It's just that if there's a way to put my foot in something, I'm the man to do it.' He swiftly changed the subject, before he dug himself in any further. 'So it was a broken engagement that sent you here looking for a new start? That sounds unpleasant.'

Nell grimaced. 'It really was. We were only a month from the wedding too.'

'So I guess I shouldn't ask, right?'

She smiled. 'Well, I'll tell you my miserable break-up story if you tell me yours.'

'OK. But you go first.'

'I found out he'd cheated on me,' she said with a sigh. 'Right before the wedding, that old cliché. But this was a bit different.'

'Why was it different?'

'Well it was on his stag do, for a start.'

'Shit, really?'

'Yep. With the stripper his mates had booked for him. In Blackpool. While dressed as a sumo wrestler.' Nell knocked back a big glug of wine. 'Which they filmed. And which then went viral on social media.'

'Jesus Christ!'

'You can search for it if you want. The hashtag's #DeepThroatSumo.'

'I'll pass, thanks. God, what a bastard.'

'Yeah.' She shook her head, her brow knitting. 'I mean, I knew he was a different person with his mates than he was with me. I knew he could sometimes be a dick when he was pissed. But I never thought he was capable of doing something like that to me. The grief over the end of the relationship was almost drowned out by the epic humiliation of it.'

'But not quite.'

Nell blinked hard. 'No. Not quite.' She looked up to meet his eyes. 'So come on then, your turn. Reckon you can top #DeepThroatSumo?'

'I'm not sure anyone can top that.' He stared into the fire's dancing flames. 'No, it was much more mundane for me – no hashtags. My girlfriend got offered a job up in Scotland. She wanted to go, I wanted to stay, so… here we are.'

'Had you been together a long time?'

'Eight years.'

'Bloody hell, as long as that?' Nell squeezed his knee. 'Tough break. I'm sorry.'

He shrugged. 'It was my fault. I'd not been an easy person to live with for about a year before she left. It was never really about the job; that was just an escape route for her. An excuse to bail out of the relationship guilt-free.'

'What happened, love?' Nell asked softly.

'I could see the two of us were heading for a massive car crash and I did nothing to fix things – pushed her away whenever she tried to build bridges.' He sighed. 'She must've been lonely. I lost my dad, you see. That was the root of all our problems – well, my problems. Marie was just an innocent bystander caught in the crossfire.'

'Aww, Xander.' Nell didn't move her hand from where it was resting on his knee. 'Stevie said you'd had a rough few years but she wouldn't tell me why.'

'It was hard,' he admitted. 'I was so… angry, afterwards. Hurt, and angry, and then there was this completely crushing, overwhelming sense of loss that just didn't seem to fit with the all-consuming rage. Marie couldn't cope with me. I couldn't cope with myself.' He snorted and finished the rest of his wine. 'But Mum was the one who really suffered. She found him.'

'Your dad?'

'Yeah. She found him…' He choked back a sob. 'Don't ask me.'

'I'm sorry,' Nell said gently. 'I won't ask anything.'

'It was… he did it to himself. I mean, he took his own life. In the fucking *house*, for Christ's sake. In my mum's house, Nell.'

'Shit! Xander, that's… oh God. I'm so sorry.'

'And now Mum has to live with that image burned into her brain, forever. Did the selfish bastard even think about that – about her? No wonder she…' He looked up, pleading in his eyes. 'We never even knew he was depressed.'

'That's OK. It's OK for you not to have known. It's not always visible.'

'Is it OK to be angry? Is it OK to still love him, and miss him, and hate his fucking guts all at the same time?'

'Everything's OK. He was your dad and this is your grief. No one gets to decide what's right and wrong for you to feel.' She put her wine glass down on the table and looked up at him. 'Would you have to give me a disciplinary for sexual harassment if I gave you a hug right now?'

He smiled weakly. 'No, we're off the clock.'

'Good, because I'm going to give you one anyway.'

She wrapped her arms around him, an action that under normal circumstances would have sent his heart pounding with anxiety as he worried about the many ways he could mess things up. But this time, it kind of felt… fine. Right. He relaxed in her embrace, his arms tightening around her perfect, reassuringly Nell-shaped body, and inhaled the fresh, smoky scent of her hair.

'Thanks,' he whispered.

She reached up to run her fingers through his hair. 'You're a lost sort of soul, aren't you, Xander Scott?'

'If that's a poetic way of saying I never quite fit in anywhere, then yes, spot on.'

Nell held him back to look into his face. He took his glasses off and ran the back of his hand over his eyes, aware they were wet with tears.

She reached up to pull his hand away. 'Don't do that. Don't hide yourself from me.'

'Sorry.'

'And for God's sake, stop apologising all the time. You've got nothing to apologise for.' She ran soft fingertips over his damp cheek. 'You know, Xander, I reckon you fit with me pretty well.'

There was a little smile at the corner of her mouth. Her fingers were still resting on his face, her eyes locked into his. And for once, every non-Xanderish cell in his body, every nerve and impulse that proclaimed they were just two people and this was right, absolutely right, joined forces to nudge him on. *For Christ's sake, kiss her!* they yelled. *Don't worry about messing it up, just get the hell on with it. Look, she wants you to.*

His eyes had started to close, his head tilt forward, when a loud rap sounded at the front door and made them both jump.

'One of them must have left something,' Nell said, disentangling herself from his embrace. 'Hang on, Xand. Hold that thought.'

She went to answer it. Xander, trying his best to hold that thought, put his glasses back on and followed her to the door.

There was a young man on the step: dark, tall, good-looking in a rough around the edges, designer-stubbly kind of way, with a big holdall slung over one shoulder. He looked sort of… trendy. And Xander realised he'd just thought the word 'trendy', which meant he was officially ninety years old.

As soon as the mystery man caught sight of Nell, he picked her up and swung her around in his arms.

'Nelliephant, you unspeakably gorgeous sight for sore eyes! Guess who's come to pay you a surprise visit?'

She laughed. 'I guess Freddie. Put me down, you daft git. What the hell are you doing here?'

The man pouted. 'I told you, surprise visit. What, are you not pleased to see me?'

'Course I am. Bit of notice would've been nice, that's all.'

'Yeah. Thing about a surprise visit, Nell…'

'Um,' Xander said.

'Oh.' Nell turned to face him. 'Sorry, Xand. This is my annoying baby brother Freddie, who likes to turn up at my house unannounced just to piss me off. Fred, this is Xander Scott, a work colleague.'

Brother. Xander almost sighed with relief. 'Hi, Freddie. Really great to meet you.'

Freddie eyed the hand Xander offered suspiciously before deigning to shake it. 'Yeah, mate. And you.'

'Nell, I'd better go,' Xander said. 'You two must have catching-up to do. I'll see you Monday at school, OK?'

'OK.' She squeezed his arm as he passed her to leave. 'Thanks for tonight, Xand.'

Xander floated dreamily back down the garden path and out of the gate, almost tripping over the sheep as he left.

–

'So, sis, who's the geek?' Freddie asked once Xander was out of earshot.

Nell shooed him into the house. 'Don't call him a geek, Fred.'

'Why not? He is a geek.'

'Yeah, but it suits him. You make it sound like an insult.'

'Who is he then? New boyfriend?'

'He's my boss. And likely to stay just my boss thanks to you, you big gooseberry.'

He laughed. 'What, seriously? Did I interrupt you about to jump his bones?'

'No you did not. We were just… lingering. You know, eye-wise. What do you want, anyway?'

'Just to see what's what. We hardly got a chance to talk over Christmas.' He looked at her keenly. 'So you found her then.'

'I told you, she found me.' Nell smiled. 'And Freddie, she's just perfect.'

Chapter Ten

'So you kissed her?' Sara asked.

'No,' Xander said. 'But I was about to. Then her brother turned up and the whole thing got shut down.'

Sara had decided a bit of father/son bonding time might be the best way to cure Jacob of his toddler-sized Oedipus Complex so the two friends were enjoying a pint together in The Highwayman's Drop, the Leyholme village pub, while Justin stayed at home with Jacob. At least, that's what she claimed. Given she was already halfway through her second pint and smacking her lips appreciatively after each mouthful, Xander reckoned that was just a handy excuse to leave her husband holding the baby while she went to the pub.

'And you think she wanted you to, do you?' she asked.

'Well, I did at the time. I'm second-guessing myself now. I might have completely misread the situation.'

'Was there any lip contact at all?'

'None.' Xander took a thoughtful sip of his pint. 'We were kind of tangled up, limb-wise, and she said something about us being a good fit. Or maybe that wasn't it exactly, but it sounded like she was saying, you know, that she liked me. And she was touching my face.'

'OK, that sounds pretty conclusive. She definitely wanted you to.'

'Dunno. I was crying at the time, which sort of complicates things.'

Sara shook her head. 'Xand, I know you're always a mess of anxiety with girls you like, but bursting into tears when you're about to kiss them is a bit much.'

He smiled. 'Come on, I'm not quite that bad. We'd been swapping break-up stories over wine.'

'Ah. So you told her about Marie.'

'And Dad.'

'How'd she take it?'

'She was… sweet. I mean, she seemed to understand. Then she gave me a hug.' He sighed. 'I don't know, maybe I did misinterpret things. I was upset, she was probably just being nice. Girls like Nell Shackleton don't go for boys like me.'

'Why don't they?'

'Because… because they can pick and choose, can't they? And when women can pick and choose, they always pick and choose men who aren't me. Men like Justin.'

Sara shook her head. 'Xander Scott, I wish you could see yourself.'

'Well it's true, isn't it? All through school, Jus blazed a trail through most of the girls we knew while I melted into the background.'

'Because you put yourself in the background and he didn't. Loads of girls fancied you at school. You were just too dim to notice even the most in-your-face flirting.'

He smiled. 'Well, it's good of you to try to make me feel better.'

'For Christ's sake, mate, I don't care if you feel better or not. This is God's honest truth.' She downed the last of her pint with relish. 'I fancied you.'

'You did not.'

'Yes I did, in Year 12. You know, that loveable loser thing you had going on was actually a real turn-on.'

Xander snorted. 'Loveable loser? Gee, thanks.'

'You pull it off though.' She put her head to one side and squinted at him. 'You're sexy, Xand.'

'Come on, pack it in.'

'You are.' She reached across to take his glasses off him, put them down on the table and ruffled his hair up a bit. 'Look at those big brown eyes, I could lose myself in them for a year. I bet this Nell Shackleton doesn't know what's hit her.'

'Sara, I can't see.' He put his glasses back on and pushed them up his nose. 'Stop winding me up, will you?'

'It's one hundred per cent true, I did fancy you at school. And I'll tell you who else. Jolene Murgatroyd.'

'Jo? Give up.'

'She did, you know. But I reckon the pair of us could've stood in front of you in nothing but black lacy knickers, begging you for a threeway, and you'd have said to yourself "oh, how kind of them to pretend they're interested in a poor, unshaggable slob like me" before bumbling off on your merry way. We both gave up on you in the end.'

'I'm not buying a word of this. Although feel free to expand on the threeway bit if you like.'

Sara shrugged. 'Ask Jo if you won't take my word for it.'

'Yeah, all right, I'll ask her next parents' evening. See you at the tribunal, eh?'

'Fine, don't believe me then. It's still true.' She slid her empty pint glass towards him. 'Go on, it's your round.'

'You're knocking them back a bit quick, aren't you?'

'My first child-free night in months? Bloody right I am.'

'Oh God, I don't believe it,' Xander muttered, peering over her towards the bar.

'Eh?'

'It's Nell. Again. She's going to think I'm stalking her.'

Sara turned to look. 'So that's the lovely Nell, is it?' She nodded approvingly. 'Nice one, Xand.'

'Don't be too obvious about it, will you?'

'Who's her hot young gentleman friend?' she asked, turning back. 'Is that the brother?'

'Yeah, Freddie.'

'Well come on then, finish your pint and we'll both go to the bar. You can chat her up, I'll have a crack at Freddie.'

Xander shook his head. 'Are you and Jus getting into swinging or something? Why are you suddenly both obsessed with dragging me out on the pull like we're all horny teenagers again?'

'What, has he been out chatting up girls with you? I'll kill him!'

He laughed. 'You massive hypocrite.'

'Wife's prerogative.' She sighed. 'Oh, he wouldn't do anything. Neither of us would. We just want to feel young and attractive again for a short while, I suppose.'

'Doesn't Justin make you feel like that?'

'He never gets the chance, Xand. Our sex life now has been reduced to an occasional quickie in the shower while Jacob's mesmerised by *Twirlywoos* for five minutes. It's hard to feel sexy with a kid in your life, what with the endless bouts of screaming and bodily fluids. Life at home these days is like the director's cut of *The Exorcist*, now with extra vomit.'

'You're really not selling parenthood to me, you know.'

'Good. Save yourself, love, while you still can.'

Xander finished his pint. 'Can I help? I'm happy to babysit every once in a while so you two can go out for some couple time.'

She stared at him like he'd just offered to pay off her mortgage. 'Would you really do that?'

'Course, why not? I do work with kids, in case you'd forgotten. I'm sure I can manage one night minding a toddler without breaking him.'

'I'd be more worried about him breaking you. I say this as the mother who gave birth to him and loves him dearly, but Xander, that boy is an absolute little shit.'

Xander smiled. 'I'll be fine. Go on, text Justin and we'll fix a date.'

'Xand, I don't say this often enough but I love you,' she said, taking out her phone. 'Thank you, thank you, thank you; you're a saint.'

–

'So?' Nell said to Freddie. 'What do you think to my new local?'

He shrugged, casting an underwhelmed look around the staid little pub with its fleur-de-lys wallpaper and old framed photos of the village dotted about. 'It's a bit dull, isn't it?'

'What were you expecting, pole dancers?'

'I don't know, live music or something. At least a pool table.' He frowned at the beer in his hand. 'I wasn't expecting £3.50 a pint, I can tell you that.'

'Welcome to the real world, student boy. It's not all £1 Jägarbombs out here, you know.'

Freddie humphed. 'Can't believe they don't do an NUS-card discount in this place.'

'I paid, didn't I? That's come out of my severely depleted house-fixing kitty so you can just bloody appreciate it.'

'All right, all right. Jeez,' said her twenty-one-going-on-thirteen little brother, rolling his eyes.

'It's got a fascinating history, you know. Local legend says Dick Turpin once stayed here.'

'Right. So that's why the prices are highway robbery, is it, in tribute to his memory?'

'Funny.'

'Are they coming then?'

'They're going to pop in briefly after they get back from the supermarket,' Nell said. 'So make sure you behave yourself, OK? I want you to make a good impression.'

'Hey. It's me, isn't it?'

'Hmm.' Nell took a sip of her wine. 'Where do Dad and Leanne think you've gone for the last of your Christmas break?'

'Potholing. Which when I saw the state of your place didn't seem like much of a fib.'

'Oi. Insult the farm, you can sleep in the outhouse and I'll let Colin have the sofa.'

Freddie nodded to a distant table. 'Isn't that your geek boyfriend-boss over there?'

'Don't say stuff like that in public, you could get us in trouble.' Nell squinted at the table. 'You're right though, it is him.'

'Who's the woman with him?'

'Dunno, never seen her before.'

Freddie nudged her. 'Looks like he moved on quickly, eh?'

'Give over.'

The two of them watched as Xander's lady friend removed his glasses and ran her fingers in a familiar way through his hair.

'That definitely looks like a date, sis,' Freddie said. 'Are you going over to scratch her eyes out?'

Nell shrugged in what she hoped was a careless fashion, turning back to her wine. 'Xander's entitled to go on dates if he wants.'

'What do you see in that guy anyway? He's nothing like your usual type.'

'Maybe that is what I see in him.'

'You're making things a bit complicated for yourself, aren't you? I'd have thought you had enough going on without jumping into bed with your boss.'

'Fred, I told you not to say stuff like that,' she whispered. 'Seriously, I'm not kidding. This place is hell for gossip.'

Freddie lowered his voice. 'Well, why are you making things complicated?'

'Because... because I like him, all right? I didn't mean to let myself like him, but that's the thing about Xander Scott, he creeps up on you. At first you just want to hug him; he looks so adorably rumpled and lost all the time. You think you're safe enough, then before you realise it, you find yourself wanting to... do other things to him.'

Freddie watched her face for a moment. 'Be careful, Nell.'

'I know what I'm doing.'

'I really hope you do.' He nodded behind her. 'Looks like you'll be able to ask him if it's a date yourself in a minute.'

'Eh?'

'The pair of them are heading this way.'

'Shit,' Nell muttered.

She hadn't seen much of Xander since whatever had or hadn't happened between them at the farmhouse the Friday before, except in the company of other teachers in the staffroom. She wasn't really sure what to say to him. And if she felt awkward, she could only imagine how he must be feeling.

Still, he was coming over. With the girl, too.

She looked nice actually, with a fun, cheeky grin. She was also tall, blonde, curvy and very, very pretty.

Perhaps Nell had been wrong about Xander Scott. Perhaps sweet and awkward was all an act and Nell was just one of many in a very big field he was playing. She'd been fooled like that before.

And if he did have a steady girlfriend... what an idiot she must have seemed, making assumptions that he might like her. Practically throwing herself at him the other night at the farm, because she'd thought his reticence was shyness when it was actually just plain lack of interest. Of course someone who looked like Xander would have interest from other women. *Nell Shackleton, please do get over yourself.*

'OK, Fred, I need you to do me a favour,' she whispered.

'What is it?'

'Just find out if that's his girlfriend for me, will you? Before I make an even bigger tit of myself than I might nearly have done last Friday night.'

'Fine, I will. But that cancels out the pint you bought me.'

93

Chapter Eleven

Sara nudged Xander as they headed over to Nell and Freddie. 'Hey. I think you're in there, Xand.'

'What?'

'Nell just asked her brother to find out if I'm your girlfriend. Sounds like she must be keen on you.'

'Are you using your lip-reading powers for evil again?'

She shrugged. 'It's one of the few bonuses of teaching sign language as a career, I might as well get some use out of it.'

'Did she really say that?'

'Yep. She's worried she made a tit of herself with you last Friday.'

Xander blinked. '*She's* worried about that?'

'Why not? Just because people don't seem as obviously nervous as you doesn't mean they aren't. Some of us are just better at hiding it.'

'So she did want me to? Kiss her, I mean?'

'That would be the obvious conclusion, yes.'

But there was no time for Xander to process this new information and what it might mean for him. He fixed on a smile as the two of them reached the bar.

'Nell. Hi again. Er, we must stop meeting like this.'

Nell smiled back, and he thought he could detect the faintest hint of a blush. 'Hi yourself. You remember Freddie, my brother.'

'Of course.' Xander shook hands with the younger man.

The barmaid approached them and Xander ordered a couple more pints for himself and Sara.

'So Xander, are you going to introduce us to your gorgeous girlfriend?' Freddie asked when they were all sorted with a drink, flashing a smile dripping with charm in Sara's direction.

'Oh, I'm not his girlfriend.' Sara pinched Xander's bum. 'Although we are lovers, but that's more of a casual thing.'

Xander slapped her wrist. 'Oi. Wandering hands off.' He turned to Nell and Freddie. 'This is my friend Sara. Just ignore her, she thrives on humiliating me in public.'

'Right,' Nell said. 'So how do you know each other?'

'We were at secondary school together. Sara's Justin's wife – you remember him. It was his turn to stay at home with the baby tonight.'

'Ah, I see.'

'You've met my mister then, have you?' Sara said to Nell.

She smiled. 'I've had that pleasure, yes.'

Sara rolled her eyes. 'Go on, love, offer me your sympathies – everyone does. And I more than deserve them.'

Nell laughed. 'How many kids have you got?'

'Only the one, and he's plenty. Jacob. He's just gone kicking and screaming into the Terrible Twos so it's nice to have a night off.' She smiled at Xander. 'Actually, our mutual friend here just offered his babysitting services so me and Justin can grab a night out sometime.'

'More fool me, right?' Xander said.

'He'll make a great dad one day,' Sara said. 'You know, Nell, he's quite a catch.'

Xander glared at her and she shrugged. 'What? You are. Take a compliment, Xand.'

'So, what brings you two down into the village?' Xander asked Nell, swiftly moving the conversation into safer territory. Bloody Sara, she was about as subtle as a wrecking ball.

Nell nodded to Freddie. 'Somebody kept whinging he was cold and bored and gagging for a pint.'

Freddie shrugged. 'Well I was. Seriously, how do people live like that? I mean, what are you supposed to do at night without a TV?'

'Read a book, maybe?'

Freddie stared at her like she'd started speaking Martian.

'Freddie's a student,' Nell told Xander and Sara. 'Naturally he regards books with a sense of loathing and dread.'

'Don't you all get bored though, out here in the middle of nowhere?' Freddie asked. 'No cinema, no bars, no clubs. The same old faces every day. I'd go insane.'

'Yeah, I used to feel that way when I was young,' Xander said. 'I mean, not bored exactly, but it did feel stifling growing up in a little village where most people had known you your whole life. All I wanted was to get away and find out who I was, spread my wings in a new place with new people. George Bailey syndrome.'

Nell smiled. 'I love that film.'

'Do you? It's my favourite.'

'Why is it your favourite?'

'Dunno, just… everyone expects it to be all twee and Christmas-schmaltzy, but it's kind of raw, I think. Emotion laid bare.'

'I know exactly what you mean,' Nell said. 'Best bit?'

'George and Mary sharing the telephone. You?'

'The speech he gives to the board of directors after his dad dies.'

'God, yeah, that's a great bit.'

There was silence for a moment as the pair of them stared at each other, for all the world as if they were the only two people in the room. Freddie rolled his eyes in Sara's direction and she shook her head, smiling.

'What changed then, Xander?' Freddie asked, dragging them back to reality. 'I presume something did, since you're clearly still here.'

'He fell in love,' Sara said. She glanced at Xander. 'But we don't talk about that.'

Nell caught his eye, radiating concern, and Xander smiled to let her know it was OK.

Freddie looked at the clock behind the bar. 'What time are we expecting your friend, sis?'

'Any time now, I think.'

'Who, Stevie?' Xander asked.

'Yeah, she's popping in briefly with Milly. I want to introduce them to Freddie before he heads back to uni tomorrow.' Nell glanced at the door. 'Ah, she's here.'

Stevie waved when she caught sight of the little group at the bar.

'You again?' she said to Xander when she'd joined them, clapping him on the shoulder.

'Yep, I'm like a bad penny. This is my friend Sara, by the way, Justin's wife.'

'Oh yeah, that guy.' She grimaced at Sara. 'My sympathies, love.'

Sara laughed. 'Thanks, I'll add them to my collection.'

Stevie turned to Freddie. 'And this must be the Shackleton brother I've heard so much about.'

'Hi, Stevie. I've heard a lot about you too.' Freddie held out a hand, and Xander noticed there was none of the affected charm he'd displayed when he was talking to Sara. Like Justin, Freddie seemed to be one of those men who, generally speaking, only addressed women they weren't related to in tones of flirtation. But the smile he flashed at Stevie was different to the charm-dripping grin he'd given Sara – polite, respectful; even deferential.

Nell watched the pair of them anxiously as they shook hands. Xander could sense this meeting was important to her.

'I'm leaving tomorrow, but I couldn't go without saying hello to the famous Stevie,' Freddie said. 'Our Nell never stops talking about you.' He smiled at Milly, who was gripping her mum's hand, eyes wide and curious at being in this unfamiliar grown-up space. 'Or this little person. Milly, right?'

Milly nodded, jabbing a thumb into her mouth. 'Are you Miss Shackleton's brother?'

'That's right, I'm young Master Shackleton. But you can call me Freddie.'

'You don't look like her.'

'No, well, it'd be unlucky if we'd both turned out that ugly, wouldn't it?'

Milly sniggered. 'Miss Shackleton's not ugly.'

'Ah, but brothers always think their sisters are ugly, you know. That's the way it works.'

Milly glanced up at her mum, who nodded. 'It's true, Mill. Ask your uncles what they think of me sometime.' She smiled at Freddie. 'I can see you and Nell inherited the same way with kids anyway. Nell, I'm so sorry I have to make it a flying visit but I need to get off. Milly should really be in bed by now. I just wanted to pop in and meet Freddie before he goes.'

'Yeah, thanks, Stevie. It was good of you to squeeze us in.' Nell stood up from her barstool to give her friend a hug. 'See you tomorrow, love.'

'Sara, we'd better get off too,' Xander said, finishing his pint. 'Have a good journey back, Freddie. See you, Nell.'

'So, what did you think?' Nell said when she was alone with her brother.

Freddie nodded. 'You're right, sis. Perfect.'

–

'Mum?' Xander called when he got home.

There was no answer. Had she gone to bed already? He peeped round the living room door to see if she was there, then headed to the kitchen.

'Oh my God,' he muttered.

Liquid and shards of broken glass covered the floor, the smashed remains of a bottle of gin. A fresh one sat open on the side.

'Mum! Where are you?'

Anne appeared at the kitchen door, looking cross. 'There's really no need to shout the house down like that, you know. I was only in the loo.'

'What the hell is all this? What happened here?'

'I... broke it. I'd have thought that much would've been obvious.'

'By accident?'

'No.' She turned her face away from him, her features crumpling. 'Xander, why must you humiliate me in my own home?'

'What? I... what did I do?'

'The water. Did you really think I wouldn't notice?'

He flushed. 'I'm sorry.'

'How long have you been doing this?'

'A while,' he mumbled. 'Few months.'

She turned back to look at him, her cheeks burning. 'Why? Am I an embarrassment to you? Is that why you think it's acceptable to treat me like a child at your little school who can't be trusted to make her own decisions?'

'What? No! Mum, don't talk like that. I'm not embarrassed by you, I'm proud of you.'

'Then why?'

'I just worry. You... you've been overdoing it a bit lately, don't you think?'

She shrugged. 'So I have a few drinks in the evening. Plenty of people do, Xander; it's normal. And where have you been tonight?'

'To the pub.'

'Exactly. Yet you still feel qualified to patronise your mother.'

'Your hands, Mum...'

She held them up and looked at the bleeding cuts with a glassy-eyed detachment probably brought on by whatever she'd had to drink so far tonight. 'Oh, it's nothing much. I cut myself trying to pick up the glass, that's all.'

'Leave the glass, I'll sweep it up. Can we go sit down?'

She made no sign of moving. 'I think I'm OK where I am, thank you, young man.'

'You're getting through a bottle every couple of days, Mum. Neat. That's... really not that normal.'

'So you think I've got a problem, do you? Like the tramps on park benches cuddling their bottles of meths?'

'I don't know. I just know it's not good for you – for your health.'

'Oh, my *health*,' she said, waving a dismissive hand. 'Don't you worry about my health. Who wants to live forever?'

'I mean your mental health as well.' He came forward to rest his hands on her shoulders. 'I know why,' he said gently. 'And I get it, I do. If I'd seen what you saw, I'd probably have crawled into a bottle of something too.'

She winced heavily. 'Xander, please don't.'

'We need to talk about this, Mum. It's been nearly two years. You can't keep using booze as a crutch, it's bad for you.'

She dropped her eyes and let out a strangled sob. 'It's getting harder, Xander. I... can't stop seeing him, everywhere I look, just as he was that day.'

'Then let me help you.'

'You? What can you do?'

'I can listen. Talk. And maybe if you got yourself out and about again instead of being shut up at home, joined a club or something...'

She scoffed. 'Like what, the Knit and Natter group at the mechanics' institute? I'm not quite an old lady yet, Alexander.'

'I know you're not, and that's exactly what I mean. I was thinking maybe a singles club or something. Where you can meet people that... you know, that you might like.'

'Oh.' She looked away. 'No, I don't think so. Not now.'

'Or you could go back to doing WI, you used to love that. And there are other groups too, I've been doing a bit of research. Specialist groups, for people like us. People who've lost someone like we lost Dad. We could go together.'

The tears his mum had been holding back forced their way out, and Xander pulled her into a hug.

'Mum, I'm sorry if I humiliated you, I didn't mean to,' he whispered. 'I want you to be well and happy, that's all. I love you.'

'I just wish I could talk to him one more time,' his mum's muffled voice sobbed from his shoulder. 'I do talk to him, sometimes, when you're at school. I shout at him at the top of my voice, ask him what the hell he thought he was playing at, why he didn't tell me how he was feeling. But it's no good, is it? He can't hear me.'

'I wrote him a letter,' Xander confided. 'A few months after it happened.'

Anne drew back to look at him. 'What did it say?'

'Well, it was more of a rant really but writing it made me feel better. I was so angry, I had to channel it into something.' He sighed. 'It was Marie's idea. She did try to help me, in the early days.'

'Xander, I'm sorry,' his mum whispered. 'I've let you down, haven't I? Marie left and when I should've been a shoulder to cry on, I was just another worry to you.'

'Don't be daft, you did everything you could. Put me up, looked after me. You've been brilliant, Mum.'

'You'll meet someone else, you know.' She smiled through her tears. 'A clever, handsome boy like you won't be alone for long.'

'There is a girl,' he admitted.

His mum raised an eyebrow. 'Is there now?'

'Yes. Nell Shackleton.'

'The new teacher? You kept that quiet, you sly devil.'

'We're not… it isn't really anything at the moment. I'm not even sure she sees me that way.'

'Of course she does,' Anne told him firmly. 'Why would she not? She's a lucky young lady to have caught your eye.'

Xander laughed. 'Mum, you're the only person in the world who makes me feel like I might be somebody pretty amazing.'

He planted a kiss on her forehead. 'Go get some plasters on those cuts while I get this glass swept up, eh? We'll watch *Pointless* on iPlayer and you can shout at the contestants, I know how much you enjoy that.'

'That sounds nice,' his mum said. 'And you're right, Xander, I have been overdoing it a bit. I'll cut down, I promise.' She made her way gingerly around the mess of glass to the open bottle on the worktop and twisted the lid back on. 'There. Not a drop more for me till Friday night.'

'What about the counselling group?' Xander asked. 'Will you think about it?'

'I… maybe. Maybe.'

Chapter Twelve

'Come on, Mill,' Stevie said as she bustled into her daughter's room one morning to find her still in her pyjamas, arranging her stuffed toys according to whether they were bipeds or quadrupeds. 'No time for those games now. I want to see that school uniform on in ten minutes flat or there'll be trouble.'

'It's OK, Mummy,' Milly said. 'It's trainer day.'

Stevie frowned. 'What, another non-uniform? You only had one a few weeks ago. What's it for this time?'

Milly rolled her eyes. '*Trainer* day.'

'Less of the sass, young lady,' Stevie told her sternly. 'Are you sure? I never got any letter about a trainer day.'

Milly giggled. 'You did, Mummy. You put it in the muppet jar.'

'Muppet jar,' Stevie muttered. 'Of course I did.'

She had a simple yet efficient filing system, which was to shove any letters, bills or other printed materials of note into Angela's giant Cookie Monster biscuit barrel in the pantry and promptly forget all about them. She did remember Milly giving her something a few weeks ago now she mentioned it, but the school were always sending some note or other home and they were rarely important.

There was a knock at the front door.

'That's Deb,' she said to Milly. 'Duckling, can you pick out something you want to wear if it's a non-uniform day? The bus'll be here any minute.'

Stevie dashed downstairs, swallowing back the last of her coffee, and yanked open the door.

'Deb. Hi,' she said. 'Welcome to Chaos Central. Do you want to come in for a second while I finish running round like a panicky chicken who thinks the sky's falling in?'

'Is that OK?' Deb nodded to the five dogs at her feet. 'I don't want this lot destroying your lovely house.'

'Oh, don't worry about it. Twenty dogs couldn't cause as much mayhem as Red does on a daily basis. Here, come into the kitchen.'

Deb followed her through. She took a seat at the dining table, looping the dogs' leads around one of the legs.

'Oh. A newbie.' Stevie crouched to stroke the new addition to Deb's brood, a small tan whippet, while Red sauntered over to give the stranger a thorough sniffing.

'Yeah, this is Holly. She's taken Nutty's place.' Deb reached down to give the dog a pat. 'Not sure how long I'll have her though. She might be in the family way pretty soon, if she isn't already.'

'Really?'

'Yep, her mum and dad are trying to breed from her. Never had one of my bitches give birth before. I'm feeling a strange sense of maternal pride about it, like I'm about to become a granny.'

'I always thought the thing about Yorkshiremen breeding whippets was an urban myth. You know, like Paul McCartney being replaced by an exact double in 1966 or the "Twangers" episode of *Rainbow*.'

'Ah, but the evidence is all there for the McCartney double. Have you never listened to *The White Album* backwards?'

Stevie laughed. 'Funnily enough…'

'So no Nell this morning?' Deb asked, flicking idly through a copy of *The Guardian* on the dining table.

'Nell? No, she'll be halfway to school around now, I guess.'

'Don't you know?'

'Well, no. I'm her friend, not her minder.'

Deb blinked. 'Right. Sorry. I kind of thought… never mind.'

'Where the hell is Milly?' Stevie muttered. She went out into the hall to yell up the stairs. 'Mill, come on! The bus is here right now. It's literally at the door waiting for you.'

She went back to Deb in the kitchen. A second later there was the sound of thundering steps on the stairs and Milly appeared, dressed in her flower-embroidered jeans and favourite jumper.

She frowned. 'Mummy, that was a fib, I bet my life.'

'It wasn't really. The bus is here. Practically. It'll be here any minute.'

Milly rolled her eyes. 'The bus isn't even coming today. I told you, Mummy, it's trainer day.'

Stevie shook her head. 'What's got into you this morning? What is this trainer day, did you dream it?'

'Could she mean training day?' Deb asked.

Stevie eyes went wide. 'Shi— sugar! Milly, is that what you mean, training day?'

Milly nodded. 'Yup, trainer day. For the teachers. They have to go to school and all the children get to stay at home.'

'Bollocks. Bollocks, bollocks, bollocks,' Stevie muttered under her breath as she got Angela's Cookie Monster from the pantry and rifled through. She yanked out the letter she was looking for and groaned. 'She's right, it is a training day. Bloody Nell, she could've reminded me.'

'Here,' Deb said, sliding Stevie's mobile across the table.

'Thanks.' She pulled up Nell's number and went out into the hall to make the call.

'Nell, I'm going a bit mad here,' she said when her friend answered. 'Is today a teacher training day?'

'Well, yeah,' Nell said. 'Ryan Theakston's bright idea; he's got us doing some naff team-building thing at Cavendish Hall. Thinks it'll help keep up staff morale while Jeremy Illingworth's still off work. Xander's driving us over there now.'

'Well no one bloody told me!' Stevie wailed. 'Why didn't you remind me? You know I can't be trusted to remember my own name for longer than five minutes.'

'Stevie, I was literally talking to you about it two days ago.'

Stevie groaned. 'That's what that was? I didn't realise it was today.'

'Have you not got a babysitter then?'

'No, and I'm not likely to get one this late in the day. Angela's mum's on holiday.'

'What will you do?'

'God, I don't know. I'll just have to ring work and tell them I need to book an emergency day off.'

'Will they be OK about it?'

'They won't have much choice, unless they want to organise an impromptu bring-your-daughter-to-work day.'

When Nell had gone, Stevie rang her office, fumbling out excuses and apologies and promising she'd happily swap holidays with any of her colleagues to make it up to them. Her boss grudgingly granted the holiday, and when it was all sorted, she went back into the kitchen.

'Well, kidder, looks like we're stuck with each other for the day,' she said, ruffling Milly's hair. 'Where will we go?'

'I want to see what Red does at dog school.'

Stevie laughed. 'I'm not sure it's really a school. More of a playgroup.'

'Can we go with her, Mummy?'

Deb beamed at them. 'Yeah, do, please. We'd love to have you along with us, wouldn't we, gang?'

The dogs didn't have much to say to that, but a couple wagged their tails and Red started licking her crotch, which seemed to be about as much welcome as Stevie and Milly were likely to get.

'Deb, are you sure?' Stevie said. 'We'd hate to get in your way.'

'Nah, you'd be doing me a favour. I spend so much time with dogs instead of humans, I actually think I'm in danger of barking rather than speaking sometimes. Here, Milly, listen to this and tell me I don't sound like a genuine canine.'

Deb lifted her face to howl, wolf-like, at the light fitting, and Milly erupted into a fit of giggles.

'Can I try?' she asked her mum.

Stevie shook her head at Deb, smiling. 'You're a bad influence, you are. Go on then, Mill.'

'Woooooo!'

Stevie laughed. 'It needs work, I think. Duckling, go get your trainers and coat on. Then you can have a quick bit of breakfast while I pack the three of us up a picnic.'

—

In the conference room of Cavendish Hall, Ryan Theakston produced an egg from somewhere and held it aloft.

'This,' he said, 'is an egg.'

'He's right, you know. It is an egg,' Xander said.

In the seat next to him, Frank nodded. 'I recognised it almost immediately.'

'Aha!' Ryan rounded on them, grinning dangerously. 'But that – Alexander, Francis – is where you're wrong. Because this is not an egg.'

'Right,' Frank said. 'What is it then, a kipper?'

'It is in fact a human child. And one that all of you, as the guardians of young minds and lives in our community, will now be responsible for.'

He nodded to Mrs Rhodes in the chair behind him, and with a world-weary expression she got up and started distributing uncooked eggs among the assembled teachers and classroom assistants.

'I want all of you to guard these with the same tender, precious care you would show to one of your pupils as we pursue our activities,' Ryan told them, looking very pleased with himself and his child/egg analogy. 'I expect to see twenty-one unbroken eggs back here at the end of the day. The only rule is, you must keep them on your person at all times.'

'What do we get?' Frank demanded.

'Eh?'

'What do we get if we don't break them? Do we win a prize?'

Ryan shot him a look. 'No, but Mrs Rhodes gets to have an omelette for her tea. Stop being a smart-arse, Frank.'

'Thing is, though, children aren't actually as breakable as raw eggs, are they?' Callum, the Year 5 teacher, called out. 'And we don't have to keep them on our person at all times either. Actually, I think it's actively discouraged.'

'It's a metaphor, Callum, I'm not suggesting you crack the kids into a bowl and scramble them.'

Kimberley put her hand up. 'What about me then? I'm vegan.'

Ryan turned to fix her with a killing stare. 'You're what?'

'Vegan. That means I can't do it.'

'No one's asking you to eat the thing, are they?'

Kimberley folded her arms. 'I bet they're not even free-range. Sorry, but I refuse to handle unethical animal products.'

'Christ on a bike, whatever did I do to deserve this lot?' Ryan muttered. 'Fine. You can use a ping-pong ball then.'

'Can I?' Callum said. 'I bloody hate eggs, they make me gag.'

'No. You can shut up and do as you're told.'

'Can't believe this is his idea of team-building,' Nell whispered to Xander. 'He's nicked this from an old episode of *Buffy the Vampire Slayer.*'

'Oh yeah, teen pregnancy? They did that one in all those American high school shows.'

'That was it.' Nell took her egg from Mrs Rhodes. 'Thanks.'

'What're you going to do with yours?' Xander asked her.

She shrugged. 'Put it in my bra and hope for the best. I'm assuming none of these activities we're going to be doing will involve falling flat on my face. And if they do, I've got a bit of padding round that side.'

Xander glanced down at her chest. 'That's cheating, that is.'

'Yeah, you're just jealous.'

'What am I supposed to do with mine then?'

'I don't know, do I? Tuck it in your sock or something.'

After patting himself all over to try to ascertain the best place for his egg, Xander eventually decided to wrap it in a hanky and stick it in his trouser pocket.

'OK. So first up, we're going to try a trust exercise,' Ryan announced. 'Into pairs, please.'

'You trust me?' Xander asked Nell.

'Not an inch. But I'll be your partner if you want.'

'Where do you think Ryan gets this stuff?' Frank said as he paired up with Callum next to them.

'I think he's got a subscription to *Marketing Bullshit Monthly*,' Xander whispered.

Nell nodded. 'Fiver says he's used the phrase "blue-sky thinking" at least once before we all get out of here.'

'Seems to me that if he wanted the team to bond, he could've put a few hundred quid behind the bar at the Highwayman's this Friday and left us to it,' Callum muttered. 'Now that's some blue-sky thinking we could all have run up the flagpole and saluted.'

'Right,' Ryan said. 'OK, trust.' He frowned at them. 'No, hang on, you can't trust each other yet, you're nowhere near ready. You have to communicate first. Mrs Rhodes, blind drawing. Give out the pads and pictures, please. Now can all of you sit on the floor, back to back with your partner?'

Xander turned to face away from Nell and sat down cross-legged on the floor, trying not to laugh. As much as he felt this was a complete waste of his staff's time, it was sort of fun. Nell sat too and leaned back against him.

That felt nice as well. Almost like they were a couple.

'Don't fall asleep,' he told her.

'I'll try not to. Although you are very comfy.' She glanced over her shoulder. 'Xander, what's the bulge in your pocket?'

'I'm not pleased to see you, if that's what you're thinking. It's an egg that represents young minds. Don't break it.'

'Oh. You know, I'm actually kind of hurt.'

Mrs Rhodes came round again, putting a blank pad and pencil in front of Nell and a laminated picture in front of Xander. It showed a basic line drawing of a tall mountain flanked by a couple of hills, a river running through the little valley they created.

'Now, half of you should have a simple picture in front of you,' Ryan said. 'I want you to describe this as best you can to your partner, who will attempt to draw it. One minute is all you're allowed. And you must describe the shapes only – no naming anything in the picture. So if your picture showed an oven, words like "hob" or "ignition" would be banned.' He clicked a stopwatch. 'Go.'

'OK, well, it's a sort of... er, there's a couple of little curved bits at the bottom,' Xander said, squinting at the image. 'And then a... a squiggly bit.'

He could feel Nell shaking with laughter against his back as she scribbled away.

'And then there's a big sticky-uppy bit. Um, sort of protruding against the hi— curvy bits. Sorry, I'm not very good at this.'

'Where's the sticky-uppy bit?'

'I don't think you're allowed to ask questions. But it's in the middle, kind of. With...' He looked at the mountain, which was capped with snow. 'Er, with something on top.'

'Time's up!' Ryan shouted. 'OK, describers, you can now show your partner what you were describing.'

Xander held his picture up over his shoulder for Nell to see.

She snorted. 'That's it? That's what you were describing?'

'Yeah. Did you get it?'

'No. Not exactly.'

She slid her pad round to him.

He stared at her drawing. 'Nell, this doesn't look like two hills and a mountain.'

'Does it not?' she asked innocently.

'This looks like something very different.'

'I don't know what you mean, Xand. All I did was follow your instructions.'

'Oh, Miss Shackleton, you are in so much trouble.'

Xander hastily ripped the top sheet off the pad and stuffed Nell's blue picture in his pocket before Mrs Rhodes came to collect the bits and pieces up again.

'Right. Now for the trust exercises,' Ryan said. 'First of all, we're going to practise our trust falling.'

'Eh?' Frank said.

'One of you will be given a blindfold and will fall backwards into your partner's arms, trusting them to be there to catch you. OK?'

Frank looked Callum up and down. 'Do you fancy being blindfolded and falling into my arms then, Cal?'

'Have you been reading my diary?'

Xander turned to Nell. 'So, faller or catcher?'

'Catcher, I think. I trust me to catch you more than I trust you to catch me.'

'Well at least I know the difference between mountain valleys and genitals.'

'Hey. It's a fact universally acknowledged that from the earliest cave paintings onwards, if you give any human being a pencil and tell them to draw something, you're going to end up with a cock and— er, hi, Mrs Rhodes.'

Xander turned to see the school secretary standing behind him, eyebrows raised as she held out a blindfold.

'Just, um, a private joke,' he said, smiling weakly. 'We were actually discussing the theories of Professor Freud.'

'OK, I'm going to have to put you on a timeout,' he muttered to Nell when Mrs Rhodes had gone. 'You just said cock and very nearly balls in front of a much-respected colleague and old friend of my mum's.'

'She works in a school, she's heard worse. Shut up and get your blindfold on.' Nell turned him round and tied it on for him. 'Hey, this feels a bit kinky, doesn't it? Do you think this whole thing was just a cover for Ryan to lure us into some kind of orgy?'

'Oh no, I'm sure he wouldn't try that again.'

'OK, get ready,' Nell commanded. 'On the count of three, fall into my arms. One. Two. Three.'

Steeling himself, Xander fell backwards. There was a crunching sound, and he felt a wetness against the back of his suit jacket as he landed on something soft.

'Um, Xand,' Nell said in a pained voice. 'I think you just broke my egg.'

Chapter Thirteen

'Can I feed the ducks?' Milly asked, pointing to the park's duck pond. A couple of mallards and a goose were on the bank, arguing over a leftover bit of sandwich.

'I thought you'd ask so I packed some duck food.' Stevie swung her rucksack off her shoulder and took out a plastic container. 'There you go. Mind that goose, he's a nasty little sod.'

Milly skipped off to the pond, where she started throwing generous overarm handfuls of little pellets towards the ducks.

'What's in this duck food then?' Deb asked.

'Not sure, they sell it down the corner shop. I think it's mainly grains – wheat and barley and that. You're not supposed to give them bread, apparently.'

'Why, what happens?'

Stevie shrugged. 'Dunno. Maybe they sink.'

Deb picked up a stick and chucked it for the dogs. Six streaks of fur went shooting after it, yelping their heads off.

'Thanks for coming out with me, Stevie,' she said. 'I'm not used to human company during my working day.'

'Thanks for having us.' Stevie turned her face up to the thin but welcome February sun. 'I could've throttled Milly this morning when she dropped the training day on me, but I have to admit, this beats being at work.'

'What is it you do?'

'I'm a chartered accountant. And yep, it's exactly as exciting as it sounds.'

Deb laughed. 'Well, I can't say I envy you. Dog-walking might not pay much but I wouldn't swap being out in the open air for anything.'

'Have you always done this?'

'No, I used to be a veterinary nurse. I don't think I was really cut out for it though – not tough enough. I couldn't bear it when we lost an animal.' She cast a fond glance at her dogs. 'This is what I was made for. So are you a single mum then?'

'Yeah. Didn't you know?'

'I sort of thought, that girl Nell... I had the idea she lived with you. I mean, that you were a couple.'

'Oh. No, Nell's just a friend. She's actually Milly's class teacher.'

'Sounds like my gaydar was off the mark for once. Sorry, shouldn't have assumed.'

'No, I am... I mean, Nell's not. But your gaydar was spot on for me.'

'Phew, thank God for that,' Deb said with a nervous smile. 'Thought I'd dropped a bit of a clanger there. I'm known for faux pas in my family.'

'Where do you get them anyway? Is there an online shop or something?'

'What, faux pas? You can have any of mine you want for free.'

'No, gaydars. I've always wanted one.' Stevie laughed. 'Tell you what, it would've made my teen years a bit easier.'

'Sorry, I think you're either born with one or you're not. I seem to be one of the happy few.'

'I've never had much luck trying to guess,' Stevie said. 'That's where the straight girls have it easy, isn't it? Like my friend Nell.'

'Why does she have it easy?'

'Oh, you can read her and Xander like a book. I've always thought all that love at first sight stuff was the biggest load of guff, but even so, he must've set a new world speed record when it came to falling for her. And she can't keep her eyes off him either.'

'Who's Xander?'

'Another friend. And you see, it's all simple for them. They don't need to play the guessing game, since everyone just assumes you're straight by default. All one of them has to do is say "So can I get you a drink?" The other knows what that means and says, "Ta very much", then after a bit of hand-holding and a kiss it's job done. If you're not straight – unless you've got one of these legendary gaydars in your pocket – you can be dancing about for ages trying to work out who is and who isn't, if you're going to offend them by suggesting it, if you'll make a prat of yourself by asking them out.' She looked at Deb. 'I almost thought you might be actually, when we met. Shows how far off the mark my gaydar is.'

'You thought I was gay?'

'I thought you might be. Sorry, hope you're not offended.'

'And now you think I'm not?'

'Well, no, not after you mentioned your ex-boyfriend. Served me right for assuming.'

Deb blinked. 'Ex-boyfriend?'

'Didn't you joke about having an ex-boyfriend who was always chasing something?'

'No, I said I had an ex. Katie. Er, she's not a boy.'

'Oh. Right. Well, double sorry for assuming then.' Stevie smiled awkwardly. 'I'm pretty useless at all this, aren't I? Sometimes it feels like there must've been some sort of special lesbian school that all the others had access to but me. You know, like a gay Hogwarts.'

'What, you mean you didn't get your owl-delivered letter letting you know you were one of the lucky few who'd been selected to fancy girls?' Deb said, laughing.

'Nope, must've got lost in the post. I ended up stranded here with all the heterosexual muggles.'

'Here, let's sit down for a minute till Milly's done duck-bothering.'

They took a seat on a bench overlooking the pond, where they could keep an eye on Milly and the six frisking dogs.

'Have you always brought her up on your own?' Deb asked. 'That's pretty brave.'

'I know it is. And if I'd realised I would be doing it on my own, there's no way I would've considered it. But I'm glad this is how my life turned out, obviously.'

'You were with someone when you became a mum then?'

Stevie nodded. 'Angela, my wife. Late wife.'

'Oh, I'm sorry.'

'Thanks.'

'So did you or she... or neither? Sorry, that's kind of personal. Just interested.'

'I had Milly.' Stevie sighed. 'She wasn't even one when we lost Angela. I think part of what makes living with the grief so hard is having to go through it on my own. Milly talks about "my other mummy" all the time – she even gives me pictures she's drawn of the three of us, outside our house. But she doesn't remember when we were a family.'

Deb was looking at her with sympathy in her eyes. 'That's a pretty unfair thing to have happened to you.'

'Yeah.'

'Do you mind if I ask how she died, your wife?'

Stevie swallowed. 'Car crash.'

'Oh God. Sorry, Stevie.'

'The worst thing was she...' She stopped, shooting Deb a curious look. 'Shit, why am I telling you this?'

'Because you need to, maybe?'

'Hardly anyone knows this. Not my best friends, my dad, my brothers, nobody.' She ran a hand over her eyes. 'She cheated on me.'

'Fuck! Sorry. I mean, God, that's awful.'

'I found out right before it happened – before she died. She said she felt bad about it, that it was years ago, before we were married, but it had been preying on her mind since Milly had

116

been born. Said she wanted to confess everything so the three of us could make a fresh start.'

'What did you say?'

'I was blazing mad, obviously. Milly was screaming, I was yelling… I told Ange to get out. *Stay the fuck away from me and my baby.* Those exact words, I'll remember them every day of my life.' Stevie choked back a sob. 'So she did, forever. She drove off, saying she'd give me some space to calm down, and she… she never came back. The next thing I knew the police were on the doorstep, breaking the news to me that she was gone.'

Deb didn't say anything. But she took Stevie's hand and held it tightly.

'Do you know how difficult it is to grieve for someone when the last thing they ever told you was that they'd been unfaithful?' Stevie said. 'The anger, the guilt, the loss? Loving them… hating them? Angela had been the one who… Deb, there was a time in my life when I thought I'd never be able to have a relationship, or to fall in love. Angela was the one who helped me love myself again. Love her. After she told me what she'd done, it felt like our whole relationship had been a sham.'

'Oh, sweetie, I'm so sorry. Why did you think you couldn't ever fall in love?'

Stevie stared into the distance. The pond, Milly, the dogs, were just a fog of colour behind the water in her eyes.

'Something that happened when I was younger,' she said in a quiet voice. 'Something that made me hate myself for a little while, until Angela… she was so gentle. So patient with me. I never would've believed she was capable of a betrayal like that.' She frowned. 'Why did I just tell you that?'

'I don't know. Why did you?'

'Because… I suppose because you seemed like you might get it.'

'Well, I do get it.' Deb pressed Stevie's hand, her eyes full of sympathy and understanding. 'Sorry, Stevie. You didn't deserve that, any of it.'

'Only one other person in the world knows what I just told you, Deb.'

'Nell?'

Stevie gave a wet laugh. 'Xander.'

'Nell's Xander?'

'Yeah. He knows what it feels like to grieve for someone you hate and can't stop loving. Or love and can't stop hating, whichever way round makes most sense. I'm not sure either way makes much sense.' She pulled out a tissue and blew her nose, forcing her tears under control before Milly noticed them. 'Don't say anything in front of Mill, will you? She doesn't remember Angela but she idolises her, all the same.'

Deb patted her hand before letting it go. 'What happens on trainer day stays on trainer day.'

'Thanks, Deb.'

'Hey. You like 99s? I'll eat them any time of year.'

Stevie smiled. 'With monkey's blood?'

'You what?' Deb said, laughing.

'Monkey's blood. That's what we used to call strawberry sauce when I was a kid.'

'Yep. Flake, strawberry sauce, hundreds and thousands, the works. And I'm buying. They sell them at the little kiosk by the kiddies' playground.'

'Oh, Milly will just love you,' Stevie said. 'Come on, let's go get her. Ice cream and swingboats will make her day.'

–

'Well, thanks for our unscheduled day out,' Stevie said to Deb after she'd accompanied them home from the park.

Deb smiled. 'Here, you've got monkey's blood on you.' She reached out to wipe a bit of strawberry sauce from the side of Stevie's mouth. Stevie flushed at the unfamiliar touch; the finger so close to her lips.

Milly giggled. 'Mummy, you're so messy. Come on, Red, let's go play Mountaineers.'

She disappeared into the house, holding her canine friend by the collar.

Deb raised an eyebrow. 'Mountaineers?'

'Yep. She's got hiking poles and everything, she asked Santa for them.'

'Strange child.'

'Tell me about it.'

'So I had fun today,' Deb said softly.

Stevie smiled. 'Me too.'

'And I wondered… um. I don't scrub up too badly. There are times when I actually don't smell of dog at all. I own two skirts, one of which is from Monsoon.'

'Posh. Why are you telling me?'

'I just thought, if you ever had a free evening, maybe… dinner? You know, in a restaurant? I'd offer to cook but I really quite like you.'

'Oh.' Stevie flushed again. 'Look, Deb, this was great and… and thanks for listening. But I'm not really dating right now. I mean, ever. I'm not really dating ever.'

'OK,' Deb said slowly. 'Any reason why not?'

'I kind of put all that behind me when Ange died. I've got Milly to focus on now, and… I don't want to get hurt again. I still haven't healed fully from the last time.'

'Right.' Deb turned away, her features crumpling slightly. 'Well, that's a shame. Because I wouldn't, you know.'

'Deb, I didn't mean I think you'd ever – I can't, that's all. It's… complicated.'

'I'm sorry to hear it.'

'You understand, though?'

'Of course. You've had a lot to deal with, I can see that.'

'And we can still be friends, can't we?' Stevie called after her as she turned to go.

'Sure. Friends. See you tomorrow morning, Stevie.'

Chapter Fourteen

Quite a lot of Ryan's team-building activities seemed to involve blindfolds, Xander couldn't help noticing. First there was the Blind Obstacle Course, in which partners took turns to verbally guide a blindfolded partner through a load of cones, hula hoops and other assorted crap. Then came Trust Pinball, with poor Caroline selected to be the ball and pushed, blindfolded again, around a circle of her colleagues. By the time they broke for lunch, the warm room was filled with a less than fresh eggy whiff and even Ryan seemed ready to admit that egg babysitting might not have been one of his best ideas.

Xander was feeling rather smug. He still had his egg. Maybe his staff didn't much rate him as a head, but by God, he could guard fragile breakfast foods with the best of them.

'Smells like young minds round here, wouldn't you say?' Nell whispered.

'Smells like a zombie buffet's worth of them to me.'

'Dear Lord, I need a shower.'

So did he, but despite the pong, Xander had really enjoyed the team-building day. He and Nell had spent the morning laughing and joking together like old friends – and, he was positive, doing some quite sexy flirting as well.

It almost felt like they'd been on a date. A good date, one that had gone well and would certainly lead to another. He was currently toying with the idea of asking her to the pub later after they'd both been home and de-egged themselves. Maybe there was even an outside chance she'd invite him back to the farm so they could pick up where they'd left off the month before when Freddie had unexpectedly shown up.

The rest of the staff seemed to have enjoyed the experience too. There'd been a lot of laughter and banter, even between the ever-battling Caroline and Frank.

Maybe Ryan was right and this had been a good idea. He probably wouldn't be too pleased if he knew that most of the laughter and banter had been at the expense of him and his daft bloody games, but the day was certainly doing what he'd intended and bringing them all closer. The team had formed a real bond over their shared belief that the chair of governors was very probably off his rocker.

They'd all removed their blindfolds and were starting to drift in the direction of the buffet when Ryan got up on stage, clearing his throat.

'Now, ladies and gents, before we officially break for dinner, I've got a surprise for you,' he announced.

'This is where he throws a few handcuffs in with his blindfolds and suggests a gang-bang as a great way of team bonding, right?' Nell whispered to Xander.

Xander frowned. 'Well whatever it is, he didn't discuss it with me.'

'There's someone here I know you'll all be pleased to see,' Ryan said. 'Jeremy, do you want to come on out?'

There was a gasp as Jeremy Illingworth, the 'real' head, emerged from an adjoining room. He was pale and a little gaunt, supporting himself with a stick, but he was waving jauntily and sporting a broad smile.

'Oh my God,' Frank muttered. He shot forward to shake his old boss vigorously by the hand. 'Jeremy, my old mate. Great to see you up and about.'

The other staff quickly followed, and within minutes there was a little throng surrounding Jeremy. Ryan brought him a chair so he could hold court in comfort.

'Did you know about this?' Nell asked Xander.

He shook his head. 'Ryan never breathed a word.'

'You'd better go say hello, hadn't you?'

'Give it a minute, he's a bit crowded,' Xander said, scanning the gang of well-wishers. 'I'll grab some food first. I'd rather talk to him alone.'

He headed for the buffet and started picking out the least curly-looking sandwiches, loading them onto a paper plate. Ryan, spotting him there, came to join him.

'Ryan,' Xander said, nodding. 'This was a nice surprise. You inviting Jeremy along.'

Ryan helped himself to a sausage roll. 'I thought everyone would like to see how well he's doing.'

'Er, it might've been nice to be told in advance, you know. With me being the acting head and everything.'

'Well, lad, then it wouldn't have been much of a surprise, would it?'

'It's just, um… I can't help feeling it might make me look a bit weak in front of my staff, when it's obvious the governors don't keep me in the loop. Undermine me, type of thing.'

'Yes,' Ryan said, frowning. 'It was actually on the subject of being kept in the loop that I came over to speak to you.'

'Oh?'

He took Xander's elbow and guided him out of earshot of a couple of teachers who'd peeled themselves away from Jeremy to explore the buffet.

'Because I have been hearing things on the old village grapevine,' Ryan said. 'Things I might have expected to hear from you directly.'

'What things?' Xander asked, his body tensing. Could Ryan have heard some rumour about him and Nell?

'World Book Day.'

'Oh, right, that. What about it?'

'Don't get too daring with it, I'm sure I recall myself saying to you the first day of term. Then Jolene Hancock casually mentions that we're looking at holding a full-scale village fete to celebrate it.'

'Well, not full-scale really, just something small in the school hall,' Xander said. 'We're planning to raise money for a literacy charity. What's wrong with that?'

'And it didn't occur to you that you ought to get this passed by the governors before steaming blindly ahead with it?'

Xander frowned. 'No, it didn't. The staff and parents were all keen, and so was I. I didn't think I needed to get approval from the governors on every decision. I mean, I am the head, aren't I?'

'No, Xander, the head is over there in that chair. Your job is to—'

'—to stop the ship going under. Yes, I remember. So what're you saying, Ryan, that you want me to shut it down? Because classes have already started preparing. It wouldn't be very fair on the kids.'

'Hmm. Perhaps it is a little late for that. But I expect a full briefing about any plans, all right? Before decisions are made, not after.'

'Right. Fine.' Xander put his untouched plate of food down, his appetite disappearing along with his good mood. 'I need to say hello to Jeremy. See you.'

Jeremy's gang of well-wishers had thinned out now. Xander approached and shook the headteacher warmly by the hand.

'Good to see you out and about again,' he said. 'How are you feeling, boss?'

'Can't complain, can't complain. You know, given that this time three months ago I was bashing my baldie bonce against the pearly gates. How are things then, young man?'

'Ticking along nicely, I think. Everyone's keen to have you back where you belong, I'm sure you've picked up on that.'

'Yes.' Jeremy cast a glance in Ryan's direction. 'Xander, can I have a word with you in private?'

'Of course.'

Xander offered the older man his arm while he stood and reclaimed his stick. Jeremy guided the pair of them to a small meeting room that adjoined the conference hall and closed the door behind them.

'Son, I've been hearing some things. Around the village, and from the other members of staff just now. Things about you.'

Xander grimaced. 'I'm so sorry.'

'Yes, I thought you might be.' Jeremy hobbled to a seat at the long central table, indicating the chair opposite for Xander. 'These were actually good things. But feel free to apologise unnecessarily if it puts you at ease.'

'Good things? About me?'

'Not all good things, I admit. Karen Doneen tells me she believes you actually hide behind your desk when she knocks on the door of your office and pretend you're not in.'

'Ah. Yes. Maybe once.'

'Well, I can't deny I might've done the same thing myself. More than once,' Jeremy said, grinning. 'But yes, I have been hearing good things – many more good than bad. I'm told you're friendly and approachable, when you're able to conquer your nerves. Never high-handed, always keen to explore suggestions from both staff and parents. Enthusiastic when it comes to pursuing those suggestions – everyone's very excited about your plans for World Book Day this year. Hardworking, of course. And the biggest thing, I think, in a job like this – people *like* you, Xander. You're part of the fabric of this village. They feel as though you care and they want to see you succeed.'

'Did the other teachers say that?'

'Certainly, and a number of the parents too. I'm paraphrasing, of course. Your biggest problem, it seems to me – and to everyone who has any dealings with you – is your complete lack of belief in yourself.' Jeremy leaned forward and laid a hand on Xander's arm. 'Lad, I'm going to tell you a secret. One not even Ryan Theakston knows.'

'OK.'

'I will be coming back to Leyholme Primary next term, when the ticker's ticking properly again. I'd like to do one last year, go out with a bang rather than a whimper. But after that, I'll be taking early retirement. I love this job, but I don't want to be doing it until I'm in a box.'

'Why are you telling me?'

'Because I'd like you to be my successor. I want you to apply for the role.'

'Me? No.' Xander shook his head to reinforce the point. 'I'm not your man. Wendy, she's the one. She's been deputy head for years.'

'Wendy won't be coming back after her maternity leave's up. She's quitting work to be a full-time mum for a while,' Jeremy told him. 'Can't say that I blame her either. I've realised recently how important it is not to assume your loved ones are always going to be there to pick up at a time you feel it's convenient. None of us know how long we've got.'

'No, but… I'm not like you. I'm nobody's idea of a leader, honestly.'

'And yet quite a number of our colleagues have just been telling me that you are,' Jeremy said, smiling. 'Being a strong leader isn't bawling and throwing your weight about. Ryan Theakston might believe that because it's basically his entire philosophy, but I don't and I've been in this business a lot longer than he has. You need to be a people person.'

'I don't know, Jeremy. It's nice of everyone to believe I've got it in me but I really think I'm better suited to the shop floor, teaching Year 3.'

'You've got the makings of a great head, Xander. With training, mentoring, a bit more experience, you could be just what our school needs. That's what I'm offering you – I want you as my new deputy head, on the understanding that the headteacher role will be yours when I'm gone.'

'You really think I could do it?'

'If I didn't, I wouldn't offer. I love that school and I want to leave it in the best hands possible.'

'I love the school too,' Xander said, half to himself.

Jeremy smiled. 'I know you do. Just think about it, will you? You don't need to make a decision straight away.'

'Thanks, boss, I will.'

'And don't let Ryan bully you,' Jeremy said. 'For as long as I've known him, he's been a blustering, pompous, overbearing arse who can't get enough of the sound of his own voice. Just remember, you're the head, not him.'

'I'll... try.'

'Empathy and compassion don't make you weak, son. Nor does fear, if you don't let it rule your life. Prove me right, eh?' He patted Xander's arm. 'Go on, go have your lunch.'

Xander didn't know quite what to say. He felt a bit choked up. But he managed to mumble some sort of acknowledgement as he stood up.

'Oh,' Jeremy said as Xander turned to leave. 'How's that new girl in Reception working out for you? She came very highly recommended by her last school.'

'Well – really well. Yeah. She's...' He paused, trying to remember what Jo Hancock had said that night at the farm. '...she's a real diamond. Don't know what I'd do without her.'

Jeremy smiled. 'Yes, I'd heard something about that too. Bye, Xander. And good luck.'

Chapter Fifteen

'You missed a spot,' Nell said as she came into her living room with a tray bearing two steaming cups of tea, a beaker of squash and a plate of custard creams.

Stevie glanced around the room's half-painted walls. 'Perhaps that's because I'm doing all the work while the actual home-owner, *hem hem*, swans about enjoying herself.'

'Hey. I was gathering badly needed sustenance for us.' Nell delivered the beaker of squash to Milly, who was colouring in on the sofa with Red watching her intently. 'Here you go, Mill.'

'What is it?' Milly asked.

'It's Vimto, same as you get at home. I was reliably informed it's your favourite.'

' 'K. Please can I have a biscuit to go with it?'

'Better ask Mum.'

'Go on, Mill, just one,' Stevie said. 'I do mean just one though, or you'll ruin your tea.'

'Hooray!' Milly jumped up and went to claim one of the custard creams. 'Thank you, Miss Shackleton. Can Red have one too?'

Red's tail thumped the floor hopefully.

Nell laughed. 'How can I resist those big brown eyes?' She reached into her pocket for a doggy treat. 'Here you go, Red, catch.'

'Mill, why don't you take Red and play Mountaineers in the back garden for a bit?' Stevie said. 'I don't like the two of you inhaling all these paint fumes.'

'But I need my poles to play Mountaineers.'

Stevie looked at Nell. 'Any suggestions, Miss Shackleton? With a name like that, you must have some mountaineering equipment lying around.'

'Is your name a mountaineer name?' Milly asked Nell.

Nell smiled. 'Sort of, yes. There was a very famous explorer called Ernest Shackleton who was one of the first people to visit the South Pole, over a hundred years ago now.'

'Where the polar bears are?'

'No, sweetie, they're in the north. Where the penguins are, though.'

Milly looked suitably impressed by this information. 'Was he your grandad?'

'No, no relation as far as I know. But I'm proud to carry the name.' Nell paused for a moment. 'Heh.'

'What?' Stevie said.

'Scott and Shackleton. Just occurred to me.'

Stevie smiled. 'Meant to be, eh?'

'What is, Mummy?' Milly asked.

'Nothing, duckling,' Stevie said, ruffling her hair. 'Just a grown-up joke.'

'Hang on, Mill,' Nell said. 'I think I've got just the thing for a budding mountaineer in my walk-in wardrobe.'

She went into her bedroom and came back carrying a hiking pole. 'My brother bought this when he was visiting then promptly left it behind. I think he had an image of himself roaming the hills like a wise old hobbit or something, except his epic laziness got in the way.'

'S'pose we can play Mountaineers with just one,' Milly said. 'Red, come on. Colin's in the garden, we can play at rescuing him.'

'Stay near the window where we can see you,' Stevie called after her. 'And keep Red on her lead so she doesn't run off.' It was a rather bizarre fact that tiny Milly, Red's partner in crime, was one of the only people the dog actually behaved herself for.

'What does poor Colin need rescuing from, do you think?' Nell asked Stevie when they were alone.

'From them, in about five minutes.'

Nell smiled. 'Here. Sit down and drink your tea, I'll allow it.'

'Thanks, Miss.' Stevie chucked her roller back in its tray and threw herself onto the sheet-covered sofa with Nell.

'Well, thanks for keeping me company on Valentine's Day,' Nell said.

Stevie shrugged. 'Not like I've got anything better to do.'

'You think we'll finish the first coat before you have to go?'

'Most of it, I hope. I'll come round this weekend and help you with the rest.'

'You don't need to do that.'

'I can hardly leave it to a klutz like you, can I?' Stevie said, nudging her. 'You pick up a paint roller, next thing you know, the house has blown up.'

'My reputation for chaos precedes me,' Nell said, laughing. 'Thanks, Stevie, you're a godsend. And you have to let me pay you back.'

'Oh, buy me a drink sometime,' Stevie said, waving her away.

'I was thinking I could treat you to a girls' night out. They're doing a *Mamma Mia!* singalong at the mechanics' institute in a few weeks, what do you think? Tickets and all your drinks on me.'

Stevie curled her lip. 'ABBA? I'm not sure I ABBA, Nell.'

'Come on, I thought that'd be right up your street. I bet you were well into them in the seventies.'

Stevie laughed. 'How old do you think I am?'

'Ah, go on. It'll be a laugh.' Nell batted her eyes hopefully. 'Cheesy singalong fun, just the girls?'

'All right, all right,' Stevie said, smiling. 'But I'm not singing "Waterloo". I bloody hate that song.'

'Deal.'

Stevie shuddered, hugging her mug to her, as a gust of wind shook the back door.

'Doesn't that creep you out?' she asked Nell.

'It did when I first moved in. I'm used to it now.'

'Nell, you need to get that door fixed. A box stuck in front of it hardly constitutes household security. I worry about you up here on your own when literally anyone could wander in.'

Nell shrugged. 'One of the benefits of being up on the moors: the only people likely to wander in are Swaledale sheep or the ghost of Cathy Earnshaw. And I reckon I could take her.'

Stevie shook her head. 'Pretty young woman, all alone in an abandoned moorland farmhouse, wind rattling the doors… you know you're basically in the opening scene of a horror film here?'

'*Charmingly gothic*, my estate agent called it.'

'And you know what happens in scene two of this particular horror film, right? I'll give you a clue: it not infrequently involves axe murderers.'

'Does Leyholme have a lot of axe murderers then?'

'I'm serious, chicken. Do me a favour – go out and buy yourself a good, sturdy lock, will you? If we can't work out how to install it between us, I'll hire a locksmith for you.'

'I'm fine, Stevie. You worry too much.'

'Nell, please. For me.'

'OK, OK, I'll pick one up from the hardware shop this weekend,' Nell said, giving her a squeeze. 'But only because I think it's sweet that you worry about me. Are you and Milly all ready for World Book Day then? Three weeks to go.'

'Yep. Picnic basket, three packets of red dye and an old hairdressing cape all set to be transformed into an adorable cut-price Little Red Riding Hood costume.'

'What about you? I hope you'll be in fancy dress for the fete. Don't forget I've volunteered you for raffle ticket sales.'

'I'm the Big Bad Wolf. Fake fur coat and a headband with ears on it. Less than twenty quid for the lot off eBay, a fact

I'm disproportionately proud of.' Stevie dunked a custard cream into her tea and sucked on the end. 'How are the school's plans coming along? For weeks Milly's been talking about nothing but this Wonka's Chocolate Factory the Reception kids are doing.'

'Has she now? That's supposed to be top secret, that is.'

Stevie laughed. 'Well, for a four-year-old she kept it pretty top secret. She only told me and Red. And her nana. Oh, and the milkman. And Carmel at the post office. And she drew a picture of it for Deb. But apart from that, not a single soul.'

'Just you and half the village. Right.'

'Once Carmel knows, it's basically the whole village. So how's it going?'

'Really well,' Nell said, reaching over Stevie so she could help herself to a custard cream. 'Actually, the fete thing's run away with us a bit – we were thinking in the early days that it'd be just book stalls, guess the name of the teddy, that type of thing, but it's really caught everyone at school's imagination. All the classes seem to have big plans.'

'So that's good, right? That's the whole idea, to spark a bit of creativity in the kids.'

'Mmm. It is good, but...'

'Xander?'

'Yeah,' Nell said, grimacing. 'Poor lad's been having a recurring nightmare about it all going tits up.'

Stevie raised an eyebrow. 'You'd know, would you?'

'Yes I would because we're friends and he told me,' Nell said, elbowing her. 'So less of the eyebrow-dancing, Missus.'

'Come on. What is going on with you two?'

'That's just it. Nothing.' Nell dunked her custard cream and cursed silently as half of it dissolved into her tea. 'It's like we're... I don't know, best friends. And that's all.'

'Oh, right. Thanks a lot.'

Nell smiled. 'Second-best friends then, if you're going to be all jealous.'

'And you don't want to be just second-best friends. Do you?'

'Well, no.'

Stevie twisted to face her. 'So what are you waiting for then? He's obviously smitten with you. Trust me, I know that boy.'

'I'm waiting for him, aren't I?'

'Bloody hell, love. If you're waiting for Xander to make a move, you'll be single till kingdom come.'

Nell sighed. 'I know. It feels like he needs to be the one to ask me, that's all.'

'Never took you for the traditional type.'

'It's not a gender thing, it's a Xander thing,' Nell said. 'I just think it'll help with his confidence issues if he asks and I say yes.'

'Hmm. You think he will ask?'

'I think he's nearly there. And I'm in no rush. Let him bide his time if that's what it takes for him to feel comfortable.'

'And what if somebody less concerned about having to make the first move snaps him up in the meantime?'

'Like who?'

Stevie shrugged. 'Jolene Hancock, for one. Her divorce just became final. Wouldn't surprise me if she set her sights on him again now she's officially back to being single.'

'Jolene? No way.' Nell frowned. 'Wait – again?'

'Yeah, her and Xander go back a long time; they were at school together. She's carried a torch for him for years, not that he's ever noticed. Now her marriage is over and Marie's out of the picture, I can't see her dragging her feet.'

'Really, you're serious? Mega-glamorous, Shellac-manicured, kitten-heeled Jolene Hancock fancies Xander?'

'She's not the only one either. I'd get in while you can if I were you.'

Nell shook her head. 'Are you honestly telling me that Xander – our Xander, Xander Scott, who can barely speak to the opposite sex without having a panic attack – is a major village sex symbol?'

'I don't know why you're so surprised,' Stevie said, laughing. 'He's a good-looking lad, isn't he?'

'Well yes, but… he's just so shy and awkward all the time.'

'So what do you see in him then?'

'I suppose he's… sweet, in an unpredictable sort of way. He makes me laugh. Eminently huggable. And kind of oddly sexy, I guess, for reasons I've never quite been able to pin down.' Nell frowned, trying to put her finger on just what it was about Xander Scott that had got him haunting her thoughts almost from the moment they'd met. 'It's that sense he's never quite comfortable in his own skin. You feel sort of special when you can get him to relax with you, show you the real him.'

'Exactly. And you thought none of the other straight girls round here would've noticed these things?'

'I still think he needs to ask me rather than the other way round,' Nell said, nibbling meditatively on what remained of her biscuit. 'And he will, I think, once he's got his courage up. He did actually ask me to the pub after the training day, but then I think his nerve went and he extended the drinks invitation to the rest of the staff so we weren't tête-à-tête.'

Stevie rolled her eyes. 'And to think I thought you muggles had it easy.'

'Nothing that involves Xander Scott was ever going to be easy.'

'I got asked out the other day,' Stevie said.

'Did you? By who?'

'Deb. You were right, she is a lesbian.' She shook her head. 'See, even you've got this bloody gaydar thing. Whereas for poor old Stevie, somebody who might actually have been able to get some use out of it, life is one constant guess-again humiliation.'

'So how come you're spending Valentine's Day painting my living room in miserable singleness then?'

'I told you, Nell, I'm not dating any more. I turned her down.'

'How'd she take it?'

'Well, she said she understood, but I'm sensing she was a bit hurt.' Stevie sighed and finished her tea. 'I feel bad. I'd have liked to be friends, at least. We kind of bonded when we took Milly and the dogs to the park.'

'You could've said yes. You like her, right? I mean, you fancy her?'

'Well, yes, I do, but… I mean, there's Milly to consider. Even now she's at school, she still needs so much of my time. And it feels too soon after losing Angela to be thinking about new relationships.'

'How long has it been?' Nell asked softly.

'Nearly four years now.'

'And you think that's too soon?'

'Too soon for my survivor's guilt to have worn off anyway.'

'You want my opinion?'

'No.'

'I think you ought to go for it.'

'Funny, I could swear I said no just then.'

'Angela would want you to be happy with someone else, wouldn't she?'

'I don't know, Nell. She's dead so I can't ask her.'

'But you must know what she'd have wanted for you.'

'I thought I knew her inside out,' Stevie muttered, half to herself. 'Who she was, how she felt, what she was capable of. But the people you love can surprise you, and not always in a good way. And now it's not just moving on, it's… back to square one, almost. Right back to where I was when I met her.'

'Where were you?'

'Not in a good place,' Stevie said, looking down into her empty mug. 'A mess, if you want the truth. It took me a long time to trust Angela enough to let her in, and then she—' She bit her lip. 'I just don't know if I can do that with someone else. Not now.'

Nell put her mug down on the table and covered Stevie's hand with hers.

'I didn't know it was so complicated,' she said quietly. 'You want to talk about it?'

'Not really. I'm a bit sick of the subject.' Stevie summoned a smile. 'But thanks.'

'You know where I am if you change your mind.'

Nell's phone buzzed and she fumbled about in her overall pocket until she located it.

She frowned at the screen. 'Xander.'

'You reckon this is it then?' Stevie asked. 'Has he been swept away by the romance of Overpriced Flowers Day and finally plucked up the nerve to ask you out?'

'Unless he wants to tell me he's eloped with Jolene Hancock. He's exactly the sort of person to marry someone out of social embarrassment because he didn't want to hurt their feelings.' She swiped at the screen. 'What's up, Xand?'

'Oh God, Nell, you have to help me,' he said in a strangled voice.

'Xander, what's happened?' Nell said, alarmed. 'Are you OK?'

In the background there was an almighty din, the sounds of metal objects crashing together and a little voice screaming, 'MummyMummyMummyMummyMummy...'

'A toddler with an Oedipus Complex is trying to kill me,' Xander gasped.

'What, your friends' kid? Are you babysitting?'

'Jacob's not a kid, he's Satan incarnate. Please, Nell, I'll give you anything. Double your salary, as many packets of plasticine as you can eat, whatever you want. All you have to do is tell me how I can make him stop screaming.'

'Why are you asking me?'

'Because the only other friends I've got who might be able to help were responsible for conceiving the little hellspawn.' He sighed. 'Plus I don't want to ruin their night out.'

'OK, text me the address and give me half an hour. I'll come over and see what I can do.'

'Nell, I love you tenderly, do you know that?'

The cries of 'Mummy!' in the background were louder now, and so high in pitch they were in danger of becoming audible only to sheepdogs. It sounded like Jacob was gaining on him.

'For the love of all that's holy, hurry up,' Xander hissed as he hung up.

'Sorry, Stevie, I have to go,' Nell said, stashing her phone away again. 'Would you be able to drop me off in Morton on your way home?'

'Course. Did he ask you out then?'

'What do you think?' Nell said, rolling her eyes. 'No, he's got a toddler trying to murder him.'

'Of course he has. How very Xander.'

Chapter Sixteen

Around half an hour later, Nell knocked at the door of Xander's friends' house in Morton. There was a yell and a loud crash from inside, then Xander appeared at the door. His face was flushed, his shirt open to the waist, and his glasses sitting cock-eyed on top of some very tousled hair.

'Right,' Nell said, holding up a shopping bag. 'I brought story books, a pan-pipe CD and some biscuits to help soothe the savage beast.'

'Did you bring a crucifix and a couple of gallons of holy water?'

'Come on, he can't possibly be that bad. He's only a kid. What was that crash I heard?'

'He threw a Tonka truck at me.'

'Ah.' Nell pushed past him into the house. 'Well, we're bigger than he is. Plus there's two of us and only one of him. We can handle him.'

'The little bugger's hidden my glasses as well. Now I can't even see what he's up to properly.'

'They're on your head, Xand.'

'Oh.' He groped around for them and pushed them back onto his nose. 'Well, he must've put them there. His deviousness knows no bounds.'

'He in there?' Nell said, pointing to a door from behind which the din seemed to be emanating.

'Yeah.' He grabbed her arm as she went to open it. 'Be careful, Nell.'

Nell peeped round the door into the kitchen. A stark-naked toddler with golden curls and a bright purple face was sitting in the middle of the floor banging a couple of upturned pans with a wooden spoon, only occasionally pausing to check his genitals hadn't disappeared before he carried on.

'He doesn't look so bad,' she whispered to Xander.

'That's what he wants you to think.'

She tiptoed forward, smiling her very brightest Reception-teacher smile.

'Hello, Jacob,' she said in a friendly voice. 'That's a pretty tune you're playing.'

Jacob spun to look at her and his brow knit into a black frown.

'Not! MUMMY!' he yelled, standing up only so he could throw himself dramatically on his face in a pile of Duplo bricks.

'He really, really wants Mummy,' Xander told her.

'I'd picked up on that. When are they back?'

He groaned. 'Not for hours. I told them to stay out as long as they liked and not to worry about a thing. Idiot.'

'Did you try CBeebies?'

'Course I did. It worked for five minutes, then off he went again.'

Jacob sucked in a lungful of air so he could really get a handle on some good, solid screaming.

'Um, Xand,' Nell said. 'You don't happen to know...'

'...what school his name's down for? I do, and you won't like it.'

'Oh God. That means he'll be mine in two years.' Nell squared her shoulders. 'Right, young Jacob. As your teacher-to-be, I insist you stop this racket right now or it's a timeout for you, m'lad.'

Xander shook his head. 'You can't timeout this one. He just sits on the step and screams.'

'Well, I can confiscate that bloody spoon off him anyway.' Nell approached Jacob and prised the spoon from his hand.

'Want it back?' she asked, waggling it at him. 'Well then, all you have to do is stop crying for me and Uncle Xander.'

Jacob looked up at her, his lips and eyes wobbling with disgust, before doubling the volume of his wails.

She glanced at Xander. 'We could let him cry himself out. He's bound to get exhausted eventually.'

'Heh, you reckon, do you? He's been at it for two hours.'

'OK, then I think we're going to have to try bribery,' Nell said. 'Work out what he wants that isn't Mu— the M word and let him have it.'

'Isn't that like negotiating with terrorists?'

'Well, have you got a better plan?'

'God, no. Negotiate away, please.'

Jacob chose that moment to stop crying and sit up. He looked at Xander and started forming his fingers into shapes.

'What's he doing now?' Nell asked.

'It's sign language,' Xander said. 'Sara teaches it, he must've picked some up. He's been trying to talk to me like that all evening.'

'What does it mean?'

'I'm not sure but from the look on his face, I bet it's obscene.'

Nell shuffled so she was kneeling in front of the temporarily quiet Jacob. His frown had lifted and he actually looked sort of cute, with his big, tear-stuffed eyes staring at her in mute appeal.

'Aww. Look at him.'

'Careful,' Xander whispered. 'It might be a trick.'

'Jacob, sweetie, can you show me what you just did again?' Nell asked gently.

She frowned as he made the same three shapes with his fingers.

'They're letters,' she said.

'How do you know?'

'At my last school we had someone come in to show the kids how to sign their names, I still remember some of the alphabet. B-E-N, he just spelled.'

'Ben?'

'Yeah. Do you know a Ben?'

'No, I – oh! Yes! That's what his favourite teddy's called.' Xander dashed from the room and came back carrying a sad-looking, floppy blue rabbit with one eye.

He held it up to Jacob. 'Is this what you want?'

Jacob's eyes lit up and he nodded vigorously, stretching out both arms for the toy. Xander put it in his hands and he cuddled it to him, beaming.

Xander flashed a delighted smile at Nell. 'We did it. He's stopped crying.'

Nell laughed. 'You'd almost think we were childcare professionals.'

'You reckon we're up to the challenge of getting some pull-ups and a pair of pyjamas on him or will we be overstretching ourselves?'

'Hey. Team Us can do anything.' She looked at Jacob. 'Sweetheart, do you want to come upstairs?'

Jacob's scowl returned. 'Want Mummy.'

Xander sighed. 'And it was all going so well.'

'Mummy's coming home soon,' Nell lied. 'She'll think you're a very good boy if you've got your pyjamas on.'

Jacob pondered this for a moment. Then with an enquiring look at the pair of them, he started opening and closing his hands in a triangle shape.

'OK, I think even I might be able to guess that one,' Xander said. 'Book, right?'

'Yeah. I guess Mum or Dad usually reads to him while the other one's getting him ready for bed.' She looked at him. 'Well, Uncle Xander, what do you think? You're the one who's good at doing the voices.'

'Really? You're volunteering yourself for pull-up and pyjama duty? Because this kid really does not like wearing clothes.'

'Go on, since it's you.'

He smiled. 'Nell, it means a lot that you'd wrestle a semi-feral toddler just to help me out.'

'Well, what are friends for if not some emergency toddler-tussling of an evening? Come on, let's get him up the stairs.'

Chapter Seventeen

'Right, Mill, come on,' Stevie said when she'd parked up in their drive. 'I need to get the tea on tout suite. We're late tonight.'

Milly giggled. 'Toot sweet. Like in *Chitty Chitty Bang Bang*.' She opened the door and tugged Red's collar. 'C'mon, Red, let's go play in my room.'

But Red didn't move from the back seat.

'Red, come on!' Milly yanked at her collar again.

'Milly, don't,' Stevie said. 'You'll hurt her. Let her get out in her own time.'

Milly jumped out of the car, but no Red followed. Stevie looked over her seat, frowning.

'What's up, hound?' she murmured. 'Tired out from all that mountaineering?'

Red lay with her feet on her paws, looking up at her with sad brown eyes. Stevie got out of the car and patted her knee for her to heel.

After a moment's hesitation, the little spaniel leapt heavily from the seat and started following her mum to the house. But when Stevie had unlocked the door and turned to check on her, she discovered Red lying in the middle of the drive, whimpering quietly.

'What's wrong with her, Mummy?' Milly asked in a frightened little voice.

Stevie approached Red and knelt down beside her. The little dog looked up at her with pleading, pain-filled eyes.

'Milly, did Red seem OK today when you two were playing?' she asked in a voice that was as casual and unworried as she could make it.

Milly nodded. 'She was good. She did everything she was told and didn't run off once.'

'Did she eat anything off the floor?'

'No.' Milly paused. 'She drank some water though.'

'Where was the water?' Stevie asked, struggling to keep the worry from her voice.

'In the thing. The thing where the sheep water is.'

'The sheep water?' Stevie cast an anxious look at her whimpering dog. 'You mean where they drink or where they get washed?'

'Dunno. It was in the field next to Miss Shackleton's house.'

'Oh God,' she whispered. 'Red, sweetheart, what did you do?'

She blinked a couple of times, forcing herself to be composed, then smiled reassuringly at Milly.

'I think maybe Red's a bit poorly,' she said. 'Just a tiny bit, that's all.'

'Does she need Lemsip?' Milly whispered.

'Lemsip's only for people. She might need some special dog medicine from the vet though. Sweetie, do you think you could quickly pack your PJs and a toothbrush? You'd better sleep over at Nanny's tonight while I take Red to someone who can make her better.'

It said a lot for how worried Milly was about her best friend that she didn't stop to argue or question: she just darted into the house and started getting ready without a word.

While Milly was packing her stuff, Stevie googled the number for their out-of-hours vet.

'Hi,' she said to the woman who answered her call. 'I'm trying to get hold of Mr Mukherjee, is he there?'

'He's on a job at one of the farms, I'm afraid,' the woman said. 'Always a busy time, lambing season. What's it regarding?'

'My dog. She…' Stevie cast a worried glance at Red, curled up awkwardly with her eyes half open, and lowered her voice. 'I think she drank some dirty water from a farmer's field. It might've had sheep dip or chemicals or… I don't know, but she's very weak. Do you know when he'll be back?'

'It could be a while,' the woman said. 'Look, can I give you the number for the out-of-hours vet in our sister surgery over in Dewsbury? She might be able to fit you in.'

'Dewsbury? But that's over an hour's drive! What if it's an emergency?'

'I'm sorry. I don't know what else to suggest.'

'OK. Right.' Stevie hesitated, skimming through her options. 'Could you ask Mr Mukherjee to call me on this number as soon as he gets in? Thank you.'

After she'd hung up, she tapped out a text.

> **I've got a Red emergency. Can I come over? I need your help.**

It buzzed almost instantly with a reply.

> **Of course. See you soon x**

Ten minutes later, she was knocking at the door of Nora's place, Milly next to her clutching an overnight bag and looking pale.

'I'm so sorry to do this to you, Nora,' Stevie said when her mother-in-law opened the door.

'Never you mind about that.' She cast a glance at Red, laying on a towel on the back seat. The poor thing had lost control of her bladder now and looked utterly miserable. 'Will she be OK?' she asked in a low voice.

'Oh yes, it's nothing,' Stevie said, with a bright smile in Milly's direction. 'Just a bit of doggy flu, I think. Still, best to get her looked at.'

'Are you taking her to the vet?'

Stevie shook her head. 'He's not available at the moment. I've got a friend who used to be a veterinary nurse, though. I'm hoping she'll know what to do until the vet can get to us.'

'Well, don't you worry about me and Mill. We're going to have a great time.' Nora laid a hand on Milly's shoulder and guided her into the house. 'Fish fingers and beans for tea, Milly Vanilli, what do you say?'

Milly managed a little twitch of a smile, but her eyes quickly flickered over her shoulder to Red again.

'Try not to worry her,' Stevie whispered as Nora turned to go into the house. 'I'll call you as soon as I know what's happening.'

-

She was soon pressing Deb's doorbell, Red cradled in her arms, swaddled in the towel. Within seconds Deb opened it, as if she'd been waiting right in the hall for them.

'What is it, Stevie? What's the emergency?' She took in Red's half-conscious form. 'Oh God, no. What happened, she didn't get hit by something?'

'No. She... Deb, I think she's been poisoned.'

Unable to stop herself, Stevie burst into tears.

'Here. Get yourself inside,' Deb said, ushering her into the house.

She guided Stevie down the hall and into the living room.

'On the sofa,' she said. The businesslike tone felt like just what Stevie needed. She wiped her eyes, forcing her tears under control.

'Are you sure?' she said. 'She's struggling to control her bodily functions, and she's vomited a couple of times. I don't want her to make a mess of your furniture.'

'Never mind that. Go on, put her down.' Deb eyed her with concern. 'You're not looking far off falling over yourself, Stevie.'

'It's just worry. I'll be OK.'

Stevie lay Red down on the sofa and stroked her head. 'Good girl,' she whispered soothingly. 'No need to be frightened. Here's someone who can help you.'

Life had jumped up from her place by the fire to greet her friend. She headbutted Red a couple of times, tail wagging, but it stilled when her usually boisterous playmate didn't respond.

'Come on, Lifey,' Deb said gently. 'We'd better shut you in the bedroom for a bit, just in case it's anything catching.'

She patted her thigh and Life followed her from the room, casting a worried doggy look back at Red lying on the sofa.

While she was out of the room, Stevie hugged Red around the neck, choking on sobs.

'Please get better, pup,' she whispered. 'If you'll just get better for me then I'll never tell you off again, I promise.'

Red wagged her tail limply in response, and Stevie laughed through her tears. 'Good girl,' she whispered. 'Good girl, Red.'

'Did you call your vet?' Deb asked when she came back in.

Stevie wiped her eyes and looked up. 'Yes but he's out on a lambing job. Sorry, Deb, I didn't know who else to turn to.'

'You did right.' Deb knelt down and pushed open each of Red's eyelids to get a look at her pupils. 'Tell me what happened.'

'She was out playing with Milly today while I helped Nell with some painting. I told Milly to keep her on the lead, but she must've let her wander because she said she drank from the sheep water in the field next to Nell's place. I don't know if she means the drinking water or the dip but whichever it was, it obviously didn't agree with her.'

'What time was this?'

'About five, I guess, so two hours ago.' Stevie looked up from Red to meet Deb's eyes. 'Is it bad?' she asked in a whisper.

'It'll be absolutely fine,' Deb said in a firm tone. 'I don't mean to sound brutal, Stevie, but if she'd ingested the sort of dangerous chemicals that could be lethal, she'd already be dead.'

'So what is it?'

'Giardia, most likely, from drinking infected water. I've seen this in plenty of dogs. It's almost never fatal.'

'*Almost* never? You mean it sometimes is?'

'Not in a young, healthy animal like Red. A course of antibiotics, she should be fine.'

'And it couldn't be anything worse?'

Deb hesitated.

'Deb, tell me, please! I need to know.'

'Well, there's a chance it could be leptospirosis. That's less common, but it is spread through water used by livestock.'

'What happens if it's that?'

'Most dogs survive it, if they're treated right away. But...' She grimaced. 'I won't lie to you; it can cause organ failure.'

'Oh God. Oh God!'

Deb put a hand on her shoulder. 'Please don't worry,' she said softly. 'It's much more likely to be the other thing. I'll help you take care of her till the vet can get here.'

Stevie flashed her a shaky smile. 'Thanks, Deb.'

'Right.' Deb went back into businesslike mode. 'First things first. Is she up to date with her worming treatment?'

'She is due one this month. Will that help?'

'It might, if it's Giardia. Hang on.'

Deb left the room. She came back in five minutes later with a packet of worming tablets, a thick blanket and a steaming cup of tea.

'Here,' she said, pushing the tea into Stevie's hands. 'Hot and strong. You look like you need it. Get that down you while I see to Red.'

Deb stripped out of her shirt, leaving her in just a vest top, and crouched by Red. First she wrapped her up in the blanket, then forced open her mouth so she could administer the worming tablet. It said a lot for the poor girl's weak state that she submitted to having it pushed into her jaws without even a whimper of protest.

'That's a brave girl,' Deb whispered, stroking her head as she swallowed it down.

'I hate seeing her like this,' Stevie said, sinking onto the carpet with her tea. 'She's got so much life in her usually, and now she's… the pain in her eyes. It reminds me of when Milly got sick as a baby. That helplessness when they look at you pleading for relief and you can't explain you've got none to give.'

Deb came to sit by her on the floor and wrapped her up in her arms.

'I promise it'll all be OK,' she whispered, pressing her lips to Stevie's hair. 'I'll be here for all of it. I won't leave you alone until we've seen it through.'

That was what she needed to hear. The idea of being alone with Red, of watching her die slowly and in pain while she sat helplessly by, was terrifying to Stevie.

She wrapped her arms around Deb's waist and gave her a squeeze.

'Thanks, Deb. Thanks for being here when I needed you. I know I don't deserve it after—' She bit her lip. 'You know.'

'You don't feel guilty about that?'

'A little.'

'It's OK, you know. I'm happy to be just friends, if that's what you want.'

'But you were hurt, I could tell.'

'Maybe,' Deb admitted. 'I like you a lot, Stevie – not just as a friend. But I'd never push for something you weren't comfortable with.'

'Deb, it's not that I—' She took a deep breath. 'I mean, I like you too. You're funny and kind and sort of adorable, and you must know you're bloody gorgeous. I was flattered as anything that you'd even think about me like that, and if it hadn't been for… if I'd met you years ago, before Angela and Mill and…' She sighed. 'Ugh, I don't know what I'm rambling on about. Sorry. Worry and paint fumes talking.'

Deb drew back from the hug to look into her face. A little smile flickered at the corner of her mouth.

'Say that again,' she said softly.

'What?'

She brought a finger up to trace the shape of Stevie's ear. 'That bit about me being bloody gorgeous.'

Stevie smiled. 'You know you are. It'll be a lucky girl who eventually makes an honest woman of you.'

Deb's gaze had settled on her lips. Self-consciously, Stevie ran her tongue-tip over them.

'Deb…' she whispered. 'I think I probably ought to… that we should…'

'Stevie, it's OK. You don't need to feel guilty about this, or about anything.' She leant forward and left a soft, lingering kiss on Stevie's mouth. 'You've been a widow for four years. This, us, what we feel for each other – it's the most natural thing in the world.'

Stevie reached up to touch her lips. Was that how kissing had always felt? So… tingly? She could still taste the heat of it.

Hardly knowing what she was doing, she brought her hand up and ran her fingertips along Deb's neck and shoulder. Deb closed her eyes at the touch.

'It's been a long time since I was with anyone,' Stevie whispered.

'I know it has. Maybe too long.' Deb's gaze lingered once more on Stevie's lips. 'Can I kiss you again?' she whispered.

'I…' Stevie hesitated. 'Yes,' she whispered. 'Yes please.'

Deb brought her lips back to Stevie's. The fingers of one hand caressed the back of Stevie's neck as they kissed, the other gliding over her hip.

'You know, it's Valentine's Day,' Deb whispered when they broke apart. 'What do you think about staying over with me? No funny business, just a kiss and a cuddle.'

Stevie smiled. 'Dunno, I've kind of missed a bit of funny business.'

'Well, I think I could manage that too.'

Deb planted gentle kisses along her neck while her hands slid over Stevie's body, exploring. Stevie shivered at the touch, but she tensed when one hand found its way to her breast.

Deb pulled away at once.

'What?' she murmured. 'Stevie, what's wrong?'

'I… can't.' She closed her eyes tight, trying to fight back the sudden surge of anxiety; the tinny ringing sound in her brain that made her feel as though she might be about to pass out. 'Deb, I can't do this, I'm sorry.'

Deb looked confused by her sudden shift in mood. But before they could say anything else, Stevie's ringtone cut through the moment.

'The vet. Thank God,' she said with a sigh of relief.

She answered and gave the man directions to Deb's house. In no time, he was on the doorstep.

'I'll have to get these samples analysed, but it looks like Giardia all right,' Mr Mukherjee said when he'd examined the poorly dog. 'Ms Madeleine, I'm going to give Red an anti-inflammatory by injection and prescribe a course of antibiotics. I'll have the samples sent for testing tomorrow and give you a call when we have a firm diagnosis, then you can bring her in during practice hours for a check-up.'

'So she'll be OK?'

He smiled. 'I'm sure of it. Rest, fluids and antibiotics, she'll soon be back to her old trouble-causing self.'

'Oh, thank you. Thank you so much,' Stevie said, pumping his hand. 'My daughter would've been devastated if anything had happened to her. So would I.'

'Lots of TLC is what she needs now.' He looked from her to Deb. 'I'm sure you and your partner can provide that.'

'Oh, she's not my – um, thank you.'

'That's my job,' the vet said, smiling. He gave Red a pat. 'I'll see you both soon, Ms Madeleine.'

He grabbed his coat and left.

'Thank God,' Stevie said when he'd gone. She threw her arms around Deb and gave her a tight hug of sheer relief.

Deb laughed breathlessly. 'Stevie, you anaconda, you're squeezing me to death.'

Stevie let her go. 'Sorry. Just relieved she's going to be OK, that's all. I'd better ring Nora so she can give the good news to Milly, then I'll take Red home.'

'I thought… aren't you going to stay over?'

Stevie flinched. 'Look, Deb…'

'Oh God.' Deb sank down onto the sofa next to Red. 'No good ever comes of conversations that start "Look, Deb". I'm not getting grounded, am I?'

Stevie felt a stab of guilt.

'It's just… I really like you. I mean that. I do, a hell of a lot.'

'But?' Deb said in a toneless voice.

'You've been brilliant tonight, absolutely amazing. Honestly, I don't know how I can ever pay you back for looking after us both. But…' She swallowed. 'I shouldn't have said I'd stay. That was… foolish. I was tired and worried and you were being so nice and… I let myself get carried away. I'm sorry.'

Deb gave her head a frustrated shake. 'Stevie, I don't get this. That's fine if you don't want to stay, but I know you like me. I completely know I like you. Did I go too far before, is that it?'

'No,' she murmured. 'It wasn't anything you did. It's me. And… and Angela.'

'Angela's dead, Stevie,' Deb said in a softer voice. 'It's not wrong to want to be with someone new.'

Stevie flushed, looking down at the carpet.

'It's daft, isn't it?' she said. 'The last thing Angela ever told me was that she'd been unfaithful. And yet here I am nearly four years later, scared to move on because it still feels like cheating.'

'But you aren't cheating. You're not doing anything wrong.'

'It's not just Angela,' Stevie whispered.

'Then what is it?'

She looked away. 'Something… something that happened a long time ago.'

'Tell me.'

'I… can't.' She shook her head. 'I'm sorry, Deb. Please don't be hurt, but we can be friends and… and that's it. It's all I've got left to offer.'

Chapter Eighteen

By the time Justin and Sara arrived home from their Valentine's night out, Jacob was fast asleep in his *Paw Patrol* pyjamas, sucking his thumb like butter wouldn't melt in his deceptively cherubic mouth. Xander was in a half-doze too, on a chair by Jacob's cot with Nell beside him. She'd dropped off completely with her head resting on his shoulder.

'Hiya,' Xander said, smiling drowsily at his friends. 'Did you have a good night?'

'We did.' Justin shot an enquiring glance at the sleeping Nell. 'Looks like maybe you did too. Been having a sleepover?'

'Sorry. Jacob turned out to be a two-man job. Don't mind, do you?'

Sara bent to give him a kiss on the cheek. 'Of course we don't mind. Thanks so much for doing this, Xand, we appreciate it. Drinks are on us for the next five years.'

'Did Jacob behave for his Uncle Xander then?' Justin asked.

'Oh, yeah. Good as gold.'

-

'So are you feeling broody after that?' Nell asked Xander when they were outside.

'Are you kidding? I'll be booking myself in for a vasectomy next week.' Xander smiled. 'He was cute when he was asleep though, wasn't he?'

'Yeah, and I bet he knows it too. That's how they get you. I'm convinced all toddlers are secretly evil overlords with plans for world domination.' She checked her phone and frowned. 'Hm.'

'What?'

'Text from Stevie. Red's ill, apparently. She's apologising for not being able to help me paint this weekend like we'd planned.'

'Red's ill? Is she going to be OK?'

'Stevie says the vet's given her antibiotics, but sounds like she had her pretty worried for a while. I hope it was nothing she picked up at my place. She seemed fine earlier.'

'Well, if you need me to fill in with a paintbrush in lieu of Stevie just let me know. I certainly owe you a favour after tonight.'

She squeezed his arm. 'Thanks, mate.'

'So... pub?' he said, trying not to dwell on the epically friend-zoney sound of that 'mate'. 'There's still time for a quick one. I'm buying, obviously.'

She shook her head. 'Sorry, Xand, I'm kind of exhausted. And it's a school night too – last day before half-term tomorrow, which you know means they'll be even more hyper than on your average Friday. I should probably get home.'

'Oh. OK,' Xander said, trying not to sound too disappointed. 'Maybe another time.'

Nell looked up at him. 'You, er... you want to walk me back? I can offer you a nightcap, at least.'

'Um, yeah. That sounds nice.'

She tucked her arm into his as they headed in the direction of Leyholme.

When they reached Humblebee Farm, they said good evening to Colin, dozing in the outhouse as usual, then Nell unlocked the front door to let them in.

'Sorry about the paint fumes,' she said, leading the way down the hall. 'First coat's still drying in the living room. Never mind, we can sit in the kitchen.'

'So can I help?' Xander asked. 'It wasn't an empty promise, I'm more than happy to pitch in.'

'I could certainly use another pair of hands. How about tomorrow after school, we— oh my God!'

The back door, which Nell usually kept blocked with a big cardboard box weighted down with bricks, was hanging open. The box was on its side, bricks spilling out over the kitchen floor.

Xander frowned. 'What's happened, Nell?'

'The door – someone must've forced it! No sheep or gust of wind could have done that.'

She started darting around the kitchen, yanking open drawers and rifling the contents. Then she ran out to check if anything was missing from the other rooms.

'Has anything been taken?' Xander asked when she came back.

'The keys to my scooter. And my scooter.'

'Oh God, so someone really was here. Anything else?'

'Doesn't look like it,' Nell said. 'There's not much else worth stealing.'

'Have you got home insurance?'

'Xand, I haven't even got a lockable back door. No, I haven't got home insurance.'

He went to the back door and peered out. 'I'd better have a scout around, make sure whoever it was is gone. You call the police and file an incident report or whatever. Got a torch?'

'Yes.' She was visibly shaking, but she managed to fumble it from out of the kitchen drawer. 'Here. Be careful, Xand.'

He headed out, shining the torch into every corner of the front and back gardens, into the outhouse where Colin slept on obliviously, the field of sheep next door and finally back down the road. All he could see were the tyre tracks from Nell's scooter.

'Looks like they're long gone,' he said when he came back in. 'I'm sorry, Nell.'

She still looked very shaken. He came forward to give her a hug.

'Did you call the police?' he asked.

'Yeah, gave them the reg number and stuff in case they manage to recover it. I told them not to bother sending anyone out though. There's nothing they can do now.'

'And are you OK?'

She shuddered in his arms. 'The worst thing is thinking about someone in here. In my home, going through my stuff.'

'You think they targeted you deliberately? It's hardly a secret that this place is falling to bits.'

'Maybe. Or maybe they saw the scooter outside and thought they'd try their luck.' She groaned. 'Stevie tried to warn me earlier too, and like an idiot I just laughed it off. What do you think would've happened if I'd been in?'

Xander held her a little tighter. 'It doesn't bear thinking about.'

'Xander... you're not an axe murderer, are you?'

'Not that I'm aware of. Although I'm always keen to explore new hobbies.'

She looked up at him with wide, frightened eyes. 'Then will you... will you stay with me?'

He blinked. 'Stay over, you mean?'

'I really don't want to be on my own tonight.'

Xander drew himself up a little taller.

A damsel in distress was asking for his help. He was a man and protector, bane of any scooter thieves or axe murderers who might happen to be roaming around. A defender of womenfolk and a kicker of ass. Yes he was.

Or he would be, just as soon as he'd cleared it with his mum.

'Of course, if it makes you feel safer,' he said gently. 'Let me just call home and tell my mum I won't be back tonight.'

'Will she mind?'

He laughed. 'I'm thirty-one, Nell. I don't have a curfew any more.'

She squinted a sceptical eye. 'What, not even on school nights?'

'Nope, I'm allowed to stay out as late as I like. Impressed?'

'Very.'

'Mind you, I wasn't planning on telling my mum exactly where I'll be staying,' he said, smiling.

Nell laughed. 'Why, wouldn't she approve?'

'Oh, she'd approve and then some. In fact, she'd probably be round tomorrow to help you organise the wedding. I'll tell her I'm sleeping over at Justin and Sara's.'

A few weeks ago he might have worried about leaving his mum alone for the night, but she'd really been much better since their confrontation the day she'd smashed up her watered-down gin. She was far from teetotal, but she did now have at least a couple of drink-free nights a week, and she rarely drank until she blacked out. Xander was feeling very encouraged by her progress, especially with the anniversary of his dad's death rapidly approaching – although he still hadn't managed to talk her into joining the counselling group for people bereaved by suicide that he'd found online.

'OK, all sorted,' he told Nell after he'd made the call. 'Let's get this door barricaded as best we can, then I'll hunker down on the sofa with the poker.'

Nell shook her head. 'You can't sleep in there. I told you, there's paint drying. You'll asphyxiate or something.'

'Right. So… you don't have a spare room, do you?'

She flushed. 'Well, no. I was actually asking… I mean, I thought you could sleep with me.'

He blinked. 'With you?'

'I'd feel safer with you there. And the poker.'

'In your bed?'

'Yeah. Is that OK?'

'Er… what do I do if an axe murderer comes?'

She smiled. 'Tell him three's a crowd.'

Chapter Nineteen

'So you call yourself a man, do you, Scott?' Xander muttered to himself in his office next day. 'Even a mouse knows what to do when it finds itself in bed with another mouse it likes on bloody *Valentine's Day*.'

While the night he'd spent with Nell had been reassuringly free of axe murderers, it had been quite depressingly free of anything else either. Specifically, anything bedroom-related that wasn't sleep.

'This is kind of nice,' Nell had whispered when they'd climbed under the duvet spread over her air mattress together, Nell looking adorable in her giraffe pyjamas, Xander still fully clothed. And she'd snuggled into him like all his dreams were finally coming true, gazed up at him with those gorgeous green eyes while all the curves he'd fantasised so many times about kissing and caressing into fits of sexual ecstasy were pressed right up against him, and his heart — not to mention other parts of his anatomy — had leapt.

'Yeah,' he'd said. 'It is nice. Night, Nell.'

Then he'd kissed the top of her head and — oh, couldn't he just punch himself? — he'd bloody well gone to sleep. Or rather he'd pretended to go to sleep, lying there hard and frustrated while Nell had drifted off in his arms.

She'd wanted him to. He knew she'd wanted him to. So why the hell *hadn't* he?

He groaned and buried his face in his hands.

Mrs Rhodes popped her head around the office door. 'Would you like a coffee, Alexander?'

'No. I don't deserve coffee.'

'OK then.'

'Actually, could you bring me one of those planks they give self-flagellating monks so I can bash myself in the face with it a few times?'

The secretary looked puzzled. 'Well, I could take a look in the art cupboard...'

'It's fine. Never mind.'

'I've got a message for you from Miss Shackleton, by the way.'

Xander's head shot up. 'Have you? What?'

'She wants you to trot along to Reception and join them for their last fifteen minutes today, if you've nothing more urgent on. Something she wants to show you.'

'Right. Yes, I can do that. Did, er... did she say anything else?'

'No, that was all. Give us a bell if you change your mind about the coffee, won't you, pet?'

–

When the clock hit quarter past three, Xander headed to the Reception classroom, wondering what it was Nell wanted to see him for. He had the vague idea he owed her an apology, although he wasn't sure apologising to women for not making a pass at them was really a thing you were supposed to do.

When he reached the classroom there were a couple of kids outside – Morgan Hancock, Jolene's little lad, and Milly Madeleine.

'Hi guys,' he said. 'What's up, have you done something naughty?'

Milly shook her head. 'We're head Oompa-Loompas,' she told him proudly. 'Miss picked us 'cos we got the last two Star of the Weeks.'

'Did you? Well done.'

'Only we'll be orange when we do it properly,' Morgan said. 'This is just for practice.'

'Ah, I see.' Xander glanced down. 'Do Oompa-Loompas normally hold hands?'

Milly giggled. 'No, that's because Morgan's my boyfriend,' she whispered. 'But shush 'cos Miss Shackleton doesn't know.'

'I've got four girlfriends now,' Morgan announced, looking pleased with himself. 'Milly's got one other boyfriend and a girlfriend so I'm winning.'

'Wow, impressive,' Xander said. 'I haven't even got one girl-friend. Any tips?'

Morgan looked thoughtful. 'Well, girls sometimes like it when you kiss them,' he said. 'But you're s'posed to ask first in case they don't.'

Xander nodded. 'That's good advice. Where do I go now then?'

'We have to take you into the chocolate factory,' Milly said.

'OK, Oompa-Loompas, lead on.'

He followed the two of them into their classroom, where a painted card archway bearing the name 'Willy Wonka's Chocolate Factory' had been set up. Nell, who was standing next to it wearing a top hat, nodded solemnly to him.

'Welcome, Golden Ticket-holder, to our chocolate factory.'

There were giggles from behind the arch.

'Um, thanks for having me,' Xander said.

Milly tugged at his sleeve. 'Come on, Mr Scott.'

He headed through the archway, where the other Reception kids were lined up in two rows.

'OK, you lot, now,' Nell whispered, and they launched into a verse of 'The Oompa-Loompa Song'. A snaking twist of brown sugar paper ran down the back wall and across the floor, where it was dotted with toy boats, representing Willy Wonka's famous waterfall and river of chocolate. All around the classroom, painted candy canes, chocolate bars and Golden Tickets decorated the walls. Even Oinky, the school guinea pig, had a little paper top hat on as he watched proceedings in a bemused sort of way from his cage.

'Guys, this is just amazing,' Xander said when the kids had finished singing. 'Did you make all this yourselves?'

The kids nodded, beaming at him.

'I painted the letters on the arch!' Robbie Doneen called out, his hand shooting into the air. 'Miss Shackleton said I could 'cos I was neatest.'

'I noticed how neat they were straight away,' Xander said. 'Well done, Robbie. And all of you. I'm super impressed.'

'This is our game for the fete,' Nell said. 'People pay fifty pee to come into the chocolate factory and win a prize.'

'How do they win?'

'Here.' She led him to a brown inflatable paddling pool at the end of the chocolate river. 'Fifty pee please, Sir.'

'Oh. Right.' He fumbled in his pocket and handed over a fifty-pence piece.

'Olivia, do you want to come and show Mr Scott what to do?'

The little girl came skipping over.

'It's dead easy,' she told him. 'You just have to put your hand in the chocolate pool and try to find a Golden Ticket. If you find one, you win a Wonka Bar. If you get a plain not-gold one, you win a candy cane.'

'So it's a prize every time?' Xander said. 'Sounds like a bargain.'

He bent to rummage in the paddling pool, pulled out a ticket and unfolded it.

'Aww. Just plain, I'm afraid,' Nell said. 'But you still get a candy cane.'

He smiled. 'I'll let you save it for me till World Book Day.'

The bell rang for the end of school.

'OK, everyone, coats on and lined up by the door,' Nell called out. 'Nobody leaves this room until someone's here to collect them.' She hastily gathered up the bits and pieces of their chocolate factory and either hid them under her desk or turned them to face the wall so the surprise wouldn't be ruined for mums and dads.

'So what's in the Wonka Bars?' Xander asked Nell as they went to stand behind her desk. 'Because as I remember it, visiting the chocolate factory didn't work out so well for four out of five Golden Ticket-holders.'

She laughed. 'It's just a Dairy Milk. We made special wrappers for them though.'

'So much for not doing anything big, eh?'

'Oh, but they've had so much fun making it all. We've got some good lessons lined up for the day too. I'm going to get them designing their own magical sweets; that should fire up their greedy little imaginations.'

'It's great, Nell. You've done a fantastic job, all of you.'

She squeezed his arm. 'Nervous?'

He stared at her.

'About World Book Day,' she said.

'Oh.' He ran a finger under his shirt collar. 'Well, yes, but I think I'm managing to keep a lid on it.'

'I heard the governors weren't too happy.'

'If by the governors you mean Ryan Theakston, you're right. But he's grudgingly agreed to support it.'

'What's his problem with it?'

'Mainly that it wasn't him who came up with the idea, I think.' The kids had all disappeared with their parents now. Xander turned to face her. 'Nell, about yesterday – last night.'

'Oh yeah, I wanted to say thanks for that. Looking after me in my hour of need.' She smiled shyly up at him. 'And, er… for being such a gent. You know, when you could see I was frightened. Some men might have taken advantage, but not you.'

'Right. Um, no problem.'

OK, now he felt worse. Because he wasn't a gent, was he? He'd definitely wanted to make a move. Cowardice rather than gallantry had stayed his hand.

'So does that offer to help with the house still stand?' Nell asked. 'I'm going to pick up a lock from the hardware shop after work. I don't know how much you know about doors, but I could use a hand fitting it.'

She was still looking up at him, just as she had when they'd been cuddling in bed together. His eyes locked into hers, and Xander was swept with a sudden, overwhelming desire to pull her into his arms and kiss her senseless, like he knew she'd wanted him to last night.

There was a knock at the classroom door. He turned away, remembering where he was.

'Come in,' Nell called, looking a little flustered herself as she patted her hair into place.

Mrs Rhodes peeped around the door. 'Ah, Alexander, there you are. You're not going home yet, are you?'

'Not for a little while, why?'

'Mr Theakston called. He says he's stopping by in half an hour and he wants to see you as a matter of urgency.'

'Oh, peachy,' Xander muttered.

–

When Ryan arrived, Xander was at his desk. He'd hurried back to his office to notch the height up on his swivel chair, so he could feel a bit more like Alan Sugar in *The Apprentice* and a bit less like a schoolboy called to the head's office for a bollocking. He, Xander, was on the head's side of the desk and Ryan could just bloody well remember that.

'Ryan. Good afternoon.' Xander rose to shake hands in that subtly hostile way where you grip just a bit too hard for a bit too long. 'I wasn't expecting to see you today.'

'Yes. Well I wasn't expecting to be here today, not after the chat we had so very recently about you making sure I was kept in the loop on this World Book Day thing,' Ryan said, scowling as he helped himself to a seat.

Xander frowned. 'Eh? But I sent you an update last week. The Reception kids are turning their classroom into a chocolate factory, we've got the Year 5s doing snozzcumber and frob-scottle tasting, the Year 4s have made a Giant Peach bowling game—'

'But you left out one key fact, didn't you? Which is that this fete will be taking place in lesson time.'

'What? No I didn't. I told you that right at the start, I'm sure.'

Ryan flicked an invisible speck of dust from his shirt collar. 'I'm sorry, Xander, but we can't afford to take a whole afternoon out of the children's learning time for frivolities.'

'It's not frivolity, Ryan, it's literature. Anyway, we're not taking a whole afternoon. The fete starts at two thirty and finishes at four thirty. That's only an hour out of scheduled lessons.' Xander frowned. 'And you had no problem taking a whole day's worth of lesson time away from us so you could get the staff pointlessly carrying bloody eggs around Cavendish Hall, did you? Without consulting me, I might add.'

Ryan cleared his throat. 'Yes, well, be that as it may, I'm afraid there've been complaints.'

'From who?'

'From parents. They're concerned about the amount of time their children are missing this term, what with the training day and now this.'

'Which parents? Nobody's complained to me. All the parents I've spoken to have been very supportive of our World Book Day plans.'

'I'm not at liberty to say which parents. Suffice to say, there are some.'

'And when did you get these complaints, Ryan?' Xander demanded. 'Recently?'

'That's right.'

'OK, well the newsletter announcing the date and time of the fete went out weeks ago. So that seems like a bit of a delayed reaction from these parents, doesn't it?'

Ryan glared at him. 'Are you calling me a liar, lad?'

'I'm not calling you anything.'

That was completely untrue. In his head Xander was calling Ryan all sorts of things, top of the list being that he was a puffed-up, interfering, micro-managing, egomaniacal, spiv-moustached tosser. But he was pretty sure he'd managed not to say any of that out loud.

'Right, well, I'm afraid I've really been left with no choice,' Ryan said. 'I'm sorry, Xander, but we're going to have to shut the whole thing down after all.'

'What? No! No, you can't do that!'

'The children can still run their games and things during the dinner hour if they like, for the staff and pupils. But this fete nonsense has to stop. I'll leave you to make the announcement after the holidays.'

'Ryan, no! Seriously, if you'd seen how hard they'd all worked... the Reception kids have made this whole waterfall and an archway and everything, and there was a song they'd learnt, it was amazing—' He stopped, narrowing his eyes. 'Hang on.'

'What?'

'Why so sudden, Ryan? Why today?'

'I'm sorry?'

'This isn't about the fete at all, is it? Did Jeremy Illingworth happen to speak to you?'

'That's... none of your business.'

'He did, didn't he? He told you he was planning to retire, and that he'd like me to be his successor.' Xander laughed. 'This isn't about the fete, it's about me. You don't think I'm up to the job and you're trying to undermine me. Make me look weak in front of the staff and parents.'

'Rein in the ego, eh, son? I told you, we've had complaints.'

'I'm the head. If people have complaints, they can bring them to me. I run this school.'

'Jeremy's the head,' Ryan snapped. 'You're the acting head, that's all, so you can drop the delusions of grandeur.'

'Exactly, I'm the acting head. That means it's my job to act like the head in Jeremy's absence, doesn't it?'

'It's your job to do as you're told.'

Xander thought back to the Reception kids earlier – their happy, excited little faces as they'd shown him everything they'd worked so hard to make and learn – and clenched his fists under the desk.

'Ryan, tell me this,' he said. 'Can you make me shut this down?'

'I'm asking you to shut it down.'

'But can you make me? Do you, as chair of the board, have the power to overrule the headteacher on this matter?'

'Young man, I am the elected representative of the board of governors.'

'That's not answering my question.'

Ryan's eyes narrowed. 'Perhaps not. But I have the power to make life very difficult for you if you refuse to cooperate.'

'How, by relieving me of my command?' Xander demanded, standing up and leaning his fists on the desk. 'This is mutiny, Mr Theakston. I'll see you hanging from the highest yardarm in the British fleet.'

'Eh?'

'It's a literary reference. *Mutiny on the Bounty*. Join us on World Book Day, you might find out more.'

'Look, can you cut out the pirate crap?' Ryan demanded.

'You started it. A school is like a ship, right? And I'm the captain. Which makes you a mutineer, I'm afraid, Theakston.'

Ryan stood up too. 'The fact is, *Mr* Scott, you just don't have the authority to run an event on this scale.'

'Well, I'm the head so clearly I do,' Xander said, smiling brightly. He was awash with testosterone now and he was rather enjoying the sensation. 'Or are you sacking me? Because I'm pretty sure you don't have the authority for that.'

'Don't be ridiculous. No one's getting sacked.'

'OK, good to know. In that case, perhaps you can let me get on with doing my job.' He sat back down and tapped at his computer to wake the screen up. 'Now if you don't mind, I've got a lot to do. We're having a fete here in a few weeks, you know.'

Ryan pointed a finger at him. 'You know why the governors wanted you for this job, Xander?'

'Because everyone else had already turned it down?'

'No. Well, yes. But mainly because we thought you were the company man, a safe pair of hands. We thought we could count on you to follow orders.'

'Yeah, I bet you did. Like Karl Dönitz, right?'

'Who?'

'He was the leader of the Third Reich. Look, get out, can you? I've got a school to run here.'

Ryan leaned forward, lowering his voice. 'Son, you do not want to take me on. You haven't got the balls for it.'

'Yes. Well, thanks for that.' Xander didn't look at Ryan as he tapped out fake emails on his keyboard. 'Like I said, I am very busy. I'm sure you can show yourself out.'

'You haven't heard the last of this,' Ryan said as he stood to leave.

Chapter Twenty

'Yeah, that's right, Private Walker, jog on,' Xander muttered as he watched Ryan skulk off down the corridor. 'My school, my rules, my fete. Ha!'

The adrenaline generated by the confrontation was still coursing through his veins. He'd fought for something and, it seemed, he'd won. This was not a thing that happened to him very often.

He felt amazing. He felt like he could do anything. He felt...

He jumped up from his desk, grabbed his coat and left the office.

'Oh, Alexander, have you got two minutes?' Mrs Rhodes asked as he strode past her desk.

'Not now, Janet, I'm being manly.'

'He's been inhaling Tippex fumes again,' she muttered as he flung open the door and walked out.

'Oh,' he said, sticking his head back round the door. 'Do me a favour, will you? Get a message to Jeremy Illingworth. Tell him I've thought about it and it's a yes.'

He didn't slow down as he marched through the village, striding purposefully towards the track that led up to Humblebee Farm.

'Hi, Xand,' Stevie Madeleine said, spotting him as she came out of the post office. 'Are you OK?'

'Better than OK, Stevie.' He stopped to give her a peck on the cheek. 'I'm a man.'

'Are you going to see Nell?' she called as he walked off again.

'You're goddamn right I am!'

When he reached the farm, the front door was propped open. He marched straight in without knocking.

'Not now, Colin!' he called as a resentful *baa* sailed after him.

In the living room, Nell was in her baggy denim painting dungarees on a stepladder, giving the upper part of the wall a good rollering. She had her hair tied back in a vintage-style red headscarf, making her look like a cute ginger Rosie the Riveter.

'Hi Xander,' she said, glancing down at him. 'Didn't hear you knock.'

'Nell, I'm a man. I wanted you to be the first to know.'

'OK,' she said, blinking. 'Well done.'

'And you, you are a damsel in distress. Now show me to a toolkit and let me loose on that back door lock.'

She laughed. 'Macho, I like it. But you're too late, I've arranged for a locksmith to come and do it tomorrow. I decided after thinking about the little visit I got last night that I couldn't afford to trust this one to the amateurs.'

'Oh.'

'What's brought all this *being a man* business on then, Xand?'

'Well, I've actually been one for a while.'

'You seem particularly preoccupied with it this afternoon though.'

'Yeah. Just had a set-to with Ryan Theakston. Kicked his ass.'

Nell frowned. 'Not literally?'

'Don't be daft, I'm not that much of a man.'

'What happened?'

Xander snorted. 'He wanted to shut down our Book Day fete.'

'What? He can't do that! The kids'd be devastated.'

'That's what I told him.'

'Why does he want to shut it down now?' Nell asked. 'There's less than three weeks to go.'

'Because Jeremy Illingworth told him he wants to promote me to deputy head and train me up as his successor,' Xander said.

'Ryan's trying to throw a spanner in the works by undermining my authority in front of the staff and parents.'

'Bastard!' Nell stopped rollering and looked down at him. 'Wait. Jeremy wants you to be the next head of Leyholme Primary?'

'Yep. He's retiring next year.'

'That's fantastic, Xander! You'd be a brilliant headteacher, didn't I always say so?'

He smiled. 'Nell, come down here.'

'What for?'

'I'll show you in a minute.'

'OK.' She climbed down from her ladder and put the roller back in its tray. 'This new you's a bit different, I must say. So what did you say to Ryan then?'

'Oh, I was very masterful; you'd have been proud. I said I was the head and he had no authority to challenge my decision on this. Then I told him to toddle along home because some of us had a school to run.'

'Seriously?'

'Yep.'

She laughed. 'Bet he didn't like that.'

'You're right, he didn't. He said they'd only picked me for the role because they thought I'd be good at following orders.'

'Like Karl Dönitz.'

'Yeah, I said that too.'

'Sounds like you two had a proper cock fight in there.' She squeezed his elbow. 'You're right, I am proud of you. Did Ryan actually get his dick out and ask for a comparison at any point?'

'No, but it was touch and go.' He smiled. 'You know, you've got a pretty dirty mouth for a Reception teacher.'

She shrugged. 'I defy your stereotypes.'

He reached out and drew her to him. 'I like it.'

She looked down at the arms around her. 'What's this, Xand?'

'I told you, I'm being manly.' He lowered his voice to a whisper. 'How am I doing?'

'It's working for me.'

'Come on, give us a kiss then. I've been waiting long enough.'

Nell smiled, reaching up to stroke his cheek. 'Xander Scott, what on earth has got into you?'

'Something that should've got into me long before now.'

He put one finger under her chin and brought his lips to hers. She pressed herself against him as they explored each other and Xander knew, as he'd never quite allowed himself to believe before, that this – that *he* – had always been what she'd wanted.

His hands slid into the small of her back, moulding her hips to his, and he felt her shudder.

'Go lock the front door,' he whispered when he drew back from the kiss.

'What for?'

'Because I'm going to make love to you pretty thoroughly now and it'll put me off if Colin's there watching.'

She tilted her head to give him better access to the neck he'd started nuzzling. 'Thoroughly?'

'Very thoroughly.'

'I like the sound of that.'

Xander pressed her against an unpainted bit of wall and ran his hands over her body, caressing each delicious curve while he planted hot kisses along her collarbone. His fingers whispered over her breasts and up to her shoulders, where they unhooked the eyelets of her dungarees.

He stripped the dungarees off her, leaving her in just a shirt and her knickers, and slid exploring fingertips up the inside of her bare thigh.

Nell moaned slightly, biting her lip.

'And I thought you were such a nice boy,' she whispered.

His hand ventured further, parting her legs a little, his thumb playing with the elastic of her underwear. 'Mmm. Well we know what it makes when we assume, don't we, class?'

'You don't mess about when you're being manly, do you?'

'Door. Then bedroom.'

She saluted. 'Yes Sir.'

—

Nell lay on the airbed, Xander's head snuggled into her chest as she traced shapes on his naked back. Her body ached all over in absolutely the best way possible.

She hadn't been expecting that.

She hadn't been expecting to have sex today, although by a stroke of luck she had planned to go for a swim after work – postponed due to her lack of scooter – so she'd shaved her legs. She certainly hadn't expected Xander Scott to turn up on her doorstep, behaving like an exceptionally polite caveman and insisting with the most immaculate manners that she immediately remove all her clothes for a long and satisfying bout of lovemaking. Not after he'd failed to pick up on what had to be the world's least subtle signals in bed the night before.

And the biggest surprise of all was that sex with Xander had been far and away the best she'd ever had. Twice.

He'd been... incredible. Tender, daring, and surprisingly knowledgeable about how her body would respond to the nuances of his touch. Not that that should surprise her really – she knew he'd been in at least one long-term relationship. Somehow he just hadn't seemed the type.

Apparently he was the type. Nice boys could surprise you.

But still so sweet – naughty and nice in the most thrilling way, whispering to her all the while he ran his soft fingers and teasing tongue over every inch of bare skin that she was beautiful, how much he appreciated her, being with her, her body. That night, Nell had made the happy discovery that sex was the one area of his life in which Xander was very confident indeed.

She smiled down at him as he slept, brushing the curls of bed-ruffled hair away from his eyes. It was getting long, but it looked good on him. She'd tell him. Maybe he'd keep it long, if she liked it.

She presumed she wasn't making any kind of ass out of either of them by assuming they were a couple now. That was what she wanted. It was, she was pretty sure, what he wanted.

What that meant for her other plans in Leyholme, she didn't know. But now hardly seemed the time to worry about that. Anyway, if everything worked out as she hoped – and why shouldn't it, when it was all going so well? – then she'd be here for a good long time. Forever, that was the idea.

'Hey,' Xander whispered, smiling sleepily at her as he woke up.

God but he looked adorable, with his cheeks flushed and his hair falling into his eyes. Glasses suited him, but Nell loved how natural he looked without them. Those eyes…

'Hey you,' she said, leaning down to give him a kiss.

'Sorry, did I fall asleep on you?'

She smiled. 'I'd say you earned it.'

'Happy?' he asked.

'Very happy.'

'Satisfied?'

'Thoroughly.'

He gave her a tight squeeze. 'Can't believe you're mine finally.' He looked up. 'I mean, are you? I was sort of assuming, after I went to all the effort of showing you a good time.'

She twisted a curl of his hair around her little finger. 'I am.'

'Then I must have done something right.' He lifted her hand to kiss the tips of her fingers, one by one.

'You're a surprising man, Xander Scott,' she told him.

'Am I?' He turned her hand around and started planting soft kisses across the palm.

'Yes you are. You know, I think you've proven me wrong in every assumption I've ever made about you. Except when I told you there was someone pretty impressive inside you trying to get out.'

'So you're impressed then, are you? I presume we're talking about my bedroom performance here.'

She laughed. 'Not sure I should say. I'd hate for you to get a big head.'

'Too late. My prowess is godlike, that's what you said. You said it and now you can never take it back.'

'That's what I said, is it?'

'It's fundamentally what you said.'

He finished kissing her hand and moved on to her arm.

'You think anyone will notice?' she asked, relishing the feel of warm, wet lips on her flesh. 'Us, I mean?'

'I don't care what they notice,' he whispered against her shoulder.

'Ah. Because you're a man.'

'Damn right I am.'

'Still, love, we'd better be careful,' she said, running her fingers through his hair. 'Keep it quiet at school and around the village, just for the time being. You're on Ryan Theakston's naughty list already; you don't want to give him an excuse to make trouble for you.'

He shuffled up to kiss her on the lips. 'If that's what you want. Personally, I feel like right now, I could walk straight up to Ryan and spit in his eye.'

'Lovely. Don't though.'

'OK, for you.' He kissed her again. 'Right, staff appraisal time. Miss Shackleton, it's my solemn duty to inform you that you're unbelievably sexy and drop-dead gorgeous.'

She ran her hands over his naked body. 'Not so bad yourself, boss.'

'Come here.' Xander pulled her into his arms and rolled her on top of him. He started nibbling her ear, his fingertips trailing lazily over her breasts.

She laughed. 'Mr Scott, it's my solemn duty to inform you that you're sexually insatiable.'

'Lucky for you, right?'

'It is now I'm your girlfriend.'

He smiled, stopping the foreplay to trace the shape of her face. 'Not sure I'll ever get enough of hearing you call yourself that.'

'Took us long enough to get here, didn't it? But we made it in the end.' She leaned forward and claimed his lips for a kiss.

Chapter Twenty-One

It was around half past five when Deb knocked at Stevie Madeleine's front door one Tuesday. Half unconsciously, she reached up to yank out her bobble and shook her hair free around her shoulders.

'So, Stevie,' she muttered to herself as she waited for her to answer the door. 'I just, um... I wanted to see if Red... ugh! Why is this so *hard?*'

She'd rehearsed this about five hundred times before setting out. It was the simplest thing in the world, wasn't it? She was worried about Red. She'd wanted to come round and see how she was. She'd been Red's dog-walker for over two months now, so what could be more natural than that?

Any suggestion that she couldn't stop thinking about Stevie and the two kisses they'd shared – that she was haunted by the evident desire in Stevie's eyes before something had spooked her and she'd shut the whole thing down – was ludicrous. She was here for Red, that was all. And she'd brought Life along to visit her poorly friend too, so that proved it.

She'd sort of hoped Stevie might call her, or at least text, if only to let her know how Red was doing. But she hadn't heard a word since that night at her house.

'Hi, Stevie,' she said as the door opened. 'I just came over to – Jesus Christ!'

Stevie was standing in the hallway in a pair of red-splattered dungarees, her hair sticking up wildly. She had tears running down her cheeks and her hands were glistening red.

'Bugger me,' Deb said. 'Who'd you kill, love?'

'It's… the… dye,' Stevie sobbed. 'It won't *fucking* dye. Well, no, it will. It'll dye me, the kitchen, everything it happens to splash against. But it won't dye Milly's Red Riding Hood costume and Deb, I'm at the end of my rope.'

OK. Deb hadn't been expecting this. But it was fine. If she could handle a cocker spaniel at death's door, she could handle a crying woman in butcher's getup with fairytale costuming problems.

'Now, come on. It can't possibly be so bad it's unfixable.'

'It is. Oh God, Deb, it is. There's only two days until World Book Day and she'll sob her heart out if she can't be Red Riding Hood. I'm a bad mother, that's all there is to it. A bad mother who's going to break her little girl's heart.'

'Here.' Deb mounted the step and gave her distraught friend a hug. 'We'll sort this. OK?'

Stevie snuffled into her shoulder. 'You probably shouldn't hug me. I'll get red on you.'

'Oh, who cares about that?'

'Why are you always so nice to me, Deb? I'm a horrible person. Really I am. I don't know why you're even still speaking to me.'

'No you're not. A mixed-up one, maybe. Come on, let's go inside.'

'You're right, we should probably get off the streets before someone sees me smearing this stuff all over you and calls the cops.'

'Bloody *hell*,' Deb muttered as she followed Stevie into the kitchen. 'Good time at the prom, Carrie?'

Stevie laughed through her tears. 'It is a bit of a bloodbath, isn't it?'

'Where's Milly?'

'Having a sleepover at Morgan Hancock's, thank God, so she doesn't have to witness her mummy having a meltdown over bastard fancy dress.'

Deb bent to stroke Red, who'd come trotting over to greet her.

'Well, someone's looking a lot better. Shame the same can't be said for her human.' She straightened up again. 'Stevie, is there wine in here? I think you need to have wine.'

'In the fridge.'

'You know, I've never known a girl like you for drama,' she said, smiling. 'Every time I see you, you're in the middle of some crisis. How do you do it?'

'It's just a gift.' Stevie went to the sink and fished out the hairdressing cape she was attempting to dye. 'Look at this.'

'Hmm,' Deb said, glancing up from the fridge. 'Not exactly red, is it? Dirty-Pink Riding Hood's not got quite the same ring to it, somehow.' She paused. 'Well, unless you're an adult filmmaker. I should copyright that.'

'I don't understand it,' Stevie said, rinsing her hands off. 'I put two packets of dye in. Followed the instructions to the letter. My hands are redder than the sodding cape.'

Deb pushed a glass of wine into her scarlet fingers. 'All right, show me the packet.'

Stevie picked up the last unopened packet of dye and passed it to her to inspect.

'Stevie, it says this dye won't work on synthetic fabrics,' she said. 'What's that cape made of?'

'God, I don't know, I picked it up at a church jumble sale. Some sort of shiny stuff.'

'Well, I guess that's probably synthetic. Sorry.'

Stevie groaned. 'Serves me right for trying to be a domestic goddess and have everything home-made. I should've just bloody bought one.'

'Can't you?'

Stevie shook her head. 'Too late to order online, and I doubt there'll be anything book-related left in the costume shops. Every school in the country will be in fancy dress on Thursday.'

Deb looked thoughtful. 'Hey. You're not going out tonight, are you?'

'With my big red hands, are you kidding? This whole evening was reserved for costume-making.'

'OK, wait here for me then. I think I've got something at home that might do the trick.'

Stevie smiled. 'You'd donate clothing just to help me out of a jam?'

'Course I would.'

'Deb, you're a proper knight in shining armour, you know that? I mean, lady knight. Knightess.'

She laughed. 'Knightess. I like the sound of that.'

'I really don't deserve to have you—'

'Oi. We'll have none of that, not when I'm knightessing. You mind Life for me and I'll be back in a jiff.'

When Deb had gone, Stevie sat down at the kitchen table to dry her eyes and drink her wine. She wasn't quite sure what Deb was likely to come back with, but she felt relieved that somebody had turned up offering solutions.

Not that she really deserved them, after everything that had happened the night Red got sick. Deb must have thought she was out of her mind, backing off like that for no apparent reason.

Maybe she was. She couldn't deny that Deb had been in her thoughts a lot since that night. A hundred times Stevie had pulled up Deb's number, then thrown her phone down in frustration when she couldn't think of the right words to explain how she was feeling.

Half an hour later, she heard the front door click open.

'I'm back!' Deb called.

The dogs barked a welcome as Stevie stood up to greet her.

'So what have you brought?' she asked.

'OK, well, it's not ideal, but it is cotton, so natural fabric. Here.'

She rummaged in a rucksack she was carrying and produced a white hooded poncho emblazoned with the words 'Summer Solstice 1998' in black lettering.

Stevie stared at it. 'What on earth's that?'

'I went out with this flower-child type for a couple of months back in college. Bought this at some Druid sun-worshipping thing she convinced me to go to.'

Stevie laughed. 'Really, you were a Druid?'

Deb shrugged. 'Briefly. Thought it might be a laugh, but to be honest it was all a bit boring. Not sure I'm cut out for chakra-balancing and all that, I'd rather go for a pint.'

'Are you sure you don't mind us having it? Sounds like it's got sentimental value.'

'Oh God, please, take it off my hands,' she said, laughing. 'I brought a sewing kit and some dressmaking scissors I had lying around too. If we cut a sort of triangle shape out of the front, it'll make for a perfectly serviceable Little Red Riding Hood costume. The letters should pick off.'

'Deb, you're an absolute lifesaver,' Stevie said, smiling grate-fully. 'Here, let me get you a wine too. Then you can show me what to do, since you're clearly more up on this stuff than I am.'

While Stevie poured her a glass of wine, Deb cleared the dining table and laid the poncho out.

'Got a pencil and something with a straight edge?' she asked.

'Hang on.' Stevie handed over the wine and disappeared upstairs to raid Milly's pencil case, returning with a soft lead pencil and a ruler.

'Thanks.' Deb took them from her and sketched a needle-like triangle down the centre of the poncho, stopping just before the neck so it was still joined by a thin collar. 'OK, nurse, scissors.'

Stevie smiled and fetched the dressmaking scissors Deb had left on the worktop.

Deb cut away the triangle, methodically and with a steady-handed neatness. Stevie loved that confident, businesslike quality Deb always assumed when she was problem-solving; her unconsciously commanding tone. If she was being completely honest with herself, she actually found it sort of sexy.

'Right, just need to get the letters off now,' Deb said. 'Come on. I'll take left of the opening, you do right.'

Deb nodded to the chair next to hers. Stevie sat down and started picking at the letters with her fingernails, her head almost touching Deb's as they concentrated on their work. It was tough to get the black plasticky stuff away from the material, but once she'd managed to prise a corner loose, she found the letters did eventually peel off.

'How's that new dog of yours?' Stevie asked, as much to break the slightly tense silence as anything. 'Pregnant yet?'

Deb laughed. 'Nope, the whippet-breeding plan's gone up the spout, if you'll pardon the expression. You'll never guess.'

'What, can't she have pups?'

'I suppose she could if she was so inclined. But no, turns out our Holly's one of the gay girls – strictly bitches only. The last boy who tried to knock her up got a bite on the bollocks for his trouble.'

Stevie laughed too. 'One of us, eh? Good lass.'

'Guess who she's got a crush on.'

'Who? Not Life?'

'Nope, your Red. Follows her round all over the place and cries when I drop her off home at the end of the day. Poor lovestruck pupster.'

'Aww.' Stevie stopped peeling to wag a finger at her dozing dog. 'Red, you rotten little tease. You let Holly down gently.'

'When do you think she'll be back in the gang?' Deb asked. 'We all miss her. I'd hoped we would've had her back with us by now.'

Stevie flushed as she leaned over the letters she was picking at. The truth was, Red had been well enough to rejoin Deb's little gang for over a week now. Stevie just hadn't been able to bring herself to contact Deb and face a conversation about what had happened between them the last time they'd seen each other.

'She's just about back to her old self now,' Stevie said, not making eye contact. 'I think if you pick her up tomorrow, she'll be up to her usual tricks again.'

'Glad to hear it. Was it Giardia then?'

'Yeah.'

'Thought so.' Deb finished peeling off her first letter. 'Well, so long, Summer Solstice 1998. You'll always live on in my memory as being a waste of perfectly good beer-garden weather.'

'What happened to the hippy girl you were going out with?'

'Heh. She became a civil servant. So much for casting off the oppressive shackles of the Establishment.'

'First girlfriend?'

'Nah, I was a slayer of the fairer sex from an early age,' Deb said, grinning. 'Alice Jefferies was my first, back in Year 10. We made a secret pact to practise French kissing ready for when we had boyfriends – only, you know, turned out we preferred each other. How about you?'

'I was a bit of a late starter compared to you. No one was out at my school. It was uni before I started dating.'

'When did you realise? That you liked girls?'

'When I realised I didn't like boys, I guess. All my friends were salivating over Bros in their *Fast Forward*s and I was like "meh". Bananarama all the way. What about you?'

'Oh, had to be when I was twelve and I saw *Alien* the first time. Sigourney Weaver kicking arse in her pants must've been the downfall of many a girl.'

Stevie laughed. 'I'm with you there.'

'So, er, you ever visited the dark side?' Deb asked, stripping back an O.

Stevie looked down at the C she was trying to get off. 'Just once. It… wasn't fun, let's put it that way.'

Deb glanced up from her letter-picking. 'Why, what happened?'

Stevie kept her eyes fixed on her work, watching her nails scrape against the fabric.

Did she want to share this? Deb certainly deserved an explanation for how she'd behaved the night Red got sick. She'd understand, Stevie knew she would, and a hundred times in the last few weeks she'd been on the brink of calling her to explain. But when it came to it, she hadn't been able to go through with it. The memories were so raw, still; the words so hard to say.

'Stevie?' Deb said, dipping her head to catch her eye.

Stevie took a deep breath.

'OK. I can do this,' she muttered to herself.

'Do what? Stevie, what is it?'

'Deb... you remember I said that when I met Angela, I didn't know if I'd ever be able to learn to trust someone with my body in that way? I mean, as a lover?'

'I remember.' Deb frowned. 'You're not saying it was because of this thing that happened?'

'Yes,' Stevie mumbled. 'It messed me up for a long time.'

'Can you tell me?' Deb said gently.

'It's tough to talk about. But... yes. Yes, I want to tell you.'

'If you're sure. Take your time.'

Stevie looked down at her fingers picking away at the letters.

'I wasn't very experienced as a teen,' she said. 'I'd never even kissed anyone. People had started talking, you know, the way teenagers do. All the girls I hung out with had at least snogged a boy. I tried the usual fibs: fake holiday romances, boyfriend at another school. But I had this one friend, Victoria, who just wouldn't let it lie. Well, I say friend. She was bloody awful.'

Deb frowned. 'I get you. That kind of friend.'

'Yeah. It wasn't just her but she was the ringleader. Kept going on and on about it, whispering to everyone who'd listen about Stevie the Virgin. "Oh, Stevie's totally frigid. Locked at the knees. Definitely a lezzer," et cetera. You know the sort of thing, casual playground cruelty for no reason at all.'

'Ugh. Nasty little bully.'

'I just wanted to keep my head down and get through school,' Stevie muttered, talking half to herself as she let her fingernails rhythmically scrape, scrape, scrape. 'One night, Victoria... she'd hooked up with this lad in Year 12, and she

183

got us into a party with some older kids from our school.' She laughed. 'Before that night, I'd never been kissed. Never had an alcoholic drink. By the time I got home, I was drunk out of my skull and I wasn't a virgin any more. Victoria practically shoved me into the arms of this mate of her boyfriend's, Reuben. He could tell I was hammered – it didn't take much to achieve that, when I wasn't used to it. And my loss was Reuben's gain, so to speak.'

'Shit! What, he forced himself on you?'

'No, I consented. I didn't know what the fuck was going on, but I was fully conscious and I never asked him to stop.'

'How old were you?'

'Fourteen.'

'Jesus, Stevie!'

She laughed bleakly, finally peeling away the C. 'You know, even now, nearly thirty years later, I can remember every touch and scent of it. I remember feeling sick from the booze and the pain. I remember holding in my breath to shut out the nauseating scent of sweat and fags and rancid teenage deodorant, praying I wouldn't vomit. And yet the main thing going through my head as I was pinned there underneath him was that after this, she'd shut up. After this, if I can just get through it, Victoria will finally get off my fucking back.' She gagged slightly, and swallowed a mouthful of wine to take away the bitter taste that had flooded her mouth. 'It took me years to recover from that night.'

'Sweetheart, I'm not surprised.' Deb stopped peeling to give her a hug. 'You poor little girl.'

'And then it didn't even work. First thing Monday, Victoria just switched tactics and had it all over the year that I was a cheap slag who'd spread my legs for anyone. Jesus Christ, after practically raping me by proxy.' She gagged again, fighting against swelling nausea. 'Fuck, that girl was evil.'

Stevie tried to relax her tensed fingers. Her nails were digging hard into the flesh of her palms as every feeling of guilt and shame and anger she'd experienced at the time hit her afresh.

'I guess you were practising kissing with your girlfriend at that age, weren't you?' she asked Deb.

'I was, yeah.'

Stevie sighed. 'All that innocent, exciting experimentation that ought to go with your teen years. That night robbed me of all that. By the time I started dating, I already felt jaded and world-weary.' She smiled. 'Till I met Ange.'

'You miss her.'

'Every day. That's what makes the grieving process so tough. Angela was the one who helped me finally put that night behind me, learn to enjoy my body again – to love myself. Then when I found out she'd cheated, it was like all the trust issues I'd had when we met came flooding back. And the one person who...' She swallowed a sob. 'The one person I needed to talk it through with, to get some closure from, was gone.'

'Oh, Stevie. I get it totally now, why you were so afraid of letting someone in.' She stroked Stevie's hair. 'But that's not me, you know,' she whispered.

Stevie looked up to meet Deb's sympathetic, swimming eyes. 'Not crying for me, love?'

'Bloody right I am.'

'Please don't.'

'How can I not? I mean, you were a child, for Christ's sake.'

'I've never told anyone except Angela that story, Deb.'

Their eyes met for a moment.

'Stevie...' Deb reached out to cover her hand.

She hesitated, then slid her fingers away.

'Well, Summer Solstice 1998's all gone,' she said. 'Shall we give it a whirl?'

'Be my guest.'

Stevie stood and pulled the robe on over her clothes. She yanked the hood up.

'So? How do I look?' she asked, spreading out her arms.

'Er, like the KKK's newest recruit,' Deb said, grimacing. 'Better get it in the dye.'

Stevie held a hand up next to her, trying to gauge Milly's relative height. 'It'll be much too long. I'll have to hem it pretty drastically once the dye's on.' She took it off and, after removing the original, failed robe, put it in the dye-filled sink. 'Still, for a last-minute Little Red Riding Hood costume it looks pretty good. Thanks, Deb.'

'Stevie. Love. Come here.' Deb stood up and rested her hands on Stevie's shoulders. 'Look, I know you've been through an absolute emotional shitstorm what with one thing and another, but the fact is, I like you too much to just walk away. We can take things as slow as you want, but I don't want to give up on this – on us. And I don't think you really do either, do you?'

'I've been by myself a long time,' Stevie muttered.

'So have I.' Deb smiled. 'I think I might've been waiting for you actually.'

Stevie looked up to make eye contact. 'As slow as I want?'

'If that's what you need to work through whatever it is you need to work through.'

'And you'd be patient enough to put up with a bitter, cynical, set-in-her-ways old boiler like me?'

'I'd be lucky enough to keep company with a gorgeous, life-affirming, funny young woman like you.' Deb leaned forward and pressed a soft kiss to her lips.

Stevie smiled, running one finger over her mouth where Deb had kissed her.

'Hey,' she said. 'Have you eaten yet tonight?'

'Not yet, why?'

'How about you let me buy you a Chinese to say thanks for helping me out? We can eat it on the sofa with a few glasses of something, once I've had a go at scrubbing all this red off in the bath. Maybe watch a film.'

'Like… a date?'

'Exactly like a date.'

Deb smiled. 'I'd love to. Thanks, Stevie.'

Chapter Twenty-Two

'Morning, Alexander,' Mrs Rhodes said as Xander arrived for school on Thursday.

He was starting to think she lived at that desk on reception. No matter how early he arrived at work and no matter how late he stayed, there she was, always with what looked like a freshly brewed mug of tea.

'Morning,' he said. 'How are we doing?'

'All set, I think. The main hall's looking very festive.' She smiled. 'You know, I do love World Book Day. This must be the only time of year you can see a parade of little Gruffalos, princesses, cats in hats and suchlike walking solemnly down the main street.'

'I loved it too, till I was suddenly responsible for pulling it off,' Xander said in a low voice.

'Oh, it'll be fine,' she said, waving a dismissive hand. 'You've got all the staff there to help you. That Miss Shackleton seems to have been very hands-on with it.'

He coughed. 'Er, yes. She has been quite hands-on just lately.'

Mrs Rhodes cocked her head to examine him. 'Are you all right, pet? You look tired.'

He felt tired. But this was the sort of tiredness that arose from a new girlfriend who liked to keep him up at night in the best possible sense of that phrase, so he wasn't about to start complaining.

'I'm fine,' he said. 'Just missed out on a bit of sleep recently.'

'Will you be OK, Alexander?' Mrs Rhodes asked in a soft voice.

'I'm sure I will. You're right, it's not a one-man operation, is it? I'm worrying myself over nothing, as usual.'

'No, I mean will *you* be OK?' she said. 'It's today, isn't it?'

He flushed. 'Oh. Yes.'

'How's your mam?'

'She's… had a rough few nights, I think. But she was fine when I left her. Buoyant, even, considering. We're taking some flowers later.'

'Is she coming to the fete?'

'I doubt she'll be feeling up to it, but she's got all the details.' He sighed. 'Hate leaving her alone today.'

'You're a good boy.' She stood up. 'You go get settled, I'm sure you've got lots to do before this afternoon. I'll bring you in a drink.'

Xander smiled. He'd known Janet Rhodes his whole life and he knew that tea and sympathy were her eternal solutions to all the world's ills.

'Thank you,' he said. 'I'd appreciate that.'

There was really nothing to worry about. He'd talked it all out with Nell in bed the evening before, between other helpful stress-relieving activities. Everyone knew what they needed to do today – the staff, the kids, the parents who were volunteering. All he had to do was be on hand to coordinate things. Easy breezy. He was a teacher, coordinating was his middle name.

But he couldn't help being nervous. Ever since his run-in with Ryan, this had begun to feel like so much more than a simple World Book Day event. Somewhere down the line, it had become career-defining for Alexander Coordinating Scott. And with the eyes of Ryan and the rest of the governors on him, not to mention the staff and parents, he had a lot riding on it being a success.

Nell glanced at the clock as the hands sped towards two o'clock.

'OK, gang, there's not long now,' she said to her class. 'Only half an hour till mums and dads get here.' She checked a list on her desk. 'Milly, Robbie, Olivia, Henry, McKenzie and Morgan, you're going first as Oompa-Loompas. Five minutes to finish your pictures, then we'll get you into your costumes.'

The idea was that the children would man the chocolate factory six at a time in half-hour shifts so the rest could enjoy the fete with their parents. She was on rotation as Willy Wonka too, with Mrs Rhodes taking over the top hat after the first hour. Nell couldn't wait to see the games and stalls the other classes were running.

She wanted to be on hand to help Xander if he needed it as well. He'd been quiet the last few days – worrying about today, she guessed – and just because her new status as his girlfriend was top secret didn't mean she couldn't show him some much-needed support.

Her brother might be coming over too, she'd invited him down on the phone last week. There was no guarantee he'd remember, Freddie being Freddie, but she hoped he'd make it. She was longing to introduce him to her colleagues, and the kids in her class. And to Xander, again. It felt more important this time, now she and Xander had made the jump from friends to lovers. As different as her boyfriend and brother were, she hoped they could find something to bond over.

She smiled to herself when she thought about Xander. It had only been three weeks but things were going well – really well. He couldn't seem to get enough of her, a feeling that was very much mutual. And God, did that boy have some energy. They'd hardly got out of bed over the half-term break.

Which reminded her, she thought, as she rubbed her aching hips. She really must buy an actual bed next payday, now she was in a relationship again. Constant sex on an air mattress was not doing her poor bones any good. Not that the pain wasn't worth it.

It was funny, really. If anyone had told Nell a year ago that her perfect man was someone like Xander Scott, she'd probably have laughed in their face. And yet here she was, falling harder and faster for him than she had for any lad before. She could barely keep the daft grin off her face these past few weeks; she was sure people must have noticed. Mrs Rhodes had been shooting her knowing smirks every time they bumped into each other.

The first parents started showing up in dribs and drabs just before half two, and by three there were people queueing out of the door to have a turn on Willy Wonka's Lucky Dip. A lot were clutching purchases and prizes they'd got from other stalls and games – bottles of frobscottle (homemade lemonade with green food colouring) from the Year 5 classroom, jars of Marvellous Medicine (rose water) from a stall run by the mum who owned the village apothecary. Plus, Nell was pleased to see, plenty of books. They had stalls selling them both new and second-hand, to suit all budgets.

There were some fantastic costumes too. She'd been pretty impressed by her own class, who'd shown up that morning dressed as everything from Bruce Bogtrotter to Fantastic Mr Fox. But visitors to her chocolate factory covered a whole range of Dahl characters, including all five of the original Golden Ticket winners – pretty brave, given the fate of four of them last time they'd visited – and an absolutely adorable trio of toddlers dressed as The Giraffe, The Pelly and Me.

She squinted at the little blonde-mopped pelican as he stared up at her with wide eyes.

'Oh,' she said. 'It's Jacob. Hello, my lamb.' She hadn't recognised him now his bright purple face had settled into a more normal colour.

'Hiya Nell,' Sara said, turning from a display of children's work she'd been admiring with the parents of the other two kids. 'Xander said we'd find you in – Jacob, no! Those candy canes are card, they're not for eating – sorry, in here.'

Sara and Justin, along with Stevie Madeleine, Nell's brother Freddie and Xander's mum, were the only people who'd been officially informed about the change in their nearest and dearests' relationship statuses. It was nice to chat to someone without feeling she had to watch what she gave away.

'Yep, still Wonka-ing it up,' Nell said. 'Fifteen minutes more, then I'll have done my time.'

'Chocolate factory going well, is it?'

'Yeah, great. Trade's been non-stop. We must've made a tidy sum for the charity.'

'Well, here's our contribution.' Sara handed over a pound. 'One go each for me and Jacob, please. Although I suspect he's going to end up with both of our prizes.'

'Thanks.' Nell chucked it in her tub. 'Just pop through the arch when you're ready. There's a couple of parent helpers minding the Oompa-Loompas; they'll show you what to do.'

'Right, cheers.'

'How's Xander doing out there, before you disappear?' Nell asked. 'Hard to tell how busy it is in the hall.'

'It's heaving, but he seems to be handling it like a trouper. I did worry, with the fete being today and everything.'

Nell frowned. 'How do you mean?'

'Oh. You mean he hasn't... OK, sorry, you'd better ignore me,' Sara said, looking alarmed at her slip.

'Sara, what's going on? What don't I know?'

'Honestly, forget it, I shouldn't have said anything. Shooting my mouth off as usual. Jacob, no!'

She ran through the arch after him as he galloped towards the lucky dip paddling pool, apparently with the intention of throwing himself in.

Quarter of an hour later, Mrs Rhodes turned up to relieve Nell as Willy Wonka and she was free to seek out Xander in the main hall. She spotted him watching the Giant Peach bowling – a miniature skittle alley the Year 4 kids had made.

'Wow,' she said after she'd fought her way through the crowd. 'Xander, this is amazing! There must be half the village in here.'

'I know, I can't believe it. We actually pulled this off, Nell.'

She smiled. 'Course we did. I always had faith in us.'

'How's the chocolate factory getting along?'

'It's not had a quiet moment. Although I thought it might all come crashing down when Jacob turned up.'

'Oh, don't worry about him,' Xander said, laughing. 'He only goes the full Damien when he can't have sole access to Mummy. With Sara here and his dad at work, he'll be fine.'

Nell nudged him. 'Hey, is there a Roald Dahl story about a case of sour grapes? Because I just saw Ryan Theakston and he seems to have come dressed as one.'

Xander smiled. 'Shush, you,' he whispered. 'You'll get me in trouble.'

She looked him up and down. He was in a shabby tweed suit and a large flat cap, with a couple of toy pheasants strung around his neck.

'Who are you then, the pheasant plucker's son?' she asked. 'You look like that *Peaky Blinders* bloke, only with fetching roadkill accessories.'

'I'm Danny, Champion of the World, clearly.'

'Is that what he wears?'

'It's what he wore after he grew up and became a professional poacher.'

'Hmm.'

'OK, OK, then it's all I could get in my size. It's all very well for you shorties.' He looked over her shoulder and groaned. 'Oh God, Stevie's spotted us. You wouldn't think anyone that tiny could be such an aggressive saleswoman, would you?'

'Is she?'

'Yeah, she's been on the rampage since we opened the doors. No one's safe from her and her damn raffle tickets.'

Stevie was in her Big Bad Wolf costume: a full-length, fake-fur coat and a headband sporting a pair of pointy ears. Nell was surprised to see that the dog-walker, Deb, was with her, the two of them swinging little Oompa-Loompa Milly between them.

'Hiya Nell.' Stevie waved her book of raffle tickets. 'Time to put up or shut up.'

Nell sighed. 'Fine, if I must. What's the prize?'

'There's loads of stuff. A complete set of Roald Dahl books, beer vouchers for the pub, tickets for a head massage at that reflexology place – oh, and Deb's offering a free dog.'

Deb nudged her. 'Oi. No one raffles off my dogs.'

'How much then?' Nell asked.

'A pound for a strip, or give me a fiver and I'll keep my clothes on,' Deb said, grinning. Milly giggled.

Stevie rolled her eyes. 'She's done that joke at least fifty times today and she's still not tired of it.'

'All right, a fiver's worth, if it'll preserve Deb's modesty,' Nell said.

Stevie nodded her approval. 'That's what we like to hear.'

'You got roped into helping too then, did you?' Nell asked Deb as she handed over a five-pound note.

'I think I might've volunteered,' Deb said, tearing off Nell's strips. 'Although I've only got Stevie's word for that.' She coloured slightly when she said Stevie's name, and Nell smiled.

'Yeah, she's a hard woman to say no to.'

'How're you doing, love?' Stevie asked Xander, resting a hand on his arm. 'Not finding it all a bit much today?'

Xander smiled. 'I'm fine. Actually, it's good to have some-thing else to focus on.'

'And your mum?'

'She's OK, I think. I doubt she'll be down to the fete though.'

'No, I wouldn't really have expected her to be. Let me know if you need anything, eh?'

'I will. Thanks, Stevie.'

Milly tugged Stevie's arm. 'Mummy, can I be Red Riding Hood again? I'm finished being an Oompa-Loompa now.'

Stevie laughed, looking at Deb. 'This is your fault. She may never wear anything else but that cloak you made her.'

'Er, *we* made her. You're not pinning this all on me.'

'Please, Mummy!' Milly begged. 'I've been an Oompa Loompa for *aaages*. I want all the new people who weren't at school this morning to see my Little Red Riding Hood costume.'

'Well, I suppose we need a Little Red Riding Hood if we're going to have a Big Bad Wolf,' Stevie said. 'OK, come on. You can change in the girls' loos if you're quick.'

Chapter Twenty-Three

When the three of them had gone, Nell turned to Xander.

'Look, are you OK?'

'I'm fine.'

She took his elbow and found them a little space where they could speak without being overheard.

'Xander, what's going on?' she said in a low voice. 'Why does everyone seem so worried about you?'

He sighed. 'That first night in the pub, when you asked about World Book Day – it wasn't that I'd forgotten exactly. It's just that today's date is... kind of already fixed in my mind for other reasons.'

Nell stared at him. 'Oh my God. Your dad.'

'Yeah. Two years ago today.'

'Sweetheart, why didn't you say something?' she asked, squeezing his arm.

'Well. We had stuff to do, didn't we? I didn't want to bring you down with it when there was so much to get done.'

'I thought you were just worried about the fete being a success. I didn't realise...' She winced as she thought back to how quiet he'd been over the last few days. 'God, I'm sorry, Xander, I should've worked it out. Bad girlfriend.'

'I told you, it's OK. Honestly, it is. Me and Mum are going this evening to put some flowers on the grave, then... well, we'll cope. It's going to come round every year; I need to learn to deal with it.'

She shook her head. 'I can't believe you didn't tell me.'

'We've just been so… happy,' he muttered. 'You were my escape, Nell. Like a perfect little island where this godawful thing had never happened to me. To be honest, I liked you not knowing. Everyone in the village knows, I've been getting the pitying looks for days.'

'But you were upset. I could've helped. That's what people do.' She looked up into his eyes. 'It's what couples do.'

He sighed. 'I know. Sorry. Maybe I'm just thinking about what went wrong with Marie. How I drove her away with my miserable face.'

'You did no such thing. You were grieving.'

'It feels that way sometimes though.'

'Well, I can promise you I'm not going anywhere.'

'Good.' He nodded to the hall's main door. 'Isn't that your brother?'

'Oh yeah.' Nell waved across the crowd to him. 'I didn't think he was going to make it.'

Freddie waved back when he spotted her, but even from this distance she could tell he looked kind of sheepish. Guilty, even.

She frowned. 'What's up with him?'

That question answered itself a second later when a middle-aged pair appeared behind him, carrying a couple of bottles that suggested they'd just visited the Year 5 classroom for frobscottle.

'Oh my God,' she muttered.

'What's up?' Xander asked.

'It's my bloody parents!'

'Oh right, brilliant. So you've got the whole family along to witness your success.'

'Xand, you don't understand. They can't *be* here!'

He frowned. 'Why not? I knew you had issues with your stepmum, but I didn't think things were that bad between you.'

'No, it's not her. It's—' She fixed on a smile as her dad spotted her. 'Shit, they've seen me. And now they're coming over. Look, just… be cool, right?'

'Aren't I always?'

197

'Er, yeah.'

Freddie trudged along behind his parents, raising his hands in a 'What?' motion as Nell glared at him.

'Dad. Leanne,' she said when they reached her. 'This, er... this is a lovely surprise.'

Leanne smiled at her. 'Well, you know our Freddie, can't keep a secret.'

She glared at him. 'Mmm. I do know our Freddie.'

'Hey. It's not my fault,' he said. 'I had to bring them, sis, they made me.'

'Anyone would think you're not pleased to see us,' her dad said.

'No, it's not that. It's just... the house is still in such a state. I really wanted to get it presentable before you made the trip.' Recovering herself, Nell came forward to give her dad a hug, then exchanged an awkward embrace with Leanne.

'None for me?' Freddie asked.

She scowled at him. 'No. I'm not talking to you.'

'Don't worry about the house, Nell,' Leanne said. 'We're not staying over – flying visit, that's all. Your dad was just keen to meet your friends, see you doing your new job. Well, I mean, we both were.' She smiled at Xander. 'Who's this young man?'

'Oh. Right. This is Mr Scott – Xander. He's my er... my, er, boss. And my friend.'

Nell's dad glanced at Freddie. 'He the one?'

Freddie nodded miserably, looking thoroughly ashamed of himself.

'I don't believe this,' Nell said. 'How many of my top-secret secrets did you spill, Fred?'

'Hardly any. One, maybe two, max. None of the major ones.'

'You call that not one of the major ones, do you?'

'It wasn't my fault, Nell. I was under duress, OK?'

She shook her head. 'Last time I tell you anything.'

Xander held out his hand to Nell's dad. 'Well, it's nice to meet you, Mr Shackleton.'

'Colin, please,' Nell's dad said, shaking his hand firmly.

Xander raised an eyebrow. 'Colin?'

'Anything wrong, lad?'

'No. You, er… you just don't meet many Colins nowadays.'

'What?' Nell whispered when Xander caught her eye. 'Come on, you know there's a resemblance.'

'I'm Leanne, Nell's stepmum,' Colin's wife said, shaking hands with Xander too.

'Lovely to meet you. Nell talks about you both all the time.'

'All good things, I hope,' Leanne said, catching Nell's eye.

'Of course.' Xander nudged Nell. 'Looks like Stevie's smelt the fresh meat. She's heading back over with her bloody raffle tickets.'

Nell didn't answer. She'd actually gone a bit pale. Freddie looked uncomfortable too.

'Nell, are you OK?' Xander asked.

'I'm… fine.' She summoned a smile. 'Fine. Sorry, I was miles away.'

'Well, well, well, what have we here?' Stevie said when she reached them, grinning. 'New customers, I do believe. Could I be addressing Mr and Mrs Shackleton, parents of one Nell and one Freddie Shackleton?'

'Hiya,' Leanne said. 'Well-guessed. Are you a friend of Nell's?'

'I am,' Stevie said, smiling in Nell's direction. She nodded down at Milly. 'And Little Red Riding Hood here knows Miss Shackleton very well too. She's in her class.'

Milly mumbled a hello, muffled by the mega everlasting gobstopper she'd just shoved in her mouth from a themed bag of pick and mix. She was back in her Red Riding Hood costume, which rather clashed with her still Oompa-Loompa-orange face.

'Um, Dad,' Freddie said, tugging his sleeve. 'Shall we go see this chocolate factory thing Nell's class have made?'

'In a minute,' his father said, waving him down. 'Don't be rude, Fred. I'm talking to Nell's friend.' He held out a hand to Stevie. 'Colin Shackleton.'

She blinked. 'Colin?'

He laughed. 'I'm sensing it's an unusual name round these parts.'

'Actually, it's more common than you might think.' She seized the hand he'd presented and shook it vigorously. 'Stevie Madeleine.'

He blinked. 'Sorry – Stephanie Madeleine?'

'Only to my dad,' she said, laughing. 'No, it's just Stevie.'

Colin looked at Freddie, who didn't meet his eye, and then at Nell, who glared defiantly back. Something strange seemed to be going on that Xander couldn't work out.

'What's up, Colin?' Leanne asked, looking as puzzled as Xander felt.

'Nothing.' He forced a smile. 'Sorry. So Stevie, how well do you know my daughter?'

'Oh, very. We hit it off right away, didn't we, Nell? Shared interest in delinquency, I think.'

'Stevie's my… actually my closest friend in the village,' Nell told her dad. She wasn't pale any more. Now, her cheeks looked like they were on fire.

'Is she?' Colin glanced from Stevie to Xander. 'Is she? Well, it's lovely that you've been able to make new friends so quickly. You seem to have quite a little gang here.'

'You know, it feels like she's been in Leyholme forever.' Stevie seemed oblivious to the strained atmosphere, beaming round at them all. 'I've been saying to everyone, however did we cope before Miss Shackleton? She's really become part of the place.'

'I'm… glad to hear it.'

'And all this is her doing. It was her idea, you know,' Stevie said, waving a hand around the hall. 'You must be very proud of her, Colin. We certainly are.'

Colin turned to look at Nell. 'Yes. I always was.' But his eyes were hard and stern rather than glowing with paternal pride.

'So how many tickets?' Stevie said.

'Sorry?'

'Raffle tickets. All for a good cause, some great prizes on offer. Pound a strip. My friend Deb says I'm supposed to do a joke about taking my clothes off now, but since you're with Nell I'll spare you the graphic imagery.'

'Right.' Colin fumbled out his wallet. 'Er, here's a tenner. Don't worry about the tickets, just chuck them back in if we win.'

'Wow. Thanks very much.' Stevie smiled at Nell. 'Hey, I like these guys, chicken. I've been trying to get Yorkshiremen to part with their money all afternoon and believe me, it's rarely as easy as that.' She peered over Leanne and rubbed her hands. 'Aha, there's Karen Doneen just turned up. I smell money to be made. See you later, Shackletons and Xander.'

'Nell, can I have a word?' Colin said when Stevie and Milly had been absorbed back into the crowd.

'I should really go check on my class,' Nell mumbled.

'That can wait two minutes.'

He took her arm and marched her to the exit, out into the corridor. Xander stared after them.

'Sorry,' Leanne said, smiling apologetically. 'Honestly, I don't know what's got into the pair of them today.'

–

'OK, Nell, what the hell do you think you're playing at?' Colin hissed when there was no risk of them being overheard.

She flushed. 'I don't know what you mean.'

'Don't give me that.' His eyes darted over her pink cheeks. 'Was this it, why you didn't want us to come here? Was this whole move a… a set-up, or what?'

'Dad – look, I'm sorry, OK? It was Freddie's idea.'

201

'Oh, it was *Freddie's* idea,' he said, rolling his eyes. 'Last time Freddie had a good idea, he… Nell, Freddie has never had a good idea.'

'I had to, didn't I?' she mumbled. 'Once I knew she was here. Eventually, I had to come.'

He groaned. 'And she doesn't know.'

'Not yet. But soon.'

'The kid's in your class, for Christ's sake! And that boyfriend, your boss, what about him?'

'He doesn't know either. No one knows but Freddie and me – and you, now. You won't tell her, will you?'

'No, but you'd bloody better.' He frowned at her, wearing the stern face she still associated with being imminently grounded. 'I'm disappointed in you, Nell. I'm used to these sort of madcap schemes from Freddie, but I expect you to make grown-up choices.'

'Please don't say that.' She looked up at him, her throat convulsing. 'Dad, I had to. I'd lost so much, and she… wouldn't you have done the same, if you were me?'

'Nelly, I love you, but this isn't right. It's not right and it's not fair. I raised you to do better.' He bent to kiss the top of her head. 'Sort it out, before you get in any deeper.'

Chapter Twenty-Four

'Come on,' Colin said when they'd rejoined Xander and the rest of Nell's family. 'Freddie, Leanne, we're going home.'

'You don't need to do that,' Nell said, looking at him with pleading in her eyes. 'Stay, Dad, please. We'll go out to dinner or something before you all head off.'

'Sorry, Nelly. I don't think we can.' He glanced at Xander. 'Er, something urgent's just come up. Sorry to have to dash off. Hopefully we can get better acquainted another day.'

'OK, what was that all about?' Xander asked Nell when they'd gone.

Nell had turned pale again, but she smiled at him. 'Nothing. Something silly. I kind of lied to my dad about my scooter after the break-in the other week.'

'Your scooter that got stolen?'

'Yeah. I told him it was covered by the insurance and I'd had it replaced. He bought it for me, and I knew he'd be worried sick if I confessed I'd been sleeping in a house with a broken door for the best part of four months.'

'That's why he stormed off like that? Because you 'fessed up about your door?'

'He's not too happy with me,' she admitted. 'That's the reason I was so keen to avoid them coming till I'd got more of the repair work done. Dad only worries.' She scowled. 'Bloody Freddie, I could throttle him. Nearly all his life he's been dropping me in it.'

Xander examined her face. 'Nell, are you telling me the truth?'

'I… Xand, it's just family stuff, OK? Shackleton stuff. It's like you with the anniversary of your dad's death.' She looked up at him. 'It's not that I want us to have secrets from each other. It's just that right at the moment, you're my happy place. I like to keep you separate from all the weird.'

He smiled. 'Well, that I get.'

'It's OK, isn't it? For us to let ourselves just enjoy this bit, when it's all new and beautiful? There'll be plenty of time for sharing life stuff.'

He met her eyes. 'All the time in the world, Nell,' he said softly.

'Xander, you're incredible. I mean it. You really are.' She patted his arm in lieu of the kiss she would've given him if they'd been alone. 'We should go mingle. We are actually supposed to be running this event. Plus I want to give that frobscottle a try.'

'We should also probably stop lurking in corners together. Given we're trying not to give rise to gossip.'

'Mmm.' Nell nodded to Mrs Rhodes, who was eyeing them with a knowing simper from across the room as she queued for a cuppa. 'I'm not sure that's really a strength of ours, is it?'

He laughed. 'Well, come on, let's try this discretion thing on for size. You go that way, I'll go this way. See you later.'

There was only half an hour of the fete left to go now. The visitors had started to thin out a little, but numbers were still very healthy.

As she weaved through the crowd, Nell wondered how much they'd raised so far for the charity they were supporting. Lots, judging by the attendance. Perhaps when it was all counted up, they could get one of those giant cheques to present for a photo op. Xander could be in the paper with some of the kids, maybe in fancy dress. She guessed he'd hate the idea of that, but it would be good publicity for the school and the charity. Plus it'd be one in the eye for Ryan Theakston and anyone else who hadn't believed he could do it. Xander might be above such petty thoughts, but she bloody well wasn't.

She could see Ryan actually, face like a Force Ten hurricane, being dragged around by a woman she presumed was the lady lucky enough to have been granted the honour of becoming Mrs Theakston.

Nell couldn't resist. She just had to go up and have a bit of a gloat.

'Hi Ryan,' she said, smiling brightly as she approached him browsing the Marvellous Medicines all-natural handmade smellies stall. 'So, what do you think?'

'Bit pricey for my purse,' he muttered, drawing an offended 'humph' from the mum running the stall.

'Of the event, I mean,' Nell said. 'You must be pleased by how well-attended it's been. I reckon we could turn it into a yearly thing, don't you?'

'Hm. Not bad,' was all the grudging praise she could draw from him.

'I'm considering sending a write-up to the *Halifax Courier*,' she told him, just to see the look on his face. 'I bet they'd run a story, don't you think? I thought maybe we could ask for a photographer to come and get a snap of Xander presenting a cheque to the charity.'

His frown grew deeper. 'What?'

'You know, one of those big ones. I know Xander won't like it, the modest lad he is, but he's worked so hard that I think we should press him to take the credit he deserves. Don't you agree?'

Ryan was silent, but his smiley, pleasant-looking wife – who surely went to prove the truth of the phrase that opposites attract – looked up from the organic bath hampers to nod in agreement.

'It's certainly an impressive feat,' she said. 'You know, I don't mind admitting I had my doubts about that young man when Ryan told me he'd been offered the role of acting head. Always looked like he couldn't boo a goose to me. But he seems to have really found his voice lately.'

'Yes, well thank you for your contribution, Martha,' Ryan snapped. 'The next time I need your advice on—'

At that moment a woman stumbled forward from the crowd, falling heavily against the table. There was a crash as a couple of jars of rose water fell to the floor and smashed to pieces, filling the air with a sweet, slightly sickly perfume.

'Oh my goodness, I'm so sorry,' the woman gasped, looking horrified. 'I'll... I'll pay for those.'

'Anne?' Martha Theakston said. 'We hadn't expected to see you today.'

Nell frowned. Anne Scott – Xander's mum? Was this her?

Anne leaned forward to peer at Martha.

'Martha,' she said at last. 'Yes. Well, I had to come and support my boy, didn't I? You know, he's worked ever so hard.'

'Are you all right?' Martha asked. 'That fall into the table looked like a bruiser.'

'Fine,' Anne said, glancing vacantly around her. 'Fine, yes, just fine.'

Her wandering gaze fell on the smashed jars again and she looked up in horror at the parent running the stall. 'Oh, I'm so sorry. Here, let me clean that up. I'll pay, I promise. Do you take cards? No, no, of course you don't, how silly. My son... I didn't bring any money, but he can give you some when he comes. This is his school.'

Wobbling slightly, she knelt down and started trying to pick up the glass with her fingers. Martha cast a worried look at her husband, who shrugged.

Nell got to her knees beside Anne.

'Don't,' she said gently, resting her hand on the other woman's arm. 'You'll cut yourself. Let me fetch a dustpan and handbrush, eh? I can clean it up, I work here.'

'I didn't mean to... just fell, that's all.'

'I know. It was an accident. Mrs Scott, let me, please.'

Anne stopped picking at the glass to stare at her. Her eyes were glazed and red-rimmed.

'You're her,' she mumbled. 'The girl. Xander's girl.'

'Um, I'm Nell.' She summoned a smile. 'Hello.'

'He said you were beautiful.' Anne stared hard at her, as if struggling to focus. 'You are rather, aren't you? That's not really important, though. Do you make him happy?'

'Er...' Nell glanced helplessly up at Ryan and his wife.

'Anne, why don't you let me take you out for some fresh air?' Martha said, smiling kindly. 'It's ages since we had a lovely long chat. We never seem to see you at WI meetings these days.'

Nell nodded. 'That sounds like a good idea. I can get this mess cleaned up and go find Xander.'

Anne grabbed Nell's arm and held it hard. 'I said, do you make him happy?' she said in a loud voice. Heads were starting to turn now. 'I should be allowed to know, if you're going to be taking him away from me.'

'I... hope we're good friends, yes.'

'His father made me happy. Very happy, once. But I didn't make him very happy, did I?' She let out a hysterical sort of laugh. 'I made him... made him...'

'Mrs Scott, you're hurting me,' Nell whispered.

Anne looked down at her fingers digging into Nell's arm and dropped it at once, staring in horror at her own hand. 'Oh, my dear, I'm so sorry.'

Then she buried her face in her hands and burst into tears.

–

Across the room, Xander had discovered Sara and Jacob queueing for the Giant Peach bowling and stopped for a chat.

'Having fun?' he said, ruffling Jacob's hair. The toddler eyed him resentfully as he sucked on Ben the Bunny's foot.

'We're flying by the seat of our pants, aren't we, Jacob?' Sara said. 'We've been to a chocolate factory, we've met the BFG, we've eaten a snozzcumber and Mummy's going to pick up a bottle of wine on the way home that she's not going to share with Daddy tonight.'

Xander smiled. 'Sounds like Mummy's earned it.'

'Has it all run smoothly then, Mr Scott?'

'Yeah, it has actually. All that worry, and it's been and gone in a flash.'

'It's been a triumph. Hope you're proud, Xand.' She glanced down at Jacob. 'We're proud of Uncle Xander, aren't we, kiddo?'

Jacob wasn't old enough to shrug, but he managed to convey the same sentiment with his eyes.

'I am feeling pretty pleased with myself. Although Nell really deserves most of the credit.' Xander looked around for her, but she'd disappeared into the crowd. 'I met her parents today, Sar.'

'Nice?'

He frowned. 'Well, the stepmum seemed pleasant, although Nell said things were a bit strained between the two of them. But her dad... I'm not sure what to make of him. He might be a bit of a bully. Nell seemed sort of afraid of him – Freddie too.'

'Why, what happened?'

'She introduced him to me and Stevie, and he was pretty weird about her having a group of new friends. Then he dragged her off for a private word and she came back white as a ghost.'

Sara blinked. 'Odd. Are they still here?'

'No, he took his wife and son and flounced out after that. He told us something urgent had come up back at home.'

'What did Nell say?'

'She tried to dismiss it. Said they'd had a row about her scooter or something, but I didn't like it. I'm sure there's more to it than she's saying.'

'How come you never told her about your dad? I mean, about today? I put my foot right in it before.'

He flushed. 'Just... you know, Marie and everything. I didn't want to put her off with unrelenting misery when we've only been together a few weeks. I really like her, Sar.'

'I know you do, love.' She frowned. 'Hey. Isn't that your mum over there by the smellies? I didn't think she was coming.'

He turned to look and grimaced. 'Oh God. It is and she's talking to Nell. I hope she's not telling her how amazing I am.'

'Looks like something's been broken.' Sara watched the scene with a worried expression. 'Um, Xander. I think you'd better get over there.'

He turned back to look at her. 'What's up, can you see what they're saying? Are they talking about me?'

'Your mum… the way her lips are moving.' Sara lowered her voice. 'Xand, I think she might be drunk.'

'Shit! Oh, *shit!* No, not here. Not today.'

Xander pushed his way through the crowd. All the people close to the smellies stall had stopped to look at his mum and Nell. His mum had started sobbing, rocking on her haunches, while poor Nell crouched beside her, looking horrified.

'Mum?' he said.

She rubbed her face and looked up at him, forcing a smile. 'Xander. You see, here I am.' She wobbled sideways, putting her hand down to steady herself. 'Whoops.'

'Mum, careful, the glass!'

'Oh,' she said, holding her cut hand up in front of her and staring at it in a puzzled sort of way. 'I'm bleeding.' She laughed. 'Silly old thing. Always in the wars, aren't I?'

'Here, let's get you up.' Xander came forward and held out his hand. She seized it with her uncut one and he helped her to her feet.

Her skirt had hitched up at the back when she'd fallen into the glass. Xander winced when he noticed her underwear was visible.

'Mum, your skirt…'

'Skirt. Yes.' She tried to straighten it, but only succeeded in yanking it down at one side.

'Let me,' Xander said, flushing bright red as he tugged it back into place for her. 'There. All smart again.'

'Came to see your fair,' she mumbled. 'And the girl. I like her.'

The hall was deathly silent now. Everyone had turned to watch the scene that was unfolding.

Xander looked at Nell, who'd got to her feet and was blinking in shock along with everyone else.

'What the hell is everyone staring at?' Anne demanded, turning unfocused eyes on her audience.

'They're not staring, Mum,' Xander said in a pained whisper. 'It's your imagination.'

'They're staring. Staring at the weirdo family. Wondering what goes on behind closed doors, what we did to drive him to it – I know.'

'Honestly they're not. You're just tired.' She tottered slightly and Xander put a supportive arm around her.

Anne gasped out a sob. 'I am sorry, Xander, I couldn't help it. It was... too hard. Every time I close my eyes, I see him there.'

'I know,' he said gently. 'Let's go back home and get something on that cut, eh? I'll look after you.'

'Flowers.' She clutched at his arm, leaving a bloody mark on his jacket. 'Xander, we have to take them to him.'

'I think you ought to get a bit of sleep first. We can take them tomorrow when you're... better.'

He felt his mum's body sag against him. She seemed smaller suddenly, frailer, as if their roles from his early years had now reversed and he was the parent, she the child.

'I hope... I hope I won't get you into any trouble, Xander,' she whispered. 'You're all I've got.' She laughed. 'Soft old baggage, aren't I? Still embarrassing you in front of your friends just like when you were a boy.'

'Don't be daft. I've never been embarrassed by you.' He gave her a squeeze. 'Come on, old lady, let's go home.'

She smiled. 'Oi. Less of the old, you.'

'Well, young lady then,' he said, bending to plant a kiss on her hair.

'You were always a good boy. Exceptional.' She let out another sob. 'You know, they... they put that on your school report once.'

There was silence. All eyes followed the tall young man, glowing with a quiet inner dignity as he supported his sobbing, stumbling parent out of the hall.

Chapter Twenty-Five

When Xander got up for work the next morning, his mum was just waking up.

He'd had to leave her in the living room. Getting her home had been hard enough – he'd hurried her through the village, trying his best to ignore the stares and whispers of their neighbours, and she'd been practically falling over by the time they reached their front door. Xander had made a valiant effort to get her up the stairs, but she was a dead weight. He'd had to settle for making her as comfortable as possible on the sofa, bringing the duvet and pillows down from her bedroom then dressing her cut hand while she slept.

'How are you feeling?' he asked gently, pulling the armchair over so he could sit by her.

Anne smiled weakly, wincing at the pain of moving her face muscles. ' "A bit rough" would be something of an understatement.'

'How much did you have?'

She rubbed her head. 'I don't know. I think… quite a lot. What did I do, Xander?'

'Don't you remember?'

'Not all of it. I remember…' She groaned. 'I wanted to come and support you. At the fair.'

'That's right, you came to see me at school.'

'Did I… did I get you into any trouble?'

'Don't you worry about that,' Xander said, although he'd been awake most of the night worrying about it himself. He was dreading what might be waiting for him at work today.

'Xander, I don't know how I can ever show my face in the village again,' she mumbled. 'Was everyone there? Did they see?'

'Quite a few people did,' he admitted. 'But they'll understand, Mum. Everyone knows the stress you would've been under yesterday.'

'Your new girlfriend – was she there? I remember I wanted to meet her...'

'No,' Xander said, deciding a little white lie was allowable under the circumstances. 'No, she didn't see.'

A sob bubbled from her throat. 'I've ruined everything, haven't I? I don't know why you're still speaking to me.'

'Because I'm quite fond of you, maybe?' Xander said with a smile, hoping he could lighten the atmosphere.

But Anne wasn't listening. 'Your career. Everything you've worked so hard for...'

'Mum, please. I really wish you wouldn't think about that. You just concentrate on getting better.' He leaned down to kiss the top of her head. 'And... you won't drink today, will you? I worry about you.'

'No. I promise, Xander.' She looked up at him, her brow knitting with sudden determination. 'In fact, I want you to get rid of it.'

He blinked. 'What, the gin?'

'Tip it down the sink. Then I won't be tempted. You're right; it doesn't make anything better in the end.'

'Well, OK, if you really want me to.'

She put a hand on his arm. 'Xander, love, I'm so sorry.'

'You've got nothing to be sorry for,' he said gently. 'I understand. Everyone does.'

'I just can't stop asking myself the same questions. Why did he do it? Why didn't I see it coming? Could I have stopped it if I had?'

'I know, Mum. Me too.'

'Xander. That group, the one you mentioned before...'

Xander sat up straighter. 'The counselling group, you mean?'

She nodded. 'If you want to… I mean, I hate the idea of talking about it in front of strangers, but maybe if we were both to go that might not be so bad. If you really think it might help with the… the dreams and everything.'

For the first time since his mum had shown up at the fete, Xander broke into a smile.

'Mum, that's the best news I've heard all year,' he told her. 'Thank you. You won't regret it.'

He left her to nurse her hangover and headed to the kitchen to get rid of her gin stash, trying not to think about what the working day might have in store for him now all his secrets had been spilled.

–

Xander tried to keep his head down as he walked to school. Maybe he was paranoid but it felt like everyone he passed was staring at him, or whispering to each other about him. A couple of people tried to stop and talk to him, but he just mumbled something about being late and carried on.

He could guess what would be waiting for him at school. The staff, their curious faces plastered with manufactured pity. The pupils – the littler ones who'd witnessed yesterday's events perhaps greeting him with stares of worried puzzlement, some of the more unpleasant older ones with barely concealed jibes. And he just knew there'd be an email from Ryan, probably demanding his instant resignation.

And Nell… Nell. What the fuck did she think of him now?

He'd been haunted through his sleepless night by the image of her face, that look of shock as his mum had slurred and sobbed out her grief in front of everyone. And while his mobile was currently showing missed calls from Sara, Justin, Stevie and any number of others besides – none of which he'd chosen to answer – he hadn't heard anything from Nell.

It was hard to believe that just yesterday he'd been on top of the world, with a gorgeous new girlfriend, a successful, maybe career-defining event under his belt and well on his way to a bright future as the fully fledged headteacher of Leyholme Primary. Then just like that, with a snap of Fate's fingers, it had all come crashing down.

Not that he blamed his mum. No, she had every reason to try to block out the flashbacks he knew she suffered from every day. He did blame his dad, though. The flatlining of Xander's career – and quite possibly yet another romantic relationship – had now been added to the long list of things he felt he had to resent his dead parent for. His resentment was muddled together with the guilt he felt over not detecting the telltale signs of depression in his father before his suicide, all of his conflicting emotions making dealing with the loss so very, very much harder than a regular bereavement.

'Morning, my love,' Mrs Rhodes said as he walked into reception, smiling in her understanding way. 'I didn't know if we'd have you today.'

'No, well, it's my job,' he said, rubbing his hair. 'Have, um… have there been any messages?'

'A few,' she said, looking down at her pad. 'Some of the parents are anxious to speak with you urgently. I've pencilled the first one in for ten.' She grimaced. 'And, er, Mr Theakston's on his way.'

'Mmm. I bet he is.'

She reached over her desk to put a hand on his arm. 'How is she, Alexander?'

'Not too good,' he confessed. 'But she knows there's a problem, at least. I can get her help, now she's admitted it.'

'How long has this been going on, love?'

He sighed. 'Since we lost Dad. Since she found Dad, I mean. Wouldn't you?'

'Yes. Yes, I think I probably would.' She opened the top drawer of her desk and handed him a Tupperware container. 'These are for you.'

He opened the lid to look inside. 'Buns?'

'I made them last night. Well, I wanted to do something.'
She flashed him another understanding smile. 'And you tell
Anne that we'd love to see her at Monday's WI meeting if she's
free. Everyone's missed having her there, helping us old biddies
with all that social media business she's so good at. Tell her she's
welcome back any time.'

Xander blinked, feeling a little choked up. 'Thank you,' he
said quietly. 'Thank you. She'll appreciate that.'

'Oh, nonsense,' Mrs Rhodes said, waving a hand. 'Nothing
to appreciate. I'll be over to see her just as soon as she's feeling
up to having visitors.'

He rubbed away a tear as he headed to his office. Lovely
Janet Rhodes. She'd known how he'd be feeling this morning
and like a true friend, she'd been waiting for him with sympathy
and homemade buns. If only everyone in Leyholme was like
her.

At his desk, he turned on his computer and groaned. Fifty
emails. He turned it off again.

He hadn't been in his office ten minutes when there was an
aggressive-sounding knock at the door and, without waiting for
an invitation, Ryan Theakston strode in.

'Well, Xander, I expect you can guess why I'm here,' he said,
clearly relishing the opportunity to switch on extra-pompous
mode.

'Enlighten me,' Xander muttered. He was in no mood to
make things easy for the bastard, not today.

Ryan helped himself to a seat. 'I'm here to talk to you about
the irreparable damage to your reputation, and to the reputation
of this school, brought about by recent revelations.'

'Look, Ryan, my mum's—'

'I don't just mean that little performance, although Christ
knows it was painful enough for all of us,' Ryan said, raising a
hand for silence. 'There's everything else as well. The fete you
insisted on continuing with against my wishes—'

'It was a success, wasn't it?'

'That's neither here nor there. And of course most of the village is talking about how you're sleeping with that new girl, the Reception teacher.'

'OK, and what if I am?' Xander said, frowning. 'I don't see why we should have to hide it. I'm not the first headteacher to begin a relationship with a colleague.'

Ryan ignored him. 'So really, the fact that your mother's a lush prone to flashing her knickers at public events is just the cherry on top of a pretty shite fairy cake at this point, isn't it?'

'You son of a—' Xander sprang to his feet. 'If we weren't in school, I'd punch you for that.'

'OK, I don't mind adding threatening the chair of governors to the charge sheet if you insist,' Ryan said, examining his nails calmly. 'That doesn't alter the facts though, does it?'

'My mum walked in from shopping one day two years ago to find her husband swinging from the attic rafters by his belt, Ryan. Everyone in Leyholme knows that. How she's been trying to deal with it is none of your fucking business.'

Ryan got to his feet too, his anger erupting finally. 'Watch that filthy mouth of yours, Scott. This is a school, or have you forgotten?'

'What is it with you?' Xander demanded. 'Why do you hate me so much? You begged me to do this job when I'd far rather have stayed with my class. Is it because I wasn't the puppet you expected me to be, is that it, Ryan?'

'If that's what your ego chooses to believe, by all means go ahead,' Ryan said, shrugging. 'In point of fact, this is about the school, not you.'

'You're really enjoying this, aren't you?'

Ryan turned away. 'We were going to wait until after the Easter break, but Jeremy Illingworth is well enough to come back to work now if necessary. If the acting head is judged not fit for purpose.'

'What are you saying, I'm being sacked?'

'I've called an emergency governors' meeting this evening at which I'll be tabling a motion of no confidence. If it passes, then yes, I'll be recommending to the Local Education Authority that you be immediately removed from your position. Of course, you could always save me the trouble and offer your resignation now.'

'For what, Ryan? For my mum? For Nell? Neither of those things has anything to do with how I do my job.'

'They have a lot to do with the reputation of this school and its head. I won't stand by and see us become a laughing stock.' He went to the door. 'Goodbye, Xander. If you do decide to take the gentleman's way out and resign, you know where you can reach me.'

—

'Bad news?' Mrs Rhodes said when she poked her head around the door a few minutes later.

'Not really,' Xander muttered. 'He's trying to get me sacked, that's all.'

'Is he now?' The tiny woman looked fierce under her pink-rinse perm. 'Well, if he does then he can find himself a new school secretary.'

Xander looked up. 'You'd do that for me?'

'I would, and so would others, I'm sure.'

He smiled. 'That's lovely of you. Don't though, please. You're the only one who knows how to keep this place running.'

'Well, that's certainly true. But no one's getting sacked if I have anything to do with it. Now what did I come in for?' She frowned for a moment. 'Oh yes. There's a parent who wants to see you but she hasn't made an appointment. Are you free?'

'Who is it? Not Karen Doneen?'

'No, the one who's always done up like a dog's dinner. Daft name.'

'Jolene Hancock?'

'That's her.'

'Yeah, send her up,' he said with a sigh.

What could Jo want to see him about? Was she coming to tell him she was pulling Morgan out of Leyholme Primary? That she didn't want him educated in a place where the head's alcoholic relatives turned up to make a show of themselves at school events? If she was, he'd resign on the spot.

'Come in,' he called when there was a knock on the door.

Jolene entered, smiling warmly. Even by her standards she was pretty dressed up, in an off-the-shoulder red jumpsuit, huge sunhat and leopard-print heels.

'Hiya Jo.' He gestured to the chair on the other side of his desk. 'What's up?'

'I, er...' Was she blushing? 'I, er, just popped in to bring you this really.' She put a ceramic pot down on the desk.

'What is it?'

'It's a casserole. For you and your mum. Chicken, I hope that's OK.'

Xander blinked at it. 'You didn't have to do that.'

'I'm not much of a cook but I wanted to bring you something,' she said, her flushed cheeks clashing terribly with her jumpsuit. 'It was very sweet, Xander, the way you looked after her. None of us had any idea she was still... suffering. You know. Um, how are you doing?'

'I'm OK. Well, I'm probably about to lose my job, but other than that.'

Her eyebrows lifted. 'Lose your job?'

'Ryan's tabling a no-confidence motion at your emergency governors' meeting tonight.'

She frowned. 'Hmm, we'll see about that. He certainly won't be getting my vote.'

'Jo, I don't know what to say,' Xander said, glancing at the casserole. 'This was very kind of you. Thank you. Was that all you came for?'

'No. No, there was one other thing I wanted to talk to you about.'

'Is it about Morgan?'

'Not as such.' She pushed the casserole to one side and leaned towards him. 'Xander, me and you – we've known each other a long time, haven't we?'

'Well, yes.'

'So I wanted to ask… I just wanted to ask, are you free next week at all?'

'I don't know, Mrs Rhodes keeps my diary. She can schedule you an appointment if you ask at reception. Assuming I'm still head by then, of course.'

Jolene laughed. 'Not professionally, dummy, in the evenings. I thought it might be nice to go out for a drink or something. You know, catch up.'

'Oh. Right. Well, I guess we could—' Xander stopped, suddenly remembering what Sara had told him about Jolene having had a crush on him when they were all at secondary school together. 'Hang on. You don't mean like… are you asking me out on a date?'

'Um, yeah. You want to?'

He shook his head, feeling dazed. 'I… can't. Sorry, Jo. I mean, I'm very flattered, obviously, but…'

She smiled. 'So the rumours are true then, are they? I did miss my chance. Serves me right for not getting in sooner.'

'What rumours?'

'You and Nell Shackleton.' She waggled her eyebrows, making him laugh.

'Well, you might think that. I couldn't possibly comment.'

'In that case, I'm very jealous. But I'm glad someone's making you happy, Xand. Nell's a lovely girl.' She stood up. 'Enjoy the casserole, eh? And we'll still grab that drink. As old friends.'

'Definitely.' He came round his desk to give her a hug.

Mrs Rhodes appeared at the door again. 'Alexander, there's another one. Stevie Madeleine's here to see you.'

As soon as the bell went for dinner, Nell headed to Xander's office. She took a deep breath and put down the yucca plant she was holding so she could knock.

'Come in,' Xander called.

'Hi,' she said, peeping round the door.

He smiled, looking as awkward as she felt. 'Hi.'

She entered and closed the door behind her. There was a loaded silence.

'I, er, like your plant,' Xander said, nodding to it.

'Oh. Yes.' She held it out. 'It's for you.'

He took it from her. 'Right. Thanks. What's it for?'

'Well, photosynthesis and stuff, mainly.'

He laughed. 'I mean, why is it for me?'

'I just… wanted to get you something.' She blinked at the spare desk that sat under the window in the corner. It seemed to be covered with assorted foodstuffs, flowers, boxes of chocolates and other bits and pieces. 'What's all this?'

Xander shook his head. 'I don't know. People keep stopping by to bring me food and presents.'

'All women?'

'Er, yeah. Why?'

She smiled. 'And here was me thinking I'd be the only one.'

'I've had parents coming to see me all morning,' he said. 'The shepherd's pie is from Stevie. Karen Doneen brought the big bouquet. And on top of that, three different mums have asked me out.'

Nell laughed as she added her plant to the table of gifts. 'So are you going?'

'I don't know. Have I still got a girlfriend?'

He was smiling as if it was a joke, but Nell knew him well enough by now to see there was worry in his eyes.

'Is that a serious question?' she asked, frowning.

'You just looked so shocked, yesterday. And then when you didn't phone…'

'I was shocked because I didn't realise my boyfriend had been quietly coping with something completely heartbreaking,' she said softly, coming over to take his hands. 'And I didn't phone because it seemed like you needed some time alone with your mum to deal with things. Stevie said there was no answer the couple of times she tried you. I thought you'd have called if you wanted me.'

'I did want you.' He looked down at his hands clasped in hers. 'I just didn't know if you'd still want me, after what you'd seen.'

'Aww, Xand, I'm sorry. Of course I still want you. I—' She bit her lip. 'How is she, your mum?'

'She's agreed to join a suicide bereavement group and asked me to throw out her gin supply. So that's progress. When she's feeling better, I'm going to see if she'll consider AA as well.' He closed his eyes. 'If this was the wake-up call she needed to finally get herself some help, then Nell, it'll all have been worth it. Whatever happens to me.'

'Love, I'm so sorry,' Nell whispered, reaching up to trace the bags under his eyes. 'I had no idea what you were going through.'

Xander sighed as he rested his forehead against hers and she wrapped her arms around his waist. 'Ryan wants me to resign.'

'Don't you bloody dare.'

'I might not have a choice. He's putting a no-confidence vote to the other governors tonight.'

'It'll never go through. The staff and parents at this school have complete confidence in you.' She gestured to the table of gifts. 'There's your proof.'

'He thinks my family problems and our sex life are bringing the school into disrepute.'

'Let him sack me then,' Nell said stoutly. 'I'll go before I'll let you leave this place.'

Xander laughed. 'God, I love you.' He flushed. 'I mean… sorry. That just slipped out.'

'It's OK.' She lifted his hand and pressed it to her lips. 'So you're the village's resident heart-throb now, are you, Mr Scott? Who do I have to fight then?'

'I'll make you a list,' he said, smiling. 'I'm starting to think women are like buses – you go a year without one and then a whole fleet turns up at once. Why does everyone suddenly want to go out with me?'

Nell laughed. 'You really don't know?'

'No. Did I get sexier?'

'Yeah, kind of. When you helped your mum, yesterday at the fete, the way you cared for her...' Nell blinked back a tear. 'Xander, it was adorable. I think every woman in the village is ready to mother or marry you today.'

'What about you?'

'Well, I'm the lucky girl who gets to take you home, aren't I?'

Xander shook his head. 'I thought... I don't know, I suppose I thought everyone would sneer at us. Me and Mum, I mean. I had visions of parents queueing up to pull their kids out of school.'

'Are you kidding? Xander Scott's a hero in Leyholme this morning.' Nell gave him a squeeze. 'And tonight, I'm going to march right into that governors' meeting and tell them so.'

Chapter Twenty-Six

Xander sat outside the classroom where the governors' meeting was taking place, fiddling with his tie.

He hated wearing ties. What a completely pointless item of clothing. Still, he reflected, they did at least give you something to do with your hands when you were nervous.

Ryan had requested Xander's presence at the governors' meeting where his no-confidence motion was due to be discussed. 'You'll want to make your case, I suppose,' he'd said in a bored sort of voice over the phone that afternoon. Personally, Xander thought the chairman just wanted to watch him squirm.

Well, it was Ryan's lucky day. Xander was certain that once he got in there, he'd be squirming away like impaled fishbait.

He checked his mobile to see if there was anything from Nell. She'd said she was coming along to support him – there didn't seem much point hiding their relationship now everyone in the village seemed to know, especially as it was one of the things Ryan was using as an excuse for the no-confidence vote. Xander did think she'd have been here by now though.

Nope, nothing. No messages, no missed calls.

He hoped she was still coming. He needed her badly tonight. She was the only person, apart from maybe his mum, who made him feel like he counted for something. With Nell by his side, Xander felt like he could do anything.

The door opened and the governors' clerk appeared.

'OK, Mr Scott,' she said. 'If you'd like to come through, I think we're ready for you.'

'Oh,' Anne said when she answered her front door. 'Hello. Can I help you?'

Nell smiled awkwardly. She knew Anne Scott didn't remember talking to her at the fete the day before, so now she needed to act as if she was meeting her boyfriend's mother for the first time.

'Hi, Mrs Scott. It's Nell.'

'Xander's Nell?' she said, blinking. 'Well, dear, I'm afraid he's not in right at the moment. There's a meeting at the school tonight.'

'I know. It's actually you I'm here to see. Can I come in?'

'Yes.' Anne seemed to recover from her initial surprise and waved her into the house. 'Yes, of course. I'll get the kettle on.'

'So, um, how are you feeling?' Nell asked when they were seated in the living room.

Anne flushed, looking down into her mug of tea.

'Oh, I didn't mean – I meant, with the anniversary of your husband's death and everything,' Nell said hurriedly. 'Sorry, I know I'm a stranger, but I thought I should ask.'

'Yes. Well. I'm feeling… better than I was, let's say.'

'I'm sorry to just turn up unannounced like this. I hope you won't think I'm horribly rude.'

'It is rather a surprise.' Anne smiled. 'But a nice one. I had thought we'd meet when Xander brought you over for dinner. You know, when he was ready. He can get himself a little worked up about these things.'

'I think that was supposed to be the plan. He, er… he doesn't actually know I'm here,' Nell said. 'I wanted to talk to you about him in private.'

Anne frowned. 'Nothing's wrong, is it? I hope you two are still getting along.'

'Oh, it's nothing to do with me and him.' Nell looked up to meet her concerned gaze. 'Mrs Scott—'

'Anne, I think, dear.'

'Anne. Did Xander tell you what the meeting's about tonight?'

'Well, no. It's just school business, I suppose.'

'It's a governors' meeting,' Nell said. 'I'm sorry, but Xander's in a bit of trouble.'

'Trouble? Xander?' Anne looked worried. 'Not because… because of me?'

'No, because of me. Ryan Theakston doesn't think it's appropriate for colleagues to be in a romantic relationship with one another. He thinks it's giving the school a bad reputation.'

'Oh, what nonsense,' Anne said, waving a hand. 'Lots of people meet their partners through work.'

'I think that's just an excuse really. Ryan seems to have it in for Xander, for some reason. I reckon he's jealous of him or something.'

Praise for Xander seemed to be the way to win his mum over. She favoured Nell with a warm smile.

'Yes, I think you might be right. So what is the meeting about?'

'It's about Xander. Ryan's trying to get him sacked. He's planning to bully the other governors into voting for a no-confidence motion.'

Anne's brow knit into a frown. 'Oh, he is, is he?'

'That's why I came. You know pretty much everyone in the village, don't you?'

'Well yes, I suppose I do. I've lived in Leyholme all my life, you know.'

'I thought that was the case,' Nell said. 'Anne, I'm going to need your help.'

–

'OK, Mr Scott, take a seat,' Ryan said as Xander entered the classroom. He nodded to an empty chair that had been placed opposite the tables where the twelve governors were sitting in one long row like a jury, with Ryan in the middle to act as judge. And, very possibly, as executioner.

Xander looked down at the chair. 'Ryan, this is a kid's chair. I'm six foot four.'

Ryan glanced up from his notes to frown at him. 'Please just sit down. This won't take long.'

'I'm sorry, but if I'm getting sacked then I want to be sacked in a big-boy chair with my knees at a respectable distance from my nose. I'm not going to let you humiliate me for the sake of it.'

Ryan sighed and turned to the clerk. 'Mrs James, could you fetch a bigger chair from the store cupboard? Sorry to have to put you out.'

Mrs James let out a very audible 'humph' as she passed Xander to go get the chair.

'Happy now?' Ryan said when Xander had been provided with a chair more suited to his height.

'Yes. Thank you.'

'Now, we all know why we're here,' Ryan said to the room at large. 'I have scheduled a no-confidence motion in our acting headteacher, following recent revelations regarding—'

'Nay,' Jolene Hancock said.

Ryan frowned at her. 'I'm sorry?'

'I was casting my vote. Nay. Or wait, is that saying I have no confidence? In that case, aye. Whichever is a vote for Xander to stay.' She smiled at Xander. 'I have every confidence in Mr Scott as the acting head and I wish that to be minuted.'

Xander smiled back. 'Thanks, Jo.'

'Jolene, we haven't got to the voting yet. Please keep quiet until requested.' Ryan frowned at Xander. 'And you needn't think your popularity with the ladies is going to get you out of this either. Please try to keep your dubious charms under wraps and behave like a professional for five minutes.'

Xander blinked. 'Charms?'

'Right, where was I? Oh yes, recent revelations. To wit, that the acting headteacher's personal life has now become a distraction from his duties and a black mark against the good name of this school. I therefore move that if a no-confidence vote is passed today, we as the board of governors make a recommendation to the LEA that the acting head be relieved of his responsibilities with immediate effect.'

'Then what happens to me?' Xander said. 'I mean, are you sacking me as acting head or are you sacking me completely?'

'I'm sorry, Xander, but if you fail the vote then we really don't have a choice but to recommend your complete dismissal. Parents' confidence in you will be shaken to too great an extent for you to continue teaching here. The education authority doesn't have to accept our recommendation, of course, but there is no reason to believe they'd go against the will of the school governors.'

'Seriously? You're letting me go?' Xander pushed his fingers into his hair. 'I've worked here for seven years, Ryan. I was a pupil here. I love this place.'

'I'm sorry,' Ryan said again, although his eyes shone with vindictive glee. 'I don't believe you could realistically continue in your previous role after failing a vote such as this.'

'Would I be provided with a reference from the governors?' Xander asked.

'If you'd resigned when I requested, certainly, I'd have been glad to arrange one. Now... I don't see how that can be allowable given the circumstances, do you? Not when a teacher is let go following a no-confidence vote.'

'Ryan, why are you doing this?' Xander demanded. 'This isn't just my job, it's my whole career you're flushing away! You must realise that. Are you seriously going to be that petty, just because I wouldn't jump through your hoops like a good puppy?'

'I have to say I think this is all very irregular,' said one of the parent governors, a Year 6 dad who was a relative newcomer to the village. 'In my experience, no-confidence votes are reserved for heads who have shown gross incompetence in the execution of their duties. I've never heard of a headteacher being taken to task for their private life in this way.'

'What you have to remember, Mike, is that Leyholme is a small village,' Ryan said. 'While it's not ideal, this is the sort of community where people do know one another's business. The head's private life is something that can, unfortunately, impact upon the school as a whole.' He glared at Xander. 'Especially when it crosses the threshold of the school gates. The first duty of any headteacher ought to be to keep their personal and professional lives separate.'

'But that's not always possible, is it, Ryan?' Jolene said. 'Not in a place like this, where – as you rightly point out – nearly everyone knows everyone else.'

One of the other governors cleared his throat. 'May I say something at this juncture?'

It was Donald Brady, Ryan's business partner, fellow parish councillor and – because this was Leyholme – also his brother-in-law. The two of them were kindred spirits, united in pomposity and petty bureaucracy, so Xander wasn't expecting anything approaching support from him.

Ryan nodded. 'Go ahead, Don.'

'Young man, you mustn't think we're doing this merely to be spiteful,' Donald told Xander in a condescending tone. He steepled his fingers and rested his double chin on them. 'Our job as governors is to protect the reputation of this school. Pupils aren't here merely to study the three Rs, they're also here to learn what it takes to become a valuable member of this community. The head ought to be setting an example to them in that respect, as well as academically.' His lip curled. 'Which he certainly isn't doing when he's dragging other staff members into the art cupboard for a bit of how's-your-father every playtime, is he?'

'What? I haven't had any how's-your-father in the art cupboard. There isn't room.'

Donald frowned. 'This is hardly the time for levity, son. In your position you ought to be a role model for the children, not behaving like some sort of… staffroom Casanova.'

'Look,' Xander said, drawing himself up. 'If you're referring to my relationship with Miss Shackleton, I can assure you our behaviour in school is always professional. As to what we do in our own time, that's our own business.'

'Plenty of our teachers have had relationships with colleagues,' Caroline, who was there in her capacity as a staff governor, chipped in. 'I don't see why it should be one rule for Xander and another for Jeremy Illingworth.'

'Perhaps so, when the relationships are kept strictly off school premises,' Ryan said. 'But I have heard reports of…' He glanced around the table. 'Well, as we're in mixed company, I'll just say "embracing" in the headteacher's office during school hours.'

Xander frowned. 'What?'

'One of the lunchtime supervisors spotted you and Miss Shackleton through your office window this afternoon, looking very cuddly and cosy.'

'That was… we weren't doing anything. Nell gave me a hug because I was upset. I didn't know anyone could see. And yes, perhaps it wasn't that appropriate, but there had been, um…' Xander flushed. 'Well, after what happened at the fete yesterday…'

'Mmm. And that's the other issue, isn't it?' Ryan said. 'Your suddenly very visible family problems.'

'Now, Ryan, that's not fair,' Caroline said. 'Xander's family has had a lot to deal with these last two years. As a community we ought to be supporting him and his mum, not censuring them.'

'Look, I don't want to sound unduly harsh,' Ryan said. 'But there is the school to think about. Admissions are already on the decline. How do you think prospective parents will feel when they find out our headteacher's the son of a suicide and an alcoholic?'

'Ryan, for Christ's sake!' Jolene snapped.

'It's true, isn't it? If you'd heard that, if you weren't' – he coughed, in what Xander felt was a very suggestive way – 'a *personal friend* of the head, would you have sent your son to this school?'

Jolene met Xander's eyes. 'Yes. Yes, I would.'

'Well I wouldn't,' one of the other parent governors said. She shot an apologetic look at Xander. 'I'm sorry, love, I know it's not your fault. And I don't care if you're going to bed with half your staff in your own time, honestly I don't. But as a parent you have to put your children first, don't you? When your mum turned up at the fete – my little lad saw that. I had to talk to him about it, try to explain, long before he was old enough to understand those issues. So yes, if I'd known beforehand that she was... ill in that way, it would have influenced my decision to send him here.'

Another governor nodded. 'And me. I'm sorry, Xander.'

Jolene looked around the table, shaking her head. 'Come on, what's wrong with you all? Haven't we always looked after our own in Leyholme? Xander and his mum need us and instead of helping them, we're trying to bring down a highly competent young man's career.'

'We're not talking about our responsibility as a village, Jolene, we're talking about our responsibility as governors of this school,' Donald said. 'And as governors, we must be seen to hold the headteacher accountable. I'm sorry, but I'm going to vote with Ryan.'

There were a few nods and mumbles of assent around the table. Some of the others were shaking their heads, but it looked to Xander as if the ayes were going to have it.

He wasn't sure what was stopping him from hiding his face in his hands and sobbing at this point. Just when his mum had made a commitment to starting again, finally moving on from the horror of his dad's suicide. What would she say when Xander told her he'd not only lost his job, but that after failing a no-confidence vote, he was unlikely to ever get another one? What would she do when she heard on the gossip grapevine – as she inevitably would – that her breakdown on the day of the fete was the cause? Look for solace at the bottom of a bottle again?

Fucking Leyholme. He never should've come back here after university. He should've set up somewhere new, somewhere no one knew him or his family, where he would have been free to just be Xander Scott.

But then he'd never have met Nell. Never have fallen in love with Nell. And… and where the hell was Nell?

'So, are we all ready to vote?' Ryan said.

There was a knock at the door. Xander's head jerked up.

But it was only Mrs Rhodes, as permanent a fixture of the school as ever she had been.

'I just wondered if anyone wanted fresh drinks before I took myself off home,' she said.

'No, no one wants drinks,' Ryan said impatiently. 'Mrs Rhodes, we are in the middle of an important meeting. Could you not interrupt us for tea-lady duties?'

'Right you are, love,' she said. 'Oh, and I wanted to drop this off while I'm here.'

She approached Ryan and handed him a sheet of A4.

He stared at it. 'What's this?'

'It's a… now, what do you call it? A subscription. Prescription. No, a petition, that's it.' She pointed to the list of signatures. 'There's me right at the top, look.'

'Petition? Why are you giving me this?'

'Oh, well, I had to get it organised in a bit of a hurry, since you didn't bother to ask the opinions of the other teachers yourself. It's been signed by every member of staff who'll resign on the spot if you pass a vote of no confidence in our Mr Scott.' She smiled brightly. 'It's nearly all of us, by the way. Well, I'd better be getting off.'

Xander stood up and put his hand on her arm as she passed. 'Janet…'

232

'Now, don't thank me, Alexander. Just you be back at your desk on Monday morning. I'll have your coffee ready.' She smiled. 'And I think you might like to go look out of the window.'

'The window?'

'I'll see you Monday, pet,' Mrs Rhodes said, turning to go.

'Mr Scott, sit down,' Ryan said. 'We're not done here.'

Xander ignored him and went to the window. He stared for a moment. Then he burst out laughing.

'What is it, Xand?' Jolene got up to join him.

'Seriously, can we have a bit of order, people?' Ryan demanded. But no one paid him any attention, the other governors all standing now to find out what was going on.

'Xander.' Jolene squeezed his arm. 'It's... everyone.'

'Not far off,' Xander said, his dazed eyes fixed on the crowd that had gathered outside the school gates.

His mum and Nell stood at the head of it, both carrying *Keep Mr Scott!* placards that they must've made in a hell of a hurry. Behind them was... well, it looked like nearly every parent at the school, a lot of them hand-in-hand with their kids. Not to mention most of his staff, all waving signs of their own, and many, many others besides. In the crowd he could see Justin, Sara, Stevie – even Martha Theakston, who'd obviously decided her duty as an old friend of his mum's trumped any responsibility to show solidarity with her bullying husband.

'Jeremy's there,' he muttered, catching sight of the head-teacher leaning on his stick. 'Jo, did you know about this?'

She smiled. 'Yeah, kind of. I didn't think she'd be able to get this many at such short notice, though.'

'Who? Nell?'

'And your mum. They organised this together.'

'Why are they all here?'

She laughed, playfully punching his arm. 'For you, dummy. Xander, people love you.'

'For Christ's sake!' Ryan yelled. 'What is wrong with everyone? Sit down, this is a meeting!'

Jolene grinned as she resumed her seat. 'Don't you want to take a look, Ryan? Your missus is out there.'

'This doesn't change anything,' he muttered.

'When we've got nearly every member of staff threatening to walk if he goes, and what seems to be an army of parents outside protesting his dismissal?' Donald shook his head. 'I'm sorry, Ryan, but I'd say it changes a heck of a lot. Now this is the sort of bad press the school doesn't need, having it get around that we let a popular staff member go in the face of public opinion.'

Ryan shot his brother-in-law his best *et tu, Brute?* glare. 'It doesn't change the fact that the boy's a liability: that his mother's a drunk, his dad topped himself and he can't keep it in his underpants during school time.'

'Ryan, what is this really about?' Caroline demanded. 'You seem to have made this personal. You thought you were getting a head you could bully when you pressed for us to appoint Xander, didn't you?'

'I only ever wanted what was best for this school,' he told her stiffly.

'You wanted a performing monkey who'd dance to your tune, that's what you wanted.' She turned to Xander. 'I'm sorry, but I actually voted against your appointment. I didn't think you were up to the job, if I'm honest.'

Jolene nodded. 'Me too. Sorry, Xand. I was worried you'd let him push you around, that's all.'

'That's OK,' Xander said. 'I had pretty similar feelings about it myself at the time.'

'Well, I for one am happy to have been proven wrong,' Caroline said, smiling. 'So it's a nay from me, I'm afraid, Ryan.'

'And me,' Jolene said.

There were mutters around the table as the other 'nays' raised their hands. One, two, three… all twelve of the other governors, even those who'd expressed concerns before. Even Donald, Ryan's right-hand man.

'Well, Ryan, looks like there's just you in the aye camp,' Jolene said.

Ryan threw down his clipboard. 'Fine. Have it your way. But you'll regret it, all of you, when he's driven this school's reputation into the ground with his sex shenanigans and bloody freak-show family.' Refusing to look at Xander, he stormed out of the room.

Jolene stood up and went to link Xander's arm. 'Well done, Mr Scott,' she said quietly.

'I won.' He stared at her, glassy-eyed. 'Jo, did I win?'

'Yeah, Xand. You won.'

'So, um, what do I do now?'

'Get out there to Nell and your mum, of course. You've got some good news to give them.'

Chapter Twenty-Seven

'Someone's in a good mood,' Xander said.

It was a balmy Saturday morning three weeks later, early spring sunshine streaming through the kitchen windows and the scent of blossom and bluebells hanging in the air. Anne was humming to herself as she arranged a bunch of daffodils in a crystal vase.

'And why not?' She pecked his cheek as she passed him. ' "I'm always most religious upon a sunshiny day." Lord Byron said that, the poet – you know, the mad, bad and dangerous one. Even if you don't have much religion, you can sort of see what he means, don't you think?'

'You can.' Xander filled in three-down on the crossword he was doing at the breakfast bar. 'Hey, one of my class is called Byron. I hope he won't grow up too mad and bad.'

'You miss them, I bet. Jeremy's still planning to come back after Easter, isn't he?'

'Yep. Just one more week of school, then after the hols I can go back to being a common factory-floor slob.'

Anne smiled. 'Ah, but you won't be, will you, Mr Deputy Head?'

'I suppose that'll be a bit different,' he said, his pen hovering over the next clue. 'It'll feel good to be teaching again though. I've talked it through with Jeremy and he's going to discuss with the governors the possibility of more teaching time for the head when I take over from him next year. Having my cake and eating it, if you like.'

'I hear Ryan's resigning as chairman at the end of the school year too. Just what that school needs, a new broom. Who's the new chair going to be, do you know yet?'

'Caroline Fairchild's offered to do a stint from September. She'll be good, I think.'

'I'm certainly not surprised Ryan feels he ought to go after the way he behaved.' Anne tutted. 'So childish, the way he targeted you like that. I wonder he doesn't leave now and spare you all his sour face.'

Her face had puckered like she was sucking on something pretty sour herself. Trying to get her son the sack would always be the ultimate unforgivable offence in her book.

'So the last stressful thing I have to deal with before we break up is the Parents versus Teachers Bunny Hop Race on the final day of term,' Xander said. 'I hope we won't have any punch-ups this year. Are you coming?'

'No, I've arranged a shopping trip with Martha, Janet and some of the other WI ladies. We're all in need of a new spring wardrobe now the weather's starting to turn.' Anne looked up from her daffs to beam at him. 'Oh, Xander, I haven't told you my exciting news.'

'Go on, what?'

'I'm going back to work.'

Xander glanced up from his crossword. 'Back to Curl Up and Dye? Are you sure you're ready for that? You've not been sober a month yet, Mum. I don't think you should put yourself under too much stress in the early days.'

'Oh no, I'm not going back to that old place,' Anne said, wrinkling her nose. 'I'm going into business for myself.'

'What, like, mobile hairdressing?'

She laughed. 'Yes, kind of. But not people. Dogs.'

'You mean you're going to give them perms and highlights and that?'

She cuffed him affectionately. 'Dog-grooming, you daft apeth. I'm going into partnership with that doggy friend of

Stevie Madeleine's, Deb – well, I think they might be more than just friends between you and me, not that it's any of my business.'

'You're going into partnership with Deb?'

'That's right. She's got the contacts and I've got the transferable skills, so to speak, so I'm going to do a bit of retraining and then we'll have some business cards done. I think it'll be fun, don't you?'

'Er, yeah. It could be good for you actually. What are you going to call this business?'

'Well, Deb suggested Doggy Style, which I thought had a nice ring to it.'

Xander nearly choked on his coffee. 'What?' he gasped.

'Doggy Style. Sounds sort of classy, wouldn't you say?'

'Mum, I'm sure Deb was joking. You can't call it that.'

She looked up at him. 'Why not, love? Don't you think it works?'

'It's just, er… do you know what it means?'

'Well, yes. What else could it mean? Stylish dogs.'

'No. No, it… it means something else as well. Something a bit, well, rude.'

'Does it?' She smiled knowingly. 'No it doesn't. You're teasing me, aren't you?'

'Honestly, Mum, it does.'

'I don't believe you.' She reached across the worktop for her tablet. 'Here, let me check.'

His eyes went wide. 'You're not going to Google it?'

'Well, yes.'

'Please don't do that. And whatever you do, don't make it an image search.' His cheeks were flaming now. 'It's a sexual position, Mum. I think Deb was making a joke. She'll have thought you knew.'

'Sexual position, is it?' His mum looked thoughtful. 'Well, you learn something new every day. I should probably stop using it as a hashtag then.'

Xander spluttered a bit more coffee over his crossword. 'You didn't!'

'Don't be such a prude, Xander,' she said, laughing as she ruffled his hair. 'I'm sure my followers will think it's funny. Now, what are your plans tonight while I'm at my AA meeting?'

'I'm staying over at Nell's.' Xander folded up his newspaper. 'I told her I'd head up there after lunch so I should probably get showered and dressed. There's some big surprise she wants to show me.' He stood up and kissed his mum on the cheek. 'Hope it goes well at your meeting, old lady. Give me a ring if you need me.'

She smiled. 'Xander, you worry too much. Be sure to give Nell my love, won't you?'

–

Stevie sighed as Deb snuggled into her back, moulding their bodies to one another.

'This is nice,' she whispered. 'Saturday cuddles.'

'Mmm.' Deb brushed her lips against Stevie's neck, one hand snaking under her pyjama top. 'I could definitely get used to a bit of spooning at the weekend.'

'Oi. Those are naughty cuddles.' Stevie tapped her wandering hand. 'I can hear the pitter-patter of tiny feet next door. Milly's up, we have to behave.'

'Unless you fancy a shower together? I'll let you scrub my back.'

'You're a bad influence, you are.' Stevie rolled to face her and pressed a kiss to her lips. 'Thanks for staying over.'

'Thanks for having me. I was a bit worried Milly might resent the invasion, but she seemed pretty unfazed by it.'

That was an understatement. Milly had been so excited at the idea of a sleepover, it was with great difficulty that Stevie had stopped the little girl from commandeering Deb herself and forcing her to sleep on the top bunk in her room.

It had felt like a milestone though, Deb's first night staying over at their place. Before, Stevie's girlfriend had felt like something separate to home stuff, another part of her life. But last night, with the three of them snuggled up on the sofa watching TV, then getting Milly bathed and put to bed together, it felt for the first time like they were starting to become a little family.

'Are you happy, Deb?' she asked.

'Very. Are you?'

'Yes. Yes, I really am.'

'Stevie Madeleine,' Deb said softly, running one finger over the bridge of Stevie's nose. 'Tell me how I ever got a girl as far out of my league as you to look at me twice.'

'Mainly I think it was your talent for flattery.' She played idly with a strand of Deb's hair. 'I never thought I could have this again, Deb. With you and Milly and Nell in my life, I feel like I've finally got everything I ever wanted. And Red, of course.'

'Nell means a lot to you, doesn't she?'

'She does. It's funny, we only met five months ago, but I feel like I've known her for years.'

'How come?'

'Not sure really. I never found it easy to form close bonds when I was young, or as an adult either. I wasn't that kid who had a best friend, you know? But with Nell... I suppose she feels a bit like a little sister. Which is something you dream of when you're growing up in a house full of boys.'

'Well, I'm glad. I'm looking forward to getting to know her better too.'

Stevie looked up to meet Deb's eyes. 'Sweetie, I— can I tell you something?'

'Course you can. Is it something good or something bad?'

'Something... old.' Stevie took a deep breath. She'd been working up to this for days. 'Something I should really have shared before now.'

'OK,' Deb said. 'You have to let me go first though.'

Stevie frowned. 'What, you've got something to tell me?'

'Yep. I'm kind of hoping it might be the same thing as you've got to tell me.'

'What is it, Deb?'

Deb leaned forward for a kiss. 'Just that I love you,' she whispered. 'You knew that, right?'

Stevie smiled. 'Aww.'

'Was that what you wanted to tell me?'

'Yes,' she whispered. 'I mean, no; that was something else. But I do, though.'

Deb laughed. 'I'm not sure how flattering it is that loving me was only second on your list. So what was the other thing?'

'Oh... nothing. I'll tell you another day.'

Deb looked into her eyes. 'You're sure? It sounded important.'

Stevie hesitated. But before she could say anything else, the door swung open and two little feet bounced onto the bed, closely followed by four little paws.

'*DUMBO!*' the two-legged thing yelled. The four-legged one joined in with an excited bark.

Deb laughed, sitting up to give Milly a hug. 'OK, mini thunderbolt, I haven't forgotten *Dumbo* day. There's ages till the film starts, don't worry.'

'Packed your tissues?' Stevie asked Deb. 'If the live-action version's anything like the cartoon, you'll need them.'

'Yeah, that bit where his mum rocks him with her trunk through the prison bars gets me every time. Not sure I can cope with seeing real elephants doing it.'

'Mummy, why aren't you coming to the cinema with us?' Milly demanded.

'Because I have to look after Red.' Stevie glanced at Deb. 'And I thought it might be nice for you two to have some fun without Mum there to tell you off. I bet Deb will spoil you rotten without me around.'

'Will you?' Milly asked Deb.

Deb shook her head. 'Absolutely not. Your mum's trusting me to take care of you and I intend to be completely responsible and grown-up.' She lowered her voice to a stage whisper. 'Wait till she's gone and we'll talk Slushies, 'K?'

Milly grinned and nodded.

'Right then, you lot,' Stevie said, pretending she hadn't heard as she swung the duvet off them. 'Time to get up. I've got to head into town and pick something up for Nell while you two are getting *Dumbo*-ready.'

'Come on, Mill,' Deb said. 'Race you to the kitchen. Last one there gets cabbage for breakfast.'

'No way!' Milly leapt off the bed and ran as fast as she could to the door, Red at her heels and Deb hot on hers. Stevie smiled as she watched them go.

–

'Oh,' Nell said when she answered a knock at the farmhouse door to find Stevie on the doorstep with a parcel in her arms. 'Hiya. I thought you might be Xander.'

'Hey. What can Xander give you that I can't?'

Nell laughed. 'You don't want to know.'

Red snuggled against her human's calf as Stevie turned to look out over the horizon. The sun, hot for the time of year, bathed the moors in gold as insects buzzed lazily around Nell's overgrown little meadow-garden. She plucked a sprig of lavender from a clump near the fence and held it to her nose.

'Glorious wilderness,' she sighed. 'You know, Nell, I'm actually jealous. This place'll be paradise in spring and summer.'

'And freeze-your-jubblies-off Baltic in autumn and winter,' Nell said. 'That's the price I agreed to pay when I bought it, I suppose. You coming in for a glass of wine?'

'Go on, just a quick one. Let's sit out though, make the most of the nice weather.'

'Good idea.'

Nell fetched a couple of fold-up chairs and plonked them down by a freshly sheared Colin, who was enjoying a sunbathe in his new fleeceless state, then headed inside to pour herself and Stevie a glass of white wine each.

'That is one weird sheep,' Stevie said as she took her seat, leaning down to tickle Colin's ears. 'Normally they run a mile at the sight of a human, but this one seems to think he's a dog or something. Who does he belong to anyway?'

'The farmer who owns the field next door. He doesn't seem to mind Colin adopting me, as long as I send him back for clipping,' Nell said. 'He told me Colin was a sickie lamb – orphaned at birth and couldn't be matched with another ewe, so the family hand-reared him as a kind of pet.' She gave her contented sheep a stroke. 'Nice to know he won't be going anywhere.'

Stevie smiled. 'What on earth made you call him after your dad?'

'Something in the eyes, I think. They both look like they're constantly disapproving of me.' Nell nodded to the parcel. 'Is that my costume then?'

'Yep, I picked it up this morning.'

'Ta, love.' Nell took it from her and eyed it with trepidation. 'I'm actually pretty nervous about this Bunny Hop thing. Xander says it gets really competitive.'

'Heh, he's not wrong. It's full-on Thunderdome some years. This'll be my first year as a competitor too so better watch yourself, Miss Shackleton.'

'I'll make sure I sharpen my elbows.' Nell started peeling off the parcel tape. 'Where's Milly today?'

'Out with Deb. I wanted them to do a bit of bonding on their own so she's taking Mill to see the new *Dumbo*.'

'I take it that means things're going well.'

Stevie's cheeks pinkened a little. 'They are actually. Really well. Thanks, Nell.'

'Me? What for?'

'For talking me out of committing to a life of chaste, boring singledom. I forgot it could be like this. You know, love and all that.'

Nell looked up from her parcel to raise an eyebrow. 'That's a big word.'

'Yeah,' Stevie said with a sigh. 'And not one I'd expected ever to use again. But I'll shut up before you have to go dig the sick bags out. How are you and Xander getting along?'

'Great,' Nell said, smiling. 'I think we're at the big word stage ourselves, except neither of us wants to go first. Well, he kind of already did go first accidentally, but then he took it back straight away so it doesn't count.'

'Oh, get on with it. You two are made for each other.'

Nell shrugged. 'There's no hurry. When the time's right, we'll know.'

'Are you spending Easter together?'

'No, not this year. Xand's got plans with his mum, I think. Holidays are always a bit rough when you've lost someone, aren't they? I'm going home to do the family thing.'

'I guess your Freddie will be back from uni too, won't he?'

'He will, but he tends to spend Easter with his mum's family. She gets him for Easter and we get him for Christmas, that's the deal.'

'Your mum?' Stevie said. 'I thought you didn't have much contact.'

'No, not her.' Nell frowned with concentration as she struggled with the stubborn layers of tape on her Bunny Hop costume. 'I mean Alison, his birth mum.'

'What, is Freddie adopted?'

'Yeah.' Nell looked up from her parcel. 'I told you that, didn't I?'

'No, I don't think so.'

'Oh. Sorry, could've sworn I did. Yes, he tracked her down a few years ago. It was a rocky road, all those issues to work through, but they've got a pretty strong relationship now.'

'How do you feel about that?'

'Pleased for him, obviously. But…' She sighed. 'Stevie, am I a terrible person for being just a bit jealous?'

'Of course not, chicken.'

'It's just, Fred always had this close bond with Leanne, and now with Alison in his life too, it feels like he's got mums coming out of his ears and…'

'…and you haven't got any.'

'Yeah.'

Stevie gave her shoulder a squeeze. 'Why don't you talk to Leanne over Easter? Whatever's happened between you two in the past, that shouldn't stop you from building a better relationship as adults.'

'I'm just worried it's too late.'

'It's never too late to fix what's broken. She definitely wants you two to be closer; I could sense it at the fete.'

'You only spoke to her for a minute.'

'Still, I could tell. Mum instinct. So will you talk to her?'

'Well… maybe. If I can find a way to open the conversation.' Nell finally got the last piece of tape off the well-packed costume and shook it out of the wrapping. 'Um, Stevie. What the hell is this?'

Stevie snorted. 'Oh God.'

Nell turned the strapless black leotard around to examine the little white pompom tail on the bum, then picked up the matching ears and bow tie that went with it.

'Stevie, when you said you'd be able to pick me up a rabbit costume…'

'I didn't do it on purpose, Nell, I swear.'

'I can't do the race dressed as a bunny girl, can I? It's only three weeks since Ryan Theakston was trying to paint me as the official school harlot so I'd say this is the last thing my reputation needs.'

'Honestly, that's not the one I hired,' Stevie said, struggling to keep her face straight. 'They must've muddled the costumes or something. Here, give it back and I'll exchange it for you.'

Nell squinted down the track, where she could just make out Xander's tall frame striding towards them. 'Er… yeah. Actually, you mind if I hang on to it? Just till tomorrow.'

Stevie followed her gaze. 'Oh, I see. Well, just remember you'll lose your deposit if he rips your cotton tail off with his teeth in the throes of passion.' She finished her wine and stood up. 'Come on, Red. There's about to be some muggle-type shenanigans around here and I don't think we want to be present when they happen.' She ruffled Nell's hair. 'Have fun, you two.'

Chapter Twenty-Eight

When Xander joined Nell in the garden, he pulled her into his arms.

'Hiya beautiful,' he said, greeting her with a long kiss.

'Mmm. Nice. Now get off me, you're making Colin blush.' She pushed him back and tapped his nose. 'You're early.'

'Well, I wanted my surprise, didn't I?'

'It's actually two surprises. A planned one and an accidental one.'

Xander raised his eyebrows.

She laughed. 'Oh God, don't worry, not that kind of accidental surprise.'

He gave a low whistle. 'Bloody hell. You had me panicking for a second there.'

'OK, surprise number one.' She wriggled out of his arms so she could fetch the bunny girl outfit from her chair. 'Courtesy of Stevie and a mix-up at the costume shop, tonight's sexy fun gets to be in fancy dress.'

Xander took the leotard and held it up against him. 'I don't know, Nell. It's going to be a tight fit.'

She smiled. 'Well, do you want your other surprise?'

'Is it sexy?'

'Of course.'

He rubbed his hands. 'In that case, surprise away.'

'OK, close your eyes,' Nell commanded.

'Yes Miss.' Xander closed his eyes obediently and Nell took his hand to lead him into the farmhouse.

'Right, you can open them,' she said when they reached her bedroom.

'Wow,' he said, blinking. 'That is sexy.'

'Yep. Biggest one I could fit in the house. They did it in four sizes: queen, king, emperor and deputy head.'

Xander laughed and pulled her down onto the mattress of her brand new bed.

'Springy,' he said, nodding approvingly.

'You can do a lot of bouncing on it. I asked the man in the shop.'

'I like the sound of that.'

'Yeah, so did he.'

'So shall we christen it now, or do you want to slip into something less comfortable first and go get that bunny girl costume on?'

'If our sex life is supposed to be bringing the school into disrepute then we want to do it in style, don't we?'

'Hey.' Xander rolled on top of her, suddenly serious. 'Nell.'

'What's wrong, love?' she asked, stroking his hair away from his face.

'Nothing.' He smiled. 'That's just it, nothing's wrong at all. I don't think I've ever been so happy.'

'Aww.' She planted a soft kiss on his lips. 'Or me.'

'Nell, I...' He laughed, rubbing his hair like he always did when he felt awkward. 'I'm trying to say something important to you here but I'm making a mess of it. Which you could probably say is our entire relationship in a nutshell.'

Nell buried her face in his neck and flicked the tip of her tongue over his earlobe. 'I'm listening,' she whispered. 'Take your time, Xand. I've got plenty here to amuse myself with.'

'I just wanted to say... when you came to Leyholme, every-thing was the same. I mean, for me. Everything had always been the same here, and I was always the same; always uncertain of myself, afraid, out of place. All my life, I'd dreamed of leaving. And when you came I realised it wasn't Leyholme that was the problem – it was me. You made it all new, Nell. You made *me* new. Made me see myself in a different way, as a man I didn't need to feel ashamed of being – a man who was worth something. You saw that in me, and you made me believe in it too.' He took a deep breath. 'So I wanted to say, thank you, Nell Shackleton. For believing in me and fighting for me and making me happier than I've ever been in my whole life and… Jesus, Nell, for that thing you're doing with your tongue right now because it feels fucking magic.'

Nell laughed. 'It's kind of sexy when you swear, you know. For some reason it sounds extra naughty when you do it.' She looked up from his neck. 'Anyway, I'm the one who should thank you.'

'Why should you thank me?'

'Well, because you do some pretty magic things with your tongue too.' She drew her fingers over his cheek. 'And for making me fall in love with you.'

–

Xander was awake long before Nell had stirred the next morning. In the six weeks they'd been a couple, he'd learnt she was a dreadful slugabed on the weekends.

He liked that he was always awake first. It meant he could watch her sleep for a little while. Which depending on how you looked at it was either kind of adorable, like that bloke with the signs in *Love Actually*, or kind of creepy, like that bloke with the signs in *Love Actually*. He was hoping to weigh in on the side of adorable, since Nell was actually his girlfriend and not his best mate's wife. If he was sitting outside Justin's window with a long-lens camera, watching Sara sleep, that'd be slightly less romantic.

Not that Nell was an especially cute sleeper. She usually had her mouth wide open and quite often honked like a pig. But Xander was looking at her through the eyes of love, so to him

249

she was perfect no matter how much drool had escaped in the night.

She was cute right now though. Her cheeks were pink, hair tangled and *Dynasty* huge after their bed-testing exertions of the night before (further testified to by a crumpled bunny girl outfit tossed over the bedroom door). Xander bent to leave a kiss on her parted lips.

Nell grunted and swatted at him. In her dreams, she was probably being attacked by some slimy face-sucking insect. So much for romantic gestures.

Last night had felt significant. Their lovemaking had felt significant, despite the costumed fun. Like it meant something... new. The next stage. Nell had said she loved him, and later as she'd cried out and climaxed and he'd wrapped her up tight in his arms, Xander had whispered it back. He'd felt it for so long – since before they'd become a couple, although he'd hardly dared admit it to himself, then. But he'd waited until last night to finally say the words. They had power, even more than sex. After them, nothing could ever be the same.

He stroked gentle fingers over Nell's hair. Beautiful girl. He loved her a hell of a lot, in fact, and that in itself was pretty damn miraculous.

After Marie had left he'd thought that was probably it for him and women. He found them hard enough to talk to at the best of times, and it said a lot for Marie's dogged pursuit of him in the face of his social incompetence that he'd managed to find himself in even one long-term relationship. And it had hurt so much afterwards, for so long, he really hadn't felt like he could muster the energy again.

But then Nell had come along and made it all seem so easy. It had just needed the right person; that was all. The right fit.

He was seized with a desire to do something for her, to show her what she meant to him. Quietly so as not to wake her, he snuck out of bed and tiptoed into the kitchen.

He'd make her breakfast. Breakfast in bed. Wasn't that the sort of thing boys in Richard Curtis films did when they weren't stalking people with signs? Anything Hugh Grant could do, Xander Scott could do better.

Just inside the pantry hung a striped apron that Nell always forgot to wear. Xander grabbed it and pulled it over his naked body, tying it in a bow at the back.

After all, Nell had dressed up for him, and very sexy it'd been too. Now he could pay her back with a bit of naked butlering. Plus, sizzling fat and exposed genitals: probably not a good combination. He didn't fancy having to explain that one down at A&E.

Right. Breakfast for Nell. What could he make? He opened the fridge to explore.

Slim pickings but there were a couple of eggs, a block of butter and some milk, and a few slices of bread in the bread bin.

Scrambled egg on toast it was then. Everyone liked that, didn't they?

He took out the ingredients and started hunting around the kitchen cupboards for other useful equipment.

It didn't take him long to locate a pan, then he started pulling open drawers looking for a fish slice or a wooden spoon or something.

He had to smile at Nell's system of organisation – or rather her lack of system. In the top drawer, where most normal people kept their cutlery, she had a microwave instruction manual (although she didn't own a microwave), a torch, a packet of crayons and a tin opener. The middle drawer just seemed to be piles of old bills and other bits of correspondence.

Xander was about to close the drawer when he did a double take, spotting a signature on the letter sitting at the top of the pile.

Dominic Leary. Why did that name ring bells?

He looked more closely. It was a letter to Nell, saying how sorry they'd been at St Margaret's to receive her resignation.

Of course. Dominic Leary was the headteacher there. Xander had known the man a little when he'd been at St Mags' on placement, although Dom had only been a humble Year 6 class teacher then.

Hang on. Resignation? Hadn't Nell told him she'd been made redundant?

He jumped when he felt a pair of hands sliding over his bare buttocks.

'Mmm. I could get used to this view in the morning,' Nell murmured, kissing the back of his neck.

Xander turned to give her a proper kiss. 'Now you've spoiled my surprise. I was making you sexy breakfast in bed.'

'How about you come back to bed and make me sexy something else? Then we can both cook breakfast.'

He smiled. 'Sounds good to me.'

She glanced at the open drawer. 'Reading my post?'

'I was looking for a fish slice. Why don't you put things in normal drawers like normal people?'

'Because I'm me.' She opened a cupboard over his head and nodded to the pile of assorted utensils shoved in there. 'There you go.'

'You keep fish slices in the cupboard?' He shook his head. 'You're a monster.'

'Come back to bed, Xand,' she whispered, nibbling his earlobe. 'I'll make those noises you like.'

'Do you want me to keep the pinny on?'

'I shouldn't even need to dignify that with an answer.' She planted a soft kiss on his lips. 'Hey. Love you, OK?'

'I know.' He kissed her back. 'I love you too.'

Chapter Twenty-Nine

'This is wrong,' Xander muttered to himself as he held his office phone against his ear. 'What the hell are you playing at, Scott? She's your girlfriend, for Christ's sake!'

Nell was his girlfriend, and he was on the brink of doing something that technically amounted to stalking. Or at the very least, to spying. Whichever way you looked at it, it was a total breach of the trust that ought to exist between them as a couple.

But she wasn't just his girlfriend, was she? She was a member of staff at a school he was still technically the head of.

Yeah, for one more day, his inner voice reminded him. If only he'd never seen that letter, his stint as acting head would have been done with and it would've been someone else's problem.

Except he had seen it. He had seen it, and now he couldn't ever unsee it.

He put the phone handset back in its cradle. This was the fourth time he'd picked it up, listened to the dial tone until it had started making that siren noise and put it back down again.

It was the last day of term and Leyholme Primary was in festive mood. Afternoon lessons had been suspended so the staff and pupils could enjoy some fun Easter activities on the school field – egg-rolling, chocolate hunts, and of course the highlight of the spring calendar: the annual Parents versus Teachers Bunny Hop. Xander was due out there himself in half an hour. He cast a glance at the creepy Roger Rabbit-esque bunny suit hanging on his filing cabinet and shuddered.

His hand hovered over the phone again.

She wouldn't lie to him. Not Nell. Anyway, why should she? She had no reason to lie.

Nell had come to Leyholme with a glowing recommendation from her last school; he'd seen it with his own eyes. There was no logical reason why she would resign and then tell him she'd been made redundant. It was probably just a slip of the tongue.

Except it wasn't, was it? She'd specifically told him she'd been made redundant after changes to the catchment area at St Mags'. Why would she say that if it weren't true? Such a pointless lie, and such a stupid one given that he could so easily double-check its veracity. It didn't make sense.

It had been preying on Xander's mind all week, ever since he'd caught that glimpse of the letter in her kitchen drawer. No matter how often he tried to tell himself it was all nothing, most likely just a misunderstanding, he couldn't get it out of his head.

He knew it was wrong to distrust Nell, to look into her affairs behind her back. But he needed to know. He was still head of this school, he had responsibilities, and he needed to know. Steeling himself, he picked up the handset again and dialled the number he had up on his PC screen.

'Um, good afternoon,' he said to the school secretary when she answered. 'Mr Leary, please. Tell him it's Alexander Scott at Leyholme Primary.'

'Xander! Well, well, well, it's been a long time,' the head-teacher of St Margaret's said when the secretary had put Xander through. 'Good to hear from you, mate. How are things in the wilderness? I'm told congratulations are in order.'

'Sorry?'

'You've been promoted, haven't you? Deputy head? Or have I been misinformed?'

'Oh. Yes,' Xander said. 'Well, it doesn't take effect till after Easter, but thanks.'

'So what can I do you for?'

'Dom, this is going to sound like an odd question, but humour me. Is your catchment area at St Mags' the same as it was when I was on placement there?'

There was a pause. 'Well, yes. Essentially. Why?'

'So you haven't seen a decline in pupil numbers at all? Or had to let go of any staff?'

Dominic laughed. 'God, no. We're fighting the kids off with sticks here – I mean, not literally, obviously, although it is the last day of term so it's a close-run thing. You know how they get.'

'OK,' Xander said quietly. 'Thanks. That's all I wanted to know.'

'How's our Miss Shackleton getting along up there? You know, we may never forgive you for stealing her from us. Especially some of the male members of staff, if you know what I mean.'

'Fine, Dom. She's doing fine.'

'Tell her we miss her, won't you? We were very sorry to lose her. But our loss is your gain, eh?'

'Yes.'

'Why the sudden concern over our pupil numbers then, Xander?'

'Oh, Chinese whispers. Nothing to do with Nell, just... something an old colleague mentioned. I thought there must have been some misunderstanding.'

'Well, it certainly sounds like it,' Dominic said. 'Anyway, better get on. Stay in touch, won't you?'

'Yeah. Bye, Dom. Thanks.'

Xander put the phone down, feeling like the bottom might just have dropped out of the rose-tinted new world he'd been building for himself with Nell.

So she had lied to him. For absolutely no reason that he could see, she'd been telling him falsehoods almost since the day they'd met.

Of her own volition, Nell had quit a good job – a great job, at one of the country's best state primary schools, apparently for the sole purpose of living in a broken-down old farmhouse in the middle of nowhere. In Leyholme, for Christ's sake! Taken a job at a school with a mediocre reputation and falling pupil numbers when she could have picked her own role anywhere in the country. Why?

And then there was that weirdness with her parents when they'd come to visit. There was a mystery somewhere here that Xander couldn't put his finger on.

His fingers hovered over his computer keyboard, reluctant to take the next step.

She'd be angry if she found out. Maybe he should just talk to her.

But then, how would he know she wasn't lying to him again? How would he know anything was real – her love for him, anything?

His feelings for Nell, his responsibility to the school – everything was so jumbled up, he didn't know what the right thing to do was any more. Maybe Ryan had been right after all. Things got messy when headteachers fell for members of their staff.

Making his decision, he typed Nell's name into Google.

There was nothing much for Nell Shackleton, or for Eleanor Shackleton either. Just the usual odds and sods of professional references, social media accounts, occasional mentions in the local papers in relation to school events, that sort of thing. Nothing that pointed to what was going on here.

He paused for a moment, then typed in the name of her brother, Freddie Shackleton. He'd been acting oddly at the fete too, although subsequent events with Xander's mum had all but pushed that out of his mind. Whatever was going on, Freddie seemed to be in on it.

There was more for him than for Nell, despite his relative youth. Twenty pages of results.

Xander thought for a moment, trying to remember exactly what had happened at the fete. Freddie had turned up with Nell's parents and she'd seemed… horrified, that was the only word for it. He could still remember how the colour had drained from her face when she'd spotted them. *They can't be here*, that's what she'd said. And then her dad had acted so strangely when she'd introduced him to Xander and Stevie.

Xander frowned. No. It hadn't been him, had it? It was when Stevie came over with Milly. That's when Nell's dad had started looking stern and dragged Nell off for a private chat.

Stevie. Nell's best friend. And that had sprung up pretty quickly. When? How?

Nell… she'd pulled Milly from the road. She and Stevie had become pretty inseparable after that. Was Stevie part of this mystery too, whatever it was?

Surely not. Xander had known Stevie Madeleine for over thirteen years. They were friends, very good friends. She'd helped him through his grief after he'd lost his dad, even though he'd found it so hard at the time to talk to Marie about it. And then she'd confided in him how emotionally confused she still felt years later because Angela had been killed right after confessing to an affair. He trusted Stevie inside out and back to front.

Feeling a surge of foreboding, Xander added the name 'Stephanie Madeleine' to his Google search after Freddie's.

Five matches for the two names together. Deeply uneasy about what he might be about to find out, Xander clicked on the top link.

—

Nell turned around when she felt someone flick her cotton tail.

'I like it,' Stevie said, nodding. 'Do bunnies usually wear gingham pinnies?'

'Have you just come over to mock me?'

'Of course. What else are friends for?'

'I look like Bugs Bunny when he dresses as a Southern belle to seduce Elmer Fudd,' Nell said, straightening the straw hat that had come with her baby-blue bunny suit. 'Can't believe I have to let Xander see me in this.'

Stevie shrugged. 'It always turned Elmer on, didn't it?'

'Yeah. You know, you have to wonder about that guy's obsessive, quasi-sexual relationship with rabbits.'

'Where is Xander?' Stevie asked, scanning the school field for him.

An assortment of rabbits – or in their more familiar guises, the mums, dads and teachers of Leyholme – were chatting and drinking lemonade, giving no sign of the carnage to come when the race heats started in quarter of an hour or so. The kids were already lined up on the forms that had been placed either side of the race track, glaring at one another. There was a lot of family honour at stake when it came to the school's annual Parents versus Teachers Bunny Hop.

'Hiding in his office,' Nell said with a smirk. 'I've got a strong suspicion his costume's hugely embarrassing.'

'What, haven't you seen it?'

'Nope. He's been keeping it top secret all week.' She frowned. 'He's been a bit quiet generally actually. I hope everything's OK at home. Have you seen his mum recently?'

'Yeah, I saw her yesterday when she came round ours to talk to Deb about their new dog-grooming venture. Seemed as happy as Larry, whoever that jolly bastard was. She's a month sober now.'

'Hmm. Maybe he's just worried about today then.'

'So, are you prepared to be annihilated?' Stevie asked. 'I had Janet Rhodes fix it so we're in the same heat.'

'Aww, come on,' Nell said, pouting. 'Aren't you going to let me win? I'm your best friend.'

Stevie shrugged. 'Sorry, family comes first. I made a solemn promise to Milly that I'd do everything in my power to kick your arse.'

'What do we win anyway?'

'Oh, some naff little trophy. It's not about that, though.' Stevie clasped a fist to her bosom. 'This is about honour.'

Nell scanned Stevie's costume, which basically amounted to a fluffy tail and a pair of ears on top of her normal clothes. 'I reckon you should be disqualified for that.'

'Hey. This is perfectly serviceable rabbit gear.'

'It's not right, you know. Leaving all of us teachers who can't get away with that kind of blatant cheating to sweat like hogs.'

Stevie grinned. 'Yep. Told you, by fair means or foul, I've got some staff bottom to kick this afternoon.'

Nell peered over her. 'Oh, there's Xander, look.' She snorted. 'Oh God, that is horrendous. He looks like a pink-and-white version of the creepy ghost rabbit in *Donnie Darko*.'

'Oof,' Stevie said, grimacing at Xander in his fluffy bunny outfit. 'Nell, if he suggests any sort of kinky role play in this gear, you need to get that boy looked at.'

'I'll go say hi before the race starts.' Nell leaned over to peck Stevie's cheek. 'Good luck, eh? May the best bunny win.'

'And the best bunny is of course me. I'm off to do some training.'

Nell laughed as her friend hopped away.

Deciding she'd save her own hopping technique for the race itself – you never knew who might be about, making notes on tactics – Nell went to get a couple of lemonades from the refreshment stand and joined Xander by the track.

'Nice,' she said, nodding to his costume.

'Cheers.'

He looked sort of pale, his eyes glassy as he focused on the finish line ahead. Nell sensed the old anxiety was kicking in and held out a lemonade to him.

'Here you go, Harvey, got you a drink.'

'I'm fine, thanks.'

'Oh. Right. Yeah, it probably is a good idea to avoid anything gassy when we're about to be hopping.' She fanned herself with one hand. 'It's so hot in this costume though.'

'Oh God, I can't do this,' he muttered to himself.

'Xander, don't worry yourself about it,' Nell said gently, putting one hand on his shoulder. 'It's only a daft race. I know everyone takes it too seriously, but it's a bit of fun at the end of the day. Nothing to get worked up over.'

He snorted. 'Nothing to get worked up over. OK.'

'What's up?' Nell said, frowning. 'Is something wrong, sweetheart?'

'Nell, I can't… look, talk to me after. I can't do this now.'

'Right,' Nell said, blinking. She knew Xander's nerves were always one step away from sending him into a blind panic, but she hadn't expected him to get quite so upset about a silly novelty race.

'You're still coming round later, aren't you?' she said. 'I made lasagne for us and got some red wine in. Celebrate the last day of term and all that.'

'I said not now, Nell.' He shrugged off her hand and walked away, his face twitching feverishly.

Nell stared after him. What the hell was the matter?

He'd been fine earlier – a bit quiet, but he hadn't seemed like he was about to go into meltdown. Now… she hadn't seen him this bad since the day of the governors' meeting when Ryan had tried to get him sacked.

But she had no time to ponder Xander's inexplicable shift in mood. Just then Mrs Rhodes, who was umpiring, blew the whistle for the participants in the first heat – which included Nell and Stevie – to line up at the end of the track.

'All right, this is how it will work,' Mrs Rhodes said through her megaphone. 'Each heat will have a winner, scoring one point for either the staff or the parents. The team with the most points wins, and there'll also be a final heat with all the winners taking part to decide today's overall champion. Are we ready, everyone?'

Nell shot a look at Stevie and narrowed her eyes. 'Game on,' she mouthed.

'Bring it,' Stevie mouthed back.

260

'OK, on your marks,' Mrs Rhodes said, whistle poised. 'Get set. Go!'

They did go: Stevie, Jolene and two of the dads on one side of the track versus Nell, Frank, Caroline and Callum on the other. Then they all stopped and went back to the beginning when Mrs Rhodes declared a false start because Callum had set off too early. In the end, it took three attempts to get all the participants off hopping in a fair and equitable way.

Nell soon saw what Stevie and Xander had meant about the spirit of healthy competition between parents and teachers. It was so healthy it was almost deadly, in fact. Jolene Hancock was particularly brutal, showing no compunction about running with her elbows at right angles and nearly elbowing Callum – who, according to popular gossip, she'd recently begun dating – where no male bunny ought to be elbowed.

Nell had never been a PE-type person, her desire to win far weaker than her desire not to do anything that amounted to strenuous physical exercise. But she did like a novelty race, if only because it took fitness out of the equation to some extent and gave her a chance of actually coming first.

At the start she was trailing in second-to-last place, but a lot of the other competitors had costumes heavier and hotter than hers. Many didn't seem to have practised their hopping technique either – Frank and one of the dads were actually disqualified for skipping when they ought to be jumping. The upshot of it all was that as she bounced towards the finish line, Nell found herself hopping neck and neck with Stevie Madeleine.

Stevie looked across at her, her face fixed into a determined frown. For a moment, it looked like it was going to be a photo finish. Then Stevie smiled and slightly, ever so slightly, hung back as Nell hopped through the ribbon.

'And the winner of the first race: Miss Shackleton!' Mrs Rhodes declared, to cheers from Nell's pupils on the forms nearby. 'Well done. That's the first point to the staff.'

'Congratulations, chicken,' Stevie said to Nell as they all staggered to the refreshments laid out waiting for them.

'Not that I deserve them.' Nell lowered her voice. 'Why'd you let me win, Stevie?'

'What? Scurrilous lies. You beat me fair and square.'

'Come on.'

Stevie laughed and pulled her into a hug. 'Well, perhaps I couldn't bear to see your sad, losery little bunny face if I won. I am sort of fond of you, you know.'

'Aww.' Nell gave her a squeeze back.

Stevie frowned as she released Nell from the hug, nodding to Xander. He was lining up with the rest of his heat at the start line, watching the pair of them with a worried look on his face. 'What's up with Bunny Boy?'

'I don't know,' Nell said, helping herself to an orange wedge. 'He was being weird before the race as well. Nerves, I think.'

Nell waited for Xander to finish his heat, hoping he'd come and talk to her, but as soon as he'd crossed the finish line he disappeared back inside.

'Something's wrong,' she whispered to Stevie. 'I'd better go find him.'

'You'll have to stay for the final race first. The winners' heat, remember?'

'Oh. Yeah.'

Stevie squeezed her arm. 'I hope he's OK. Call me later if you need me, eh?'

'I will. Thanks, Stevie.'

Feeling unsettled, Nell went to sit with her class while she waited for the final race.

Chapter Thirty

Nell managed to invalid herself out of the winners' race in the end. Filled with worry about what might be wrong with Xander – who never did reappear after losing his heat – she hadn't been concentrating properly and managed to trip on another competitor's flailing limb. She'd had to sit out the rest of the race, a handkerchief filled with slightly lemonadey ice pressed against her swollen ankle.

After it was all over, Nell unbunnied herself and limped to Xander's office. But there was no familiar 'come in' in response to her knock.

He hadn't gone home, had he? They were supposed to be leaving together.

'Xand?' she said, peeping round the door. 'You there?'

Yes, he was there, although he didn't speak to answer her. He was sitting behind his desk, back in his regular work suit, staring blankly at the computer screen with his glasses on top of his head. His eyes were red, like he'd been crying.

'What's up, love?' she asked, coming in. 'Why'd you disappear? Me and Stevie were worried about you.'

'I needed to be on my own.'

He still wasn't looking at her. Something was wrong. Seriously wrong.

'Xander, did I do something to upset you?' she asked, frowning.

'Well. It's not really about me, all this, is it?' He pressed his face into his hands. 'Christ, I've been blind!'

'Blind? Xander, I don't understand. What's going on?'

'I should've seen. It was all there for me to see. But like a moon-eyed schoolboy I was falling in love, so all I could see was you, Nell.' He rubbed his face and pulled his hands away. 'Or do you prefer Jemima?'

She staggered backwards, pain she barely registered coursing through her sore ankle.

'What?' she whispered, clutching at a chair for support.

'That is the name you were born with, right? Jemima Madeleine? I don't think there's much point trying to deny it now.'

'How... who told you that?'

'It's all here,' Xander said, nodding to the screen. 'Your brother's not quite so discreet in making enquiries on your behalf as you might have hoped, I think. He's left a trail as long as your arm on various genealogy sites and forums, looking for information about a Stephanie Madeleine and her family. Mother to one Jemima Madeleine, who was given up for adoption at birth when her mother was just fifteen. That's you, right?'

'You've been checking up on me?'

'Yeah, and you've been lying through your teeth for months so don't come the moral high ground angle with me. I know you weren't made redundant, Nell; I spoke to Dom Leary.'

'Xander...' Nell came forward and put a hand on his arm, but he jerked it away.

'Don't touch me.'

'Please don't be angry. Sweetheart, I'm sorry. I never wanted you to find out like this.'

'Nell, do you have any idea how unethical this is?' he exploded. 'You engineered this! This job, the move to Leyholme, this whole so-called new start...' He paused. 'Me?'

She winced. 'No. No, you were just... something that happened.'

He pressed his fingers against his eyelids. 'Jesus, she's in your fucking class,' he muttered. 'Your own sister, and she doesn't

264

know. That's wrong on so many levels, I don't even know where to start with it.'

Nell sank into a chair and swallowed a sob.

'Why'd you do it?' Xander demanded. 'Why did you lie?'

'I just… I couldn't be sure you'd understand. And you were the head, it would've compromised you professionally if I'd asked you to keep secrets for me. I lied about being made redundant to stop you getting suspicious and asking questions about why I came here – I mean, I wouldn't have if I'd known you had a St Mags' connection, but it was too late then. I felt guilty about it, but… Xander, I didn't see any other way.'

'Not why did you lie to me, why did you lie to Stevie? She had a right to know – to choose.'

Nell gave up fighting and let her tears flow.

'Because… because she didn't want me,' she gasped.

'She was a child, Nell.'

'I mean, she still didn't want me. She registered a wish for no contact on the Adoption Contact Register.'

'What?' Xander stared at her in disbelief. 'She registered to say she didn't want any contact with you and you… you thought you'd go and trick her into it instead? Christ, Nell!'

'I just thought, once we had a relationship…' Nell looked up at him, her eyes drenched. 'Xander, my adoptive mum walked out on me and Freddie when we were small because she discovered my dad had been the one firing blanks and not her. Who wants an adopted family when you can have a real one, right? That's how she saw it – we were always second-best, the consolation prize. In her mind, we always belonged to someone else.'

Xander's expression softened slightly.

'Here,' he said, passing her a box of tissues from his desk.

'Do you know what that feels like, to be rejected by not one but two mums before you've even turned ten? To be thrown away twice, like a used fucking hanky or something?' Nell looked down at the tissue in her hand and paused to blow

265

her nose. 'All my childhood, especially after my mum left, I dreamed about my birth mum.' She coughed out a sob. 'Oh, she was so perfect, Xander. Beautiful, loving, fun, kind – everything I didn't have.'

'Is that why things were tough with your stepmum?' Xander asked in a gentler voice.

She nodded. 'Every time Leanne tried to be a parent to me, I couldn't help comparing her with the dream mum I'd created. It wasn't fair, but neither was I at that age. I felt badly about it when I was older, but even so, I never let go of the dream.'

'So what happened?'

Nell tossed her saturated tissue in the wastepaper basket and started mopping her eyes with another. 'When I became an adult, with my dad's blessing I looked up my birth mum on the Adoption Contact Register. And there she was: Stephanie Madeleine. I was ecstatic when I saw the name.' She snorted. 'But then I read the entry. *Stephanie Madeleine wishes for no contact.* And it felt like she'd given me away all over again. Another rejection, another kick in the gut.'

Xander still looked hurt, but his eyes had filled with sympathy.

'I'm sorry, Nell.'

'It was Freddie's idea, my coming here,' Nell murmured. 'He got in touch with his birth mother Alison when he was eighteen – she'd wanted contact and in the end it had worked out really well. He thought, if my mum just got to know me then she'd change her mind. So two years ago he found her for me.' She laughed through her sobs. 'But it was just another daft Freddie scheme. I never seriously thought of doing it, not back then.'

'And the fiancé, did he know you'd found your birth mum?'

'Shawn?' She snorted. 'No. Although you might say he's the reason I ended up here.'

'Why?'

'I knew she lived in Leyholme – my mum and her other daughter. With my brother's help I found out all I could about them. I knew she'd been widowed, who her wife had been, what her job was. I even drove here once and looked around the village. Saw their house. Them. Ages ago, when Milly was a toddler.' She sniffed. 'I know it sounds kind of stalkery, but... I'd dreamed about her for so long. I just wanted to know what her life was like. If she looked like me, spoke like me. If the reality matched the fantasy I'd nursed all through my childhood.' She looked up at him, her eyes pleading for reassurance. 'Wouldn't you?'

'I... don't know,' he said in a low voice. 'I've never had to think about it.'

'And I've had my whole life to think about it.'

'So Shawn never knew.'

'No, I never told him. Like I said, it was just a fantasy. I came here once to satisfy my curiosity, then I told myself that was it, all there could ever be. I knew my mum didn't want to know me. I suppose I could have hated her for that, but I never did.' Nell smiled a bittersweet smile. 'She was still my secret dream.'

'Did it hurt?'

'Yes, Xand, it hurt. I used to think about her life here, in this beautiful place with her beautiful little girl, the little girl who wasn't me. Make myself cry with it after Shawn was asleep. Happy they were happy, and miserable because I couldn't ever be part of it.'

'So you made yourself a part of it.'

'Yes. Yes, I...'

She stopped for a moment, her body shuddering with sobs.

'Don't go on if it's too hard,' Xander said softly.

'No, it's OK. I want you to know.' She took a deep breath. 'I saw there was a job opening here for an Early Years teacher. I was an Early Years teacher. Fate, right? And in the very year my own little sister had started in Reception at the same school. It would've been the perfect way for me to build a relationship with her and her mum – our mum – without them suspecting who I was.'

'So you went for it.'

She shook her head. 'No, not then. I was tempted for maybe a nanosecond, but I knew it was madness. I was about to get married, build a life and family of my own. So I pushed it to the back of my mind, convinced myself I'd forgotten all about it. Then I found out Shawn had cheated on me and… everything changed.'

'And we still had a job opening.'

She nodded, looking down at her feet. 'Freddie said I should go for it. That the job and Shawn cheating must've been a sign from the universe, like it was just… meant to be. I thought, why the hell not? I literally had nothing left in my old life.'

'And what about what Stevie wanted, Nell?' Xander asked quietly. 'Didn't you think about that?'

'I thought… I hoped if I could get to know her as a friend first, she'd change her mind about no contact.' She laughed bleakly. 'And it went so well, better than I could ever have hoped. I mean, I didn't even need to seek her out – she came to me. Then we hit it off right away, like that was the way things were always supposed to happen, and she turned out to be just as perfect as I'd always dreamed she would be. Better even, because she was so completely real and human.' Nell looked up to meet his eyes. 'I was always going to tell her, Xand. I just needed to wait until the time was right. Another rejection would've broken me.'

To her surprise, Xander flinched as he succumbed to tears of his own.

'Nell, Jesus Christ, this is… I wish you'd told me.'

'How could I tell you? What would you have done?'

'I don't know what I'd have done but I feel like I had a right to know before you started sleeping with me, don't you?' He wiped his swimming eyes. 'Why did you?'

'Why did I what?'

'Why did you want to be with me? To cover your tracks? Get the boss into bed, avoid any inconvenient questions?'

'What? No! Xander, you can't really believe that. I just...
fell in love with you.'

He winced as if he was in pain. 'Please don't say that. Not
now.'

'I swear to you, it's true. It wasn't in my plan – actually it was
pretty bloody inconvenient – but I couldn't help it.' She choked
on another sob. 'You became part of the dream too. You, and
Stevie, and Milly, and the farmhouse, and Leyholme. And me.
Somewhere to belong. You have to believe that whatever lies I
told you, the way I feel about you wasn't one.'

He buried his face in his hands again and she saw him shaking
as he struggled with strong emotions.

'You betrayed my trust, Nell,' he whispered. 'I honestly don't
know what to believe.'

She looked down. 'I'm sorry.'

'And now I have to make a choice. A choice between what
I want to do and what I know I ought to do. I can't even think
straight to work out what's right and wrong any more.' He
looked up at her, his face soaked. 'Nell, as head of this school it's
my moral duty to take this to the governors. Your professional
behaviour, exploiting your position to build a relationship with
your biological family against their specified wishes – it's beyond
unethical, you must know that.'

'I know,' she said, hanging her head. 'I knew that's what
you'd have to do.'

'And if I do, I doubt you'll ever get another teaching post.
It'll ruin your career.'

'I know that too.'

'Did you even think about that when you hatched this
ridiculous plan?'

'Yes,' she whispered. 'I knew it could come to this and I
didn't care. I just wanted my mum.'

He fell silent.

'Miss Shackleton, I want your resignation on my desk before
you leave today,' he said finally in a toneless voice, looking away

from her. 'Make up any excuse you like – family problems, illness, anything. The governors will see that you're provided with a reference, I'm sure, and with your experience at St Mags' you should walk into another job.'

'What?'

'You heard what I said. And then you need to tell Stevie the truth, before I do.'

'Xander...' She reached for his hand, but he pulled it away.

'You'd better go,' he said in the same flat voice.

'Xander, I'm sorry. I'm so, so sorry.'

'Nell, please.' His voice quivered with hurt. 'Just go, can you?'

'If that's what you want.' She stood and hobbled to the door on her sore ankle, her shoulders hunched with shame.

She opened the door, then turned back.

'I really do love you, you know,' she said in a quiet voice.

Xander didn't answer. He just stared with unseeing eyes at his computer screen, tears dripping unchecked over his cheeks.

Chapter Thirty-One

Stevie put the last bit of washing-up on the draining board and wiped her hands on a tea towel.

'Milly Angela Madeleine! Where are you and what mischief are you up to?' she called out.

'Here, Mummy.'

Milly came marching in dressed in her beloved Little Red Riding Hood cape, a hiking pole in each hand and Red trotting along at her feet as usual.

Stevie laughed. 'What, is Red Riding Hood going mountaineering again?'

Milly nodded. 'We're climbing to Grandma's house. Mummy, can I have the basket?'

'Here you go.' Stevie fished a little straw basket out of the pantry, tipping out the baking potatoes she kept in there when it wasn't being commandeered for Little Red Riding Hood duties. 'Poor old basket's getting a bit tatty, I'm afraid.'

'Deb says she's going to bring me a better one from her house, 'specially for playing Red Riding Hood.'

'Did she? Well, that was very kind of her.' Stevie looked down at her daughter's beaming face. 'Do you like Deb, Mill?'

Milly nodded vigorously. 'She's funny. I like when her and Life stay at our house and when we go out to play in the park.'

'I'm glad. I like her a lot too.'

'Mummy, can we have biscuits to take to Grandma's house?'

Stevie laughed. 'Hmm. I suspect the biscuits won't be coming back from Grandma's house, will they? But go on, since it's the holidays now and I'm in a good mood.' She dug out a couple of Jaffa cakes and a dog treat for Red and put them in Milly's basket. 'There you go. Nothing else to eat before bed now though, that's your supper.'

'Thank you,' Milly chanted dutifully, then went skipping off upstairs with her booty.

Stevie was just about to throw herself down on the living room sofa and relax with a book when someone knocked at the front door.

She opened it to find Nell on the doorstep, smiling a little anxiously.

'Hi,' Nell said.

'Hiya. Didn't expect to see you after your hard day's bunnying.' Stevie frowned. 'Anything wrong? You look strange.'

'No. Yes.' Nell was still sporting the same worried smile, and her face seemed whiter than usual. 'Stevie, can I come in? I want to talk to you about something.'

'Of course, chicken. Come on through.'

Nell limped to the living room and took a seat on the sofa, perching on the end as if she might suddenly need to make a run for it.

'How's the ankle?' Stevie asked.

'Still sore, but the swelling's gone down a bit.'

'Glad to hear it. That was quite a tumble you took.'

'Yes.'

'So, glass of something to toast the end of term? You earned a drink today, I think.'

'Thank you, no. Not now.'

'Nell, what's wrong?' Stevie asked gently. Her friend's eyes looked puffy and tired, as if she'd been crying, and she clearly wasn't her usual bubbly self. 'Is this about Xander acting oddly at the Bunny Hop? Did you two have a row or something?'

'Yes. Quite a big one.'

'Oh, sweetie.' Stevie took a seat next to her and pulled her into a hug. 'Now, don't worry, all couples have a big one at some point in the early days. This just means you've got it out of the way, that's all. If there's one thing I know, it's that that boy's completely crazy about you.'

Nell sniffed, burying her head in Stevie's shoulder. 'Thanks,' she whispered. 'But it's... I didn't come to see you about the row with Xander. Well, I sort of did, but not just that.'

'What did you come to see me for?'

Nell drew back and wiped her eyes. 'Stevie, I just resigned from my job.'

Stevie blinked in shock. 'What? Why would you do that?'

'I had to. I... I did something really unprofessional. Something that meant I couldn't remain in my position.' Nell laughed slightly manically, resting her fingers against her temples. 'And the thing is, I don't even care. I don't care about anything except... except...'

'What?'

'The argument I had with Xander. Don't you want to know what it was about?'

'What was it about?' Stevie asked, feeling more confused by the second.

'It was about you.'

She frowned. 'Me? Nell, I don't understand.'

'Xander found out...' Nell took a deep breath. 'Stevie, I'm so sorry I waited until now to tell you, but... I'm her.'

'Her?'

'Yes. I'm... I'm Jemima.'

Stevie felt the blood drain from her face.

'What?' she whispered, recoiling. 'No. No, you can't be.'

'I'm so sorry.' Nell shuffled round and eagerly took Stevie's hands. 'I know you didn't want any contact. I know how wrong it was, to trick you into a friendship that way. But Stevie, I'd dreamed of you for so long. And when a position opened up at the school here and then I had to end things with my fiancé, it just felt like fate or something. You understand, don't you?'

273

'I don't… you're her? You're that little baby?' Stevie felt like she might be about to faint.

'I'm your little baby. I know, it's a lot to take in.' Nell's eyes were shining now as she rambled feverishly. 'And I know I did a stupid, wrong thing, but I only did it because it meant so much to me to know you and be part of your world and have all the things I never had – a mum and a sister and a whole village I could belong to. And Xander… well, he's angry now but he'll come round when he knows you're not upset with me. We'll be so happy, all of us, I know it.'

'You threw your job away for this, for…'

'For you. That's right.' Nell squeezed Stevie's hands tightly. 'But that doesn't matter. Nothing matters but this. Me and you.'

'How did you find me?'

'Freddie did it. He found all the Stephanie Madeleines who could have been you on the electoral roll, then narrowed it down using forums and social media till he was sure he had the right one.' Nell laughed. 'Then he kind of gave you to me, as a present. That's so Freddie.'

'Why? Why go to all that trouble?'

'Because he knew how much I'd always wanted you. Because…' Nell took a deep breath. 'Because you're my mum and I love you and this is all I ever wanted, if you'll just tell me it's OK and you want me too. You do, don't you?'

The sharp, stabbing pain in Stevie's abdomen when Nell said the word 'mum' almost made her vomit. She snatched her hands away, anger and hurt clawing their way through her initial shock.

'Nell. Jemima. Jesus Christ!' She jumped to her feet, backing away. 'What the hell is this? You… you lied to me. You tricked me.'

Nell blinked. 'Aren't you… Stevie, aren't you pleased? I was sure you would be, now you know me.'

'You know who the first Jemima was, Nell? She was a doll, for fuck's sake. My best one from when I was a kid. I gave her my very favourite cutesy-pie name. And when I had a baby, I gave her the same name. You know why? Because I was a child. A child who'd made a child, but was still young enough to see a doll.'

'Stevie, what're you saying?'

Stevie's head was spinning dangerously, and she gripped the mantelpiece for support. Nell stood up, offering a hand to help steady her, but Stevie recoiled from it as if it was something venomous.

'Didn't it occur to you that the reason I specified no contact might have nothing to do with you?' she demanded in a shrill, choked voice. 'That there might be things I didn't want to think about – things I never wanted Jemima to know?'

Nell stared at her. 'I thought... you were so young. Wasn't that why you gave me up?'

'I gave you up because... because every time I looked at you, every time I thought about you, I remembered the night you were made and... and Reuben, the piece of shit I made you with. Even when you were a newborn baby, I suffered flashbacks to that night just from looking at you.'

Stevie shuddered as the full horror of her first sexual experience washed over her again. She could taste it, as real and vivid as it had been that night. The sweating bulk that barely seemed human, pinning her in place as she sobbed with pain and humiliation. His breath, his smell, that festering mix of sickly-sweet alcopops and cigarette smoke and body odour. The dirty things he'd slurred in her ear that had made her burn with shame. The jeering laughter of her so-called friends somewhere nearby.

Nell took a step backwards, hurt and pain in her eyes.

'What are you saying? Flashbacks of... you weren't raped?'

'No, but at fourteen I was hardly in a position to give informed consent either. He was in Year 12, two years older than me, and the bastard took full advantage of everything he knew and I didn't.'

'Oh my God.' Nell steadied herself against the mantelpiece, the blood draining from her cheeks.

'Nell, how could you do this?' Stevie whispered. 'I trusted you. I thought we were friends.'

'I didn't know. If I had I would never have... Stevie, I'm so sorry.'

'I... I can't do this. I'm not your mum, Nell, I never can be. Go now, please.'

'But I—'

'When I said I didn't want any contact with Jemima, it never was about her. It was about me – what happened to me. And now...' She put a hand to her head, which was burning with a sudden fever. 'Shit, I never wanted my baby to have to know this. I never wanted her to look at her own face in the mirror and feel the hate and disgust I felt looking at mine for so long after that night. I gave her away so she wouldn't have to grow up with the knowledge of how she'd been made.'

'Stevie...'

She clasped a hand to her mouth, feeling bile rising up her gullet. 'Nell, please. I need you to go.'

'I... Stevie, I...'

Stevie let out a gasping sob, almost hyperventilating now as the scents and sounds of that night battered her senses. 'Please. Please, just get out. I can't *do* this!'

Nell took a last horrified look at Stevie's ashen face and stumbled to the door.

As soon as she heard the front door click closed, Stevie ran to the toilet and retched up the contents of her stomach, bathing her face with tears while she vomited.

Chapter Thirty-Two

There was a hesitant little knock on the bathroom door.

'Mummy?' whispered a worried voice. 'Are you still being sick? You've been in the toilet for ages.'

Stevie gripped the toilet bowl with both hands, willing back the waves of nausea she didn't seem to have any control over. She'd had flashbacks to that night before now, the night of the party, but it was nearly thirty years since she'd had a physical reaction as strong as this.

'It's… OK, duckling,' she gasped. 'Mummy's OK. I ate something bad, that's all.'

'Did you have a fight with Miss Shackleton?' Milly asked in a trembling voice. 'I heard shouting.'

'Not… not exactly. Not really a fight.'

'Won't you be friends any more? Will I have to stop going to school?'

'Sweetie, could you give your mum ten minutes?' Stevie paused as her throat convulsed, but she managed to suppress the wave of bile pushing up from her gut. 'I'll be OK when I've finished being sick. I just need to get all the bad stuff up.'

There was silence.

'Milly?' Stevie said.

'Shall I make you Ribena?' the little voice asked.

Stevie couldn't help smiling. Whenever Milly was poorly, Stevie always made her hot Ribena in her favourite mug and the little girl had come to see it as the cure for all ills.

'I don't think this is the kind of poorly that gets better from Ribena,' Stevie said. 'I really just need to finish being sick. Tell you what, why don't you go get your PJs on and get into bed? I'll be there in no time to read you a story.'

'Promise?'

'Promise.'

There was a pause, then she heard Milly's steps disappearing in the direction of her bedroom.

When she was gone, Stevie gave in to her body's demands and retched over the bowl again. But her stomach was empty, and bitter-tasting acid all she could produce.

'This is over,' she muttered. 'It can't hurt you any more, Stevie. It's over, gone, done.'

But whenever she tried to reassure herself, another strong image – a picture, or a smell, or a sound – pushed itself to the front of her brain with such force that her body couldn't help but react.

She'd suffered for this. She'd lived this once. Why was it coming back to haunt her now?

When she'd given up Jemima, the teenage Stevie had thought that was it: she could put it all behind her and go back to being just a kid again. But it hadn't worked that way. After that night at the party, it had been years until she'd been able to make her peace with her body. The day she realised that had finally happened – the day she knew she'd fallen in love with Angela – her inner voice had whispered *victory*.

But it hadn't been victory, not really. That night was always lurking in her subconscious, waiting for the trigger that would unleash it.

She stood up and swilled her clammy face with cold water. A frightened fourteen-year-old looked in the mirror to see a pale, middle-aged woman staring back.

Eventually, after another half-hour of intermittent retching, Stevie was able to get brain and body back under her own control. After flushing the toilet, she rinsed her mouth out with mouthwash, wiped her sweat-sodden face and went to find Milly.

She smiled at the sight that met her in Milly's bedroom. The little girl was in her pyjamas, tucked up in the bottom bunk, with her clothes folded neatly over the chair and all her toys out of sight in the toybox.

Milly blinked sleepily at her mum as she took a seat by the bed.

'I tidied up my room,' she whispered. 'I was good, Mummy.'

'That was very good, duckling, to tidy it when you knew I didn't feel well.'

'Are you better now?'

'I'm... getting better. Once I've had some sleep, I think I'll be back to normal. Then we can enjoy the rest of our Easter holidays, can't we?'

'What about Miss Shackleton? Will you make friends again? I liked it when you were friends.'

Stevie winced. 'Well, never you mind about that now. What story are we having? Please God, not "Little Red Riding Hood" again.'

' "Goldilocks" please.'

Stevie picked up Milly's tatty old copy of *Revolting Rhymes* and flicked to the appropriate page. She knew every page number for every story off by heart – in fact, she pretty much knew all the stories off by heart now too. She'd remember every couplet of 'Little Red Riding Hood' long after she'd forgotten her own name.

Milly started to drift off as Stevie read to her, but she jerked suddenly awake when her mum reached Baby Bear's first line.

'Mummy, that's the wrong way,' Milly muttered drowsily. 'When Miss Shackleton reads it to us, she does it squeaky. Like a tiny mouse.'

'Sorry,' Stevie said penitently.

She looked down into her daughter's face, those innocent, wide-spaced green eyes blinking with sleep, and felt a sudden urge to sob.

As soon as she was sure Milly was fast asleep, she got up and closed the door gently behind her. Red, Milly's loyal guard dog, took her place as sentinel and lay across the front of the door like a draught excluder.

Where had she put it? In one of her old textbooks, she was sure. It must have been there since school – she'd never taken it out, never once looked at it.

Stevie went into her bedroom and pushed the mattress off her double bed to get to the storage space beneath. There were boxes of old rubbish down there, some belonging to her, some to Angela. She'd been saying for years she was going to take a load of it down to the tip, but somehow she never got round to it.

She finally found what she was looking for, buried underneath a stack of files from university. A pile of textbooks she'd hung on to from schooldays. And, tucked in the back of her GCSE Maths revision guide – her favourite subject, had she chosen that one deliberately? – there was a Polaroid photograph.

Stevie's dad had taken it. She'd told him she didn't want him to, that she just wanted to get it over with and pretend the whole thing had never happened, but he'd insisted she ought to have something. He thought she might appreciate it in the future, if she didn't then.

Stevie stifled another wave of nausea as she looked at it, remembering, this time, the almost animal pain of separation when Jemima had been taken from her for the final time.

A young girl, pale and frightened, stared at the camera with a newborn baby in her arms. Anyone looking at the photo would probably assume it showed a teenager meeting her little sister for the first time, from the older girl's awkward way of holding the baby and the teen and infant's matching red hair.

And Stevie could see clearly now that the baby was Nell, so very Nell. Those big green eyes that just hours ago Stevie had seen shining with childlike hurt – Milly's eyes, she now realised – were right there in baby Jemima's smiling face. Her baby. Her first, painful, but never forgotten little baby.

Stevie remembered how much she'd felt the absence of a mum, at that difficult time, to comfort and advise her. Nell wasn't the only one who knew what it was to grow up with that hole in her life.

And on top of all the old, painful memories, a new one was making its presence felt. A young woman's eager, hopeful face, reaching out to her, then crumpling with pain as her mother recoiled in instinctive disgust.

Stevie lifted the photo to her lips and pressed it against them. Then, after putting it carefully back where she'd found it, she gave in to emotion and burst into tears. All the anger and betrayal she'd felt when Nell had confessed her secret evaporated in an instant, replaced by a sickening sense of emptiness.

Jesus. What the hell had she gone and done?

–

'Is that the last one?' Nell's dad asked as he loaded another box of her stuff into the back of his hired van the following morning.

'Yes, that's it.'

She turned to gaze at Humblebee Farm and let out a sob.

It had meant so much, this place. The whole thing had almost seemed like a metaphor. The decaying shack she'd slowly made into her perfect home, just as she'd slowly built the relationship she'd always wanted with the mother she'd never known. Just as, quite unexpectedly, she'd found herself falling deeply in love with the last person she'd ever have believed she would fall in love with. All gone. All ended, all dead. She'd come to Leyholme to find a place she could belong, and ended up being rejected by every person here she'd learned to care for.

And each time she closed her eyes, she saw Stevie's face. The look of betrayal and disgust, the nausea Stevie had clearly been battling when she'd realised the friend she'd taken into her heart was the baby she'd conceived under horrific circumstances when she was just a child herself.

It was an image that would be burned onto Nell's brain forever. That face, that expression... Christ, she was made of that. That's where Jemima Madeleine had come from; that's what she meant. Pain. Horror. Disgust.

Of course Stevie had wanted no contact, for her own sake and Jemima's. How selfish Nell had been, how arrogant, to presume she alone knew what was best for them. And now she knew what her origins had been, she'd never be able to forget them.

'Dad, I've been such a fool,' Nell whispered. 'Why didn't I listen to you? I've hurt so many people in ways I'll never be able to take back.'

He drew her to him for a hug.

'Now, we'll have none of that talk,' he said gently. 'You did what you thought was for the best.'

'I was so wrong. So very, very selfish and wrong to come here.' She felt strangled by unshed tears, and amazed she still had any unshed tears left to be strangled by. 'If you'd seen her face, Dad. I disgusted her. Physically disgusted her. I wanted her to love me, but all I did was bring back the memory of the worst thing that ever happened to her.'

'You did act like a pillock, no arguments there,' he said, nodding. 'But for quite understandable reasons, I think.'

'Oh God, what will I do? I've lost everything. Again. Only this time it was my fault and... Dad, I'll never get another job. I've literally got nothing left.'

'That's not true, Nelly.' He held her back to look into her face. 'You know I've always supported you and Freddie on this journey of yours, wanting to know your birth parents. I knew it was only natural, perhaps especially after what happened with your mum, and I was long prepared for the day you'd ask me those questions. But don't forget you've got a parent right here who loves you to bits — who always has.'

Nell smiled through her tears. Her dad was a typical gruff Yorkshireman, never one to show affection easily. It meant a lot when he pushed himself out of his comfort zone to let his children know they were loved.

'Thanks, Dad. I love you too.'

'And you've got a stepmum at home who'd love to know you better than she does, and an idiot brother who thinks the sun shines out of big sis's backside.' He planted a kiss on her hair. 'You'll always belong to us, pet.'

'I know. I know I will.'

He sighed. 'Well, I'm sorry it didn't work out with your birth mum. It's a shame, for you and for her. But these things are always more complicated than they make them seem in the films, I'm sorry to say. The emotions triggered when you have to give up a baby go deep, very deep, and no two cases are alike.'

'But she looked so... horrified.' Nell shuddered. 'I'll never forget that expression on her face.'

'Try not to dwell on it, sweetheart. It'll only give you pain. Just remember that how she reacted really wasn't about you.'

'What will I do, Dad?'

'Come home to your family. Take some time, let us look after you. Then you pick yourself up and start again, to paraphrase the old song.'

'How? I've lost the man I love, a job I adored, and the mum I've been dreaming of since I was old enough to form a picture of her is physically sickened by me. How do I just pick myself up?'

'Well, one step at a time, eh? Let's start by getting you home.'

'Yeah.' She wiped her eyes. 'Let me just say goodbye to my sheep.'

He frowned. 'Your what?'

'My pet sheep. He was the first friend I ever made here. And the only one left still talking to me.'

'She's a strange girl but we love her,' her dad muttered as Nell hobbled off to seek out the other Colin in the outhouse.

'Well, this is it, Col,' she whispered, crouching down to talk to the stinky, warm pile of wool and limbs. 'I'm going and I don't think I'll ever be coming back. You know I'll miss you, don't you?'

Colin bleated appreciatively when she tickled his ears. Nell felt a tear escape and laughed at herself.

'Oh God, I'm ridiculous. Crying for a sheep.' She gave his head a last stroke and stood up. 'Goodbye, buddy. Look after them all for me, eh? I hope the house's new owners are nice to you – assuming I actually manage to sell the old place.'

With a last mournful look at the farmhouse, Nell climbed into her dad's van and they drove off down the track.

Chapter Thirty-Three

The unopened envelope sat on the coffee table in Anne Scott's living room. Xander dug his fists into his cheeks as he stared at it. He'd been staring at it pretty much solidly since Nell had slid it under his office door yesterday afternoon.

He'd remained at his desk as he'd watch it materialise on the carpet. Then, after hesitating a moment, he'd got up to open the door. But Nell had already disappeared.

It was addressed to Ryan Theakston, but he hadn't been able to bring himself to pass it on yet. It just sat there on the table, Nell's curly handwriting on the outside a depressing reminder of his now Nell-less state.

Once he gave it to Ryan, that would be it. The end. The end of so many things: so many hopes and dreams and promises of happy days to come.

But what choice did he have? If he covered up what Nell had done, broke his own ethical code to protect her and save her job at Leyholme Primary, he'd have to live with the knowledge of that for the rest of his life. If he demanded she confess all to the governors then he'd know he'd been responsible for ruining her career – the woman who'd lied her way into her job and into his bed, but at heart was just a damaged little girl who wanted her mum.

So he'd given her an out, the only compromise he could think of. She'd lose her job, but she'd keep her career. It was all he could do for her.

'Hello, lazy bones. Have you been sitting there all day?'

He started at the sound of his mum's voice and hastily stashed the resignation letter away in his pocket.

'Pretty much.' He managed to summon a smile that didn't at all match his miserable mood. 'Well, I am on my holidays.'

'What's that you've just hidden away?'

'Oh, nothing. A letter to the governors I'm supposed to pass on. I'm trying to muster the energy to walk over to Ryan's with it.'

'You should,' Anne said as she picked up his dirty coffee cup from the table. 'The walk will do you good. I thought you were supposed to be staying over at Nell's last night?'

'I wasn't feeling too well. Didn't want to pass on my germs if I was coming down with something.'

She examined his face with concern.

'You do look a bit green around the gills. When did this start?'

'Yesterday. I'm just run down, I think, Mum. End of term, it's always stressful.'

'Hmm. Well, make sure you get an early night tonight. And go have that walk, the fresh air will help if you're bilious.'

'Where've you been today then?' Xander asked, trying to wring some everyday small talk from his tired, overwrought brain.

'Out and about. I went into Halifax with Janet to visit some of those fancy little shops around the Piece Hall. Oh! That reminds me.' She left the room and came back in holding a folded sheet of A4. 'I picked this up for you while I was there. I spotted it in the window of the estate agent's.'

Xander took the sheet and unfolded it. At the top was a photograph of a modest little house he recognised, with a correspondingly modest monthly rent figure printed underneath.

'4 Jubilee Street?' he said.

'That's right, just around the corner,' his mum said. 'It's a lovely cottage, only one bedroom but very affordable. Perfect for a bachelor. Well, I suppose you and Nell will end up living together in the end, but it's early days for that sort of talk, isn't it?'

Xander looked up at her. 'You want me to move out?'

'No, of course I don't. But now you've got your important new job and your new girlfriend, I know you won't want to be stuck at home with your mum.' She stood behind the sofa and rested a hand on his shoulder. 'I know you stayed all this time for my sake,' she said gently. 'It's all right, I promise. You don't need to look after me any more.'

He smiled. 'I thought you were looking after me.'

'And I know that's what you wanted me to think,' she said, smiling back. 'I'm not a fool, Xander.'

'Mum...'

'Take as long as you like. But if you're sticking around for this old lady, I can promise you there's no need.' She gave his shoulder a squeeze. 'I'm getting better, love. I'll be just fine on my own.'

'I'm glad to hear it. I'm very fond of this old lady.' He patted the hand on his shoulder and stood up. 'You know, you're right, a walk will do me good. I think I'll go out for an hour or two, get some air.'

'That's a good idea. Why don't you head up to Nell's and show her your flyer, eh? See what she thinks of 4 Jubilee Street.'

'Actually, I might walk over to Morton. I've not been over to Justin and Sara's for a while.'

'Don't forget that letter you have to drop off,' his mum called after him as he left the room.

'I won't.' He patted his pocket. 'I couldn't,' he muttered.

–

'Hiya Scotty,' Justin said when he answered the door to Xander. 'What's the crisis this time?'

'How do you know there is one?'

'Your face, mate.'

Xander sighed. 'Well, you're right. Is this a good time?'

'Yeah, come on in. It's bathtime so I'm afraid chaos reigns as ever, but his Lordship'll be in bed soon.'

Xander followed Justin through to a toy-sprinkled living room and collapsed onto the sofa.

'How's Jacob's Oedipus Complex getting on?' he asked.

'Oh, loads better,' Justin said. 'I decided it'd be easier if I just relinquished alpha male status and let him be the boss. It's worth it for a quiet life.'

He headed to the kitchen and came back carrying three bottles of beer. He pressed one into Xander's hand and put the other two down on the table.

'Right,' he said. 'I'll go help Sara get him off, then we'll have a drink and you can tell us all about it.'

Half an hour later, Xander's friends were sitting either side of him with a bottle of beer each and the expression of flushed contentment that can only come after having successfully wrestled a toddler to sleep.

'What's up then, Scotty?' Justin asked. 'Work, women or a combination of the two?'

'Combination,' Xander muttered.

'Go on.'

'It's sort of confidential so I can't tell you all of it. I had a row with Nell and we kind of… we kind of broke up.'

Sara blinked. 'You broke up with Nell?'

'Yeah.'

'Aww, Xand.' She put her arm round his shoulders and gave them a squeeze. 'Why did she end it then?'

'She didn't. I did.'

'What?' Sara withdrew her arm and stared at him. 'Have you gone completely off your chump?'

Xander snorted. 'Thanks for your support.'

'Xander, you love that girl to pieces. We've known you for over twenty years and even in the honeymoon period with Marie, we've never seen you as happy as you've been with Nell.

If you let her go, you do realise you'll regret it the rest of your life?'

Justin nodded. 'She's not wrong, mate. Plus Nell's fit as, you were lucky to find her. It's mostly only the dogs that're still single when you get to our age.' He shrugged when Sara glared at him. 'What? I'm here to offer the male perspective.'

'Arsehole perspective, more like,' Sara muttered. 'What was so bad that you called off the best thing that's ever happened to you then, you stupid bastard? I mean you, by the way, Xand, not Jus cancelling his subscription to *Top Gear* magazine this morning.'

'She… I can't tell you exactly.' Xander scowled at his beer bottle before taking a swig. 'It involves other people, and work stuff I shouldn't really discuss. But she betrayed my trust in a pretty big way.'

Sara frowned. 'Cheating? I'd never have believed that of her.'

'No. No, it was nothing like that.' Xander paused, wondering how he could phrase it without betraying confidences. 'She kind of exploited my feelings for her so that in my role as her boss, I wouldn't realise she'd lied about something relating to work. She… used me, I guess.'

'She did that? Bloody hell.' Sara shook her head. 'You think you know someone, eh? She always seemed so sweet.'

'She is,' Xander muttered. He took his glasses off and rubbed his eyes. 'She really is.' He sighed. 'If you knew all the details, you might understand. I do get why she did it. But it was such a big lie, and it lasted so long… it's not something I can just get over. It hurt me a lot when I realised what she'd done.'

Justin patted his shoulder. 'Sorry, Scotty. I know how you felt about her.'

'Thanks, mate.'

'And you're absolutely sure you did the right thing breaking it off?' Sara said.

Xander ran his fingers through his hair, the hair he'd kept long just for Nell after she'd said she liked it that way.

'I don't know,' he mumbled. 'I miss her like mad, Sar. And I love her so much it hurts.'

Sara put her arm back round his shoulders. 'You soppy bugger. Yeah, we know you do.'

'What do you think, guys? Advise me, please.'

'Well, it's hard to say without knowing all the details,' Justin said. 'But…'

'…but it's been great to see you happy again these last few months,' Sara said softly, leaning round to look into his eyes. 'You've smiled more since you've met Nell than you have since – well, you know.'

'Since before Dad died,' Xander said.

'Yeah.'

Xander stared blankly at the canvas photo of Sara, Justin and Jacob that hung over the fireplace as he swallowed down his beer in silence.

'I'm thinking I'll probably resign from Leyholme Primary,' he said at last.

Justin raised his eyebrows. 'What? Why the hell would you do that when you were so chuffed about the promotion? I thought they were all set to fast-track you to headship?'

'Because I'm sick of that fucking village. Without Nell to make it special, it looks greyer than it ever did when I was a kid. I'm going to do myself a favour and get out, like I should've done years ago. Mum doesn't need me now she's in recovery, and there's nothing else I want to stay for.' He glanced at his friends. 'I mean, obviously I'll miss you guys. But you've got your own lives to lead, you don't need miserable old schoolfriends turning up every five minutes and disrupting your family routine with their woes.'

'We like you disrupting our routine,' Sara told him firmly. 'And we especially like it when you babysit.'

'When did you decide this then?' Justin asked.

Xander shrugged. 'About an hour ago.'

'Fuck me. And you don't think this is the sort of weighty decision that might benefit from a bit more mulling over?'

'Why waste time? I always wanted to get out of Leyholme. Might as well do it now, when I've got nothing left to stick around for.'

'Where will you go?' Sara asked.

'Dunno. Anywhere. Abroad, maybe, if I can get work. Far, far away.'

'At least talk to Nell before you start booking your bloody flights,' Sara said. 'You're making life-changing decisions in the throes of rebound here, which is hardly healthy, Xand. I'm sorry, but I still can't imagine Nell could have done anything so awful that it can't be worked out.'

'I just can't see how I could ever trust her again,' Xander muttered. 'It feels so… unreal now, everything that happened between us. And through it all she was nursing this massive secret.'

Justin exchanged a worried look with Sara.

'I don't like this, Xand,' Sara said. 'All this mystery.'

'No. I'm not a big fan of it either.'

'Can't you tell us any more about what Nell's done to make you consider a new life on the other side of the globe?'

'I wish I could, but it's not my secret to tell.' Xander put down what was left of his beer. 'I have to go. There's a letter I need to deliver.'

After he'd left his friends, Xander turned his steps in the direction of the Theakstons' place back in Leyholme. As he walked, he took his glasses off to let the wind dry his damp eyes.

When he reached Ryan and Martha's neat little bungalow, he rang the doorbell. It was one of those monstrosities that played a jingly tune, and he glared at it for its ill-timed jollity.

'Oh, hello, Alexander,' Martha said when she answered. 'What can I do for you, pet?'

'There's something I need to give Ryan. Is he about?'

'He's doing some work in the study. Do you want to leave it with me?'

'I'd rather deliver it to him personally, if that's OK. It's kind of important.'

'Well, all right.' She called up the stairs. 'Ryan! Alexander Scott here for you.'

Ryan appeared down the stairs moments later, looking grumpy at being interrupted.

'Yes?' he snapped.

After their face-off at the meeting the month before, Xander had been doing his best to keep things on a civil footing, but the man seemed determined to make it difficult for him. Following the announcement of Xander's promotion to deputy head, Ryan's resentment of him seemed stronger than ever.

'I brought a letter for you,' Xander said. 'One of the teachers asked me to pass it on.'

'For God's sake. Could you not have put it through the letterbox? I was in the middle of something.'

'I wanted to see it delivered personally.'

'For God's sake,' Ryan muttered again. 'Well come on then, let's have the thing. We've got lives to lead here, young man.'

'Right.'

Xander looked at Ryan for a moment, taking in the heavy scowl and the resentful glare that had fixed on him.

This man. This man who'd tried to get him sacked, who'd gone all out to destroy his career. Who'd relished bullying and humiliating him at every turn. Who hated him, still, for petty, spiteful reasons of his own.

Jesus, if Ryan could make his last act as chairman chewing Nell up and spitting her out, he almost certainly would – if only because he thought it might hurt Xander. What if he refused to provide her with a reference, what then? What if… what if somehow, he found out the real reason she'd resigned?

Xander reached into his jacket pocket, paused, and drew his hand out empty.

'You know, Ryan, I've only gone and forgotten it.' He gave a strained laugh. 'Forget my head if it wasn't screwed on, eh?'

'Xander. Are you seriously telling me you walked over here to deliver a letter you haven't got?'

'I know, what am I like? First day of the holidays and my brain's gone to sleep. And you know, now I come to think of it, it wasn't really all that urgent. I'll, er, drop it off another day.'

'Well next time, perhaps you could avoid disturbing the household by pushing it through the bloody door like any sensible human being.' Ryan shut the door in his face.

Once Xander was out of sight of the house, he took out Nell's letter and stared at it.

For about five minutes, he just stood there looking at the envelope, listening to the breeze shake the new spring buds overhead. Then, on a sudden impulse, he tore it open.

He frowned as he read what Nell had written. Then he laughed: a choked, painful laugh. Only then did he stride off towards the track that led up to Humblebee Farm.

Chapter Thirty-Four

'Hey-up tiny,' Deb said when Milly opened the door of the Madeleine household to her. 'Do you answer doors now then?'

'Yep,' Milly said, looking pleased with herself.

'Well, that's very grown-up of you. What would you do if I was a stranger though?'

'I'd yell "GET LOST, STRANGER!" and slam the door.'

'OK. Harsh but reassuring.' Deb held out the basket she'd brought. 'Here we go. One Little Red Riding Hood basket filled with Grandma treats, as promised.'

Milly took it from her and peeked into it. 'Ooh! Creme Eggs, yum.'

'Yep, for you. A week early for Easter, but every day is Creme Egg day in the world of Deb.'

Milly threw herself at Deb and hugged her legs. 'Thank you, Deb.'

'You're very welcome, sweetheart,' Deb said, smiling as she patted her head. 'Where's your mum then? I'm sure she's got a lecture she needs to give me about spoiling you rotten again.'

Milly lowered her voice to a worried whisper. 'She's sick.'

'Sick?' Deb said, frowning.

Milly nodded. 'She shouted at Miss Shackleton and then she was sick.'

'Shouted at Nell? What about?'

'I didn't hear. I was frightened so I stayed in my room with Red. But I heard yelling and then I saw Miss Shackleton go away crying from the window, and then Mummy was sick in the toilet for ages and ages. Then I woke up after she went to bed and I heard her crying lots too.'

Milly looked like she'd been crying a bit herself. Sensing she was worried about her mum, Deb crouched down and pulled her into a hug.

'When was this, my love?' she asked gently.

'Yesterday.'

'And is Mummy still sick?'

'She's not *being* sick but she's still poorly sick,' Milly said. 'She's all tired and sad and she doesn't move or do anything.'

'You'd better let me in to see her, I think, Mill. Maybe I can help.'

''K.'

Milly stood beside the door like a nightclub bouncer as Deb came in, then closed it behind her, turning the key in the lock. It was obvious the little girl took her new status as door monitor very seriously.

'Stevie?' Deb called. There was no answer.

'Mummy's in the conservatory,' Milly said in a whisper, as if she was in the presence of an invalid. She took a Creme Egg from her basket. 'We should give her this to help make her well again.'

Deb nodded. 'That's good thinking, it'll give her energy. Hey, but what do you think to going to your room for a bit while I talk to Mummy about what's wrong?'

'Why?'

'Well, then I can examine her and that. I'll be able to make her better easy-peasy, me. I look after poorly dogs all the time and I always get them better.'

'Really?'

'Really. I helped make Red better when she got sick, didn't I?'

'Do you *promise* you can make my mummy better though?' Milly demanded, looking up at her with worried eyes.

'Absolutely. Super promise.' Deb rested a gentle hand on her head. 'No need to worry, sweetheart. Everyone gets a little bit sick sometimes. Go on, go play with Red.'

When Milly had scampered off upstairs, Deb went to seek out Stevie in the conservatory.

'Stevie, Jesus! You look awful.'

Her girlfriend was sitting on the sofa in her dressing gown, no make-up on and her face deathly white. Heavy purple bags circled eyes that were bloodshot and swollen with tears.

'Oh. Hiya,' Stevie said, without looking round.

'What's wrong? Milly said you'd had a row with Nell.'

'Yes.' Stevie choked on a sob. 'Oh God, Deb, I've done the most awful thing.'

Deb took a seat on the sofa and wrapped Stevie up in her arms.

'No you haven't,' she whispered. 'You could never do anything awful, I know that for a fact. Not my girl.'

'I have. I really have.'

Deb turned Stevie's face towards her and examined the pale skin and puffy eyes with concern.

'Milly said you'd been sick.'

'Yes. Not been able to eat much since either.'

'Have you seen a doctor? She's really worried about you, you know. So am I, now.'

'It's not a doctor kind of sick.' Stevie let out another sob. 'Deb, I've told you a lot of things I've told hardly anyone else. Except… there's one thing I never told anybody. Not even Ange. I tried to tell you in bed the other week, but then after you said… well, it just didn't seem like the time.'

Deb took Stevie's hand and pressed it to her lips. 'Go on.'

'You'll never look at me again when I tell you. Not the same way you look at me now.'

'Stevie, I love you. Nothing you tell me is going to change that.'

Stevie took a deep breath. 'I told you about Victoria. About the boy at the party, Reuben. The one who...' She shuddered. 'That night.'

'I remember. What about it? He didn't get in touch or something?'

Stevie shook her head. 'I only told you half the story. I only told Ange half the story too.' She snorted. 'Because... because what I didn't say was that the union was blessed. Or cursed, if you like.'

'Shit! You mean you—'

'Yeah. My first time. As if the act itself hadn't been punishment enough.'

Deb held her tighter. 'What happened, love?'

'God, Deb, I was such a naive kid, even for my age. It took me about three months to work out what was happening – why my body was going through all these changes.'

'Did you tell anyone?'

She nodded. 'My dad, when I finally worked it out. I think, if my mum had been around, maybe things would have been different. Perhaps she'd have advised me to terminate, I don't know. But my dad was adamant I ought to keep it or I'd come to regret it, one day. And like a good little girl, I just did as I was told. Arrangements were made, a place at a special school for expectant teens, while I carried the pregnancy to term.'

'But what happened to the baby? Didn't you have it?'

'Yes.' Stevie let out a strangled sort of cough. 'I was a coward, Deb. When I saw it, this crying thing that looked like me and needed me, I... I just couldn't do it. I was too much a child myself, and I was still traumatised from the night she'd been conceived. I told my dad I couldn't keep her. That I wanted her to be adopted by a family who could give her everything I couldn't, a grown-up family, where she'd never have to find out how she came to be alive.'

Deb stroked Stevie's hair away from her face. 'Sweetheart, why on earth would you think that would make me see you any differently?'

'You only know half of it,' Stevie muttered. 'The worst thing isn't what I did to Jemima when she was born. I still think I was right to give her up. It's what I did to Jemima yesterday.'

Deb frowned. 'What?'

'It's Nell, Deb. All this time, and I never knew.'

'Nell! Your best friend Nell? She's your... daughter?'

'She's Jemima. She's the baby I gave away. She put everything on the line – her job, her relationship with Xander – all for me.'

'Oh my God,' Deb whispered. 'I can't believe it! When did you find out?'

'Yesterday, when she came over to talk to me.' Stevie swallowed another sob. 'That's when I did the worst thing I've ever done. And when I tell you, I don't think you'll feel the same about me. I don't deserve you to.'

'Try me,' Deb said, fierce at the suggestion there was anything that could change the way she felt about the woman she loved.

'It's like Nell was some sort of trigger to me. When she told me who she was, called me her mum... all the memories came flooding back. The awful flashbacks of the night she was conceived: that shameful, painful, brutal act.' Stevie's throat convulsed feverishly. 'And then the memory of having her taken from my arms the last time – overwhelming relief that it was over and I could go back to being just a kid again, mingled with the feeling that I'd lost a part of myself that I'd never be able to get back. I just felt so hurt and betrayed that someone I loved would lie to me; bring back that pain I'd spent so many years trying to forget. So I... I...'

'You rejected her.'

Stevie nodded miserably. 'I felt sick, physically sick, in the most visceral way. Not because of Nell. Because of where Nell came from. She was looking at me with all this love and hope in her eyes, and suddenly I could see her in there, Jemima, the baby I gave away. Asking me to love her. And instead of hugging her like I could see she needed me to, I... shunned her. Told her to get out.' She took out a tissue and blew her nose. 'The last time I did that to someone I loved, she never came back.'

There was silence, broken only by the sound of Stevie's strangled sobs.

'So I guess you hate me now,' she muttered.

'Are you kidding?' Deb turned Stevie's face towards her and kissed it softly, repeatedly; kissed away the tears that had dampened her eyes and cheeks. 'Stephanie Madeleine, I love you, and I think you're the bravest person I know.'

'But I… it was such a terrible thing to do,' Stevie mumbled.

'It seems to me there are a lot of people who deserve blame in this whole business, and not one of them is either you or Nell. You were both victims.' Deb stroked Stevie's hair while she clasped her head to her shoulder. 'Little girls, the pair of you.'

Stevie summoned a weak smile. 'I don't deserve you, do I?'

Deb smiled back. 'You won't say that when you see all the chocolate I slipped Milly behind your back.'

At that moment, Milly herself galloped into the conservatory, Red at her heels. Stevie turned away and hastily wiped her eyes.

'Did you make Mummy better yet?' Milly demanded of Deb.

'Well, I'm not sure.' Deb turned to Stevie. 'Did I make Mummy better yet?'

Stevie laughed. 'Much better. But I think there's one more thing Mummy needs to do before she's properly well again.'

'What is it?' Milly asked.

'Someone I need to talk to,' Stevie said. 'Mill, do you want to go upstairs and put your toothbrush and night things in your little rucksack, and some clothes and clean knickers for tomorrow? You're going to stay at Nanny's tonight.'

'Ooh, Nanny's! OK.' Milly went dashing off again.

'Not that Nanny knows a thing about it, but I'm sure she won't mind some unscheduled Milly time,' Stevie said to Deb, watching her daughter disappear. She sighed. 'After Nell left,

I still felt so sick and angry. Sick about what happened, and angry with Nell for bringing it all to the surface again. It was only when I put Milly to bed and she looked up at me... did you ever notice they've got the same eyes?'

'Nell and Milly?' Deb paused to consider it. 'Yes, I suppose they have. That same shape and shade of green.' She ran a finger under one of Stevie's red-rimmed eyes. 'Like their mother's, eh?'

'That's when it hit me. We'd bonded as adults, but deep down Nell was just a lost little girl who wanted her mum. Every lie she'd told was because it meant so much to her to have me in her life. I was her mum, and I'd sent her away.'

'Are you going to talk to her then?'

'Yes. I have to try to make it right.' She swallowed another sob. 'Oh God, the poor girl. Imagine finding out something like that about yourself. That's the thing I'm most angry with myself for, not having had enough of my wits about me to lie to her. I just blurted out the truth like it wouldn't even hurt.'

'You were in shock, Stevie. Don't blame yourself.'

'I just hope she can forgive me and we can... I don't know, take whatever the next step needs to be.'

'I think she will.' Deb leaned forward to kiss her. 'Anyway, whatever happens, you know I've got your back. Always.'

Stevie smiled. 'Always. I like the sound of that.'

—

Xander knocked again at the farmhouse door. When there was still no movement from inside, he pushed open the letterbox.

'Nell, please open up,' he called through it. 'I need to talk to you. I read your letter.'

Still nothing. Had she gone out?

He peered through the letterbox and frowned.

Today's post still on the floor. The lamp that usually sat on the hallway table... not there.

'Oh my God,' he muttered.

She might have gone home to her parents'. She'd said she was going home for the Easter holidays. But why take the lamp with her? That didn't suggest a holiday. It suggested...

Filled with foreboding, he squeezed down the narrow ginnel between the farmhouse and outhouse. In the back garden, he pressed his face against the living room window.

It looked bare. The fire was black and empty, the smaller items of Nell's mismatched skip-chic furniture all gone. Her books were gone too, and the pictures that had hung on the wall. Only the sofa and chairs remained to prove that Humblebee Farm had ever been occupied.

He went back to the front garden and sank down against the outhouse next to Colin.

'Where is she, Col?' he muttered, reaching out to give the sheep a stroke. 'Do you know?'

Colin gave an answering bleat, then got to his feet and trotted to the gate. He waited there expectantly.

'Where are you going then?' Xander said. 'Is it feeding time? Or... can you see something?'

He squinted into the distance. A silhouette – a woman's silhouette – was heading up the track towards the farm.

Nell? He scrambled to his feet.

But as the figure got closer, Xander quickly recognised the short red hair and petite frame of Stevie Madeleine. Colin, disappointed, retreated back into his outhouse.

'Xander,' Stevie said when she reached the garden. 'What're you doing here?'

'Same as you, I think.'

'Where is she?'

'Not here. Stevie, I think she might've moved out or something. I looked through the back window and half the furniture's gone.'

'Shit!'

He came forward to examine her face. 'You don't look so good.'

She summoned a weak smile. 'You're not looking too hot yourself, love.'

'What happened?'

Stevie looked down at the dandelion-strewn grass of Nell's lawn. 'I ruined everything. That's all.'

'She told you then?'

'Yes, last night. And I handled it in just about the worst way possible.'

Xander sighed. 'I was no better.'

'How did you find out?'

'She lied to me about being made redundant. I yanked at a thread and a whole can of worms unravelled, to mix a metaphor or three.'

'And now she's gone.'

'Looks like it.'

Stevie looked up at him. 'What've we done, Xand?'

'Well, I don't know about you but I'm pretty sure I just made the biggest mistake of my life.' He took the letter from his pocket, unfolded it and handed it to her. 'Read that.'

'What is it?'

'Nell's letter of resignation. The one I insisted she write when I realised what she'd been doing.'

' "Dear governors",' Stevie read aloud. ' "Please accept this as my formal letter of resignation. My position has been compromised, entirely through my own actions, and it is with great regret that I must now leave my job at Leyholme Primary with immediate effect. I have exploited my position and the trust that was placed in me by yourselves and by the community in order to fulfil my own personal ends – namely, attempting to forge a relationship with my birth family without their knowledge or desire and using my position in the school to facilitate this. I understand that this means I will now have to leave my role, and in all likelihood the teaching profession, and I also understand there may be action taken against me by the school as a consequence. I can only humbly apologise for my wrongdoing, with no excuse but an earnest wish to know my family that led to me making some very poor choices. Last of all, I would like it to be known – and will gladly swear to the truth of the statement – that Alexander Scott had no knowledge of any of this until today. This letter is written at his request, and I wish to state that he has at all times acted with impeccable professionalism in the execution of his duties. Regards, Eleanor Shackleton".'

Xander let out a pained laugh. 'Jesus.'

'What does it mean, Xander?'

'It means… it means she's fallen on her sword. For me. It means I'm an idiot and I just let the best thing that ever happened to me walk out of my life.'

Stevie frowned. 'I don't understand.'

'Stevie, it's a lie. I didn't act with impeccable professionalism. I told Nell not to write that letter.'

'What?'

'I gave her a "get out of jail free". I wouldn't cover it up, but I told her to make up an excuse about why she was resigning so she'd be able to get another job. I couldn't bear the thought of her ruining her career over this.' He met Stevie's eyes. 'She just wanted you, I think. And if she could have that, she thought everything else in the world was worth the sacrifice.'

'Oh God,' Stevie whispered, blinking hard.

'What happened with you two, Stevie?'

'I made a mess of everything. She came to me with her heart in her hands, begging me to accept her, and I… I pushed her away. Again.'

'You had it sprung on you when she'd had a whole lifetime to prepare. Whatever you did, it was understandable.'

'Still. I said things, Xander. Things I can't take back.'

Xander went back to sit against the outhouse. Stevie sank down at the other side of him.

'Where do you think she's gone?' Xander whispered.

'Home, I suppose. To her dad's.'

'Do you know where home is?'

303

'Leeds somewhere. I can't be any more specific than that, sadly.' Stevie looked at him. 'She'll come back, won't she, Xand? If we tell her we want her to?'

'I don't know.' Xander slammed his fist into the soft earth. 'What the *fuck* is wrong with me? She was vulnerable and afraid, she needed me and I… all I did was go into bloody headteacher mode. Demanded her resignation when what she needed was a hug and reassurance it was all going to be OK. It'd serve me right if she never came back.'

'I was worse than you. When she told me who she was, the physical response – I couldn't control it.'

Xander reached out to squeeze her hand. 'You had some pretty complex emotions going on to explain what you did. I'm just a bad boyfriend.' He winced. 'Ex-boyfriend. I thought maybe none of it had been real – that she'd only got involved with me to stop me asking awkward questions about why she'd moved here. Until I saw her letter.'

Stevie patted the hand he'd stretched out to her. 'Love her a lot, don't you?'

'Yes.' He let out a sob. 'God, yes.'

'Me too.' She wiped her eyes and pushed herself to her feet. 'Right. Why the hell are we sitting about feeling sorry for ourselves? Let's get off our arses and bring our Nell back home.'

'What if she won't come back?'

'That's defeatist talk. Nothing's unfixable, that's what Deb always says.' Stevie fished out her mobile and swiped at the screen.

'You're calling Nell?' Xander asked, standing up too.

'Yep. Maybe she won't answer, but she'll know I reached out to her and that's a start.'

Stevie tapped to make the call and held the phone to her ear.

'Hey,' Xander said, frowning. 'You hear that?'

'What?'

He walked up to the house and flipped open the letterbox again, bending to bring his ear level with it.

'It's coming from in there,' he said. 'Nell's ringtone, I can hear it.'

Stevie ended the call and sighed. 'She left her phone behind.'

'On purpose, do you think?'

'Maybe. I wouldn't be surprised.'

'So what do we do now?' Xander asked. 'How can we find her if we can't contact her?'

Stevie looked thoughtful. 'Xand, can you come over to my place? I might have a plan.'

Chapter Thirty-Five

Nell stood in front of the mirror on the wall of Freddie's room and ran a finger down her nose.

It wasn't Stevie's nose. It was longer, less broad. His nose, the boy who'd made her – Reuben, Stevie had said he was called. It had to be his, didn't it?

What else had she got from the bastard?

Nell had never thought much about her birth father. It had been her mum she'd wondered about, dreamt about, drawn pictures of when she was no bigger than Milly was now. If she'd thought about him at all, it was just a passing flash of curiosity about how he might have looked and little more. She already had a dad, and she hadn't experienced that same aching hollow where she'd always felt a mum ought to go.

But now she knew more of the story, she couldn't help thinking about him. The sort of boy who'd take advantage of a fourteen-year-old girl. The sort of boy... she still didn't know exactly what had happened to Stevie to trigger such fear and disgust, but whatever it was had clearly scarred her for life.

And that's where Jemima had come from. Not the sort of loving, wholesome sex that created most children, or even, as Nell had always assumed, the experimental fumbles of teenage sweethearts. She came from something seedy, something painful. Something that scarred.

Nell touched her nose again. He was in her. She had his features – perhaps she had his character. Maybe that was what had driven her to move to Leyholme; to make the catastrophically selfish decision to force a relationship with her birth mum against her wishes.

Or was she just looking for a way to shift responsibility because she knew she'd done wrong?

She'd been sure Stevie would want her when she eventually confessed the truth. They'd become so close, as friends. Nell let out a sob when she remembered how comfortable they'd always felt in each other's company; Stevie's maternal concern for her living alone in the farmhouse; the way she'd started calling her 'chicken' almost at once – a mum-type endearment, as if she could sense the natural bond between them. Nell had wondered, for a while, if perhaps Stevie did know. If Nell would eventually reveal she was Jemima only for Stevie to smile and say, 'Oh well, I know that, chicken. I always did'. And they'd hug and—

Ugh. She was dreaming again. Her brain just couldn't seem to accept that it was all over.

She looked again at her reflection in the mirror. At her eyes, her nose, her skin. She remembered – as if she could ever forget – what Stevie had said about not wanting Jemima to grow up feeling disgusted at her own reflection because she knew where she'd come from.

Well now she did know, and Stevie was right. Her own face would never look the same to her as it had before.

She felt a surge of anger and hatred towards this man – this Reuben, whoever he was now. It was his fault, all of this. He'd hurt Stevie beyond repair, traumatised her to the extent that she couldn't even *look* at her daughter without feeling the need to vomit. He'd made Nell's own face hateful to her. God, what she'd give to come face to face with the bastard, just once, and really kick him where it hurt. She could put a lifetime of rejection and pain – Stevie's and her own – into that kick.

Nell reached under the bed, yanked out her overnight bag and found her make-up case. She tipped the contents onto the mattress, grabbed some eyeliner and started applying it to her lids.

She didn't know why. All she knew was that her face was suddenly as disgusting to her as it seemed to be to Stevie, and she wanted to make it look as alien and unlike itself as possible.

There was a knock at the bedroom door.

'What?' Nell called.

Leanne poked her head round. 'Only me, love. Can I get you anything? Cuppa?'

'It's fine, I can get my own. I'm not an invalid.'

Leanne's face crumpled and she turned away. 'OK.'

Nell looked up.

'Sorry,' she said in a softer voice. 'I didn't mean to snap. I mean, no, thank you. But thanks for the offer.' She patted the bed. 'I wouldn't mind some company though.'

Leanne came to sit by her on the bed. 'Why don't you come down, eh? Let me take you out to the pictures or something. We'll have a fun girly trip, just us.'

'No, I can't. I've already got plans.'

Leanne frowned. 'Plans? But you just got here.'

'Yeah. I made them in a bit of a hurry.'

'Oh.'

Nell took her stepmother's hand. 'Lee, we haven't always been the best of friends, have we?' she said quietly.

'No.' Leanne sighed. 'I'm sorry, Nell. I wanted to be a parent to you, but you were already becoming a young woman when I married your dad. I guess it must have seemed like a liberty, me moving in and trying to boss you about.'

'I was such a little madam. All those times I yelled at you and said you weren't my mum. You must have hated me.'

Leanne smiled sadly. 'Nell, I loved you very much. I always saw you as just as much mine as Freddie was, you know. I didn't know how to get through to you, that was all.'

'I hurt you a lot. Didn't I?'

'Well, you were hurting too. Let's not dwell on it, eh? The past's the past, and I think everyone in this family needs to be thinking about the future right now.'

'You were a great stepmum, Leanne. Thanks for everything you did for me. And… I'm sorry.' Nell squeezed her hand. 'I hope we can be better friends from now on.'

'I'd like that very much.' Leanne stretched an arm around her shoulders. 'I'm sorry about what happened with Stevie, honey. I can see she caused you a lot of pain.'

'It's not her fault,' Nell muttered.

'No, but you mustn't blame yourself either. You've been rash, yes, but it's understandable.'

'I don't blame myself.' Nell glared into the distance. 'I blame Reuben.'

Leanne frowned. 'Reuben? Who's Reuben?'

'My… the boy who got Stevie pregnant. Leanne, could I borrow your car?'

'Why?'

'I'm going to see our Freddie.'

–

'So what's the plan then?' Xander asked when he and Stevie got back to her place.

'Here, come up to the den. Milly's at her nana's and Red's with Deb so we've got the house to ourselves.'

He followed her upstairs to her office. She shoved various papers that looked vaguely accountanty to one side of the desk and fired up her computer.

'Do you know how Nell found out where I lived?' she asked.

'Her brother did it. He'd posted enquiries and family trees on a load of genealogy sites, I saw them.'

'Yes. But first he looked on the electoral roll, that's what Nell told me. That would have narrowed it down a bit, area-wise. Then he just had to make sure he'd got the right Stephanie Madeleine.'

Xander frowned. 'So what are you saying? We can use it to find Nell? That'll just give us her home address.'

'Not her, her dad. Assuming that's where she's most likely to be. Him, his wife and his son will all be registered voters at the same address, and we know their names and the city.'

Xander blinked. 'Wow. Stevie, I'm impressed.'

'I know, right? I should've been a private detective.'

'Can we access this electoral roll online then?'

'Yeah, easy. It's what they use as the basis for all those directory enquiries sites.'

She pulled up a browser window, typed in the URL of a directory website and entered 'Colin Shackleton, Leeds' into the search box. In seconds, a table of Colin Shackletons had popped up on screen.

'OK, so now we scroll down the list,' she said. 'If any of the listings show the other occupants of the household as Leanne and Freddie, bingo.'

They soon found the answer they needed. Only one Leeds household contained Colin, Leanne and Frederick Shackleton.

'Harewood, Leeds,' Stevie said. 'Getting there, Xand.'

'We need to register with the website to get the full address though.'

'That's OK, I've got an account. We use this site for work.'

Stevie logged in, then grabbed a pad and copied down the address.

'Now let's have a look on Google Street View.' She pulled up the website and entered the postcode, clicking until they had the impression they were standing right outside Nell's parents' front door. The Shackletons lived in a terribly civilised redbrick semi – a far cry from the tumbledown charm of Nell's Humblebee Farm.

Stevie nodded. 'Nice place.'

'I never knew stalking was so easy,' Xander said.

She turned to him. 'So what do we do? Just turn up on the doorstep?'

Xander was silent for a minute.

'You should go alone,' he said at last. 'She came here for you.'

'What would I say?'

'You'll know, I think, when you see her.'

'I don't know, Xander,' she said in a low voice. 'I might screw it up again. Last time… the physical sensation was so strong, I couldn't control it. One more meltdown like that and I'll have alienated her for good.' She looked at him. 'And just because she came here for me doesn't mean I'm all there is in Leyholme that matters to her. Not any more.'

'You mean me?'

'Of course I mean you, thickie. She loves you. You're just as much a part of this – of Nell – as I am.'

'Do you really think so?'

'I do.' She smiled. 'Anyway, I don't need to think so. She told me.'

'Nell told you that?'

'Yep. She said we were going to be happy. Me and Milly, and her, and you. Like a family.'

Xander swallowed hard. 'God, did she really?'

'So… both of us? Now?'

He nodded. 'Now.'

'OK, then let's get going.'

–

'Oh. Nell,' Freddie's mum Alison said when she opened the door. 'Hello, love. We weren't expecting you.'

'No, sorry, I just… could I talk to my brother a minute?'

'Of course. Come on in.'

She brushed a couple of capering kids and a cat to one side with businesslike efficiency and ushered Nell into the hall. With four young children and countless pets, Alison's home always seemed to be awash with chaos, while the woman herself stood calm and unfazed in the centre of it all.

'Fred!' she called up the stairs. 'Your sister's here to see you.'

'I'm really sorry to intrude like this,' Nell said.

'Don't be daft, you're Freddie's family. That means you're always welcome. Would you like to join us for tea? I can set another place.'

'No, I can't stop. But thank you for the invitation.'

'Your parents are OK, aren't they?' Alison asked. 'I thought you'd be with them now it's school holidays.'

'Yes. I mean, I will be. There's something I need to do first.'

Freddie came galloping down the stairs, frowning.

'What's up, sis?' he asked. 'Why aren't you at home? You didn't have a row with Leanne, did you?'

'No, nothing like that.'

'Why didn't you call to say you were coming?'

'I've… lost my phone. Fred, can we talk?' She cast a glance at Alison. 'Um, in private? Sorry. Just some family stuff.'

'Yeah, if you want,' he said, looking concerned. 'Come up to my room then.'

'I'll leave you both to it,' Alison said. 'Shout down if you want a cuppa or anything.'

She gave Freddie a squeeze before she disappeared. Nell couldn't help casting an envious glance at the fond maternal arm around her brother's waist.

She followed Freddie up the stairs. As soon as he shut the door behind them, she burst into tears.

'Nell, what's up? What's happened?' he asked in alarm.

'I told her,' she sobbed. 'I told her and… Fred, she… she doesn't want me.'

'Oh God, no.' He came forward to give her a hug. 'But you guys seemed to have got so close when I came to visit.'

'We had.' She snuffled against his shoulder. 'That made it worse, I think. That she felt I'd betrayed her trust all this time.'

'I'm sorry, Nelly, it's my fault. I never should've suggested it.'

'No, it wasn't you. I made my choices, now I have to live with them.' She rubbed her tear-filled eyes, smearing panda-like rings of eyeliner around them. 'Fred, she was so traumatised she could barely bring herself to look at me.'

'Traumatised by what?'

Nell drew back from the hug, scowling blackly. 'By him.'

'Him?'

'Yeah, the bastard who got her pregnant. Fucking Reuben.'

'Why, what the hell did he do to her?'

'Forced himself on her, I think, although she wouldn't say it. Destroyed her mental health, nearly ruined her life, then skipped off into the sunset with no consequences.'

'Jesus, seriously?' Freddie muttered. 'What a prick.'

'Yeah.' She looked at him. 'Freddie, I need you to help me find him. Right now.'

Chapter Thirty-Six

It took Xander and Stevie over an hour to get to Nell's parents' place in the suburbs of Leeds. When they reached the Shackletons' cul-de-sac, Stevie parked a little way away and they walked down to the house, just in case Nell got spooked by the sight of her car.

'I'll go knock,' Xander said. 'You wait out of sight a minute. It might overwhelm her if we both turn up together.'

Stevie nodded. 'You're right, that'll be best. I don't know how I'm going to react to seeing her. I can watch through the hedge and hopefully get over any strong emotions before she spots me.'

Xander walked up to the front door and rang the bell, his heart in his throat.

'Oh,' Nell's dad said when he answered. 'It's you.'

'Er, yeah. Hi, Colin.'

'Mr Shackleton to you.'

'Right.'

'What do you want, lad?'

'Well, to see Nell. She is here, isn't she?'

'I don't see that it's any business of yours whether she's here or not.' Colin looked him up and down, oozing hostility. 'And I'm not sure you seeing her is such a good idea, are you? She's quite fragile at the moment, I'm sure you can understand why.'

'I know, I know, and no thanks to me,' Xander muttered.

'Well, I didn't say that. But you're right, it is no thanks to you.'

'I'm sorry. I came to tell her I'm sorry. Can't I just see her?'

'Look, whatever your name was—'

'Xander.'

'Look, Xander,' Colin said in a low voice. 'I don't appreciate taking calls from my little girl in hysterics because she's not only been rejected by her mum, but some wanker's broken her heart on top of it. She never stopped crying the whole drive home.'

Xander winced in shame. 'Look, I'm sorry, OK? I just want to talk to her. I… love her. Can you at least tell her I love her?'

'I don't think so, do you?' Colin started to close the door, but Xander held his hand against it.

'Colin, wait! Please. It's not just me. There's someone else here who wants to talk to her.'

He beckoned to Stevie behind the hedge and she came to join them, looking nervous.

'Hi,' she said quietly.

'Oh.' Colin's frown lifted. 'Stevie. Hello, love.'

'I, um… I was hoping to talk to your Nell. I owe her an apology and… well, a hug, I think, if she'll let me. Can you ask her if she'd like to see me?'

'I'm sorry, I'm afraid she's not here. She was, but she went out a little while ago.'

'Are you telling us the truth?' Xander asked.

'Why wouldn't I be? I know she'd want to see Stevie.' He shot Xander a look. 'You, I'm not so sure about.'

'Where's she gone, Colin? Not back to Leyholme?'

'No, to visit her brother at his mum's place. She said there was something urgent she needed his help with.'

Xander turned to look at Stevie. 'Why would she go there, do you think?'

'I suppose she might want to talk to Freddie, if she was upset. He was the one who helped her find me.'

'Hmm.' He turned back to Colin. 'What was the something urgent, did she say?'

'No idea. Whatever it was, it obviously couldn't wait. She'd only been here an hour when she practically flew out of the door again.'

'Oh God.' Stevie put a hand on Xander's arm. 'Xand. I think I know what she's planning.'

'Do you? What?'

She shook her head ominously. 'Nothing good.'

–

Nell banged again at the front door.

'Come on, you bastard,' she muttered. 'I know you're in there.'

She stepped back to look at the house, feeling a surge of rage at its offensively civilised, clinging-ivy luxury. This was the last place he'd deserved to end up settled.

Reuben lived in an innocent-looking sandstone cottage with a meticulously well-kept garden. The front lawn was surrounded by high hedges – her biological father was obviously someone who set privacy at a high price.

The door was eventually answered by a bespectacled, red-cheeked man with a bald crown and sizeable tummy. He was wearing a faded T-shirt and mud-stained jeans, with a pair of ugly plastic Crocs on his sockless feet.

'Sorry, love, I was gardening round the back.' He wiped soiled hands on his jeans. 'Can I help you?'

'Reuben Dyson?' she said, casting a look at the beer paunch filling out his old T-shirt.

'Yes, that's me. Do I know you?'

'No.' Nell brought her palm crashing into his cheek. 'But you fucking raped my mum, didn't you, you son of a bitch?'

–

'Dyson. Reuben Dyson,' Stevie told Xander as they drove out of Leeds. 'Oak Lane Secondary, left in… must've been 1992.'

'Age?'

'Forty-five or forty-six. I think he was living in Steeton back then.'

'OK. That's an unusual enough name, I can't imagine he'll be too hard to track down. Especially if he stayed in the area.'

'That's what I'm worried about,' Stevie muttered, her eyes fixed on the road. 'Shit, Xand, what if she's there now? She might be in trouble.'

Xander looked up, worry etched on his features. 'You don't think this guy's dangerous?'

'I don't know. Probably not. I'm more concerned about what Nell might do while she's angry and irrational.'

'Something illegal, you mean?'

'That's what I'm worried about. Assault, criminal damage… God, Xander, the poor kid's holding onto a lifetime of hurt. Reuben's going to feel the full force of that.' Stevie glanced at him in the rearview mirror. 'Just find him, please, before she does something she can't take back.'

'I'm on it,' Xander said, tapping at his phone. 'I'll try the social media sites first. If the school's got an alumni page, his profile might be on the list of followers. That ought to tell us where in the country he's living, assuming he's got the standard privacy settings, then we can get his full address from the directory site we used before.'

'I'll pull over while you search,' Stevie said, indicating into a layby. 'We might be driving in completely the wrong direction for all we know.'

'Aha!' Xander said after fifteen minutes' intense stalking.

'What? Did you find a match?'

'Yes, I think I've got him. Here, tell me if this guy looks familiar. He posted some old photos to Oak Lane's Facebook group.'

Stevie looked at the grinning teenager in his sports kit and flinched hard. 'Yeah, that's the bastard.'

'Nice of him to make it easy for us.' Xander frowned. 'Are you OK, Stevie?'

'I'll be fine. Just tell me where I need to go.'

'Take the second exit at the next roundabout. We're heading towards Skipton.'

'Right.' She started the engine again.

'Nell's got a head start on us though,' Xander said. 'Colin said she set off for Freddie's mum's a while ago, and that's half an hour closer to Dyson than we are.'

'But she doesn't know as much as we know. She's not got a surname, for one thing, and she doesn't know the school either. Even with her brother's help, it'll take them a little while to dig up enough about him to get an address.'

'True. If you put your foot down, maybe we can get there before she does.'

'Or before she's done anything stupid,' Stevie muttered.

It took them nearly forty-five minutes to reach the village on the outskirts of Skipton where Reuben Dyson now lived. Xander directed Stevie down a leafy rural street and she parked the car.

'This is it?' she whispered.

'No, it's the next street along. I thought we'd better park out of sight.'

He turned to open his door, but Stevie put a hand on his arm. When he looked at her, her face was white and bloodless.

'What's up?'

'Xander, the last time I saw this guy, he...' She shuddered. 'Have you ever had that thing where you wake up in the night and you can't move?'

'Sleep paralysis? Yeah, a couple of times.'

'Terrifying, isn't it? Like there's a heavy weight on your chest and all you want to do is cry out, but when you try to open your mouth you realise you can't make a sound.' She felt her gag reflex convulse. 'Like being pinned to the ground by the weight of someone's body. That's the recurring nightmare that goes with my night terrors.'

Xander closed the door again and sat back.

'I never realised,' he said quietly. 'Did you ask him to stop?'

'No, but I was crying. That's quite a clear signal, I would've thought.'

'So it was rape.'

Stevie stared down at her hands, which were trembling. 'Perhaps it was. But if I call it that, it means that's where she came from. Jemima.' She choked on a sob. 'I did love her, Xand. I hated myself for seeing *him* in something so innocent. I hated that the very thing that made her was the thing that stopped her from being mine.'

'You don't have to do this, Stevie,' he said, taking her hand. 'Let me go.'

'No.' She wiped her eyes. 'It's time. I have to face him.'

'It might be too much for you. This bastard's caused you enough pain.'

'You're right, he has. And now he might be hurting our Nell.' She squared her shoulders and opened the door. 'Come on.'

—

'Jesus!' Reuben said, holding a hand to his cheek where Nell had slapped him. 'What the *hell* do you think you're doing?'

'Giving you what you deserve, you evil bastard,' she said in a voice low with strangling rage. 'Do you even know how many lives you've ruined?'

'You're insane. I've never seen you before in my life.' He tried to slam the door, but Nell jammed her foot in the way.

'Have you got any kids, Reuben?'

'What?'

'Well, have you?'

'No I haven't. And if that was a threat, you're playing games with the wrong man. I'm actually a personal friend of our local chief inspector, if you're interested.' He called to someone over his shoulder. 'Vicky, call the police, can you?'

A person, who Nell assumed must be his wife, appeared at the door.

'Reuben, what's going on here?' she demanded, looking Nell up and down. 'Who is this woman?'

'Mrs Dyson, I presume,' Nell said, smiling brightly. 'Tell me, what's your view on coercive sex with underage girls? Reuben's a big fan. Although perhaps you know that.'

'What's she talking about?' Mrs Dyson asked her husband.

'No idea. She just turned up on the doorstep ranting and raving, then she attacked me.' He rubbed his cheek. 'Call 999, can you, and get them to send someone out before she starts running riot around the neighbourhood. She's a drunk or a mental case, I suppose. Most likely both.'

'You OK there, Mr Dyson?' a voice, presumably that of a concerned neighbour, called through the hedge as Reuben's wife disappeared back inside.

'Fine, fine,' Reuben called back. 'Don't worry, just a drunk. The police are on their way.'

'So you're really going to stand there and claim you don't know what I mean, are you?' Nell demanded, digging her foot in more firmly as Reuben made another attempt to shut the door. 'Do not close that door on me, Reuben, unless you want me to shout down the street for everyone to hear what a misogynistic piece of shit you really are.'

Reuben let go of the door and cast a worried look in the direction of his neighbour's place.

'Look, I've got no idea what you're talking about,' he said in a low voice. 'I think you've mixed me up with someone else.'

'No, I know exactly who you are. Reuben Dyson, forty-six. IT professional, vice-chair of the local Neighbourhood Watch and part-time rapist of teenage girls. That's you, right?'

'You'd better watch what you're saying,' he snarled. 'I don't know how much you know about the law, young lady, but that's what we call criminal slander. Where's your evidence for this?'

'Standing right in front of you, mate.'

He took a step back. 'What?'

'You heard. Better tell your missus to cancel that 999 call, don't you think?'

He paused a long moment, tracing her features with his eyes. They lingered on the curve of her nose; the shape of her mouth.

'Vic, can you hold that call?' he yelled into the house. 'I think she's calming down a bit. I'll handle it myself.'

'All right, you've got my attention,' he muttered to Nell. 'Now keep your voice down. What's your name?'

'Jemima Madeleine. Ring any bells?'

He shook his head. 'No it doesn't. Would you mind telling me just what you're accusing me of, Jemima?'

'What about Stevie Madeleine, does that sound familiar?'

Again, he shook his head.

'Jesus.' Nell laughed in shock. 'You genuinely don't remember, do you? She's had to live with the fallout from this her whole life and you… you don't even know her fucking name.'

A voice she recognised rung through the air from somewhere behind Reuben's high box hedge.

'Nell! Nell, where are you?'

'Oh my God,' she muttered. 'Xander?'

A second later, Xander appeared at the garden gate. He almost laughed with relief when he saw her there. As soon as he reached her, he pulled her into his arms, peppering kisses over her face and neck.

'Nell, you bloody idiot,' he sobbed. 'Oh God, I was so worried about you. What the hell did you think you were doing?'

'How did you find me, Xand?'

'We followed you to your dad's. When he said you'd gone to get Freddie's help with something, we guessed what you must be planning.'

'We? What we?'

'Sorry, who are you now?' Reuben asked him.

Xander turned to him, his arms wrapped protectively around Nell.

'I'm with her,' he growled. 'And I ought to punch you in the face right now for what you did, you bastard.'

He shook his head in bemusement. 'What the hell did I do?'

'Like you don't know.' He turned back to Nell. 'Sweetheart, why did you come here?'

'I… had to. After what he did to her, I…'

She fell silent as she caught sight of the pale figure who'd appeared behind him.

'Stevie,' she whispered.

'Nell.'

Xander stood to one side to let them talk.

'You shouldn't be here,' Nell said.

'When you were getting yourself into even more trouble than usual? Who else was going to come and save your backside?'

They looked at each other for a moment. Then before Nell knew what was happening, Stevie had folded her in a tight embrace.

'Oh Nell, I'm so sorry,' she whispered. 'I didn't do right by you.'

'No, I was wrong.' Nell let out a sobbing laugh as she wrapped her arms around Stevie's neck. 'I thought… I thought you couldn't stand to look at me.'

'Sweetie, it was me, not you. Don't ever, ever think that.'

Stevie held Nell back to look into her face. She'd been worried, on the journey over, that their meeting might be another trigger – that she wouldn't be able to control how her body reacted. But a stronger, more basic instinct than the trauma of her teenage experience seemed to have kicked in when she'd been worried Nell might have put herself in danger. The instinct to protect her child.

For the first time, Stevie became aware of her surroundings. She turned to look at the man watching the scene from his doorway and blinked a few times.

'Reuben?' she said in disbelief.

'Good God, here's another one,' he muttered. 'I should've lit the barbecue. I'm sorry, and you are?'

'Seriously? You don't know me?'

'The prick doesn't even remember,' Nell told Stevie, glaring at him. 'Can you believe this guy?'

'Reuben, what on earth is happening out there? Who are you talking to now?' Mrs Dyson appeared at his side again and blinked at the little group in front of her. 'Oh my God. Is that…' She laughed. 'Bloody hell, it is. It's Stevie Madeleine, isn't it? I haven't seen you since school. What are you doing here?'

Stevie stared at her. 'You,' she whispered.

'Who is it, Stevie?' Xander asked.

'The Ghost of Shit Friends Past,' Stevie said, glaring at the woman. 'Hello, Victoria. So you married Reuben. Well, you certainly deserve each other.'

'That's right, I'd forgotten. You two hooked up that one time, didn't you?' Victoria trilled out a little laugh. 'You've left it a bit late to come back for seconds, Stevie.'

Stevie smiled. 'Oh, Victoria. Haven't changed a bit, have you?'

'I don't remember any of this,' Reuben muttered.

'No, you were falling down drunk,' Victoria told him. 'She threw herself at you at some party; it was embarrassing.'

'*You* threw me at him, you nasty little bitch,' Stevie spat.

'What, and… did she have a baby?' Reuben said.

'Yeah. Her dad tried to hush it up but everyone knew. She had to finish her GCSEs somewhere else after that.' Victoria turned to sneer at Stevie. 'She hasn't turned up here trying to claim you were the brat's dad, has she? Don't listen to her, Reuben. She must've opened her legs for half the boys in our year.'

'Jesus,' Nell whispered to Xander. 'She's worse than he is.' She made a move to step forward, but Xander put a restraining hand on her arm.

'I think Stevie needs to do this for herself,' he muttered. 'Let her handle it, Nell. It's helping her.'

Nell looked at Stevie. Xander was right. She'd been pale when she arrived, and sort of fearful-looking, but now she was standing tall, arms folded, as she faced her past.

'I think you'd better go back inside,' Reuben said to his wife. 'This seems to be between me and her.'

'I'm not going anywhere.'

'Vicky, please! You're making things worse.' He lowered his voice. 'It could do us some damage if these people start spreading this stuff around.'

'Fine. But I'll be right next to the phone if it all kicks off.' Victoria cast a last resentful look at Stevie, then disappeared into the house.

When she'd gone, Reuben turned to Stevie, for the first time wearing an expression that might be something approaching shame.

'Look, I'm sorry,' he said. 'I don't remember. But if I did something to hurt you, I'm sorry for it.'

Stevie turned to Nell and Xander.

'Can you guys wait for me in the car?' she said quietly. 'I want to talk to Reuben for a minute.'

Nell cast a glance at Reuben. 'Are you sure? I don't like leaving you alone with him.'

'It's OK, Nell. I need to do this.'

Nell looked into her eyes and nodded once. She and Xander turned to go.

'Hey.' Reuben reached out to touch her arm, but she shuddered and jerked it away. 'Are you really... I mean, um...'

Nell nodded. 'Believe me, I'm no happier about it than you are.'

'Could I... could we... I could maybe give you my number or something.'

'Or you could stay the hell away from me. Goodbye, Reuben.' She let Xander lead her away, sagging, spent and exhausted, against his shoulder.

'So,' Stevie said to Reuben when they were alone. 'You don't remember.'

He flushed. 'No. When did it happen?'

'You were in Year 12. Sixteen or seventeen. I was in Year 10.'

'Shit!'

'That's right. Fourteen years old.'

'Did I know that?'

'You knew. And I was a virgin, Reuben, whatever your wife chooses to tell you. The fact that I sobbed through the whole thing didn't seem to put you off though.' She shivered. 'You don't remember and I have to remember every day. How helpless and scared I was. The names you called me in sordid little whispers. The pain of having to give my child away because she reminded me so strongly of that night – of you.'

'Look, I'm sorry, OK?' he said again, looking shrunken somehow. 'I must've been very drunk. If I'd been sober I never would've... that's not the man I am, Stephie.'

'*Stevie*. For God's sake, you got me pregnant. At least make the effort to remember my fucking name.'

'Stevie then,' he said. 'I swear, I'm not the boy who did those things to you. I'm... I'm a pillar of the community. I give to charities – I win prizes for my begonias, for Christ's sake! They made me president of the Rotary Club last month.'

Stevie almost laughed at the helpless expression on his face as he said this.

'You know the memory of that night nearly stopped me from ever being able to have a healthy relationship?' she said. 'I felt dirty and ashamed for so long afterwards, I honestly believed I could never fall in love. And through all the guilt and the flashbacks and the nightmares that woke me up screaming, I remembered you, Reuben. The bulk of you, pinning me down while I sobbed; holding my arms in place so I couldn't move. You became something almost inhuman in my mind, a monster forever lurking in the shadows.' She looked him up and down, taking in the supremely non-threatening Crocs, the faded T-shirt and overhanging beer gut. 'But you're nothing, are you? Just a tiny little man with tiny little thoughts. You can't hurt me, not any more.'

'I said I was sorry. I wish it hadn't happened, but I can't take it back.' He lowered his voice. 'You won't tell anyone about this, will you? I'm a respected man in this community. It wouldn't be fair to let one youthful indiscretion ruin me, I hope you see that.'

'Youthful indiscretion? For fuck's sake, is that what you're calling this?' Stevie laughed in disbelief. 'Smoking a joint's a youthful indiscretion, Reuben, not forcing yourself on a fourteen-year-old girl.'

'You won't though, will you?'

She laughed again. 'Oh, don't you worry. Your position at the Rotary Club is safe.'

He visibly sagged with relief. 'Thank you.'

'I should be the one thanking you. It turns out that all this time, this was exactly what I needed. Just to face you and see what a pathetic human being you actually are. Goodbye, Reuben.'

She turned to go.

'Er, hey,' he said. 'That girl...'

'Nell.'

'Nell? She said Jemima.'

'That was her birth name. What about her?'

'Can you tell her... I mean, if she ever wants to talk, I'll be here. We'd have to keep it quiet, obviously, but I'm sure we could work something out.'

'I'll tell her. But I doubt she'll want to be your shameful little secret, if I had to take a stab at what her answer was going to be. If you decide she matters more to you than your standing at the Rotary Club, perhaps she might reconsider.'

Stevie cast a last look at the house, with its trim, dull little garden and ivy around the door – the picture of refined domesticity. It made her laugh softly to herself, although she didn't know why. Then, her demons buried at long last, she strode off back to the car.

Chapter Thirty-Seven

Nell and Xander were sitting together on the back seat, her head resting on his shoulder.

'What on earth made you do it?' he asked, stroking soft fingers over her hair.

'I was just so angry,' she whispered. 'Not for myself, for what he did to Stevie. He destroyed her life for so long. I didn't expect remorse, but I had to confront him and hear him acknowledge it – all the people he's hurt.' She snorted. 'Never occurred to me he wouldn't even remember.'

'What exactly did you do to him?'

'Nothing too bad. Just yelled at him and gave him a pretty hefty slap. He deserved a lot worse.'

'And did that make you feel better?'

'Not better, but kind of cleansed, I guess.'

'You could've got yourself in a lot of trouble, Nell. You know he can charge you with assault?'

She shrugged. 'After losing you and Stevie and my job, it felt like I didn't have much life left. Why not chuck in a criminal record as well?'

He tilted her face up to look at him. 'I read your letter.'

She frowned. 'That was addressed to the governors.'

'Yes, well. We all make iffy choices for the people we love sometimes.' He paused. 'That doesn't make sense. I was trying to say it was a bit like the stupid things that you did.'

'Yeah, I got it.'

'Nell, why would you do that? Throw your career away for me?'

She turned away. 'Well. It was all bound to have come out in the end, wasn't it? I didn't want you getting in trouble for my idiotic mistakes.'

'You stupid… God, you're amazing.' He kissed the top of her head. 'You'll come home now, won't you? Back to Leyholme – to me?'

'I… don't know.'

'Nell, I'm so sorry for how I reacted when I found out about you and Stevie. I tried so hard to do the right thing, but I just managed to do all the wrong ones. You needed me, and when I should've been there for you I—' He turned away while he struggled with strong emotions. 'I can't take it back. But if you'll let me, I promise I'll spend the rest of my life making it up to you.'

'Xander…'

'You don't realise how much I've changed, knowing you. For the better, I mean. How much happier and… and braver I felt, just knowing you thought I was someone worth being with.' He took his glasses off and pinched the bridge of his nose. 'You always supported me, through everything, all that stuff with Ryan and my mum, then I paid you back by failing you when you most needed me. I'm not surprised you ran away.'

'Hey. No tears from you.' She reached out to brush away one that had appeared at the corner of his eye. 'You know you're not my type, right?'

'Wow. Harsh.'

She laughed. 'I mean, when we met I'd have said you weren't my type. The sort of blokes I went for… they were the cocky, swaggering ones, the boys with the cheeky grins and little black books. No one was more surprised than me when I realised I'd fallen for you.'

'I'm not sure this is doing wonders for my ego, Nell.'

'Well it should,' she said gently. 'Because what you made me realise is that I don't really have a type, not when it comes to falling in love that final, forever time. Just a Xander.'

He smiled. 'You're sweet.'

'And part of what made me fall for you was that I knew you'd always do the right thing in any given situation. Because you were Xander Scott and you couldn't not.' She stroked one finger over the back of his hand. 'I could see the battle going on inside you yesterday in your office, wanting to help me and needing to do right. I couldn't let you cover for me and be just that bit less the Xander I loved. That's why I wrote the letter.'

'Nell...' He planted a soft kiss on her lips. 'You know you're sensational?'

'Sensational. I could live with that.' She reached up to cup his cheek. 'I'm sorry I lied to you, Xander. I knew it wasn't fair to put you in that position, asking you to keep my secrets. I knew I probably never should have let myself get close to you in the first place, when I'd told myself my only goal was getting to know my mum.'

'Why did you?'

She smiled. 'Well, I suppose you must be irresistible.'

'I am pretty irresistible, aren't I?'

She kissed him. 'Hell, yes.'

'So you'll come home?'

'I don't know, Xand. I mean, I want to, but that decision really belongs to Stevie. If it's going to cause her pain to see me... I couldn't do that to her.'

'Well, here she comes. You can ask her.'

Xander opened the door and got out of the car.

'You know, I think I might just walk around a bit, stretch my legs,' he said. 'We've got a long drive back.'

He squeezed Stevie's arm as he walked off. 'Good luck,' he mouthed.

Stevie took his place on the back seat and closed the door.

'Hi,' she said.

'Hi,' Nell whispered.

'Um, was I interrupting?'

'No, course not. We'd just finished kissing and making up.'

'I'm glad to hear it.'

'So... how's Reuben?'

Stevie snorted. 'President of the Rotary Club.' She rested a hand on Nell's arm. 'It's OK, chicken,' she whispered. 'Reuben's been well and truly exorcised. He can't hurt us any more.'

'Is there an us?' Nell asked quietly.

'I'd like there to be. If that's still what you want.'

'It's all I ever wanted.'

Stevie smiled.

'Reuben's door is open to you too, apparently,' she said. 'If you don't mind being kept a secret.'

Nell wrinkled her nose in disgust. 'Oh, no. God, no, not after what he did to you. I never want to see that bastard again.'

'Nell, you mustn't think because of what happened with Reuben and the way I reacted when you told me who you were... that really isn't anything to do with you. It's not who you are.'

'But he's in me, isn't he?'

'A bit of him,' Stevie said. 'But so am I. So are all the people who've been part of your life – your dad, Freddie, Leanne. Maybe not genetically, but they helped make you all the same. And all that gives us is one completely unique, completely herself Nell Shackleton, who organises fetes and dresses as bunnies and makes friends with sheep and brightens up the life of everyone who's lucky enough to know and love her.'

Nell gave a choked laugh. 'Give up.'

'I mean it. And once the initial shock had worn off and I'd taken time to think, I knew she was exactly the sort of young woman I'd always wanted Jemima to grow up to be. The sort I hope my Milly will one day grow up to be. The sort of young woman I'd be proud to call my daughter.' She leaned forward to kiss Nell's forehead. 'Well, I suppose it's a colossal cheek to claim any credit for that when Colin and Leanne are the ones who brought you up. But I'm going to claim a little bit all the same. I am your mum after all, aren't I?'

'Stevie… you mean it?'

'I do. Do you forgive me?'

'You're the one who needs to forgive me,' Nell said fervently. 'I was a selfish cow to force a relationship like that. I never even thought how painful it might be for you. I'd spent too long building up the fantasy to think of the reunion being anything but perfect.'

'Aww, love. I'm just glad you found me. Now come here and give me a proper mum hug.'

Stevie pulled Nell to her, felt her arms wrap tight around her neck, just the way Milly's did when she was feeling sleepy and wanted carrying to bed, and stifled a sob.

It was funny. When Jemima was a baby, it had been so hard to detach her from the horror of the night she'd been conceived. Stevie had felt guilty about that, at fifteen. Sobbed when the child had been taken from her for the last time, sobbed with hurt and loss and the guilt that came from knowing she couldn't separate an innocent baby from an act that baby had nothing to do with. But now they'd faced Reuben and buried the past together, when Stevie looked at Nell, all she saw was Nell. Her best friend. Her daughter. Someone she'd come to love for her own sake, long before she'd known who Nell really was.

No wonder Nell had slotted so easily into all their lives. Leyholme was always where she was meant to be.

'It's going to be all right,' she said, making the same comforting sounds over Nell as she made over Milly when she cried. 'You can come home now.'

'My job… I lost my job.'

'We'll work it out. Perhaps… Xander's still got your letter, we can destroy it. What if I were to tell the governors I always knew who you were and asked you to keep it confidential? That doesn't sound nearly as bad.'

Nell shook her head. 'No. No, I can't let anyone else lie for me. I'll have to come clean and throw myself on their mercy.'

'Well, I can give a statement or something, saying how happy I am you found me. That has to help plead your case. You don't need to mention the no contact thing either.' .

Nell opened her mouth to object, but Stevie waved her down.

'No you don't,' she said firmly. 'The reasons for that are personal to me, not you, and I don't want to rehash the whole traumatic story for the governors.' She held Nell back to look at her. 'I do think, once they understand… it might be a slap on the wrist, but it doesn't sound like a sacking offence to me.'

'Ryan Theakston's likely to put up a fight.'

Stevie shook her head. 'Ryan's a spent force. He lost the respect of the other governors after the way he behaved towards Xander. The more he tries to hurt you, the more likely the others will be to take your part.'

'I hope you're right. I do love that old place.'

'Nell, I know the future's not going to be all sunshine and rainbows,' Stevie said softly. 'We've got a whole lot to work through, you and me. But I'm ready to give it a go if you are.'

Nell nodded, smiling through her tears.

'How did you get here?' Stevie asked.

'My stepmum's car. It's parked on the next street.'

'Well, how about you drop that off back at their place then come home with me and Xander, eh? I think you two probably have some talking to do tonight, up at the farmhouse. A whole lot more kissing and making up.'

'What happens then?'

'Well, then tomorrow I'd like to introduce you – properly – to your little sister.'

Epilogue

One year later...

'OK, this is the last one,' Stevie said as she struggled into the living room of Humblebee Farm with another box of books.

'Thanks, Stevie.' Nell climbed down from the stepladder she was using for loading books onto shelves to give her mother a peck on the cheek. 'What would we do without you?'

Stevie shook her head at Xander as he came in with a load more paperbacks in his arms. 'How can one man own so many books?'

'You can never have too many,' he said. 'Supposing there was a nuclear apocalypse and we got returned to a feudal society? You lot'll appreciate my books when all your Kindles have packed in.'

Stevie picked one out of the box. '*Lord of the Dance: My Story* by Michael Flatley?'

'OK, maybe not that one.' Xander took it from her and looked at the cover. 'This is my mum's. Not sure how it got in there.'

Stevie snorted. 'Oh yeah, a likely story.'

'All right, you've got me. I've had a closet Riverdance fetish for years. I was keeping it under wraps until after Nell had asked me to move in with her and there was no going back.'

Nell shrugged as she climbed back up her ladder. 'I could live with it. Have you got one of the costumes?'

'Of course. Velvet sequinned jumpsuit in emerald green, very me.'

She glanced around the bookshelves that now lined every wall. 'Xand, it looks like a library in here with all your bloody tomes.'

'I know, isn't it awesome? Not to mention my open fire and my sexy girlfriend. I'm literally living the dream.'

'So is that it, then? Are you all moved in?' Stevie asked him.

He scanned the room. 'Looks like. About fifty bookcases' worth of books and half a drawer's worth of clothes. I think that sums me up.'

'Well, you can just start helping me get them onto shelves,' Nell said, frowning at him. 'There's a governors' meeting tonight and I want all your books off the floor before I have to go.'

Xander shook his head. 'You a staff governor. I'd never have believed it.'

'And you a headteacher in just under a month.' Nell paused with a book halfway to a shelf. 'Hey, Xand, we're like proper adults.'

'I know. I'm very impressed by us.'

'Well, if you don't count our pretty un-adult lack of tidiness,' Nell said, looking down at the book-strewn floor. 'Don't forget we've got my dad and Leanne driving over tomorrow, and Freddie and his new girlfriend. I don't want the place looking like a tip for them.'

'OK, OK, I'm doing it,' Xander said, rolling his eyes as he started collecting up books and slotting them into some of the lower shelves.

'You're still bringing everyone round for dinner on Saturday night, aren't you?' Stevie asked Nell. 'Deb's doing her famous cheesecake for pudding.'

Xander looked up from his books. 'I thought she always claimed she couldn't cook.'

'Yep, that's why it's famously bought from the chilled aisle at Marks and Sparks. Very moreish.'

'We'll be there,' Nell said.

'Great. I'm dying to meet this girl of Freddie's.' She grabbed her handbag from the sofa. 'Right, I'll leave you lovebirds to nest.'

'Hang on, there's something I want to give you before you go. Present for our Mill.' Nell climbed down from her stepladder and left the room.

When she was gone, Stevie shot a glance at Xander.

'And should I be getting the fizz on chill for our family dinner party?' she asked in a low voice.

He smiled. 'I'll let you know.'

'Here you go,' Nell said when she came back in, handing a little packet to Stevie. 'It's a commemorative Ernest Shackleton two-pound coin, I sent off for it. To commemorate Milly's two favourite things: mountaineers and her amazing big sis.'

Stevie smiled. 'Aww, thanks, chicken. She'll love that.'

Nell gave her a hug goodbye. 'Thanks for helping with the big move, Stevie. You're a diamond.'

'More like a turnip. I don't know how I let you rope me into these things.' Stevie glanced around the cosy little room. 'You know, I'd never have dreamed the night I first wandered up here to bring a bottle of wine to the new Reception teacher that this knackered old place could turn into something like this.'

'Right? I'm thinking I ought to audition for a presenting slot on *Grand Designs*.'

Stevie waved goodbye. 'OK, see you both Saturday. Bring a bottle or four, eh?'

When she'd gone, Xander took Nell in his arms.

'Hello, roomie.'

She smiled. 'So how does it feel to be officially living in sin, Mr Scott?'

'Well, I don't know.' He nuzzled into her neck. 'Have we got time for a bit of sin before your meeting? Just so I can really get a feel for it.'

'Come on. We've got all these books to put away.'

'Yeah?' He tilted her head to one side so he could kiss behind her ear, one hand sliding up her top.

'When you put it that way, I guess we are due a break,' she whispered.

'Happy, Nell?'

'Very.'

'Couldn't be happier, do you think?'

'Not one iota.'

'Right. Because I did want to ask you something.'

Xander disentangled himself from her embrace and scanned the floor for a bit that was free of books. When he'd kicked a few out of his way, he fell to one knee. He fished in his pocket for the box he'd stashed in there earlier and held it up to her.

'Um,' he said.

'Xand, those are Tic Tacs.'

'Oh. Right, yeah, wrong pocket.' He fumbled in the other one until he found the right box, then popped it open so she could see the diamond ring he'd chosen for her.

'It's for you,' he said. 'I thought, um… you might like to marry me. I mean, please will you marry me? Because… I love you. So I'd be honoured if, er… you know. Sorry, I've never done this before.'

Nell blinked at him for a moment. Then she burst out laughing.

He shuffled towards her on his single knee, making a little channel through the books, and took her left hand.

'Is that a yes then?' he asked hopefully, pressing it to his lips.

'Xander Scott, you are still surprising me.' She smiled. 'Of course it's a yes.'

'Thank God for that. My knee's getting cramp.' He slid the ring on and stood up to kiss her.

'Thank you,' he whispered when he drew back. 'I'll make you happy, I promise. I love you very much, Nell.'

She smiled, resting her forehead against his chest. 'No matter how many times I hear you say that, it always feels like the first. I love you too, Xand.'

'When did you know?'

'That I loved you?' Nell thought for a moment. 'Honestly, I'm not sure, it came on so gradually. I think probably it was that day at the fete. Seeing how you looked after your mum. What about you?'

'Oh, I can pinpoint it to the exact moment,' Xander said, smiling. 'I was well ahead of you.'

'Go on, when?'

He laughed. 'I'm pretty sure it was at that ridiculous team-building day when you drew me a picture of a cock. Hang on.'

He freed himself from her arms and went to rummage in one of the boxes of his stuff.

'There,' he said, holding up the picture she'd drawn at the training day.

She shook her head, smiling. 'I can't believe you kept that.'

'Of course I did. It was a beautiful gift.' He held it at arm's length, tilting his head to appraise its artistic merit. 'What do you reckon, one for the mantelpiece?'

'Leave the dirty pictures and get back here and kiss me, you.'

'Yes Miss.'

He wrapped her in his arms again and kissed her heartily.

'So, about that sin we mentioned… now I've got you in the mood by showing you my erotic etchings…' he whispered.

'Hey. It was my erotic etching.' She inclined her head so he could kiss her neck. 'Go on.'

'I think we have to get it in before the wedding for it to count, don't we?'

'Mmm, you know, you're absolutely right. Shall we make a start now?'

Xander nodded solemnly. 'I think we ought to. Practise for the honeymoon.'

Laughing, Nell let him lead her to the bedroom, her new engagement ring sparkling in the April sunshine that blazed through the pristine windows of Humblebee Farm.

A Letter From Lisa

Hi there, this is Lisa! I wanted to say a massive thank you for choosing to read *The School of Starting Over*. I hope you enjoyed getting to know Nell, Xander, Stevie, Milly, Deb and their friends both human and canine, and that their stories will stay with you as they have with me.

As with *When You Were Mine*, my first book for Hera, love is the beating heart of this book – love of all kinds, whether romantic, friendly or familial. Although the characters face some tough issues, it's their strong affection for one another that ultimately brings them through. If you enjoyed this book, I do hope you'll consider checking the previous title out too.

I'd also absolutely love to hear your thoughts on this story in a review. These are invaluable not only for letting authors know how their story affected you, but also for helping other readers to choose their next read and discover new writers. Just a few words can make a big difference.

If you would like to find out more about me and my books, or contact me directly, you can do so via my website or social media pages:

Facebook: /LisaSwiftWrites
Twitter: @LisaSwiftAuthor
Web: www.lisaswiftauthor.co.uk
Thank you again for choosing *The School of Starting Over*.
Best wishes,
Lisa

Acknowledgments

As always, the biggest thank yous have to go to my wonderful agent, Laura Longrigg at MBA Literary Agents, and to Keshini Naidoo, my talented and hard-working editor at Hera.

I'd also like to thank a couple of author friends for their help with the story – Rachel Dove for her suggestion of Nell's bunny girl costume and other input, and Katey Lovell for her advice on the ins and outs of Early Years teaching. Thanks too to Catherine Wossick for her suggesting of 'Doggy Style' as the name of a dog-grooming business, which made me giggle so much I had to ask if she'd mind me borrowing it!

High fives to all of the supportive writers in my circle, especially the Yorkshire romance posse, Rachel Burton, Victoria Cooke, Rachel Dove, Katey Lovell and Rachael Stewart; the Authors on the Edge, Sophie Claire, Jacqui Cooper, Helena Fairfax, Kate Field, Melinda Hammond, Marie Laval, Helen Pollard and Angela Wren; the Airedale Writers' Circle; the ever-helpful members of The Savvy Writers' Snug on Facebook, and my fellow members of the Romantic Novelists' Association. I'm also grateful for the support of the RNA's Rainbow chapter, which provides support for RNA members who identify as LGBTQIA+ and/or write novels featuring LGBTQIA+ characters.

As ever, thanks to my fabulous family, friends and colleagues – my partner and long-term beta reader Mark Anslow; friends Robert Fletcher, Amy Smith and Nigel and Lynette Emsley; Firths, Brahams and Anslows everywhere, and my ever-supportive colleagues at Dalesman Publishing.

And finally, the amazing team at Hera, who once again have worked tirelessly to bring this book to readers – Keshini, Lindsey and the gang, thank you so much: it's been a pleasure to work with you once again!